THE BEAUTIFUL STRANGERS

ALSO BY CAMILLE DI MAIO

The Memory of Us

Before the Rain Falls

The Way of Beauty

THE BEAUTIFUL STRANGERS

CAMILLE DI MAIO

LAKE UNION
PUBLISHING

Text copyright © 2019 by Camille Di Maio
All rights reserved.

Published by Lake Union Publishing, Seattle

www.apub.com

Amazon, the Amazon logo, and Lake Union Publishing are trademarks of Amazon.com, Inc., or its affiliates.

ISBN-13: 9781542040440
ISBN-10: 1542040442

Cover design by Kirk DouPonce, DogEared Design

Printed in the United States of America

For my husband, Rob, who was the first to suggest that I write a book about Coronado, and who is the most amazing sounding board in regard to writing and so many other things. Love you!

For my in-laws, Joe and Inge, longtime residents of California who have opened my eyes to the beauty of the state and been so loving to me.

Though I met you both outside California, I associate the state with Sarah Weaver and Erin Gross. Sarah—thank you for many years of friendship. Erin—thank you for a friendship that was meant to be!

"And every day her loveliness shines pure, without a flaw; new charms entrance our every glance, and fill our souls with awe!"

—L. Frank Baum, of the Hotel del Coronado in 1906

"Three best to have in plenty—sunshine, wisdom, and generosity."

—Irish saying

November 28, 1892

Tom disappeared several stations before we arrived in San Diego, which is just as well, since I have papers in my bag that will begin the process of my leaving him for good. We quarreled, and I am embarrassed to say that it was witnessed by a gentleman in our compartment. But I believe our words were vague enough that my identity, which I have gone to considerable lengths to conceal, will not come to light.

Our argument was no different from any other since I married him seven years prior. He is a drunkard and a gambler, rapidly wasting away the sizable allowance I'm given by my grandfather. And if pilfering that is not enough, my husband brings his railroad bible—a deck of cards—and swindles innocent passengers out of their money by challenging them to games of three-card monte to pass the time on the tracks.

I tried to stop him once, and the slap that befell my face left a mark that I had to conceal by dabbing cosmetics on it and fashioning my long hair to fall over that cheek. Needless to say, I never interfered again, though I managed to avoid involving myself any further in the ruses, as he would have preferred.

Tom's abrupt departure was a greater relief than I know how to express, but it did leave me with two problems. First, he had not yet signed the documents that will dissolve our ill-fated union. And second, he absconded—perhaps intentionally—with our baggage card, and without it I was not able to retrieve the three pieces of luggage that I had checked in my name.

My real name.

I have tried for several years to escape from this monster, my most successful attempt being a feigned bout of rheumatism that sent me from Hamburg, Iowa, to San Francisco. His only contact with me was to demand more money when he'd run out of it, and I obliged with the allowance from my grandfather, forcing me to earn my own funds as a house servant. Work that I found most satisfactory after an upbringing in which I was so pampered that I never had a chance to test my own mettle.

And worth it to keep Tom from following me.

Craving the sun that regularly evaded the City by the Bay, I made my way south to Los Angeles, where I continued domestic employment, and up until last week I worked under the last name of Logan. I have received the praise of my employer, a Mrs. Grant at no. 917 South Hill Street, and after this jaunt to San Diego, it was my plan to return to what was a most generous position.

When Tom found out where I was—he could always locate me, eerily, like some villainous breed of homing pigeon—he insisted that we get out of town and find a notary to witness the signatures on our divorce papers. Why we had to leave Los Angeles to do so, I don't know. I might be some kind of bargaining chip if he got into trouble. I had my reservations about going anywhere with him but was so desperate to finish this once and for all that I agreed to go wherever he wanted to make it come about.

Tom had heard that the Hotel del Coronado was the first building in the world to be fully electric, and for all his many faults, the man has a mind that is eager for new experiences. In fact, that is the very thing that first drew me to him—he had a hunger for life that exceeded the boundaries of Hamburg. I am sure that the island's famed sunshine and spotless beaches were also a consideration. He never did take to the Iowa winters.

It was also the southernmost point before crossing the border.

How I would have loved to go even farther south and disappear into Mexico myself, but I fear that it would be too difficult for my grandfather's stipend to find me there. And for all the courage I try to cultivate, I am not as brave as I wish.

Abandoned, I continued on with the journey. I am sitting now on the third floor in my hotel room overlooking the water. Tom took with him the little satchel of money that he insisted I entrust to him while I left the train car to use the ladies' facilities, but he neglected to remember that I carried the pouch of quinine pills that relieved his early arthritis. (There is some justice, then, though maybe I'm wicked for thinking it.)

I registered here at the hotel as Mrs. Lottie A. Bernard of Detroit, grateful that they took pity on the story I told about my purse being stolen and that I would have money wired as soon as possible. A small room costs $3.80 per day, which is a reduction of their normal rate, since the busy season is not yet upon them. It includes three full meals, which I've been taking in both the ladies' lounge and the magnificent Crown Room. But the debt is adding up quickly, and as my time here draws to an end, I realize that I must take care of my bill so that I do not become the ilk of my husband, who will take advantage of people at every opportunity. I had hoped—which I see now was futile—that he would meet me at the Del as originally planned and sign our divorce papers, as this location was his idea in the first place. But I have asked for him at the front desk several times a day, and each time the answer is the same—my brother, Mr. Anderson, has not yet arrived.

Of course, Tom's name is not Mr. Anderson, and I have no brother— they are several of my fictions—but he and I had prearranged this moniker, as we are both afraid that the police will soon catch up with him if either of us reveals our true names.

Though I ache to see him behind bars, I would not embarrass those whom I love with the publicity that would no doubt spring from it.

As Tom's desertion of me is now becoming a truth that I have accepted, I have several things to attend to if I am to avoid bringing any more scandal to my already devastated family back home.

I plan to burn my divorce documents in the little fireplace in my room so that my name will not become known by the hotel staff when I am . . . gone.

I am desperate to receive funds to cover my hotel account and have telegraphed Tom's friend G. L. Allen, trusting that he will come to my rescue on this point. He was always a little in love with me, and it pains me to take advantage of him in this manner, but I am afraid I have no other choice. If I had married G. L. instead, I would now be the wife of a perfectly respectable bank clerk. Bored, perhaps, but at least not in peril as I am now.

Why did I not heed the warnings of my dear family when Tom appeared, dazzling and blazing?

My stomach groans, and I double over in pain for the fourth time today. The staff here is quite worried about me, and they have begged on more than one occasion to let them call a physician. But I told them that I have cancer of the stomach, a lie easily believed by the very real weakness that has overtaken me and the sallowness that has been carved into my once-proud cheekbones. I visited the hotel pharmacy looking for some easy relief but was met, oddly, by a real estate agent who offices in the shared space. He did offer me some whiskey, and I have drunk most of that, with the effect that it dulled the pain but failed to take it away entirely. It did, however, confuse my senses, enough that I slipped while entering the bathtub and had to call upon the housemaid to help me out and dry my hair. She insisted once again that we call the physician, but I do not want my true condition to be found out. It would be unseemly, I know, for someone of my young age of twenty-four to be dying of cancer, and he might discover what I am hoping to hide:

That I am carrying Tom's child—the result of a brief, insistent visit when he first found me a couple of months ago. And if he discovers my condition, there is no way he will ever sign divorce papers, no matter the money involved. He would have a claim on me that could not be undone, one that could be even more profitable for him.

On my part, I cannot imagine bringing a new life into a world that breathes the same air as my insidious husband.

Already I can tell that something is wrong. The pain I feel is so overwhelming that I have begun to experience spasms where I am greatly taken over by delirium, and in those moments I fear that I may do harm to myself just to stop it from hurting. Only days ago, I visited a gun retailer on Sixth Street and purchased a .44 and a few cartridges. I exchanged a silver filigree brooch to pay for it, and the revolver now sits on my hotel nightstand. More than once I have held it in my hand, knowing that with one swift action, the pain could end. But then I think about the dear bellboy who would discover what would be left and how devastating it could be for whoever would have to clean up what are now such crisp white sheets.

I am not heartless.

If I were to go through with it, I would instead walk down to the redbrick stairs by the ocean where the water might splash away all traces of the deed and maybe even take me with its tides, and I could disappear altogether.

Perhaps in doing so I will forgo any hope I have of the eternal paradise preached in my childhood, but in exchange my ghost could haunt these luxurious halls and the fancy visitors who walk them. A shadow version of a heaven I can't attain. I would not be an unfriendly phantom, scaring people who are here for the purpose of having a marvelous vacation. Instead I would welcome them, bidding them to enjoy their time here as much as I would have liked to, were my own personal circumstances not so tragic.

Yes, that's it. I can wed myself to this place even as I disentangle from Tom and my vow of till death do us part. Forever walking this beach and feeling this sunshine. As much as I imagine a drifting soul can.

There would be one more advantage to tying myself here. But that is part of my story that is known only by me and by Mr. and Mrs. Alan Morgan of 753 A Avenue, just blocks away from the hotel. They still live in that little cottage—I pay regularly for someone to tell me if their whereabouts change—and though I tried to forward some funds from my earnings to them, they steadfastly refused, believing, perhaps, that I needed the money as desperately as I do.

I intended to visit them during my time here on this island, but my pain is so formidable that I am not sure I could even walk the short distance to the door at the end of their picturesque garden.

The couple holds my secret—or one part of it that I shared with them: That this is not my first trip to Coronado.

Chapter One

San Francisco, 1958

Kate didn't hear the phone ring above the sounds of a squabble over the price of fresh flounder outside the restaurant window. Her sister, Janie, shouted over the noise.

"It's for you! Granddad again."

Janie rolled her eyes and stretched the phone away from the wall as if it were the most difficult task she'd ever been asked to do. The long cord was twisted, with the effect that one had to stand almost right next to the base to have a conversation.

Kate looked around for a towel, but the only one she could find was soaking wet from having fallen into the sink suds. She wiped her hands on her apron instead and held a finger up when a customer asked for more ketchup. Nothing came before Granddad George, and she didn't care if her tips reflected that.

Janie placed the receiver against her chest and seemed to growl. "He's getting quacky, Kate. That's the third time he's called you today, and I can only imagine that the people on his party line are fed up with his interruptions. It's a good thing we work for Uncle Mike. If we weren't family, you'd be fired by now."

"How can I say no to him?"

"Like this." Janie stretched her lips into an exaggerated circle. "Nnnnnooooo. Tell him you're busy."

"Getting more salt for whiny tourists?"

Kate's exasperation had less to do with the customers and more to do with the fact that without something significant changing the course of her life, she would be frying fish forever.

Janie shrugged and handed over the phone. "Your funeral."

Kate put the receiver to her ear and spoke as if it were the first time she'd heard from their grandfather today. Because in his mind it probably was. "Granddad? How are things going? Are you OK?"

She worried at the sound of his anxious breath.

"I figured it out, Katie-boots. It's the beautiful stranger. Find the beautiful stranger."

This was becoming a daily request. But he'd given Kate no clues as to what it meant. She covered the mouthpiece and let out a sigh, never wanting him to hear how the signs of his decline broke her heart.

"Sure, Granddad. Right after work."

"You promise?"

"I promise."

"It's *im-por-tant*, Katie-boots." He sounded out each syllable. He always did that when he wanted to stress a point.

"I know," she answered.

"OK." Kate could hear the relief in his voice, and that had to be enough for now. He hung up without saying goodbye.

Janie handed her a bottle of ketchup. "Table seven. I'm salvaging your tip for you. What did he want?"

"To find the beautiful stranger."

"Again? What the heck does it even mean?"

"I don't know. You know how he is."

"Dementia is for the birds." Janie raised her arms and retied her ponytail.

"Yeah," said Kate. "But his doctor said to just go along with whatever he says. It's easier on him than arguing."

"So if Granddad says that purple aliens are ice-skating down Lombard Street and they're handing out free cotton candy, you should pretend to take that seriously?"

Kate might have laughed at the image if it were anyone but her sister she was talking to. Janie had lost interest in Granddad long before the dementia set in. Old people and old stories were just old news to her, and she couldn't be bothered.

"Yes, if he seems to be in earnest."

Janie shrugged. "You're a better woman than I am. Now, head over to table four after you deliver this ketchup. A big family just sat down. Rent's due next week and we're short right now, so put on your happy face."

Kate opened her mouth to counter her, but this wasn't the place. Rent on their apartment was not merely due. She'd seen the notice from the landlord peeking out from a pile of bills on their dad's desk at home—eviction proceedings would begin if they didn't get caught up on their late fees. Her parents hadn't let on, but she knew that rising costs of living and shouldering Granddad's expenses were straining them to the point of breaking.

But she had no wish to worry Janie until the time came. And as unprecedented as it would be, maybe Mom and Dad had a plan to pull them out of it.

Kate finished her shift an hour later than usual. One table lingered, leaving enough trash between the seats to contribute to the landfill project in Foster City. And fifteen cents for a tip. Some people didn't have any concept of how hard waitresses worked. And for how little. Grace Kelly had never had to work like this. Or Doris Day. Everything in the movies was easy.

Kate pulled the apron over her head and winced when strands of hair got tangled in the strings. She smelled like fish and grease and cigarette smoke, but she was anxious about getting over to her grandfather's apartment and didn't want to stop at home for a shower.

A voice startled her as she left the restaurant. Dimitri Kropos cast a wide shadow next to her slim one. Any other day, she would have been happy to see her friend. But lately he seemed to want something more from her. Wanted to talk about the future. He was ready to settle down. And it descended on Kate like a suffocation from which she didn't know how to escape.

Not just from him. From her family, too. Uncle Mike wanted to train her in purchase orders. One more shackle to tie her to the family restaurant.

Did it make her a terrible person to want something different for her life than what they all offered?

"Hey, Katherine! I hoped I'd catch you before you left. Want to grab a milkshake?"

Dimitri's family owned the eight-story hotel across from Fisherman's Wharf, the latest in their growing enterprise. But he had a penchant for the french fries that her family served, a welcome break, he'd told her, from spanakopita. So he came in several times a week.

Kate pulled her sunglasses down to look at him. "I wonder what Adara would think about that?"

Not to mention Janie. Though she'd never said it, Kate suspected that her sister had feelings for Dimitri. Her usual confidence evaporated whenever he was around.

He walked next to her toward the trolley stop and put his hands in his pockets. "Aw, you know how I feel about her. That business between us was arranged when we were both in diapers. But this is America. There are laws against your parents picking out your future wife."

"You know there aren't."

"Well, there should be. Maybe I'll run for office and make it my platform."

Kate turned back toward him and smiled. Dear Dimitri had always been a pal. They'd met in grade school and spent recesses in the library, she reading Nancy Drew and he reading Hardy Boys. They plotted perfect crimes, though neither would ever dream of committing one. The librarian called their parents in for a meeting to discuss her concern over their preoccupation with mystery novels.

Kate's parents responded by shrugging it off and buying her the next few books in the series for Christmas. Dimitri's parents banned him from all fiction and decreed that he would start on Aristotle and Homer from then on.

Maybe his parents had been right. Kate's family wore themselves thin working for paychecks that vanished the day they arrived, and Dimitri was on his way to heading a small hospitality empire.

"Tell you what," she offered. "I'll volunteer on your campaign and vote for you on Election Day."

He touched her arm, but she continued on. The trolley was two blocks away, and she didn't have time to wait for the next one.

"Come on, Katherine." He lowered his voice. "We could be so good together. Be the Nancy to my Ned."

She wished she could feel the same way about him. Maybe then she'd be willing to charm his parents and convince them to break with years of tradition. Dimitri had told her on many occasions that he would take care of her and her family. Give them all jobs at the hotel. He was going to open one of his own when he turned twenty-one and was four months away from breaking ground.

It would be so easy.

But as much as it would alleviate her family's financial woes, it would only be a more comfortable version of what her life looked like now: tethered to this corner of San Francisco, working in a family business where the singular focus on survival left little room to imagine something different.

This was 1958. Life could be lived in Technicolor now, the days of black and white left behind. If one only had the brass to make it happen.

Kate jotted down her dreams in a journal that she stuffed under her side of the mattress. It was filled with film quotes, cutouts of matinee idols from magazines, and receipts from movie outings with Granddad. Someday, she wrote in it, she'd get out of here and head south. And work in some capacity around the glamour of Hollywood and under the beauty of palm trees.

That was the California that the wider world imagined, not realizing that the opposite ends of the state might as well be on separate planets. It was about the same distance from Paris to Barcelona as from San Francisco to Los Angeles (she'd measured it on a map), and no one would ever mistake one for the other.

Kate had never voiced these aspirations to anyone except her grandfather, knowing that even Dimitri would only push the boundaries of convention so far. Her family loved her. But love and understanding were not always synonymous.

Dimitri's interest was well-worn territory, as was her declination, another part of the routine that spun round and round with every year. She lifted up on her tiptoes and gave her friend a hug as they approached the trolley. "I need to go. Talk to you soon."

She found an aisle seat after she'd boarded, avoiding a window where surely he would have stayed to wave until she left. As if it were a train station instead of a trolley stop. She pulled a tissue from her pocket and dabbed her eyes, wondering again if she was being ungrateful. She had the love of her family and the friendship of a good man. And knew that she was richly blessed to be able to say that.

But she wanted the life they showed in the movies.

~

Granddad still lived in the apartment that he and Grandma Kitty had bought when they first settled in San Francisco. She'd passed away two years ago, and that was when his decline became pronounced. At first it was little things, like looking for his glasses when they were already on his face. Then it accelerated to leaving milk out until it spoiled overnight and forgetting to feed his bird. So far nothing truly dangerous had happened—nothing like leaving the gas stove on—but it was only a matter of time.

And given his recent obsession with this *beautiful stranger* business, she feared the worst was right around the corner.

The reference—whatever it meant—was just the latest. He would often grab on to her arm and get that wild look in his eyes and tell her how important it was that she go to California.

"We *are* in California, Granddad," she would say sweetly, concealing the very real concern she had for his growing agitation. Then he would rub his hand through his hair as if he somehow *knew* that but there was more to impart.

"You need to get to California," he'd insist again. "It's very important."

Important? she wondered. He may have thought so, but the burden of the family's ongoing financial troubles was more fitting of the word. Their need for Granddad to have the kind of care that they couldn't afford now. Or to pay the rent increase on the apartment she shared with Janie and their parents. To save the last of the family restaurants. Her parents used to own one of their own, but it fell victim to the failure rate that so often plagued the industry. Palates were fickle things, and the traditional American fare they served couldn't compete with the growing interest in more exotic cuisines. They might have done better farther down the peninsula—Millbrae or San Bruno, where families would have appreciated their simple offerings. But here in the city, things were changing. And her parents didn't want to change with it.

Uncle Mike's fish and chips restaurant sat in the shadow of Alioto's and Tarantino's, but it had held its own—barely.

She had no idea how Granddad's nonsensical implorations could be more crucial than the family's problems. It was more evidence, sadly, that they were losing him, one memory at a time.

Still, even in his dementia, he'd not been prone to theatrics. If he was this insistent, maybe there was something to it?

Kate pulled the key to his apartment from her pocket and let herself in. The smell of burned cheese tickled her nose, but at least there was no smoke. She was afraid that it was only a matter of time before he did something that could harm him—or others in his apartment building. She'd thought of broaching the idea to her family that Granddad come to live with them, giving him her and Janie's bedroom while they'd sleep in the living room.

Not ideal by any means, but it might be the only way to keep him safe.

"I'm here!" she called as she closed the door behind her.

"Welcome!" His macaw called out one of the two words it could say, the other being "Blimey!" No one in the family understood that reference, as they lived on the other side of the world from England and had never set foot on its shores. Granddad insisted that he hadn't taught it to him. But the bird was old and had been with the family since before even her dad was born.

"Hi, Mr. Hobbs," Kate responded. The bird bobbed its head and turned around so that Kate could stroke its bright-green tail feathers.

Then she began the maze walk.

Granddad had saved the daily newspaper for as long as she remembered. Not just the local *Chronicle* but used copies of *Screenland* and *Movie Story*, which he bought for Kate at a nickel apiece, the newest being several months old. Thrift stores were great for that. She loved to pore over them for news and gossip about the world of Hollywood. Granddad also subscribed to the San Diego *Evening Tribune*. He'd lived in Southern California long before he had a family, but his conversations about that time were few, small comments that revealed nothing personal. Simple things like how the beach seemed as if it had gold flecks in it or what sand dollars looked like before they were dried for tourist shops.

Whenever Kate would ask more probing questions, he'd change the subject, and she sensed that it pained him. But he held on to that newspaper subscription no matter what. The only tie she knew of to his youth.

He and Grandma Kitty had read the papers every morning for headlines and sports scores and, as they aged, obituaries. Their morning coffee and the stories, as they called them, were a routine that kept them married through good times and bad. Both shared the habit of sentimentality, and neither could part with things. Perhaps it was a Depression-era mentality. Newspapers were good not only for the words they contained but for kindling fire, wrapping meat, lining birdcages.

As a result, they were stacked waist-high, and as the magazines and periodicals became too tall for walls alone to bear, they wound their way into the room space until, years later, there was an actual path to get from the front door to the couch. It was a fire hazard—another concern in the possibility of Granddad accidentally doing something dangerous—but a previous attempt to remove them had caused a frantic panic in him that no one wanted to repeat.

Once in a while, Kate slipped an *Evening Tribune* into her bag, and even if its news was a month old, she liked to imagine that she lived in the colorful place that she knew only through the black-and-white print. She clipped the coupons to the local stores and cut out articles about places she'd like to see. Doing so created the tiniest of hopes that it might be her world someday, and she wanted to be ready for it.

Occasionally she'd ask Granddad about something she'd read, careful to limit the scope of her questions to the innocuous. Hoping that it might nudge him to tell her more.

It never did.

"Katie-boots!" her grandfather called. He was in good spirits today. He sauntered into the living room with a well-toasted sandwich on a chipped plate. "Want me to make one for you?"

"No, thanks. I just came from Uncle Mike's."

"You're missing out. This might be my masterpiece."

She smiled. "I know. You make the best ones."

He used to, anyway. Granddad liked to put surprises in his basic grilled cheese sandwich: ranch dressing. Bacon. Whole mustard seeds. There was always something new.

He nestled into his recliner, mindlessly humming a tune familiar only to the Morgan family. Kate could never place it among any popular radio songs. When Grandma Kitty was alive, Kate once asked him what it was. But he'd clammed up, a look of old hurt washing over him. He got like that whenever the family asked about the past. And after Grandma died, his dementia had set in enough that he couldn't have recalled those memories if he'd wanted to.

Granddad was like a diary whose key had been lost.

"Sit, sit," he insisted.

She picked up a pile of books and placed them on the floor, where a bit of the green shag carpet peeked between the stacks. She sat down and put her hand on his knee, rubbing it. It was bony—he was losing weight that his already slim frame couldn't spare, and it added to her worries.

He had an impish look in his eyes, one that usually preceded him slipping Oreos into her pocket when her parents weren't looking. But that hadn't happened in years, not since she was a child. Maybe she'd just imagined the expression—it had been a long day.

"Seen any good flicks lately?" he asked.

Their shared love of the movies belonged only to the two of them, and it seemed to transcend his illness. When they'd catch a matinee together, him plunking down a quarter for each of them, there was a sparkle in his eyes that nothing else could put there. He'd taken her to her first show when she was ten years old—*Sunset Boulevard*—complete with a large bucket of buttery popcorn. Kate didn't know if it was the magic of movies itself or the setting in Hollywood that did it, but that evening ignited her passion for all things Southern California. Her love for it all was intertwined with her love for him.

The playful look returned. Something had amused him.

She caught his eye, and he smiled as he pulled a copy of the *Evening Tribune* from the top of a pile. He folded it so that the classifieds were on top and set it on his lap.

"This is for you," he said. And he handed it to her.

One small advertisement was circled in blue ink.

> Wanted: experienced wait staff for temporary work on a movie set. Apply to Andrew Fletcher at the Hotel del Coronado, 1500 Orange Avenue, Coronado, CA. All inquiries and applications must be received by August 8.

Kate's heart raced at the notion. To work on a movie set in Southern California! Granddad knew this was as close to her dream as she could hope to get right now, and she was certainly qualified for the job.

But she knew better than to get excited over the impossible. She couldn't be spared at the restaurant—leaving would mean that an already overworked Mom and Janie would have to cover for her. And getting there had to be expensive. Lodging might eat up whatever she'd earn. There was a reason it was advertised in a San Diego newspaper: it was intended for locals.

Even if she could hope to overcome all the obstacles, the deadline—August 8—was only two days away.

Granddad probably didn't realize it. The calendar on his wall was still pinned open to January 1956. The month that Grandma Kitty died. He was hardly aware of the year, let alone the day.

Kate wanted to cry at how *close* such a possibility seemed. Yet so impossible. But the fact that Granddad understood her so well, cared so much for the desires of her heart, meant a great deal to her.

She sniffled, swiping a tissue under her nose and quickly putting it back into her pocket before he'd notice.

"Thank you, Granddad. This is very exciting. But I don't think I can do it."

"Whyever not, Katie-boots? This is exactly what you want."

She wasn't going to mention the date.

"The money. It would cost too much. This is really meant for people who already live there."

"Nonsense. I'll give you the money."

Oh no. That lapse in reality was a sure sign that he was on his way to a forgetful spell. He'd stopped working when Grandma Kitty first got sick, and Kate's parents had been giving him a stipend ever since, often neglecting their own needs.

"It's OK. There will be another opportunity." Her chest tightened in disappointment.

"No." The excited look in his eyes was replaced by a stern one. "You have to do this," he insisted, stringing out the words in that familiar way. "I want you to take the ring and sell it."

She gasped, the quick intake of air shooting its way down to her fingertips.

She didn't have to ask what he meant. There was only one ring in the family that could be called *the* ring: the one he'd given Grandma Kitty for their wedding, now sitting snugly in a blue velvet box in the top drawer of Mom's dresser. Nothing—not the direst of times—had prompted them to part with it. And she certainly wasn't going to be the one to do it, not on a whim that had no hopes of coming true.

"Granddad, I can't do that. It's Mom's now, anyway."

He shook his head, his fine white hair swishing side to side. She needed to get him to a barber. Maybe tomorrow. "It's not. It's mine.

Mine and your grandma's. Your mother only keeps it because everyone was afraid I'd lose it."

"I—I can't." But Kate knew her voice quavered as she said it, betraying any conviction that her words tried to impart. It was tempting. Too tempting.

He leaned forward, resting his elbows on his knees, and looked at her with as much clarity as she'd seen in these past two years. "Katherine Morgan, this is not something I'm asking you. This is something I'm *telling* you. Take the ring. Sell it. Use the money to go to Coronado and get yourself this job. Promise me. Promise me you'll do this. I haven't left much of a legacy for you, but dadgummit, I can do this."

Dadgummit? That was practically a curse word for an old man. Kate wanted to laugh, but he was so very serious.

"I love your dad and your mom and your sister, but Katie-boots"— his eyes were steely in their determination—"you may be the only one who can set a new course for this family. Starting with yourself."

She felt a nervous energy race through each limb of her body, charged with pride at his confidence in her as well as the daunting challenge he presented.

"Thank you," she told him. "But as exciting as this sounds, I don't see how it helps them. This is an advertisement for a waitress job. That's exactly what I do now."

"My girl," he said, pressing his fingers together until they formed a steeplelike arch. He pressed them to his lips. "Remember in Millbrae when your parents had the chance to buy the building they rented for that restaurant? I told your dad that it was a deal. A steal in a bad economy. But he had too many concerns about being an owner when calling a landlord with problems was so much easier. And fears about being beholden to a mortgage. Turns out that property *doubled* in value not three years later when things improved. And doubled again since then. If he'd only acted on that advice, they could be sitting on a tidy sum."

Kate had been too young at the time to be aware of that particular opportunity, but it had been a frequent—and heated—topic around their dinner table ever since.

"I still don't see how being a waitress at the hotel changes our situation, though."

"It's not about the *job*, Katie-boots. It's about who you'll meet. How you'll get ahead. It's not going to happen overnight. But slow and steady, I believe that you can create a new life for yourself down there, and you won't give up until you do. And maybe by your example, they'll imagine new possibilities for themselves, too."

She hadn't looked at it that way. That this job—if she even got it—was only a stepping-stone. An entryway to something more. If Granddad was to be believed—though she thought his confidence in her might be more than a tad optimistic—heading south could mean pursuing her dreams *and* encouraging her family to do the same. Maybe Janie would finally tell Dimitri how she felt about him, something unspoken between the sisters but observed by Kate. And Mom and Dad had always talked about opening a small inn. Something overlooking the water in the Sunset District, tiny in comparison to what Dimitri and his family were building. But they never acted on it.

If only it were as easy as he made it sound.

"Do I have your word?" he said. "That you won't come home until you've given it a go?"

Oh, goodness. Granddad came from a time when your word was your honor, and contracts were spoken and sealed with a handshake. He would know that she would treat her word with the sacredness he intended—and to request it of her indicated that this was as important to him as he'd insisted it was.

"I promise," she said. But a pit of worry formed in her stomach. Was she up to such expectations? How could she parlay a simple waitressing job into a foothold to the world of movies? The likelihood of failure was vast.

Then, all too quickly, she was losing him. The light in his eyes began to dim once he was relieved to hear what he'd wanted to from her. And she'd not yet asked him about what he'd called her over for in the first place.

"Tell me about the beautiful stranger, Granddad."

He gave her the bewildered look that resided on his face more often than not. He was almost gone, and it could be days before his comprehension returned. Janie was right. Dementia was for the birds.

"What are you talking about?" he asked.

"The beautiful stranger. You called me at the restaurant and told me about it. Sounded urgent."

"I don't know what you mean."

She sighed and gripped the edge of her skirt to keep from pulling at her hair. They were well-worn words that had never been given meaning beyond his desperate imploration, but she couldn't help him if he didn't give her more to go on. "Does it have anything to do with going to California?"

His eyes widened, and the lucidity returned but not wholly. "Yes! Yes! I remember now, Katie-boots."

She leaned in. Every second that the old Granddad was back was like air in her lungs.

"There is something you have to do for me. Find her. Please find her."

She sat up straighter. "Why?" She thought of the bills stacked on their kitchen counter like the Leaning Tower of Pisa. The closest she ever hoped to get to Italy. Or anywhere else. Despite Granddad's insistent tone, she could think of nothing more imperative than paying those off. Not a goose chase to appease a fading mind.

"She is at the Hotel del Coronado in San Diego. You have to find her *now*."

The Hotel del Coronado? Had the advertisement stirred up a memory in him? Or had it created a false one, and his mind was connecting things that had no relation at all? If this disease was confusing for the ones suffering from it, it was doubly so for the families.

She sighed again, dismissing any hope of his thoughts corresponding to each other. "So, what happens? I just go to the reception desk and ask for the beautiful stranger?" It sounded like an absurd task. Kate hoped she didn't come across as exasperated as she felt, but as much as she loved her grandfather, her patience was beginning to fray. This request sounded not unlike Janie's mention of a purple alien.

He looked confused by her question, but a cough took over any chance of a reply. Kate went to the kitchen to get him a drink of water. Then she sat back next to him.

"What is this woman's name, Granddad?"

The confused look returned to his face just as quickly as it had left. "What woman?"

He was slipping again. She didn't try repeating herself. It would be fruitless.

But she understood this about him—when he knew something, he *knew* it. Even if the realization only lasted for a few seconds. It was a look in his eyes, one that was honed only by spending countless hours with someone, comprehending every tiny change in expression. That had played out time and again in small matters, and Kate had grown adept at reading them. Why not bigger ones?

Or was this just a cover for insisting that she go apply for this job, knowing that if she wouldn't head down for her own pursuits, she would make the trip for his sake?

Either way, her resistance was slipping. Granddad—when he was whole and when he wasn't—could reach her heart like no one else.

She had to find a way to get to Coronado.

~

1892

I don't need to see Harry West's eyes to know that they are resting on me from across the hall. The bellboy has been exceedingly concerned about my health. So dear of him. I wish I could say that it is unfounded, but the truth is that I can barely walk due to the pain. Each step is an unspeakable agony.

He brought me matches earlier when I asked for them and had the decency not to question it out loud. Does he suspect that I am contemplating my own undoing, and is he worried that it will happen by fire? He need not fear that. I would not harm a single thread of the carpet or a splinter of the banisters of this ethereal place. The matches were merely to light the fireplace, where I finished burning the last of anything that tied me to my husband.

I am standing on a second-floor veranda overlooking the ocean, on the opposite side of the hotel from my room. It took me twenty minutes to get here. I move at a small and labored pace, and this is an immense resort. But the sun has set now, and all that remains of its light is the faintest glow that illuminates the ocean. I wanted—I needed—to see it one more time.

I know I sound calm in the face of such a permanent thought. Maybe too coherent for one in such a state. But Kate Farmer ceased the day I married Tom Morgan; I just didn't know it at the time. Yes, that is meta-phorical. I still draw breath. If you have lost, though, your merriness, your innocence, your vision of a world that is full of goodness; if bitterness has slowly fermented your youthful verve, then it is a death of the soul, and the body is merely a tail following its head.

Oh, I remember those times like they were yesterday. I was alive! So alive! The girl I was then—so rosy, so gay—looks nothing like the pitiful shell of today. And if by sunrise I am no longer here, it will be by my own hand, but only as proxy to the man who is my husband. He is my murderer, no matter how many miles away he disappeared to.

Oh, that is too much darkness to ponder, and I wish it were not so, but there it is. Maybe, though, it tells something of the state of my mind. Would a priest offer me prayers and compassion? I'd like to think so. Though I can't say that they would do any good.

There I go again. I must not slip into all that woe any longer. I was raised to keep on the sunny side. In this, at least, I need to temper my words and hope that my mother would be proud.

Chapter Two

"You're crazy."

Janie spoke in spectacularly predictable fashion.

"Are you going to tell Mom and Dad?" Kate was certain that this endeavor would not meet with anyone's blessing. After thinking through many ways to bring up the idea to her parents, her imaginary conversation always ended the same.

There was no way she'd be allowed to gallivant off to Southern California and miss valuable work shifts. But Kate had a feeling—that pestering ache in her stomach—that Granddad was onto something. Even if it seemed ridiculous.

And it would get her out of the routine of here, if only for a while. The same work, the same life, the same geography. Even the tourists blended into one monotonous voice shouting for more salt or more napkins. She might never have had the courage to leave on her own, but knowing how much it meant to Granddad that she try this, she felt emboldened enough to consider it.

What did an old man have in the waning years of his life other than his hopes for the future generations?

Janie lay next to Kate in the small bed they'd shared since their childhood. The moonlight was filtered through the San Francisco fog, and it looked merely like a glimmer in the otherwise invisible sky.

Kate tried another question. "What's the worst that can happen?"

Her sister sighed, and though it was dark, Kate could feel her eyes rolling.

"What's the worst that could happen? How about the train jumps the track on the way down? How about you get mugged in San Diego? What are you going to do for money? How long are you going to be gone? Who is going to replace you here?"

This was the exact reason her parents had trouble getting ahead. Their fears of risk bound them to the sameness and safety of the restaurant, never moving forward by testing out a new venture. Was that to be the legacy of the Morgans? Janie's warnings had indeed run through Kate's mind already. But someone had to push through apprehension if their situation was to have any chance of improving.

Otherwise her future children would be frying fish just like she was. If they were lucky enough to still have the restaurant.

Kate sat up and fumbled for her slippers on the floor. She leaned against the windowsill and looked out into the nothingness three stories below. When the fog rolled in, it erased not only the sky but everything around it. It was like living in a cloud. Kate had never cared for British literature, with its bogs and its moors and its brooding, because at times like this San Francisco made her feel strangely like those miserable heroines. She craved sun, palm trees, warm water.

So Janie's well-intentioned concerns didn't sink in enough to make her pause. Except for one.

What *would* she do for money? Granddad had offered the ring. But there were so many other things her family could do with that money.

Was there any other way she could make this happen?

Nothing came to mind.

"Kate? Are you listening to me?"

"Um-hmm." Kate turned back toward her sister and sat on the edge of the bed. She brushed her hand against Janie's long hair. As much as her sister annoyed her, she knew that no one could ever know you quite as thoroughly as a sibling.

Janie scooted over and patted the warm side of the bed so that Kate could rejoin her. She held out her arm and stroked Kate's hair in return, playing the role of the older sister, though their difference was a mere eleven months. Kate was three inches taller, though, always being mistaken for the firstborn, which irritated Janie to no end.

"I just worry about you, you know. You've never been content here. That's no secret to me. But the dream of doing something is different from the very real obstacles you will face."

"It's—"

"No, don't give me the *Granddad wants me to do this* speech. He doesn't know what he's talking about."

Kate winced and didn't know whom she felt sorrier for—Granddad for being so misunderstood or Janie for not spending enough time with him to know the difference between what was real and what was rambling. She'd not brought up the beautiful stranger again, knowing that it *did* sound like one of the crazier things he'd ever said. Though Kate was still certain that there was more to it than what it seemed on the surface.

"Granddad *does* want me to do this. And *I* want to do this. What if I wait until we have more money or until it's easier, and by that time his mind is completely gone?" She paused. "And, Janie, it's *Southern California*. Haven't you ever wanted to see the ocean?"

Janie grinned and threw a pillow at her stomach. "You ninny. You can see the ocean here."

"Not the ocean in *Pacifica*. It's too rocky and too cold. I mean the kind where you can take off your shoes and get tanned and the sun shines all the time."

"All very nice things if you actually have a roof over your head and food in your belly. But you won't. You are forgetting once again that *you have no money*."

Kate's pulse raced. She'd test the waters.

"Grandma's ring."

Janie shot up. "Tell me I did not hear what I think I heard."

"Think about it," Kate pleaded, though she was trying to convince herself as much as she was her sister. "What if this works? What if this is my start for something new—something that helps the family, too? But I have to have money to even try. What else am I supposed to do?"

"But Grandma's *wedding ring*? Even when things have been at their worst, we haven't resorted to that. It's *sacrilege*."

Granddad didn't seem to think so. He'd been adamant.

Janie lay back down and pulled the covers past her chin, the sign that she would not talk about this anymore. Her silence sat between them like a boulder.

There was only one other option. Kate could ask Dimitri for the money. He would give it to her and not even expect to receive it back. It would be so easy.

And so unfair to him.

No, she couldn't do that. Whatever she did had to harm no one.

At least as much as she could help it.

～

The morning brought clarity. The fog in Kate's head lifted just as the one outside did. She hadn't slept, and her head felt the weight of exhaustion. She lay rigidly in the bed next to Janie to avoid waking her sister. There was enough disharmony between them as it was.

It was as she heard the first early trolley outside her window that the idea came to her. It wasn't perfect, but it sat in just enough of the gray area of rightness that she decided to risk it.

Instead of selling, she would pawn her grandmother's ring.

Kate had seen her parents do it with lesser things. A neighbor moved once and gave them an old violin as thanks for having helped her carry all the boxes down four flights of stairs. Janie was the only one who had interest in playing it, and that had lasted for all of a week. So Dad went to a pawnshop and got eighteen dollars for it. He took the family to dinner with the proceeds and bought Mom a pair of inexpensive earrings with the leftover change.

Before the receipt was signed, though, the pawnshop owner had told him that if they wanted the violin back, they could put it up as collateral for a short-term loan instead. Kate hadn't thought much of it at the time, and Dad wanted the money straight-out, but that conversation resurrected itself from the dusty corners of her mind now that she was desperate for options.

Janie bolted upright at the screech of their alarm clock. She always woke like her life depended on it—full of energy, ready for the rigors of the day. She had two modes to her—on and off. In the morning she was on.

From the kitchen, Kate could hear Dad brewing coffee and Mom frying eggs. They always worked the early shift at the restaurant. Not that Uncle Mike's was open for breakfast, but when you lived in San Francisco and worked in an establishment that served fish, it was expected to be fresh, fresh, fresh. So Mom and Dad left early to check out the first catches and plan the menu for the day based on what was available and how it was priced. Janie and Kate traded off, and luckily today was her sister's turn to join them.

Kate pulled the covers up to her eyes. Janie already had her bra fastened and her hair brushed. She'd showered last night—a model of efficiency that drew unwelcome contrast to Kate's own unhurried pace.

"Lazybones," said her sister. "Didn't you hear the alarm?"

Kate groaned. "I don't feel well." She forced a cough from deep in her throat and hoped it sounded convincing.

Janie walked over with brisk steps and put her arm on Kate's forehead. Sometimes their age difference felt like eleven years, considering the authority with which she acted.

"You're not hot."

"You don't have to have a fever to be sick."

"Do you have the rag on?"

Kate was ready to agree to whatever malady got her family out of the house and left her to do what she was going to do. And the nervousness she felt inside had made her skin feel clammy. It wasn't a stretch to say she felt ill.

"Yes. *Ow*, it hurts." She curled up into a fetal position and threw in an extra cough for good measure.

"If I bring you an aspirin, do you think you'll be ready to come in for the lunchtime shift?"

"Sure." Kate figured that if she was agreeable, her sister wouldn't linger.

It took everyone another half hour to clear out. Her parents checked in on her before they left. Dad stood at the door and blew a kiss to her as if breaching the threshold would make menstruation—or a phony case of it, in this circumstance—contagious.

Mom stopped in and brushed her fingers through Kate's hair. Kate crinkled her nose. Mom was wearing that Blue Waltz perfume they'd given her for her birthday. She always sprayed twice to make up for the inevitable stink of seafood that would permeate her every strand by the end of the day, and in the morning she smelled like an overripe bouquet of carnations.

"See you at lunch, my love?"

Kate nodded and pursed her lips together to keep from crying. She wouldn't see them at lunch. She might not see them for a very long time at all.

Today she would leave for San Diego before she talked herself out of it.

～

Zabie's Pawnshop opened at nine o'clock, and Kate was its first customer of the day. After her family left for work, she'd filled a suitcase with everything she could imagine needing in Southern California:

sandals, a sun hat, a bathing suit, summer dresses, the pink sweater that Mom had crocheted for her. Just in case the evenings were cool.

She also took the slim black dress and the black high heels she'd bought at a thrift store in the hope that the time would come when she'd have a place to wear them.

Someday she'd buy herself a brand-new dress. And ones for Mom and Janie, too. Maybe even expensive evening gowns. Real diamond earrings. Mom was always admiring the ones that were placed in the fancy display windows on Union Square.

But fifteen-cent tips needed to go toward rent payments, not the finery that was meant for the sort of people who would see that as pocket change.

The last thing she took was the ring. She could pack, she could dream, and the future would still just be speculation. But she knew that once she opened her mother's dresser drawer and took out the blue velvet box, possibility would become reality. Her hands shook as she placed them on the worn wooden knobs. She had to tug to pull the drawer open—years of moist bay air had warped the furniture, and its hesitance gave her one more second to reconsider.

Was she deluding herself by believing that she possessed the fortitude to make something of this venture? Or was she really no more than anyone had ever expected her to be? The fear was giving her a headache, and she stopped to rub her temples while she fought the temptation to give up.

But there was no possibility of succeeding if she let doubt fill her. She pulled the knob harder. At last it gave. Several pairs of socks and stockings lay on top, unorganized, holes in some pairs. It felt strange to go through Mom's things, the experience reminding her that she was intruding.

She pushed the hosiery aside and found the small box in the back corner.

Kate held it in one hand and struggled to close the drawer with the other.

She didn't dare open it. Seeing the ring would make her question everything. Though they knew it as Grandma Kitty's, it had been in Granddad's family long before that. But details were few. It was old, and that was the extent they knew of it. Old and dear, adding to the feeling that she was a thief within her own family.

But Granddad's insistence reverberated in her thoughts. He was so very clear in his intentions. It was his ring. His to give. And he wanted Kate to have it. He wanted Kate to take a leap and imagine a different future—for her and for their family.

Kate closed her eyes and put it in her pocket before running out of the apartment. She locked the door behind her, then rested her forehead against its splintered frame and sighed.

She was really going through with this.

She purposely walked twelve blocks to a pawnshop that wasn't in their neighborhood. Although she'd left a note of explanation, she didn't want it getting back to her parents that she'd been here or that she'd taken Grandma's ring until the train had departed with her on it. The danger in this, of course, was that she had no idea whether the owner would be trustworthy. She didn't know what the ring was worth, and until she stood here about to walk through this grimy door, she hadn't thought about what her plan would be if she didn't get as much for it as she might need for this trip.

And what did she even need? Train fare was only the beginning. She had to eat. She needed to stay somewhere. What did any of that cost? The pawnbroker could tell her that the ring was worth ten dollars or a thousand dollars, and she wouldn't have any notion how much of her expenses it would cover. Or whether he was leveling with her.

This was the last chance to change her mind, the seesaw battle of it almost making her dizzy. The safe choice was almost more appealing than forging on. It was a couple of hours before she'd be expected for the lunchtime shift, and she could go home, put the ring back in her mother's dresser drawer, and make it to the restaurant before anyone discovered that she'd come here.

But the image of Granddad's eyes would haunt her if she didn't give this a go. He'd gotten that look—that stubborn look that had served him well in life—and she couldn't fathom disappointing him. Or waiting until it was too late for him to have any connection to them at all.

Wasn't this the privilege of youth? To do impetuous things that were not always advisable? Was this not the very definition of *now or never?*

And wasn't this the very kind of risk that her family was loath to take, condemning them to the same daily grind?

The sensation of possibility was new for Kate. Exhilaration and fear resided in the same space, a phenomenon that she'd never experienced in the day-to-day sameness of her life.

She had to be stronger than fear. More resolute than doubt.

The bell on the pawnshop door jingled as the owner opened for business.

"Buying or selling?" he wheezed with cigarette-saturated breath. He was old enough that his age could be guessed in decades—maybe sixty, maybe seventy. He had ink stains on his shirt pocket and was a good four inches shorter than Kate.

"Selling. Pawning. Whatever your program is called where I can come and get this back after a while."

He shrugged and gestured for her to walk past him.

The shop smelled dusty, though it looked tidy enough. The offerings were eclectic—baseball mitts, framed autographs of sports figures, neglected musical instruments, jewelry, watches.

"Let's see what you've got."

Kate followed him to his counter. She pulled the box from her purse and opened it, looking behind her to make sure no one else was lurking in the shop. It seemed a foolish thing to lay out a piece of jewelry that could be swiped away by the wrong kind of person. And it wouldn't surprise her in this part of town.

But there wasn't a choice. The ring had loosened itself while she was walking, and it landed on the glass counter with a quiet tinkling sound.

Until this moment, she hadn't seen it in years. Not since she and Janie had taken turns playing grown-up with Mom's wedding dress, something they were far too old to do now. Grandma had let them try on the ring. It was made of a platinum band, tapered so that it was paper-thin in the back. The front looked like a small globe. A squared diamond on top, sapphires on either side. Kate wished she'd thought to ask Granddad where he'd gotten it while he might have still remembered. It was difficult to imagine that old people were ever young. That they might have had a love story—maybe even more than one.

The shop owner grunted out a cough—a real one, not Kate's forced variety—and it returned her thoughts to the matter at hand. He picked up the ring, and Kate's throat tightened.

Janie's voice came to mind. *Sacrilege.*

She gripped the countertop and felt the blood escape from her whitening knuckles. She breathed in deeply, dust tickling her nose.

"I don't know if I can sell this," he said, holding it up to a light.

Kate's heart skipped, disappointed at this pronouncement. Everything rode on acquiring this money. But then his eyes widened, belaying the words. He liked it. She could tell. Years of practice reading Granddad's expressions had taught her something about looking beyond words.

He wrapped what looked like a magnifying glass at the end of a bandanna around his head and peered at the ring, turning it over and dragging a lamp across the counter for a better look. The tiny scrollwork in the globe sent magnified rays from the light across the glass top.

"This is old. British, maybe. Or it could be German."

Old like Granddad? Or older?

He held it up between two fingers and took the magnifier off to look at it with his own eyes.

"But it's not much more than a trinket."

She watched his Adam's apple bob up and down, swallowing, the sign of a dry throat. A nervous one, perhaps? It stilled. He was waiting for an answer from her.

"But what is it worth?"

The man pulled a handkerchief from his pocket and wiped his nose. He shrugged.

"Eh. Look at the size of the stones. They're real, but they're small."

She exhaled a breath that she hadn't realized she'd been holding. It had to be enough to get her down to Coronado and see her through until she could figure out what to do next.

"I'll give you a hundred dollars if you pawn it, with ten percent interest to be paid back in five weeks. Or I can buy it outright for one seventy-five."

A hundred dollars! Kate felt faint at the thought of such a number, despite his calling it a "trinket." One hundred dollars could have saved her family from innumerable stresses. Did Granddad have any idea? Or was it too precious to him to have let go of until now?

She looked at other jewelry in the display case. Four hundred dollars. Five. Six. But none as beautiful as Grandma Kitty's.

That was so much money, and she knew nothing of business, but she was certain that he'd be able to sell it for much more. Not that he would let on. She'd seen Uncle Mike barter at the fish market, and he never took the first price offered. He talked them down, round after round until he was quoted something he was willing to pay. Maybe it would work in reverse.

"How—how about three hundred to pawn it?" Her voice quavered, but she stood up straight, towering over him and hoping that it made her sound knowledgeable. Was tripling it too much of a leap? Or didn't people overshoot in order to reach a middle ground?

The man squinted as he looked her over, and Kate wondered if he could tell how very inexperienced she was at this sort of thing.

"Two hundred," he said. If she—God forbid—couldn't pay him back at the end of the contract, she had no doubt that he could sell it for much more.

"Two seventy-five," she tried.

He snorted. "Two twenty-five."

"Two fifty." She folded her arms, trying to appear resolute. Truth was, one hundred was already more of a sum than she'd ever seen in her life.

He held it up to the light and turned it around in his fingers once more. "Two fifty," he agreed at last. "And remember—if you don't pick it up within five weeks, you relinquish it to me, and I sell it."

His narrow eyes stared at her without flinching. Without even blinking. Like one of the fish from the market.

But she'd won. A hundred and fifty dollars more than he'd originally offered. She hoped Uncle Mike would have been proud.

Surely that amount could get her to Coronado and feed her and house her for that amount of time. Five weeks? That had to be plenty of time to see whether Granddad's notion about the beautiful stranger was any more than a wild-goose chase. And enough to test her mettle among a Hollywood crowd. If she could land the job at the hotel.

But what if it *was* a dead end? She'd never be able to afford to buy the ring back with interest. Their tiny heirloom would be gone forever. And her family would be in even more debt than they were now.

It was enough to make her claustrophobic.

This could be their salvation. Or their ruin. It *had* to work. There was no other option except giving up. Something she could never live with now that she was this close.

Kate closed her eyes and took a deep breath.

"Done. Where do I sign?"

~

1892

To say that the view is beautiful is such an inadequacy, but I am in far too much pain to conjure more poetic words. So beautiful must suffice, though I know I do the ocean an injustice.

The light has receded now, and there is little color left to indicate that I am standing in front of the mighty Pacific Ocean. But the waves can still be heard—louder, even, than they are in the daytime. Whether that is because the tides are somehow more powerful at night or the people and their frolicking noises have deserted her for the evening, I cannot say. But the sound provides a different kind of beauty altogether.

I smile—oh, even the pain that comes with a smile!—at the thought that my own life will recede tonight with the waters. Like the darkness that has overcome the sky, the shadow that I've diminished into will enshroud the girl I once was.

Harry West has disappeared from the corner he was hiding in. Duty called, I presume, and surely there are more pressing matters for a bellboy at a place such as this than to stand guard over a mysterious woman who wallows in Room 302 waiting for a man who will never arrive.

Too bad about Harry. I have one more small task to tend to, and it would have been terribly convenient for him to take care of it for me.

The pain has subsided just now. It ebbs and flows like the ocean's tides, so I do not allow this respite from it to fool me for a moment that I am somehow on the mend. But there is no mending the tiny life inside me that fights, that causes this pain.

There is no mending the marriage I entered into so unwisely.

No mending. Only ending. Only ending.

Oh my, I am rambling and even rhyming. Is that a sign of anything? Maybe only that I am losing my mind as rapidly as I lose blood.

Yes. I have begun to bleed. It runs down my legs, and I am glad that I chose black to wear tonight. A high-necked frock. It looks like I'm attending a funeral.

In a way, I am.

I breathe. The temporary break from the sharp cramping allows me the time I need to walk down the grand staircase. Look at me! I am even fully upright, and I might pass for a great lady rather than a dying domestic. There is Harry, there. Carting in luggage for a superior woman who has two strands of pearls that hang down to her waist. Is that her husband behind her? She married well, it seems. That would be me if I'd listened to Mama and Papa and Grandfather.

Hello, Harry. I am well. You need not concern yourself with me. Oh, but I do not get to say these words out loud. He has stepped into the golden lace elevator with the woman's bags. Goodness, did she pack her entire household?

I hope she tips him generously, as I would if I were not here on credit. He has been a good helper—attentive, watchful. Does he have a sweet little wife at home, stirring the soup over the stove as we speak? Lucky girl indeed. If only I'd married a Harry instead of a Tom. I could do without material goods if I had a considerate man wedded to me.

I reach the reception desk. All made of dark wood, mahogany, maybe, as are the beamed ceilings and the walls. Wood, wood, wood. Hardness all around when just outside is the softness of sand. It is no doubt considered elegant, but I would paint it all white and make it a bit more cheery.

A uniformed attendant stands behind the registration bell.

"Mrs. Bernard," he says. And I forget for a moment that this is my name. Not my real name, remember, merely the one I wrote on the paperwork a few days ago.

"A favor, please," I ask. I reach into the pocket of my coat and withdraw a small blue velvet box. "This needs to be sent in the morning to Mr. and Mrs. Alan Morgan of 753 A Avenue."

"It's not very late, Mrs. Bernard, and this address is quite close to the hotel. I can dispatch Harry within the hour."

"No. In the morning, please. It would not do to disturb them this evening."

"Do you have a note I can send along with it?"

"No. Thank you. Just give them this box. They will know what it is for."

I do not say who it is for.

But this, too, they will know.

Chapter Three

Three days of travel quickly disillusioned Kate of the romantic notions she'd placed on this adventure.

Adventure. That was one word for it. If she'd known what she would be getting herself into, she might have listened to Janie. She hated that her sister had been right. But she had come too far, suffered too much, to turn back now.

She hoped the note she left for them explaining where she was would keep them all from worrying.

How naive she'd been to think that she just needed to board a train at the Southern Pacific Depot, though, and ride it all the way to San Diego. When she'd arrived, the ticket taker had corrected her assumption but promised a carefree trip in which she would only need to change trains in Los Angeles first.

One breakdown later, plus a delay due to a freight line dominating the same track, and an electric fire that caused the café car to be out of commission, Kate had finally arrived in Los Angeles, only to learn that the train she needed was *not* serviced by Southern Pacific, and she would have to travel across town to another station that could take her south.

A long day, indeed.

The one redeeming benefit: she'd seen that infamous sign from the taxi that took her between the two depots. There in bright-white letters against the green hill stood that dear word that captured the imagination of every young girl in America, including her own.

Hollywood.

Just think of it! She was only a few miles away from where celluloid magic was made and where the greats like Cary Grant and Marilyn Monroe and Elizabeth Taylor and Jimmy Stewart lived and worked. For those minutes she forgot the tumult she'd gotten herself into and remembered that this—*this!*—was the Southern California she'd dreamed of. Why, there were even palm trees! So many of them, and they seemed to rise into the sky by a thousand stories. Orange trees, too. If she stepped out into their groves, would the air be permeated with the sweetness of citrus?

But the taxi whizzed by, and soon the sign of legend was no longer visible, even from the window in the back. Like a mirage come and gone. Ominous, maybe? Janie would have made such a comment. Kate pushed the thought from her head.

They arrived at a dingy train station, and she paid the driver, though she realized as he drove off that she'd forgotten to tip him. The Morgan family did not swim in circles where they tipped people—they were the ones receiving them. They were the ones who suffered bone-deep weariness from hours of dipping battered fish into boiling oil and scrubbing ketchup stains and bubble-gum residue from tables.

Next time she would remember and planned to put a few coins in her pocket to make it easier.

In the depot, she crinkled her nose at the stench of stale urine. It reminded her of some of the street corners in San Francisco. She hurried over to the ticket counter, gripping her suitcase and adjusting her purse so that it lay across her shoulder. She didn't need Janie to be right about the possibility of being mugged.

And this looked like the kind of place where that just might happen.

Kate bought her ticket for the remainder of the trip to San Diego, but the next one was not leaving until the morning. Fear gripped her nerves at the idea of staying in this station overnight, but she also needed to preserve her money and could not afford to take another taxi ride nor pay for a hotel.

She took a seat nearest a door where a policeman stood guard. No one would do anything in front of a policeman.

Hours passed, each second on the overhead clock ticking a temptation to turn around and go home. Kate sat, immobile, hugging her purse to her lap, placing her feet on her suitcase. If she nodded off and someone tried to take it, it would jar her awake.

Her legs tingled with the ache for movement, but she could only stretch them one at a time, as she didn't want to give up her seat in the safety of this spot.

Sleep eluded her, as there was just enough bustle in the station to keep her alert. It wouldn't do to sit like this all night, though. Her head pounded from weariness. Her stomach groaned in protest of the hours and hours spent in neglect. Her throat burned with thirst. All these she could endure, but at last, she could no longer control what else was ailing her.

She would need to find a ladies' room soon. She hadn't been since Bakersfield, and what little water she'd managed to drink was catching up with her. She tapped her foot on the suitcase to distract herself from this growing urgency.

"You too?"

A female voice echoed in the large space. Kate turned her head to see that a red-lipped girl with tight blonde curls had made her way to the benches.

"What do you mean?" asked Kate.

"You going home, too? Hollywood spit you out and you're heading back to Mom and Pops with your tail between your legs? I don't know if the taste of gasoline exhaust or of humble pie is worse."

"I—I don't know what you're talking about."

"The pictures. Aren't you here for the pictures like everyone else?"

She was probably one of the many starlets who had left Kansas or other places east to come here to pursue her big ambitions.

"Well," she answered. "Almost. I'd like to work on a set."

The girl waved her arm around, and a whiff of gardenia-scented perfume trailed her. A welcome respite from the fetor around them. "Good for you, then. Most gals our age are out here for their big on-screen break. Everyone thinks they're the next Elizabeth Taylor. And most get chewed up and thrown to the curb. It's not all it seems, ya know."

Kate's heart sped up. Hollywood. Just like the sign on the hill. She'd heard that it had an underbelly. But she'd never wanted to believe it. It was all so glossy in the theater. Kate wanted it to be so in reality, too. On- and offscreen.

The girl pulled out a cigarette case and offered one to Kate.

She shook her head. Uncle Mike's restaurant was saturated with the soot of years of tobacco use, and she had no stomach for it.

"More for me." The girl shrugged. "My name's Maisy Watson. You?"

"Kate. Kate Morgan. I'm from San Francisco."

Maisy whistled. "San Francisco. Gee, now there's a city I'd like to see. Maybe I should trade my ticket and head that way."

"Where are you from?"

"Glenwood Springs, Colorado."

"I've never heard of it."

"Yeah, most people haven't. But you've heard of Doc Holliday? From the Wild West?" She shot two fingers out like they were pistols.

"I suppose most people have," said Kate.

"Well, that's what we're known for. Hot natural waters and Wild West antics and Doc Holliday's grave site."

Kate smiled. "And home to Hollywood star Maisy Watson?"

Maisy laughed. "Ha! That's the brand of optimism I had a few months ago. You've heard of the casting couch?"

Kate shook her head.

Maisy crossed her arms and leaned in. "Producers, directors, they all do it."

"Do what?"

"Promise a girl a lead part in exchange for . . . well, you know."

Kate's blank reaction must have shown on her face.

"You really don't know, do ya?" Maisy grinned as her eyes widened. She put a hand on Kate's knee. "Starts off with them only wanting a little smooch. Just to see if you'll go along with it. Not such a big deal, right? But if you're cool . . . if you'll give them that much, then they go after more. My word, if a girl thinks all she has to do is memorize some lines to make it in this crazy town, she's fooling herself. You learn quick where to put exactly which parts of your body on theirs, and not always in the places you might think. Ha! And my parents thought I got an education at Glenwood High. That was nothing."

Kate was appalled. She'd always been taught the value of hard work, but Maisy painted a much darker picture. She found herself wondering what lay behind the mysterious eyes of the platinum-blonde idols whose pictures she cut from magazines and just what exactly she was getting herself into. Maybe it was like *Through the Looking Glass*, where their side of the mirror harbored a distorted world that was only seen by the rare few.

"I—I hope that never happened to you," Kate ventured.

Maisy shrugged. "More than once. I'm not square. I played along. But some stuff . . . it got weird. Besides, nothing came of it except for a few walk-ons and one-liners. So I had to scrape up the odd bit of money here and there however I could. Whatever it takes, ya know."

Kate's mind raced as she tried to picture what Maisy was saying. Already Southern California was a whole different world than the few square blocks around Powell Street. Even gleaned from only two train depots and the taxi ride between them.

"And it wasn't worth pushing through? Surely there are directors who don't, uh, demand so much," Kate asked.

"Sure there are. And ya gotta starve in the meantime or get gray hair waiting for them to give you a screen test. Not me. I'm down to my last three dollars, and that's got to last me until Colorado."

Three dollars. That might give the girl enough to buy food for a few days, but what if she needed more in a pinch? Kate thought about all the money she was carrying. Though she'd planned to save every penny possible, the advice Maisy had given her even in this brief time was so valuable. She unzipped her purse and pulled out the two dollars in change she'd received when she bought her ticket to get here.

"I hate the idea of you getting in a bind. Why don't you take these?"

Maisy put her hand to her mouth and shook her head. "I can't accept that. You're going to need everything you have."

Kate kept her hand out. "Then how about this? Take it for now, and when you get home, just mail it back to me. Kate Morgan at the Hotel del Coronado."

It was a gamble. What if she didn't get the job?

Maisy extended her hand and reluctantly took the money from Kate. "That is so nice of you."

Kate shrugged. Mom always said, *What goes around comes around,* and maybe this gesture would be returned if Kate were ever in need of help.

She clasped her hands into a fist and dug them into her knees. She really needed to get to the ladies' room. "Will you be here for a few minutes?"

"I'm here until my limousine arrives."

"Limo—"

Maisy threw her head back and laughed. "I'm kidding! I'm waiting for my train, just like you. Do I look like I have a limousine?"

Kate felt her cheeks heat up, feeling like the bumpkin she was in comparison. She smiled. "No."

She really needed to get there now, with an urgency that prompted her to ask Maisy to watch her suitcase for her. "I'll be right back," she promised.

Maisy shrugged again, her attention taken by a magazine left on the bench. "Sure thing. I'm not going anywhere until the conductor calls for the Eastbound Coaster. And hey—"

Kate turned around.

"Be careful who you trust with requests like that. This is the sort of town that will burn you."

"Thank you!"

Kate hurried off to the restroom down the hall. While she washed her hands, she looked in the mirror and was appalled by what she saw. She hadn't shampooed her hair in days, and if she'd had a bottle of Breck with her, she'd hold her nose and get it done right here in this sink. Instead she pulled it into a tight ponytail. In the morning she'd apply some rouge and lipstick before boarding the train. Cosmetic courage as she ventured into the exact sort of life Maisy was warning her about.

Maybe San Diego would be a good proving ground for her. It wasn't the belly of Hollywood, and she was merely trying to get a job working on the set, as described in the advertisement. A taste of it. If it was sweet, she'd stay and try to make a go of it. If it was bitter, she could head back home and never wonder what it would have been like to try.

Either way, she was grateful that Maisy's caution had given her a reason to keep her wits about her. Though, in truth, the girl's words also tempted Kate toward giving in to the fear that would make it so easy to turn around right now.

But could she live with that? Could she return to the restaurant, marry someone bland and safe, and look into the eyes of her husband and children and not boil in resentment at never having tried to see who she was on her own?

And another thought made her shudder—could she face Granddad, who'd pinned his hopes on her? Hopes about his past . . . and about her future.

Kate forced a smile at her reflection. She had to do this. Here she was, just miles away from it all! The thought made her giddy in spite of everything.

Whatever happened, she had to buy the ring back from the pawn-broker within five weeks. That meant she had to preserve as much of the two hundred and fifty dollars as possible. And she had to get the job—or any job—so as not to jeopardize that for her family.

She'd already abandoned them by leaving. She wouldn't do more by losing the only heirloom they would ever hope to have.

Kate felt refreshed after washing her face. She could do this. She could spend the night here, and tomorrow would be a brand-new day. Janie was wrong. The real adventure was about to begin.

As she walked toward her seat, a man in a bow tie sat where she and Maisy had spoken. Her pulse raced.

Where was Maisy?

Where was her suitcase?

She looked right and left and ran over to a window to see if a train was being boarded. But the tracks were empty.

Nothing.

Kate's stomach twisted.

"Excuse me," she said to the man, pushing past the fact that she felt ill.

He looked up from his newspaper, irritated by the interruption.

"Did you see a girl who was just here? Red lips, blonde curls?"

"Oh, yes. She bumped into me on her way out the door. Seemed to be in a hurry."

Out the door. Out the door.

Not toward the train.

"And did she—" Kate held her hand to her mouth to keep from crying, but her lip quivered beneath it. Every nerve in her face tingled as the truth became evident. "Did she have a black suitcase with her?"

He nodded. "Yeah, and in the morning I'll probably have a bruise on my shin to show for it. A friend of yours?"

Kate darted to the entrance, wild with worry, her heart racing, pushing like it was going to fly out of her chest. Janie's concerns were coming true after all. Kate was shoved back by a man nearing the same door. She finally passed him and made her way onto the street. It was dark—so dark—and the glow of headlights was all that illuminated the black evening. Everything was in silhouette—cars, people, palm trees. She could not make out discernible shapes.

Maisy was long gone. And it felt like the ground had been pulled from under Kate's feet.

Kate returned to the concourse of the depot and slumped into the seat the con girl had vacated. It was still warm from where she'd been, not unlike a body just after a death. That's what Kate mourned—the death of her trusting nature.

Her sister's rightness.

She unzipped her purse and riffled through its contents.

Her money from the ring was in there, as was her ticket for the rest of her trip. That was one relief. But she'd lost all her clothes, her shoes, her Brownie camera, her hairbrush, her swimsuit. Her dress. It was all replaceable, but you had to have *money* to purchase even basic things. And what money sat in her wallet didn't have much room for stretching. Not if she needed to save the bulk of it and more for the pawnbroker.

As the Eastbound Coaster was called and the station emptied, Kate curled up on the bench, caring little that it might be full of decades of grime. Caring little about anything. She put her purse under her head as a pillow, looping the strap around her arm, and tucked the money into her bra. The bills lay across her chest, protected by a rapid heartbeat that was on alert for anything that might attempt to separate them.

She wanted to retch. But she'd eaten so little that even her stomach betrayed her, and she lay with a knot in her belly that felt like a gut punch.

Had anyone ever died of humiliation?

She looked up at the ceiling. It was made of wood and painted with geometric patterns that would probably have seemed dizzying even if she weren't suffering from the deprivation of sleep and stench of betrayal. The round lights that hung from the beams looked like UFOs from the science fiction magazines that Dimitri hid from his parents. She wiped her nose with a tissue as she thought of home. Mom, Dad, Janie, Granddad, Uncle Mike. Dimitri.

She'd made a tremendous mistake going on this fool's mission.

~

1892

The halls of the Hotel del Coronado are quiet. It is even past the hour when revelers in the bar have gone home to whatever they were drinking to avoid.

I never take the drink myself, but in my marriage to Tom I witnessed enough of it from his associates and heard their blathering as they became ever more inebriated. It was not out of some pious religiosity that I abstained. Instead, it was the appalling nature of those who imbibed and the spectacles they made of themselves. I wanted no part.

My pain has intensified. The reasonableness of my words might indicate that I am of sound mind, while in fact I am feeling half-crazed with each wave of sharpness that stabs at my abdomen. I am again relieved that I purchased the gun, because there is nothing I want more than to escape this misery. But I am determined not to subject the housemaids to this folly, so instead I will gather the remnants of wits I have left, and I will go outside, where the waves should carry me away.

I do not want to be a burden. I know that when my fate is discovered, my grandfather or even G. L. will settle my hotel account, and the Del will be only minimally put out. My family will be devastated, of course. We were always so close—my parents, my grandfather, and me. They were bewildered that a man like Tom could have fascinated me as he did, but to their credit, they loved me even through all that.

But as his nature became apparent to me, I could not subject them to it, and so I disappeared and lied whenever necessary to try to hide from him, and in doing so I had to hide from them. That's why I must end things. So that he will never find me again. And so that he will never find out about . . . my secret.

My steps slow once again. But I am almost there.

I am almost there.

I am almost there.

It is agony, but I must do this. I'm heading to the westernmost corner of the hotel, nearest the ocean. The cool air hits my face as I open the door. No one is about. No one sees me leave.

With my right hand, I steady myself on the banister. My left hand slides into my coat pocket and strokes the cold, odd shape of the pistol that will bring me relief. Its smooth barrel. Its rough handle. A grip, they called it at the shop. I do grip it now, feeling its heft as my palm encircles it. And for the briefest moment, I panic at the thought of what I am about to do.

I have thought only of what it will be like to be on the other side of this disaster. The freedom from pain. The liberation from my marriage. Releasing this child in my womb from whatever is causing it to expel itself before it's even grown enough for my belly to swell.

But I have not thought until just now of the horribleness of the actual event, and I am beginning to have my doubts.

The worries spread like tendrils, perhaps as a harbinger of the blood that will do the same if I go through with this. Will the pain of it be worse than what I am already feeling? Will my family not merely feel bereft at my passing but inconsolable that it is at my own hand? Can I do that to them?

Can I really end my own life?

The idea sickens me, and hellish warnings from childhood sermons give me cause for hesitation.

I am talking myself out of it.

There must be other ways. I can accept the hotel staff's insistence on finding a doctor for me. I can talk to the police about Tom, though they have not been of help in the past. He charms even the most hardened officer. But maybe there will be someone else—some authority who will believe me when I tell them what a monster he is—and they will help me find another way out of it.

I take a deep breath of the salty ocean air, and it fills my lungs like an elixir. I smile for the first time in as long as I can remember. If there is not hope, then what is there to save us? And I must cling to hope. If not for me, then for my family. If not for my family, then for my child.

I breathe again. And one more time. I am almost euphoric, and I understand now why people are sent to the ocean when they have ailments. It is already curing me of my despair.

I turn and grasp the banister in order to walk back upstairs when I hear footfalls on the sidewalk below me. I shiver, though the air is warm.

A voice speaks.

"Kate."

All the goodwill that the air has given me leaves my body as I speak the one word that is more abhorrent to me than any other.

"Tom."

Chapter Four

It was impossible for Kate to sleep after being so violated by Maisy's unexpected theft. Was the girl a gifted swindler who used her acting skills for thievery when she couldn't use it for the movies? Or was all that Hollywood talk just a sham and Maisy was a crook to begin with? She probably wasn't even from Glenwood Springs. Anyone could find a book about a small mountain town like that and learn enough to pretend to be from there.

Maisy might not even be her real name.

Was this the reality of Southern California? Kate thought back to the glossy travel posters and the legends that surrounded it, and their memories made her feel sick in the face of this betrayal. In fact, maybe Janie's fears were right—though she hated to admit it—and it was just a cesspool of con artistry. A fabrication, like the movies on-screen.

Only hours down here, and she already felt herself changing. Maisy had taken not only her suitcase but her optimism.

As soon as the ticket office opened, she would buy a return fare home.

Kate realized she'd drive herself mad if she tried to relive the event and make sense of it, though. There was no explanation that would make her any less robbed.

Instead she picked up a copy of *The Catcher in the Rye* that had been left on a nearby bench, its cover ripped off in jagged tears. But reading Holden Caulfield's message of rebellion and running away hit a little too close to home right now, and its setting at an institution near Hollywood only exacerbated that feeling. She laid it down when she got to the part where he and Sally got into an argument because she wouldn't go live in the wilds of New England with him.

Kate's eyes burned with tiredness, and she had to blink every few seconds to keep them from drying out. Her headache rivaled the kind she'd get when she'd worked a twelve-hour day at the restaurant. The thought of returning to it reminded her of her failure. She hoped her family would all be happy to see her. But she imagined the disappointment in Granddad's eyes and the shame of telling her parents how much money she had to pay back to the pawnbroker.

There was no easy answer.

Just before dawn, Kate decided to do something that she never would have imagined in the past. She headed back to the ladies' room before it became busy with arrivals and departures. She removed her shirt and picked up a half-worn bar of soap sitting in a little pool of water. Years of such residue had stained the white porcelain basin with streaky lines.

She held the soap in her hand, remembering the rose-scented one from the five-and-dime that Mom always bought for Janie and her. Her eyes welled up at the thought.

She ran the soap under a faucet until it lathered and tried not to think about all the people who had used it before her. Instead, she considered her options. She could head home and plead with the pawnbroker to return the ring and reduce the interest. And return to the familiarity of the restaurant and the comfort of family.

And that would be a life sentence.

Granddad's voice haunted her.

Find the beautiful stranger, he'd begged. But what he hadn't said resounded even more loudly. In giving her the advertisement, in encouraging her to sell the ring, he'd told her this: go follow your dreams.

How could she ever face him if she didn't at least try? And how could she encourage her parents if she couldn't follow through with it herself?

She raised the bar to her shoulders and began to wash herself. Too late, she realized that there were no towels, so she waved her arms around to air-dry and did the same with the rest of her body.

Mercifully, no one walked in, and she vowed to be grateful for the miracle of hot water every time she took a shower in the future. Her hair was still impossible, and she was afraid that hand soap would leave it looking oily, so she combed her fingers through her hair and reset it in a new, tight ponytail.

She was surprisingly refreshed after the pitiful little routine, and it gave her fresh courage to press on. At least she would arrive in San Diego mostly clean.

This train ride was uneventful—just over an hour—and upon arrival she took another taxi to the dock that would lead her—at last!—on the ferry ride to Coronado. There was a long line of cars and even a school bus waiting to board the auto ramp. She bought her ticket at a hexagonal white booth and sat down in a section with the passengers who would be walk-ons like herself.

A waft of hot pretzels came through on a breeze, so she walked over to a concession area. Thirty-five cents. That would equal her tips from two small tables at the restaurant, which would be an hour of work. And it would take all of a couple of minutes to eat it. The injustice of it pained her, but not more so than the hollow feeling in her stomach.

She chose an extra-salty one, deciding against the ice-cold Coca-Cola to go with it. That would have been another twenty-five cents—a mere drop against the fortune she carried in her purse, but such extravagances could add up if she wasn't disciplined about it. She took it back to her seat.

"Those are my favorite, too."

To her right, a young man several years older than her spoke. He had light-brown hair, some scattered freckles, and a smile that would normally make her feel flushed. He was handsome in a different sort of way. Not the kind that would grace the covers of a magazine but the kind who looked like he would be great fun to be friends with.

Yesterday morning she might have let her thoughts dangle over a smile like his. But not after the night she'd had.

She clutched her purse and even the pretzel, as if he might take them from her.

"Mm-hmm," she mumbled in response, imagining that he might be another Maisy. She scooted away from him, though as she was sitting next to a wall, there was not much room.

The man was persistent. "Heading to Coronado?"

"Isn't everyone here?"

He laughed. "You don't make it very easy to talk to you."

She felt bad. It wasn't like her to be so snide. But this whole trip wasn't like her, either. She'd grown up in just the last few hours. Why didn't they teach a class in high school about surviving out in the world? To not be so trusting, so guileless?

Kate didn't like this version of herself. She took a breath and tried to recapture the spirit of the girl who'd boarded the train in San Francisco. The one full of hope. How was she supposed to emerge from such a betrayal and recover that piece of herself that could trust?

"I'm sorry," she said. "I am not trying to be rude. But I am tired. This is all I've eaten in the last day, my suitcase was stolen, and . . ." She couldn't finish her sentence. The tears she'd held at bay ever since bringing her grandmother's ring to the pawnshop chose this very moment to erupt, despite her best efforts.

"Jeez Louise, you've had it rough." He pulled a handkerchief from his pocket and reached forward as if he was going to dab her eyes with it, but he hesitated.

Kate looked up at him. His eyes were green like the jade baubles that could be purchased in Chinatown. He seemed trustworthy enough. But then, wouldn't a well-rehearsed con be able to become anything you wanted him to be?

The man kept the handkerchief in his palm and laid his hand flat as one would when offering bread crumbs to a timid squirrel. "Well, my name's Sean. Sean O'Donnell. Good Italian boy."

Kate almost cracked a smile at his joke. But maybe he was just disarming so he could snatch her purse.

"Anyway," he said as he continued to keep his hand out, "I have three older sisters. One is a math teacher in Pasadena, and the other two are married and live here in San Diego. And what about me? Oh, thanks for asking."

Kate hadn't asked. But he continued talking. Rambling, even. Maybe to distract her. She felt herself closer to that smile.

"I'm biding my time until the University of California builds their campus here in a few years, and in the meantime I'm working at the Hotel del Coronado."

She gasped. "That's where I'm heading," she admitted.

His eyebrows popped up, letting her see more of his green eyes. "Really? The hotel?"

Sean halted his breath like he was about to ask something else. Probably *why*, considering she looked like someone who bathed herself in a train station restroom. But maybe he was too polite to press it.

Kate pursed her lips. She had to decide to trust him or not. If there was any chance of her making it here, she had to be able to let people help her. Or her journey might as well be over. If he worked at the Hotel Del, he was as good a resource as she had yet.

She loosened her grip on her purse and tried to relax. In the distance, the ferry rolled in, and people in the waiting area started to collect their bags. She almost told him about Granddad, about the beautiful stranger, but she might lose any credibility she had by starting with such a ridiculous-sounding task. And she had a more urgent need.

"Do you know if the wait-staff positions for the movie set are still available?"

She'd brought the advertisement with her, folded and creased in the zipper compartment of her purse. The date on it might as well have been written in red ink, so much did it stand out to her. The journey had taken longer than she'd expected, and the job notice had expired yesterday.

Sean folded his arms and cocked his head, seeming to look at her in a different way. "Do you have any experience?"

"I work in my uncle's restaurant. I can do kitchen work. And waitressing."

His eyes sparkled like he was amused. "I can ask around. I can't make any promises, though."

Her spirits lifted. She had a thousand other questions she wanted to ask, but the ferry pulled up and its mighty horn drowned out any other sound. A cacophony of engines started—those exiting the ferry, those preparing to enter.

Sean's fingertips touched her shoulder so lightly that she almost didn't feel it. He guided her toward the line with the passengers waiting to board. She reached down to pick up her luggage until she remembered that it had been stolen, renewing the resentment that she'd carried for the last few hours. But the possibility of being able to get the job seemed to be its antidote, and it took little time to push those thoughts away. She gripped the handle of her purse and walked forward as he slung a canvas bag over his shoulder.

Two large American flags flapped in the breeze on either side of the boat. Passengers entered on a central ramp while the cars that drove on lined the perimeter. Men in official-looking jackets waved their arms, directing drivers to squeeze into impossible spaces so that every last one would make it aboard. She started to follow everyone up the stairs that led to a seating area, but Sean put his hand on her arm and held her back.

"Aren't we going up there?" she asked, turning her head toward the second story.

"No," he said as he winked at her. "That room is only for people who see the ferry as a means to an end. To get from point A to point B."

"Isn't that what it is?"

He clutched his hands over his heart and began to double over. "Oh, that hurts like a dagger. I pegged you for a girl who has more imagination than that."

"I—I'd like to think I do," she said. His words should have made her nervous, but despite being frazzled, despite the betrayal in the train station yesterday, she wanted to trust him.

"Follow me." He took her hand in his, a gesture that was probably casual on his part, steadying her as the ferry prepared to rumble forward. She had never held a man's hand before, and she found that she liked how it felt. Her slim, bony hand in his larger one.

They wove their way through the impossibly narrow spaces between the cars. Kate jumped when a man leaned against his car horn and yelled something that was muffled through the window.

Sean looked back. "Never mind him. Some people are just born grumpy."

At last they reached the back of the ferry, and he leaned over the railing.

"What do we do now?" asked Kate.

"We wait until she gets out a little farther."

She referred to the ferry, Kate assumed, remembering that feminine characteristics were usually attributed to boats.

"And do what?" she asked.

He turned his head and looked at her sideways. "Do, do, do. Are you always in such a hurry?"

If he thought she was always in a hurry, he should meet Janie. Still, his words stung. Both she and Janie had done their best in school, rushed to the restaurant for the evening shift, and usually worked weekends. Sometimes their efforts felt aimless, because it was understood that they'd stay on there beyond graduation. No talk of career or college for the Morgan girls.

Maybe if she'd been a boy, it would have been different. It might have seemed more natural to encourage a son to go to college. She'd never heard one word pass her parents' lips that made her think they'd wished for anything more than their two daughters, but she wondered whether she might have had different opportunities if things were reversed.

Sometimes she questioned what the point of it all was. But no other choice had been available. Until Granddad saw through her frustrations and offered her this chance.

Sean had seen right through her, too. Her epitaph might just read "Busy." It would sum up her life in a single, efficient word. That's why this trip was so out of character for her. She'd obeyed for so many years. She never took a day off. Never stopped *doing*.

It was the Morgan way, and there was little room for doing otherwise. Even if it came more naturally to Janie.

Maybe that was to stave off dreaming about other possibilities. If they stayed busy enough, if they worked enough, they wouldn't have the time to face their fears about trying something else.

It worked for Dad, Mom, Janie, and Uncle Mike. But Kate and Granddad shared a restlessness. One that bloomed during their excursions to the movies and their mutual interest in reading newspapers from elsewhere.

"What are you looking at?" Sean asked when she hadn't answered. She realized that she'd just been staring at him through her musings.

"It's my freckles, isn't it?" he said before she could answer.

"No!" she said hurriedly. Though, in fact, they were rather plentiful and part of his charm.

"We have a saying in Ireland. *A face without freckles is like a sky without stars.*"

Kate smiled. "I like that. I like—your freckles." She felt herself blush at admitting such a thing.

He stood up straight and faced her. "I have a nephew who is four years old. My sister had just taught him how to do dot-to-dot drawings. Next time I was over for dinner, he said, 'Uncle Sean, what kind of picture does your face make?'"

Kate put her hand over her mouth to keep from laughing. "What did you tell him?"

Below her, the engine of the ferry roared, and the movement jostled her. She grabbed the railing.

Sean folded his arms. "I told him, 'Why, whatever you want. Care to try?' So I gave him a pen and lay down on the couch and let him get to work."

"What did he draw?"

He traced a finger across his cheeks. "A star. He connected this one, and this, and this and this." He continued until she saw that you could, in fact, draw that shape across his face if you connected those particular freckles.

"Then the saying is doubly true for you," she said. "You have freckles *and* stars."

"Freckles *and* stars," he repeated, grinning. "What a lucky lad I am, then. Two for the price of one, all on one face."

Kate giggled and found that she felt better than she had since she'd left home.

"You don't have an accent for being Irish."

"Born and raised in San Diego to parents who immigrated when they were children. But you'd never know it. We eat corned beef like the world would end if we didn't, and the occasional 'lad' and *slainte* creep in. My parents fly the green, white, and orange year-round."

The ferry was rolling now at a steady pace. Sean pulled the bag from his shoulder and opened the top.

She peeked in. It was full of bread in paper bags. She touched the loaves—they were all stale.

"What are these for?"

"They're for the birds," he said. "I get these from the baker every day. Two days old, unsellable. But the seagulls love them."

He offered a slice to her and pulled one out for himself. "Just rip it like this and throw."

She tore the bread in half and then in half again. It wasn't so difficult, and it didn't crumble as much as she expected. She flung a piece over the stern of the ferry, and almost immediately a swarm of gulls appeared as if conjured by a gifted magician. As they sailed farther and farther from the dock, Kate marveled at the stamina of the birds, flapping on for such a distance in eager exchange for bread that people wouldn't stoop to eat.

In addition, their reflexes were sharp. She and Sean continued to fling pieces of bread into the wind, and while some landed in the water that rippled in the wake of the ferry, most were caught midair by the magnificent creatures.

For ten minutes this continued, the birds never showing weariness, the glee between Kate and Sean increasing.

"Look at that one," he shouted over the engine, pointing to a seagull that swooped almost to the water to catch a morsel in its beak.

"And there," she yelled, showing him two birds that nearly collided going after the same piece.

She and Sean reached into the bag at the same time. Their hands touched, and she shivered. She glanced up and saw him looking back at her. In place of his smile was an expression that she could only describe as wistful. He pulled his hand away.

"Last piece is yours," he offered, handing it to her. But his demeanor became more subdued. She wondered what might be going through his mind. If his heart beat rapidly as hers did when they'd touched.

"Share?" She tore it in two and gave him the other half.

When they were done, Sean turned the paper bag upside down and shook it over the edges. "For the fish," he told her, though she wasn't sure such tiny crumbs would feed anything larger than a minnow.

Sean put his bag back over his shoulder. "Let's head to the front. You've got to see this."

She followed him to the bow, curious. They wove their way among the cars once again. When they arrived, her breath caught at the sight before her. Her pulse raced in awe.

This, *this* was the Southern California she'd always pictured. Water, palm trees, seagulls. The salty smell of the air. The ferry building came into view—its arched stucco walls painted yellow, its red tiled roof set against the blue of the water, the green of the trees. If paradise existed somewhere in the afterlife, it could not be more stunning than what lay before her.

"Beautiful, isn't she?" said Sean in a tone she could hear just above the dying engines. "Coronado. It means 'crowned one.'"

Coronado. She couldn't bring the word to her lips, a sense of reverence overtaking her. For its beauty. For the mysteries it held about her grandfather. For all she'd dreamed it would be.

"It's perfect," she whispered. "What an absolutely perfect name."

Sean crossed his arms and faced her again. "Speaking of names, I'm at quite the disadvantage. We've known each other for a full half hour, and you know a lot about me. But I know nothing about you. Including your name."

"It's Kate."

"Kate," he repeated. "I like it. Does it come with a last name?"

"Morgan. My name is Kate Morgan."

Sean unfolded his arms, and his skin turned so pale that his freckles were even more pronounced. "Is that some kind of joke?"

That wasn't the reaction she'd expected. A joke? Why would she kid about that? "No," she answered, shaking her head. "What do you mean?"

He still looked ashen. "The ghost. The Hotel del Coronado has a ghost. And her name is Kate Morgan."

~

1892

"Tom," I say. I don't know what to feel at the sight of him. I've waited for days for him to come here. To sign the papers that would dissolve our disastrous marriage. But he never showed, probably spending the days cheating another poor soul or bedding another unfortunate prostitute.

But the surprise turns to fear when I look in his eyes.

"There's my wife," he says, sending chills through me. I smell alcohol on his breath, and I want to retch. "My wife, my wife, my little wife. Waiting here for me just as I told her to."

He staggers forward, and I step back, but his legs are longer than mine, and I am easily overtaken. He trips on a rock and barrels into me. He falls to his knees, and his hands slide down my side. The feel of him sickens me, just as it did when he came into my room months ago and insisted that I do my wifely duty. Maybe his coercion cursed the child, and this terrible pain is its result.

Tom grips my long black skirt, tearing its lace as he tries to steady himself and stand upright. But his hands remain at my hips, and he begins to pat them.

I want to run. But I have run in the past, and I learned that it is far better to acquiesce. Fear emboldens him. Makes the inevitable even worse.

"What is this?"

My heart beats faster. He's found it.

The gun.

He slides his right hand into my pocket, and I close my eyes tightly. Tom and alcohol and guns are lethal enough individually. Together—they are horrific.

"What is this, Katie Kate Kate?" he asks. His breath is truly wretched, and I turn my face the nearer he gets to it. "A gun? What is my Kate doing with a gun?"

I think, I have a gun so that I can escape a world that exists with you in it. But I do not say these words out loud, of course. I remain still.

"I'm talking to you, wife. I said, 'What the hell are you doing with a gun?'"

When I don't answer, he draws it out and waves it up over his head. The moonlight illuminates it, and I can see every detail of the deadly piece. What was I thinking, buying this? Was the pain so great that I thought I could have ended my life? Did I really believe I could have done that to my grandparents and my parents who love me so desperately?

My decision rendered the gun harmless. But in Tom's hands . . . in Tom's hands . . .

I can't finish the thought. He can come by a gun with no problem, but I do not want to be responsible for whoever might find himself—or herself—at the other end of this particular one. It would be my fault in some way. My fault for giving him possession of this one.

I stand on my tiptoes and reach for it, but he is too tall, too overpowering. Instead, his arm swings down and, too quickly for me to move, it lands against the side of my cheek, causing unbelievable agony.

I'd learned to expect the burn that came routinely from the back of his hand. But this hard metal is too much, and I collapse onto the bottom step. I want to scream, but the ocean waves would drown the sound—and I know better than to encourage Tom.

He leans over me. "You always were a malcontent," he spits, brandishing the weapon once again as if he'd never seen or used one. I curl my lips inward and bite them until I feel the bitter taste of blood seep onto my tongue. I force my breathing to remain steady despite the pounding of my heart that races in terror. Tom slips a finger next to the trigger and spins it around, over and over. Despite the throbbing in my cheek, I pull myself up to the next step.

But Tom follows me. I do my best not to let him see me tremble.

Maybe I can buy time if I talk.

"Where have you been?" I ask. I say it sweetly. Tom always liked when I spoke softly in our bedroom. He said loudness and crassness were for whores. Docility for wives.

He pauses, sitting down next to me, and for the briefest of moments, I think that I am safe if I only keep talking this way. He places his hand against my cheek. "Did I hurt you, Katie? It's not my fault, you know. I came to the hotel looking for my wife, and instead of her being asleep in her bed as she should be, waiting for her husband, I find her outside in the middle of the night like a trollop. With a gun. You have one chance to answer me. Why did you have that in your pocket? Did you plan to use it on me?"

His hand moves from my cheek down to my breast, and he squeezes. It is already aching from the milk that will come in fully in a few months, and his touch is excruciating. He moves in closer, his other hand starting to pull at my skirt, and I can't do this again. I can't pretend to love him when I loathe him enough to put a bullet through his heart.

My face becomes feverish—with anger, with fear—fighting off the infection that is my husband. Sweat gathers on my forehead, and I know that I can't live another minute with this man on the earth.

If I am to have any chance of freedom, I have to end this.

It's he who deserves to die. Not me.

See what he has turned me into? Someone who would take her own life. Or worse—the life of someone else.

I play along just until I'm able to pull an arm away and grab for the weapon.

But he is quick and easily angered. He springs to his feet, and I look away from the bulge that had begun to grow in his trousers as he tells me that he would have taken what he wanted right here with my consent or without. And without regard to our surroundings.

"You bitch," he says. He points the gun at me, and I tremble. I stare at that dark tunnel of the barrel and imagine the bullet sitting on the other end. I feel the darkness of delirium return, and I bite my lips again to keep myself from fainting.

My teeth begin to quake as if I am cold.

Just an hour ago, I wanted to be rid of this world. To take myself to the ocean waters and sink into them forever. Clean and simple. But to die by Tom's decree—it is more than I can take. I hold my breath and muster everything left in me.

I struggle to my feet, the pain in my abdomen reaching a crescendo. I step forward.

But then I hear it. I hear the gunshot cut above the sound of the waves into the quiet night. And then I hear myself scream.

I collapse there at the bottom of the stairs. And when I wake, it is in a world filtered by unearthly vision.

Chapter Five

"The hotel has a ghost?"

Kate didn't know if she'd heard Sean correctly above the sounds of the many car engines revving up for their departure.

He rubbed his hands across his face. "I'm sorry. Of course you wouldn't know that. She's infamous at the hotel, but I don't suppose anyone outside this area would know about her."

"Is she—is she scary?" The words sounded childish even as they left her lips. But Kate had never encountered a ghost, nor someone who believed in them.

"I've never seen her. But I know plenty who have. Sometimes she seems to be real flesh and blood, and at other times they report being able to see right through her, like you'd imagine a ghost. Sometimes she's on the beach; other times she's entering what was her room. Room 302. And it's even been said that she rustles bedsheets."

The very idea!

"She was a guest here?" asked Kate.

"Yes." He nodded. "In 1892. Right after Thanksgiving. But for reasons no one understands, she shot herself in the middle of the night."

Kate took a sharp breath, horrified by the thought of it.

"An accident?"

"A suicide. Or so the inquest determined."

"Why would she do that, I wonder?" Kate had heard of it happening, but she imagined it being the domain of truly crazy people. Or desperate ones.

"Why would anyone? We don't really know a lot about her, so it's hard to say."

A shiver went through her, though this time it had nothing to do with Sean and everything to do with the possibility that the hotel was haunted.

She was about to ask another question when Sean gestured for her to step forward. "Time to get off. Welcome to Coronado."

~

The first thing Kate noticed was the presence of so many water-skiers. She'd seen pictures of the sport, but the San Francisco waters were too cold to encourage that kind of frolicking. Boys in long black shorts and even girls wearing bikinis—*bikinis!*—were partaking in what looked like a great deal of fun. She watched as one particular girl balanced herself extraordinarily even as the speedboat took sharp turns in the bay, spraying water near her face. The girl held on with two hands, but then—*look!*—she let go with one. She turned around and was being pulled backward! Kate couldn't imagine the skill it took to perform such a trick, but it was just one more amazement that made her feel like she had finally, *finally* arrived in the California of her dreams.

"You may stay here as long as you like," said Sean, cutting into the trance that the sport had cast over Kate. "I need to get to work."

"I'm sorry," she said. "I've just never seen anything like that."

"Where are you from? The boonies?"

"San Francisco."

"San Francisco's no shabby place."

"Of course not," she answered, feeling like she'd betrayed her colorful hometown. "It's actually pretty great. But it doesn't have . . . this."

She swept her arm around, letting the scenery of the otherworldly Coronado speak for itself.

Sean's eyes followed her gesture. He put his hands in his pockets and smiled. "I know what you mean. This place has been a part of my soul since—well, forever."

He didn't elaborate, but his eyes took on a wistful look, and his thoughts seemed to be lost in something Kate couldn't understand.

"Anyway," he continued, snapping out of that trance, "I have to cross over to Orange Avenue and catch the bus to the hotel. Did you want to head that way and see it?"

"How far away is it? You can't just walk?" Kate thought of the money in her purse. Bus fare wouldn't eat into it by much, but she still wanted to preserve what she had until she secured some temporary work.

"You *could*. It's a mile and a half. No big deal. But I spend much of my long work shift on my feet, so I get a better start if I ride there. Besides, it's free. And you can't beat free."

She agreed. That was her favorite kind of price.

The bus arrived just as they stepped up to the corner. Sean offered her a window seat. As they drove, he pointed out the cedar trees—fifty-two of them—that had been donated by members of the community.

"So, you have three kinds of people living in Coronado," he explained.

Kate's mind drifted, aching from the tug-of-war between her desire to find a soft bed and sleep for a year and the exhilaration she felt with each new sight. She couldn't let her exhaustion rob her of what little she had left—the sense of amazement that this place sparked.

"You've got the old-timers who have been here for decades," Sean continued. "They bought land when there was nothing here. They're the lucky ones. Then you have the New Rich. The ones who can afford to live right smack on the beach. Then you have the part-timers. The Mexicans who come up from the border and live here nine months a year so their children can come to school in the United States. And the Canadians who come down here in the winter because otherwise they'll turn into Popsicles."

Kate laughed at the image, as much as she could without letting a yawn escape. She hoped she wasn't making a bad impression. But even that wouldn't stop her. Now that she was here, she was determined to make a success of it no matter what.

Coronado had already wound its way into her very fabric, and it was never going to let go.

Before she knew it, she saw the expanse of the Pacific Ocean. The same one that she could see from the coast near San Francisco—but different. In San Francisco the water reflected the ever-gray sky to the point where you could barely see where one started and the other stopped.

But this water . . . this water was bluer than blue, a shade entirely different from the sky above. The sand was *sparkling*, if her eyes weren't deceiving her. Just like Granddad had said. She would give anything, pay anything for him to be with her right now. To see this through his eyes and his memories.

The palm trees cast shadows on people dressed in jewel-like shades. Bikinis again, and Kate wished she could afford to buy one. To be one of those girls who seemed so carefree.

Wouldn't Janie think that was a laugh? Old Kate would be reluctant, but if this was what they wore in Southern California, then New Kate would love to try it.

She turned to Sean, who was looking at his watch.

"Are you late?"

"Nope. Fifteen minutes to go."

"I realized that I didn't ask you what you actually do at the hotel."

He smiled. "I started in the kitchen a few years ago, but now I help coordinate events and special occasions."

Her jaw opened, and she punched him lightly on the arm. "You're kidding me. You were once a kitchen rat like me?"

"I know. Funny, isn't it? I told you I might be able to help you find a job in that department. My buddy Andy is the head chef, so I'm in a particularly good position to put in a good word for you."

Andy. The name in the advertisement.

"Is that—By any chance is that Andrew Fletcher?"

Sean looked startled. "How did you know that?"

Kate bit her lip and opened the flap of her purse. She pulled out the newspaper cutting and handed it to him.

He unfolded it, and his eyes widened.

"Oh, the advertisement," he said. "He stopped accepting applications yesterday."

"I know," Kate responded, embarrassed.

He ran his fingers through his hair, and his eyes and voice softened. "Hey, don't worry. It's fine. I mean, it's *great* that it brought you here. But he's usually a stickler for interviewing as they roll in."

She felt tears begin to gather in her eyes. If there were no openings for her, she'd either have to go back home or figure out how to make something else work.

Sean must have seen the dismay on her face. He rubbed his hand across his chin. "Don't worry. Don't worry. Let me ask around. People come and go in the summer. There might be something that has opened up. Or someone who couldn't take the job after all."

Kate had little energy left to spend on hope, but she mustered what she could.

Sean grinned. "I think all semi-interviews should happen out there on the ferry. Much more informal that way. Don't you think?"

Before she could answer, a woman behind her groaned with impatience.

Kate followed Sean down the stairs of the bus. He took her hand for the last large step. She felt like Dorothy entering Oz in the movie. Granddad had taken her to see it when it returned to the movie theaters a few years ago for its fifteenth anniversary. This was like that moment when it changed from black and white to Technicolor brilliance.

Kate stepped into the saline air and took in the blue, blue sky and the blue, blue water and the trees and the people. But none of it—as breathtaking as it was—compared to the otherworldly palace that towered above her. The Hotel del Coronado was white as a bridal cake, its roof red like the feathers of the cardinals in Golden Gate Park. And perhaps related to the namesake of this town, the roof was adorned with crownlike peaks, the largest one piercing the horizon.

"Honey, are you going to stand there all day?"

Kate looked behind her to see an older woman in a pillbox hat waving an umbrella at her.

"I'm sorry. We're moving." Sean waved her on down the sidewalk, and Kate followed, trying to keep her eyes ahead of her rather than pausing for each new marvel that presented itself.

Kate's hope returned.

If I'm lucky, I'll be here for weeks, she told herself. *I don't have to take it all in right now.*

A wooden sign in the manicured grass showed that Reception was to the left. But Sean turned to the right.

"This way to the kitchen," he said.

An earsplitting roar cut through the sky, startling her. Kate held her hands to her ears and crouched down. Sean seemed unfazed and kept walking ahead. At last he looked back and laughed.

"What *was* that?" she asked.

He walked back to her and held his hand out to help her up. "It was an F-8 Crusader. A navy jet from North Island. Our metal birds, we call them here."

"I have never heard anything like that in my life."

"Coronado is only thirty-two square miles. Half of it is this paradise that you see now. The other half"—he pointed to his left—"is North Island. The naval base. You'll get used to it. The jets fly overhead pretty routinely, and we forget they're there. And out that way"—this time he pointed to the water—"you'll see all the watercraft. The battleships, aircraft carriers. Pretty neat, now that I think of it. I guess I just don't notice anymore."

"Amazing," said Kate, at a loss for any other word.

"They also test aircraft there. They've been flying some experimental helicopters lately. You'll see plenty of those. They look like birds from a distance, and their rotor blades kick up the sand when they get close."

A high-pitched voice spoke up behind them. "Well, that just won't do."

Sean and Kate turned to see a woman dressed head to toe in black. She wore stiletto heels, formfitting culottes, a button-up blouse that stretched to capacity, and a sun hat with a brim so wide that it cast its own oblong shadow on the ground.

"That won't do," she said again with bright-pink lips. "We can't shoot the film if they go on making a racket like that."

The woman pulled sunglasses off her face and glanced up, her eyes looking toward North Island. She shook her head and put them back on. Kate and Sean watched her walk over to a white-curtained cabana and close it up.

Kate's mouth went dry, and every difficulty she'd had disappeared.

"Was that—" she began.

Sean just nodded, still looking at the cabana. "Marilyn Monroe."

~

1892

The preachers of my childhood described death as seeing a light and walking toward it to a chorus of singing angels and centuries of waiting saints. Or, should one be deemed undeserving, she might find herself in a fiery pit, forever tortured as punishment for her sins.

Maybe they were wrong. Or maybe there is another state of being of which they know nothing. A limbo in which a soul is still connected to the world and yet not. Tethered to it by an invisible rope.

Perhaps it was the gun I purchased and the deplorable action I'd planned with it that kept me from the glory promised to the pious. But I changed my mind before taking such an action. And maybe that saved me from the latter.

Because here I am in some kind of in-between. I can see all. But I cannot interact.

My feelings are nothing except benevolence. Even toward Tom, if you can imagine that! So I must be closer to heaven than the other place, if there is a geography to it. I watch him arrange the gun over my fallen body, and I know already that it is his intention to make it appear to have been accomplished by my own hand. He looks left and right and then flees to the north. It is not long before his form has been swallowed into the night.

You would think that I would be irreparably bitter at the atrocity my husband just committed, but I am flooded, unusually, with a peace that permeates every part of whatever I am now. And even forgiveness. It is as if poor intentions are incompatible with this state I've been flung into.

I attempt to walk, thinking I may float, for I feel weightless, but I do take steps. One at a time. Walking, yet not walking, as I have no sensation of actually touching the steps as I alight them. I turn before reentering the hotel and gaze at the nearly full moon that is casting its light across the sparkling sandy beach and illuminating the still waters.

It takes on a beauty that is beyond what my eyes have ever seen. I find that there are no words for the new vision that I have just obtained. It is not enough to say that light is brighter or colors are more enriched or that their shapes are muted. Though all that would in some way come close to it.

All I can say is that if I have to be here forever, coming short of the eternity that was preached in my youth, I will still be in a kind of paradise.

Chapter Six

"That. Was. Marilyn. Monroe," said Kate. It was difficult to even say the words that almost tasted unbelievable. She'd come all this way because of a movie, so she shouldn't have been surprised to see a movie *star*. But expected or not, seeing her idol within minutes of stepping foot on the grounds was certainly a surprise, and it winded her.

Sean's cheeks turned pink, and she was afraid that she'd embarrassed him somehow. She didn't want to come across as yet another dream-chasing starlet, although maybe that's what she was.

"Come here," he whispered. He put his arm around her, which sent the same kind of chills through her that had been there when he'd taken her hand earlier. In another circumstance it might have held the kind of romantic notion that she'd always dreamed of, but it appeared to be no more than a way to guide her off the sidewalk to a place where he could speak more quietly. He removed it as soon as they'd stepped aside.

Was everyone in Southern California so comfortable that they acted in such a way? She liked it. It took down the barriers that were more easily constructed up north.

He spoke in a hushed tone. "I knew that she was supposed to be here later in the week, but I guess she arrived early."

"But what is she *doing* here? Taking a vacation?" Unless . . . unless she was a part of whichever movie the ad had referred to.

Wouldn't Granddad marvel at that!

"She's filming a movie."

Kate's stomach knotted in disbelief. Here she'd been excited just to pass through Hollywood on a train, imagining that she was breathing the very air of goddesses such as Marilyn Monroe. But for her to be right here—right at this hotel—was an impossibility that was somehow true.

For all she'd known, it would be some B movie in production here. A way for her to get her feet wet in that world. She hadn't even considered that a film big enough to star the legend would have been what she'd come for.

This adventure had just taken an unexpected turn for the better.

Except the positions that would get her close to it were all filled.

She took a deep breath so as to steady her voice. She didn't want to let on that she was the kind of girl who tore photographs of Hollywood movie idols out of *Photoplay* and *Modern Screen*. That the idea of working in film was so far from greasy kitchen work that she'd never told anyone of her dream for fear of them laughing at her. Or worse—discouraging her.

Except for Granddad. He'd always told her that she could do anything. It was more of the tragedy of the dementia. Kate had lost not only her beloved grandfather but her champion.

Kate composed herself and spoke at what she hoped was a normal, steady pace. "What's the name of it?"

Sean shrugged. "*Hot Summer.* No. *Hot on the Beach.* No. It's something with 'hot.' They changed the name a few times. I do know that it's being directed by Billy Wilder."

"It's *Some Like It Hot*!" She'd always thought her knack for retaining strange facts about the movie world was a useless quality. But maybe not.

"It's not just starring Marilyn Monroe," she continued. "It also has Jack Lemmon and Tony Curtis in it." Wow—would they be here, too? She'd seen Tony Curtis in *The Midnight Story* last year, and he was the *dreamiest* actor to ever grace the screen. She knew everything about him. That his real name was Bernie Schwartz. That he was from New York City. That his wife, Janet Leigh, was pregnant with their second child. That while such things were hushed up, everyone knew that he'd had dalliances with many of his leading ladies.

She wondered if he was having an affair with Marilyn Monroe.

Kate thought such behavior was unforgivable, but after seeing Marilyn Monroe on-screen and now *in person*, she could understand how even the most upright of men could fall under her spell. Her voice sounded like bells; her hair glowed like a blooming halo around her face. And her face! Perfection had kissed her creation. That was to say nothing for her body. The kind of curves that Kate envied and men seemed to adore.

All woman, her uncle might say if he were here.

Sean must have thought so, too. His eyes darted between Kate and the path that Miss Monroe—though currently she was Mrs. Arthur Miller—had shimmied down, and Kate couldn't quite blame him.

It was as if she wasn't even part of the human race.

"I don't get to the movies much," admitted Sean, turning back toward Kate. "I work pretty long shifts here. Days in the office and lots of nights when we have banquets and events."

Kate worked those kinds of hours at Uncle Mike's restaurant, but she'd gladly sacrifice a few hours of sleep if she and Granddad could catch a flick.

"Well, you'll just have to remedy that as soon as possible," said Kate. She wished she could take the words back as soon as she'd said them. That sounded as if she were asking him out on a date. Movies were such an escape, though. A cure for all sorts of ills, including the fatigue from too many hours at a job. She'd peddle that notion to anyone who would listen.

Sean's eyes widened, but then he looked down at his feet, a cloud coming over him that she'd not yet seen in her brief time of knowing him. "The hotel frowns on fraternization between employees," he said stiffly.

"I—I wasn't . . . ," she stammered. Then she quickly recovered from her embarrassment by realizing the other message in his words. "Does that mean you think I've got a good chance at getting hired?" If she could get this locked up soon, three days of worrying would vanish. Three days of anguish over how far she would have to stretch the money from her grandmother's ring, let alone how she would earn enough money to buy it back with interest. As long as she could find an affordable place to rent. But she would work harder and longer than any other employee if they would have her.

Sean's grin returned. "I think there's a good chance," he offered. "At least in the kitchen. Sorry, though. No movie stars in there."

Unable to help herself, Kate threw her arms around him and, for a moment, felt him return it, his arms wrapping around her waist and sending that newfound warmth through her body. But just as quickly, he pulled back and turned toward the hotel. "Let's go show you around."

∾

The kitchen of the Hotel del Coronado was as common as the exterior was exquisite. The walls were immaculately white, but its flooring was made of plain red tiles with black grout that served every kind of functional purpose and none that was lovely. Still, it was more impressive than any other kitchen she'd ever seen, if for no other reason than its sheer size. A long stainless steel table stood in the middle of the room, full of bowls and chopping boards and vegetables waiting to be cut.

A clock hung above the main prep area, showing her that it was nearly noon and reminding her that she'd eaten nothing but a pretzel. Her stomach groaned, but she doubted that it could be heard above the whirring of enormous mixers lined up against the wall. A man in a tall white hat walked by each one, peeking into cavernous bowls that stood as high as his chin, and he poured hefty bags of flour into each.

"That's Paco," said Sean. "He's making the rolls for a production dinner being held later today."

"So many rolls," she said in awe.

"I think that last one is for some pastries." Sean walked over to Paco, having to shout above the sound of the machines. "What's the dessert tonight?"

Paco shook the bag of flour over the last one, and a spray of white powder formed a cloud around his head. "Cream puffs," he said. "Someone said Billy Wilder's crazy about them, so we added them to the menu at the last minute."

Sean nodded. "I hope there will be some leftovers."

"You'll be the first to know." Paco grinned.

A puff of flour escaped from the mixer and covered his hair in snowlike powder, prompting a laugh from all three of them.

Sean walked on past the long table. "Kate—come through here. I'll show you around the rest of the area."

Kate followed him through the remainder of the kitchen and then a hallway.

He opened an unassuming door. Once again Kate had the sensation of being Dorothy in Oz, walking from a plain world into such an extraordinary one. Was it the intention of the Hotel del Coronado to dazzle one so effortlessly?

"This is the Coronet Room," he said. "The production company has rented this room tonight as well as the adjacent Crown Room, which is even larger and more magnificent, if you can believe it."

Kate had never seen anything so opulent in her life, and she wasn't quite sure what to look at first. The room was round, wood panels adorning the walls and the domed ceiling alike. At the front was a curved bay of windows that looked out into the lush landscaping. At the center was a chandelier that didn't merely resemble a crown—it *was* a crown, just like one she'd seen in pictures of Queen Victoria, with bulbs at its round base and all along its curved sides.

"Everyone likes the chandeliers," said Sean. He seemed amused by her awe. "You'll never guess who designed them."

"Who?"

"L. Frank Baum."

Kate was confused. "The *writer*?" The author of the Oz books. Why on earth would he have designed light fixtures here in this extreme corner of the country? Wasn't he from South Dakota or somewhere like that?

"The very one." He started walking around the room, straightening tablecloths as he spoke. Kate followed him and did the same. "He and his wife spent a lot of time here in the early part of the century. He wrote three of the Oz books right here at the hotel. They say he found the architecture whimsical, much like his stories."

No wonder her introduction to this amazing place sparked comparisons to Dorothy's world. It had been the very inspiration for the books.

"Sean." A door on the opposite side of the room opened, and a man with a clipboard walked in.

"That's Mr. Clark, one of the junior managers," he whispered to Kate. "But he acts like he's number one." The man was imposing. A wide girth, a pinched nose, and on that nose sat glasses that looked like they belonged in another era.

"Mr. Clark," he said, "this young woman comes to us with restaurant experience in the Bay Area. Her name is Kate Morgan."

"Like the ghost?" Mr. Clark looked her up and down as if trying to see whether she was pulling his leg.

"Like the ghost," Sean answered for her.

Kate wondered whether she would always be greeted with the comparison.

"Good, good," the man answered, looking away from Kate and seemingly not concerned with trivial matters. "Look," he said, pulling a chair out from a table and wheezing as he sank into it. His frame poured out over the seat by inches on either side. He pulled a handkerchief from his pocket and dabbed his nose. "I'm going over the calendar for next month, and we have some conflicts."

"Let's see." Sean pulled out a chair as well and sat next to Mr. Clark. He held up a finger behind his back, indicating that Kate should wait for just a minute while they spoke. She walked around the room, continuing the work of straightening the tablecloths, though there was little to correct. The room was pristine. She worked slowly and, without trying, overheard their words.

"Here," said Mr. Clark. "The film plans to finish their work on the thirteenth, and Wilder's assistant said they want to have a party that evening. Cast and crew, to celebrate the end of filming. They want the Crown Room."

Sean's eyebrows wrinkled, and he shook his head.

"They can't have the Crown Room on that night. It's already taken. For the wedding."

"This is a big deal, Sean. If we accommodate the likes of Billy Wilder and his company, they may book future events with us. Production or otherwise. This puts us on the map with Hollywood."

"We're already *on* Hollywood's map. This is not the first movie to be filmed here."

Sean's protest was ignored, so he continued. "They can't have that day. It's not possible, since it's already taken. Can't we move them to the ballroom? It will hold them just as well. Maybe better."

"Move the wedding banquet to the ballroom."

"It's not that easy." He was speaking faster, louder.

"Sure it is. There're still a few weeks left. Change the paperwork."

Uncle Mike's restaurant was not the kind of place people held wedding banquets, but she knew it was not merely a change in paperwork that Sean was being asked to consider. It was the feelings of the bride. Probably one who had dreamed of holding her banquet in a beautiful place like Kate imagined the Crown Room to be. And the deposit from her family. Surely it was no inexpensive proposition to rent a place like the Hotel del Coronado. Whoever she was and whoever her father was, he must have some influence to be able to plan for an occasion here.

"But—" Kate heard Sean continue the argument.

Mr. Clark pushed himself up off the table and wobbled back toward the door he came from.

"Move the wedding," he shouted, his back to Sean and Kate. "Or you can find somewhere else to work."

The door shut behind him with enough force that another door might have echoed a slamming sound, but this one closed in silence. An indication, maybe, of how well maintained the hotel was.

Sean buried his head in his hands. Kate vacillated between going over to him or staying put, but he looked harrowed after the talk with Mr. Clark. She slid into the seat but refrained from putting her hand on his arm. They were not yet friends, not really, and she dared to hope he was going to be her coworker. One she wasn't supposed to *fraternize* with, according to Sean.

"He can't switch plans like that just because someone bigger comes along and wants it." Sean seemed unusually upset.

There had to be a solution. *Billy Wilder* wanted the Crown Room. If Kate were in his shoes, she'd move heaven and earth to accommodate the legendary director. But if Sean was insisting that it couldn't be done, the scheduled wedding must be for someone very important.

"Whose wedding is it?" she asked.

He looked at her, his skin turning pale once again.

"Mine."

Chapter Seven

"Yours!" A knot formed in Kate's stomach, and she hoped that her surprise didn't show as deeply as she felt it. Of course, men didn't wear engagement rings like women did, so it wouldn't have been apparent. And he did not suggest in any way that he was considering Kate anything but someone he'd met on the ferry and for whom he'd throw in a good word for the job. So for her to feel a rush of disappointment was a thing of her own doing, and he was blameless for where her imagination had begun to go.

"Yes," he said without an explanation that wasn't owed to her anyway.

He stood up and ran his fingers through his light-brown hair. Kate liked the way it curled at the ends.

She looked away, because she didn't want him to be able to read her disappointment. A sense of aloneness descended, and missing her family felt like a knife in her side despite her happiness to be here at last.

"Do you know where I can find a pay phone?" It seemed a safe enough question when his engagement had put the proverbial nail in the coffin of any hopes that his friendliness was more than just that, and it steered her daydreaming back to what she'd come for: to live up to Granddad's hopes for her down here. And to find his *beautiful stranger*.

"Where do you need to call?" he asked.

"San Francisco. Home."

They must be worried sick. Sure, she'd left a note. But they had to be wondering if she got here safely. Mom would want to know where she was staying, what she was eating, when she was getting home.

As for the staying, Kate had no idea. And despite only eating a hot pretzel in the last day, she'd assure her mother that there was plenty to eat in Coronado.

Sean tugged at a tablecloth. One that needed no adjustment. "Leaving us so soon?" Surely he couldn't think that she'd come all this way just to turn around.

He cocked his head up, and she saw a glimmer in his eye that made her heart do a somersault, despite learning that he had a fiancée.

"No. But I thought I should let them know that I've arrived safely. My mom's a gold-medal worrier."

The edges of his mouth curled up. "Mine, too. Is it just ours who have that in common, or is it a condition of motherhood?"

She smiled back. "I wouldn't know. But I'd guess all of them."

Sean nodded. "There are pay phones in the reception area. I'm sorry—I came straight to the kitchen and didn't show you the rest of the hotel. But there will be time enough for that tour. For now, though, don't spend your money. You can call from my office. Just try to keep it to less than fifteen minutes, or it becomes more difficult to justify the charges."

"You don't have to do that." It occurred to her that she didn't even know how to make a long-distance call. She would either have to reveal her naivete over that or sit there staring at the phone, wondering how to connect to San Francisco.

"Nonsense. Here, follow me."

He led her to a different door from the one they'd come from and held it open for her. Her arm brushed against his as she walked past him. She took a deep breath and controlled the shiver that began at his touch.

Foolishness, Janie might have said.

She followed him down an unremarkable hallway into an office that had his nameplate posted in brass. Maybe he was more important here than he'd led her to believe.

But the inside was simple. There were a few historic pictures of the Hotel del Coronado on the walls. Some books about boating. Some cookbooks. And a few photographs—girls who must have been his sisters, for they looked just like him but with longer hair. Freckles and all.

And one picture sat on his desk in an elaborate silver frame. It was a stunning blonde woman in a pose that looked like she was heading for Hollywood.

"Your fiancée?" she choked out. Of course Sean would be in love with a woman like that. What man wouldn't? A girl who spent long hours in a stifling kitchen was no match for a beauty like this. Especially when that was already how he spent his own days.

His voice was measured, and he didn't give away any emotion one way or another. One would barely know that the girl pictured was the love of his life. "Yes. Cynthia. Her father hired a professional photographer to do that on the occasion of her nineteenth birthday."

A professional photographer! The girl must come from some means. Well, of course she did if she could book a reception at a place like the Hotel del Coronado. Still, when the subject looked like this one did, everyday faded printouts from a photo booth just couldn't cut it. Kate's family had never had a portrait done, but she and Janie had plenty of instant photos strung with yarn along their wall.

Even on this glossy paper, the woman—Cynthia—had a look in her eyes that said that the camera couldn't contain her. Maybe nothing could. Kate would have imagined Sean with someone more demure. Someone sweet. Someone who would kick off her shoes and roll up her jeans and toss a beach ball on the sand with him.

Someone like Kate.

Oh! She tried to hurry the thought out as soon as it came to her head.

"She's lovely," she managed to say.

Still, he was all business. "Yes, she is. Now, let's make that phone call."

Sean pulled out his chair for her and leaned over to pick up the receiver. He smelled like salt water, and she probably did, too, from the spray at the back of the ferry. "Operator, get me San Francisco." He covered the mouthpiece with his hand. "What number are we calling?"

"Nine, one, six, zero."

"San Francisco nine, one, six, zero," he repeated into the receiver. He handed the phone to Kate. "Easy as pie. I have some things to check on, so I'll leave you here. Like I said, just keep it to fifteen minutes. I'll come back then, and we can talk to Andy and see if he has any room to hire one more for the kitchen."

He shut the door behind him. The loud sound of static came through the receiver.

"Hello?" asked Kate. "Hello?"

"I'm dialing San Francisco nine, one, six, zero now," said the operator.

More static, but then she heard a familiar voice.

"Mike's Fish and Chips," said her tired-sounding sister.

"Janie?"

"Kate!" Janie shouted her name and then lowered her voice. "Kate? What are you doing? Where *are* you?"

"Didn't you get my note? I'm in Coronado. It took me three days, but I made it in one piece. Barely."

"You have some nerve running off like that. Mom and Dad are in a *fit* over your disappearing. I thought Dad was going to have a heart attack!"

Guilt washed over Kate at these words.

"I didn't disappear. I said I was heading here and here I am. Safe and sound. So you don't need to worry."

"Worry?" Janie sounded incredulous. "Worry is the least of it. When Dad called the train station and at least found out that there were no terrible accidents or explosions on the rails, we figured you were probably safe. And then it moved to anger. You took Grandma's ring, didn't you? After I told you not to."

Kate winced.

"I told you that Granddad wanted me to sell it."

"You had no right!"

"How can you say that? He *gave* it to me."

Kate didn't know if Janie was more upset about the ring itself or the fact that he hadn't given it to *her*.

She could hear the exasperation in Janie's sigh. "Yeah, and if he told you that cows could jump over the moon, you'd believe him. He's *batty*, Kate. He doesn't know what he's saying. And you're in denial."

Kate opened her mouth to defend Granddad, but she knew there was no point. And Janie had cut right to the heart of what worried Kate—what if selling the ring and coming here, which were founded by Granddad's insistence on both, were merely products of his failing mind? Quicksand decisions that had concrete repercussions on her family if she didn't succeed.

"I just can't believe you went through with it," continued Janie.

"I didn't sell it. I pawned it. It's safe for five weeks, and then I'll buy it back."

Well, four weeks and four days at this point. Kate felt the acute pressure of an hourglass that was losing its sand with every breath.

She hoped that Janie didn't hear the worry in her voice.

Her sister sighed on the other end of the line, and Kate could hear the clatter of dishes in the background. She looked at the clock on Sean's wall. Noon. She was calling in the middle of the lunch hour. She was surprised that Janie hadn't bitten her head off over that, too.

"It's not just the money, Kate. It's—Hold on." She shouted away from the phone. *"Table 10 is going to bolt if their haddock doesn't get out there right away!"*

"Janie? Do you want me to call back later?"

"No, no, I'm here. Kate—Granddad's in the hospital."

~

1892

I could not attend the coroner's inquest, of course. It hadn't occurred to me that my attachment to the Hotel del Coronado would have a perimeter. The first time I walked toward the edge of the property, all I could see beyond it was white. It wasn't the white of a cloud or of a thick steam but of nothingness. I looked behind me. The hotel still had all the colors of this new vibrancy to my vision, but before me was a void. I reached out my hand, but it was cold. Permeatingly cold.

So when the officials all gathered off-site to debate the details of the woman they'd found on the stairs leading to the ocean, I was not there to listen. But news of their discussions was all the talk in the salons of the hotel.

The aliases I'd used over the years threw them off, apparently. For days they were pursuing the demise of Lottie A. Bernard. They finally concluded that Kate Farmer Morgan of Fremont County, Iowa, had taken her own life. I don't know how they discovered my real name.

There was no mention of my husband, Tom. Not of his whereabouts. Not of his culpability. And so my family would hear this version of the tragic news instead of what really happened: that at the last moment, I changed my mind. I'd wanted to go home to them.

I'd wanted to have this baby, if it could be saved.

The baby. I am aware that I am the only one here in this odd, medial space. There was never a question in my church days that a baby owned a soul, even though it was incapable of right or wrong—it merely was. And if that's true, surely it would not have been cast to the dark abyss that existed for those who cheated, lied, stole, murdered. My child must be in the other place—the one of light.

So I do not worry about that one. Nor the one I lost six years ago, so soon after my marriage to Tom. Already by then Tom had demonstrated his callousness, and my days rotted with disillusionment and fear. But when my tiny son was born, weeks earlier than expected, I felt the first pinprick of hope that I'd had since our nuptials. I was overwhelmed with love for this sweet boy whose hand curled around my smallest finger and held fast.

He breathed for only two days before the Lord took him.

My children sleep with the angels.

But there is one other. The boy who no one knew about.

He was conceived in a drunken fit of Tom's one night. As soon as the signs of motherhood began to reveal themselves to me, I hurried away to California under the guise of lung problems that might be aided by the coastal air. I would not allow the putridity of my husband to infect another child—for I held on to the supposition that the death of the first baby was a kind of salvation for him. A salvation from becoming another Tom. Or becoming his victim.

So this child I brought into the world amid the warm air of Coronado.

Even for him I do not worry, for as I told you, there is something about this state of being that is the very definition of peace, and anxiousness has no place. I do wonder, however.

I wonder what became of George.

Chapter Eight

When Sean came back to his office to find Kate in tears, she told him about Granddad's hospitalization, Grandma Kitty's ring.

She omitted the promise she'd made to her grandfather. Giving him her word about coming down here. It seemed too dear a thing to share with someone who was still a stranger.

Kate ached to hop on the next train to be by Granddad's bedside. And even though Janie had assured her that it was only precautionary after he'd had some chest pains, Kate had picked up the phone to call the depot to check on the times. But then she imagined their conversation in that moment where his lucidity would return. She knew his eyes would brighten with joy over seeing her, then dim, his eyebrows furrowing, as he would realize what she'd left behind to get there. And then he'd fade into darkness once again, leaving her feeling traitorous for not holding up her end of the deal.

No, she would stay and fulfill her promise to the person she loved most in the world. She just hoped Sean wouldn't ask if she wanted to go home. She wasn't sure how to explain.

He didn't, and she appreciated that he just listened with a great deal of patience and understanding, especially considering he'd given her a good portion of his morning. Sean had sisters, so he probably had experience coming to the aid of a crying girl.

"I know this isn't much help, but I grabbed some towels from housekeeping, and I found an empty room where you can take a bath. So long as you don't sit on the bed they've already made up, the second-story maid said you could have it for an hour. Maybe that will help you decide what you need to do."

A bath! Despite her best efforts in the restroom of the train station, Kate was sure she looked as bedraggled as she felt, and a bath sounded like heaven.

"I'd put you up in a room for the night if I could," he added, "and in another season I could probably get away with that. But we're all booked this week."

Kate took the towel from him and smiled. "I don't know how to thank you."

He shrugged. "I'm sure you'd do the same." He looked like he wanted to say something else and decided against it.

Save for her worry over Granddad, the bath in room 210 was the best she'd ever taken. The tub was deep, the back angled perfectly for reclining, and the soap was a vast improvement over the dregs in the train station bathroom. Her hair felt silky after she rinsed off the peach-scented shampoo.

She used up most of the hour, washing away worry. Her fingers wrinkled and the water grew cold, but she was not going to miss a second of it. When the last drop had drained, Kate was careful to step out without leaving puddles so that the maid would have little to do. She rubbed her hair with the towel to dry it and looked at the perfectly made bed. Sheets whiter than snow, corners sharper than knives, pillows fluffier than cotton.

She could only imagine how comfortable it would be to rest her head there. She might never wake up.

How did people afford such luxuries? How many shifts would she have to work to pay for just one night in a room like this?

It wasn't going to happen for her any time soon. She'd been so judicious about money, but it had still cost a lot to take the train, and it would be more to take it back home. Especially if Sean couldn't find work for her to do here, near the movie set—the whole reason for coming. If that was lost, she'd have to tell her grandfather that she'd let him down. Maybe she could work longer shifts at Uncle Mike's restaurant and beg the pawnbroker to let her have a little extra time.

A knot of worry tightened in her chest and heightened her need to ask around about the "beautiful stranger." If she returned home with nothing more than an answer to whatever Granddad was asking about that, she'd have to consider it a small victory.

Kate stopped back by Sean's office, feeling refreshed in a spare uniform that the maid had left for her. She didn't wear the apron, just the black dress, which made her feel like she was preparing for a funeral. She dearly hoped that she wouldn't have need for such garb anytime soon. The news about Granddad had been unsettling.

Sean was sitting at his desk writing in a calendar. He bit his lip and erased an entry just as she walked through the door.

"Well, look at you." He grinned. "You look like you're ready to turn down the beds. Or visit a mortician."

"That's what I thought, too." Kate brushed her hands down the starch-stiff skirt and forced a smile back. "I washed the clothes I was wearing, and the maid said I could leave them in the housekeeping closet until they dry. I don't need to jinx Granddad's health by wearing something like this home!"

She thought again of Maisy, wondering what the thief had done with all her things. They'd been about the same size. Had she kept the pink sweater that Mom had crocheted for Kate for her sixteenth birthday? Had she sold the saddle oxfords that Kate bought last month with tip money she'd saved?

Maisy had not merely inconvenienced Kate and cost her money; she'd stolen memories. Kate had packed that suitcase with things that reminded her of home so that home would remain close to her even as she was far away. But Mom would have told her that bitterness would only eat her up, so she tried to back away from her resentment.

"Have a seat," Sean suggested. "I'd like to talk to you about your plans."

She sat across from his desk, relieved that it was not the large executive piece she'd first imagined it to be. It felt instead like two friends sitting across a table from each other. This might be what it would have looked like if he'd asked her out for lunch and they'd shared a milkshake.

Funny how we always wanted what we couldn't have.

Sean cleared his throat. "It's a shame for you to have come all this way just to apply for a job that has been filled. I asked Andy if anyone had backed out, but it seems our gig with the movie was a popular one."

Kate's heart sank. On the one hand, it was good news. She would return home to Granddad's bedside. On the other, she felt like she'd failed both of them.

"But," Sean continued. Her pulse raced. There could only be good news when bad was followed by that word.

"He said he did have room in his budget for a part-time floater. It means that you'd have to be on call to come in whenever he needs more hands. And it might prevent you from getting work elsewhere. I don't know if that's what you'd hoped for, but it's a start."

Stay. The very minute she'd stepped into the ferry kiosk in San Diego and viewed the shimmering waters of the bay across to Coronado, she'd known that she wanted to do just that. Stay here forever. And that was before she'd exchanged one word with Sean in the passenger area.

She wanted to give him her enthusiastic *yes.* But there was still much to determine—how many hours, what did it pay, where would she sleep?

"I can offer one more piece of hope," said Sean. He leaned across his desk. "Filming starts in two days, and in my experience, these things always take longer and need more than what we're originally told. If that holds true, I may have some odd jobs on my team as well. And that would put you on set."

Kate's heart beat faster. Andy's work would relegate her to the kitchen, something not much different from the life she already knew. She wouldn't be working on set. But it was still *here*. Here in the place she'd always dreamed of. And off time would allow her to be near the hubbub of it all. Maybe even encounter people like Marilyn Monroe again. That wasn't going to happen at Uncle Mike's. But even better, if Sean needed help, it might put her closer to it all.

"I'm so grateful," she answered. She remembered Janie's assurances that Granddad wasn't in any immediate danger and was just being kept for observation. It was a small comfort in her sea of concerns.

Sean continued, a managerial tone taking over. "For however many hours you work, I'd pay you the same as what I pay my current restaurant staff, which is a dollar thirty-five an hour. And there may be tips. Andy's would pay about the same. Without tips."

A dollar thirty-five an hour! That was significantly more than the government-regulated hourly wage of one dollar. She knew this because Uncle Mike paid Janie and her fifty cents an hour and told them they could make up the rest in tips. He wasn't unkind. But after several closed restaurants in the family, there was a general understanding that if you were related, it was just all part of pitching in and helping the group. During the busy seasons, she and Janie could usually make up the difference between them.

This changed everything. Though it broke her heart not to be at Granddad's bedside, to do so would require her missing work anyway. Here in Coronado, she could earn even more. She would give everything to the work at hand, making herself indispensable, and hope for as many hours as possible. Buy Grandma's ring back. Help her family in a bigger way.

Have the chance to be on set.

And to find the beautiful stranger.

But where would she stay? That worry nagged at her. If she could, she'd happily camp out on the beach. How blissful it would be to go to sleep to the sound of the waves and wake up to the ocean breezes.

A naive notion, certainly, void of all practicality. But so tempting.

"Mr. O'Donnell," she started, thinking that it was wise to begin this professional endeavor using his proper name. "This means so much to me. And I would like to accept. But I have a few questions first."

Beggars can't be choosers. She heard Janie's well-worn phrase echo in her head. Janie was always content with whatever she got. It was Kate who wanted something more.

He put his pencil down and looked up. Had she offended him by not jumping at the chance right away?

"Would it be possible to call my family like this once a week? Same amount of time?"

Sean smiled at her. He looked amused, not angry. She had no idea what such a thing would cost her, and she could not languish here and worry without the hope of knowing she could talk to them at least that often.

"Anything else?" he asked.

"Will I have to sign a contract or anything that binds me to a length of time? If my grandfather declines . . ." Kate pulled a tissue from her pocket. She'd taken a few from the bathroom and hadn't expected to need them quite so soon. She dabbed her eyes and felt embarrassed for crying once again in front of him.

"Kate," Sean said. He reached across the desk and took her hands in his. They felt warm on hers, and she could feel her heartbeat in the place where they touched. But it was merely a gesture of consolation.

"Kate," he repeated. "Both of those are completely reasonable requests. And I applaud you for speaking up. I have to admit that most women I work with are too intimidated to say exactly what they need.

But I have sisters. Outspoken sisters. And I, for one, think that's a good thing."

He pulled back, the warmth that was left in place of his hands making it feel like he was still holding hers.

But more than that, his words surprised her. Though she had been surrounded by the love of her dad and uncle, Granddad was the only man in her life who had ever made her feel like she could be more than a waitress in a smelly fish joint making less than what the government mandated.

Well, except for Dimitri. But the *more* she knew he would offer was just trading one family business for another. Neither fulfilling what she felt destined to do.

"There's one more thing," said Kate. She hoped she wasn't trying his patience.

"What's that?"

"Housing. Do you have any suggestions for where I can stay?"

She didn't add that it couldn't cost too much. It might come across as more needy than she wanted to appear.

"Of course." He riffled through a pile of papers on his desk and then bent down and retrieved something from his trash can. A newspaper.

He flipped through its pages.

"Here we go. The classifieds. A few days old, but they might be a start." He looked them up and down and then set the paper on the desk, pointing to one section. "There are usually rooming houses for women in here. Most are in San Diego, so you'd have to take the ferry. But look through these. You might find something closer."

"Thank you." Kate took it from his hands and already imagined how many dimes she might need to spend at a pay phone calling around to them. If any were in Coronado, she might walk to save the money.

"I'm sure you're tired after your ordeal," he offered, speaking words that she'd only begun thinking. "Feel free to stay and make some local calls so that you can find a place. No doubt you'll want to be well rested for tomorrow. Andy said he can use some help for a few hours in the morning, starting at six. We've got a full house, and you've never seen so many coffee drinkers as those who want to drown themselves in caffeine before a long day at the beach."

He stood to leave, and she began to do the same, but he motioned for her to stay where she was.

"I have to get back to the Crown Room. Take all the time you need and grab a plate lunch in the kitchen around noon if you like. Tell them that Sean O'Donnell hired you, but you don't have your badge yet."

And then he was gone. Kate felt her breath return to normal.

Was having sisters what taught him how to be compassionate? Or did he just have a heart that could recognize the need in another? Either way, Sean was the angel who countered the devil she'd met at the train depot.

Kate had once visited a Chinese fortune-teller in a crowded, narrow shop on Clay Street. The old woman had said that she would have a long life, some sorrows, but much luck in a land far away.

At the time, fourteen-year-old Kate had only gone along on the whim of a friend. But maybe there was something to the message. Something to the ten cents she'd paid for a reading.

Because already her good luck in Coronado outweighed her woes. Even if there was still much that needed to come together.

~

Fourteen calls to lodging houses for women. All filled, causing her to panic. Maybe sleeping on the beach would have to become a reality. Until one kindly owner called back and said she knew of a temporary room in a house on the north side of Coronado near the ferry. A friend of hers rented it to a family from Mexico who brought their two children up for school, but they returned home every summer.

It wouldn't be fancy, and the woman expected a strict code of decency. Kate would be given the nanny's room in an already small carriage house. But it was only a mile and a half from the hotel. Kate had been ecstatic to hear about it, and the price was right at her budget. She'd left a note for Sean thanking him and telling him where she'd landed.

The first night was fitful. Kate dreamed in images that she couldn't remember, though the sensation of floating still sat in her head. At a knock on the door, she awoke, reminding her that she was no longer at home but quite far from all that was familiar. She swept her legs across the smooth cotton sheets and lifted her head from the pillow it had sunken into.

This was Coronado. Yesterday she'd seen Marilyn Monroe in person. And she'd met Sean.

"Just a minute," she called. She wasn't wearing anything. *Anything.* That wasn't her typical sleeping attire—she did share a bed with her sister at home. But she didn't want to wrinkle the one set of clothes she had. She'd even had to wash her undergarments in the sink and leave them to dry overnight.

Kate reached behind her to fasten her Maidenform and then threw on her dress. She sauntered over to the door and opened it to the landlady, whom she'd met last night.

"Good morning," Kate said to Mrs. Rorbach, who, by her pained expression, was clearly not a friend of early hours. Though, to her credit, light had not begun to stream through the lone window.

The landlady yawned and held out a parcel, looking put out at making the delivery. "I found this on my doorstep when I went to let the dog out. Had your name on it."

Kate took it. "Thank you."

"Feels like it might be some clothes. I noticed that you only arrived with that small purse, but you paid for a week."

Kate hadn't wanted to commit to the length of the film production, given Granddad's health and her part-time status. The landlady had promised to give her first rights if someone else came looking for the rest of the summer.

"I'm trying to save money and planned to just rewash what I have." She wondered who it could be from but didn't want to be unkind to the woman, who was leaning in the doorway and seemed breathless from the effort of coming up the stairs.

The landlady crossed her arms. "If you think like a pauper, you'll always *be* a pauper, child. Saving is well and good. It's what got me this house. A husband as thrifty as myself until he died. But we enjoyed a Sunday steak dinner even when we couldn't afford it and for that one night a week lived like kings. Candles on our kitchen table and a chocolate cake in the oven. But no wine. Only the godless drink."

"That's good advice." Kate nodded and hugged the package to her chest.

The woman left, her heavy steps falling softly on damp stairs that suffered from wood rot.

Kate closed the door and placed the parcel on the bed. It was wrapped in twine, knotted too tightly. Unable to loosen it, she pulled at the paper, careful not to rip it more than necessary.

Inside there was a note. Sean's handwriting was expertly neat, as if he wrote using a straight ruler. Nothing like Uncle Mike's: anything he wrote might as well have been the Rosetta Stone—needing professionals to decipher it. At least he knew it—he'd been merciful to Janie the few times she'd made errors in purchase orders, citing his own rough scrawl.

She turned on a lamp and read.

Kate—excuse this presumption, but I asked one of my sisters if you could borrow some clothes until you can get some of your own. She was heading into Coronado anyway for dinner with her husband, so I caught her just in time. The hotel will provide your uniform, of course, but you won't want to wear that off the clock! You can catch breakfast in the employee dining room, down the hall from my office. If you want to stick around after your shift with Andy, I'll have a better idea of what work I might have for you.

Sean O'Donnell

Clothes! She was used to Janie's hand-me-downs. Kate couldn't remember many times when something had ever been her very own without being her sister's first. These might have come from someone else's sister, but there was a newness about them. New enough.

Kate sat on the bed. The room she'd rented was tiny, and its only window overlooked a brick wall and trash bins. But she'd never come from luxury and didn't expect it. Just being in Coronado was luxury enough.

Kate held up several of the outfits and chose a midcalf black skirt. A little heavy for San Diego in August, but she supposed the pair of pink gingham capris wasn't as professional. Maybe if there was free time, she could wear them around town. An emerald-green top rounded out her attire.

She showered, applied her cosmetics, and brushed her teeth, having picked up the necessary items at the hotel's gift shop the night before. When she had a chance, she'd call home from the bank of pay phones and let her family know that she'd gotten a job. She'd leave them the number for her landlady in case Granddad's condition worsened, in which case, she'd head north on the next train.

But she'd never have to wonder what it would have been like to give it a try.

Pinch me, she thought. *This is my life for now.*

~

1892

George. The only child I suckled at my breast for longer than a scant two days. Though not much more than that. He was such a good baby. He smiled at me within hours, and I thought then that my life would be over, positively wrecked, if I ever had to part with him. But even before I'd laid eyes on him, before I'd held his warm, wriggly body, I knew that I couldn't keep him.

Tom could not discover that he was a father.

Tom could not use this child to entrap me. He could not raise this child to be his unwitting sidekick. I imagined a likely scenario: Tom takes little George, newly walking, looking smart in his tiny-man knickers, on a train trip. He distracts people who stop him to say hello to his enchanting son. And while their attentions are elsewhere, Tom picks their pockets.

Or worse—Tom returns home in one of his drunken states, and the boy is crying from impending teeth breaking through. And, driven wild at the noise, Tom beats him into silence.

Of course, these were just nightmarish musings, but where my husband was concerned, there was no precaution too extreme. He always found me somehow, despite the aliases I took on to conceal my whereabouts. I came to suspect that he had a spy at my grandfather's bank. He followed the money.

That's all I was to him. I believe that's all I ever was.

If I'd tried to deny his paternity, Tom would have only decried me as a whore—a detestable word to him, though he engaged their services with frequency—and obtained a divorce based on the notion of infidelity. And received my money through that means.

No, I had no hope but to find a place for my son. Someone who would care for him the way I could not. Someone who could raise him to be upright. Kind. Safe.

When I handed George into the arms of the Morgans, what small piece of myself that was left died right then for all intents and purposes. Ask any mother who has lost a child. It takes half of her. A half that was once vibrant and hopeful.

Having lost my first child, a child who took the original half of me with him, I had only the leftover portion remaining. And that went with George.

I was dying years before Tom killed me.

Chapter Nine

The first morning passed, then the second, each turning from breakfast to lunch and to dinner. If Andy had thought he'd just needed some help when they opened, he was off by more than a little. The pace of the staff as the movie people arrived was near frantic, and a request for her to stay *one more hour* became many.

There was enough activity that Kate had no time to ask about the beautiful stranger. Most of the people she interacted with were temporary staff like herself and had no experience at the hotel or knowledge of its history. The regular employees bustled without breaks. She hadn't forgotten—it was one of the reasons she'd come here. But there was the very real need to work every available hour to save for the interest on Grandma's ring, and the good wages could even help her family get ahead of the bills that piled on the counter at home.

As little time as there was to mingle, there was no opportunity at all to interact with the movie people who were setting up on the lawn outside the hotel. She was seeing about as much sunshine in Coronado as she did in foggy San Francisco.

None.

She was happy to be here. But she couldn't let the work distract her from why she'd come. Otherwise she'd have wasted Granddad's great gift. And she dearly wanted to return to him with information about the beautiful stranger.

She just hoped that when she got home, he'd remember even having those conversations.

Andy put her to work in the familiar surroundings of the kitchen, though the recognizable features of sinks, stoves, and counters were magnified many times over in a space that supported the enormous hotel and a Hollywood-based cast and crew to boot. And it was noticeably missing the smell of fish and the bellowing of the seals at Pier 39.

By the end of the third day, Kate had only passed Sean in the halls with quick hellos, and she'd barely slept before rising again for a new shift. She was too tired to make friends, to worry about her family, or even to eat, skipping several meals and just snacking as trays were brought in from the outside.

From folding croissants to shaping burger patties to—dread—peeling potatoes, her hands were red and worn.

Shooting was about to get started, she was told.

But there was hope.

Before she clocked out for the evening, Sean stopped her outside the kitchen door.

"Hi, I'm Sean O'Donnell. I don't think we've met, though you look vaguely familiar."

She grinned. "Yes, I'm that flash who races past you as we head in opposite directions. I'm Kate."

Sean folded his arms, looked back and forth down the hall, and slid against the wall to sit down. She did the same.

"I'm beat," he said. "What about you?"

"Beat," she agreed. "And I haven't seen the sun in days."

"The sun? What's that?"

"Exactly."

"Kate Morgan, I knew that about you as soon as we met. Do, do, do."

"I thought that was an admirable quality in an employee."

He nodded and ran his hand through sweat-filled hair. "You're right. It's actually why I wanted to find you. I'm stealing you from Andy."

Her head lifted up. "What do you mean?"

"As of tomorrow, you're officially off KP duty, and you'll be working for me."

She pursed her lips to keep at bay the enormous smile that wanted to emerge. Andy was a good guy. The kitchen was the best she'd ever worked in. But if she could be closer to the set . . . it would be even better.

"Yeah, Billy Wilder wants to start having snack and drink stations outside to keep the crew from heading indoors so frequently. So I'll need you as a runner. Making sure that the tables are stocked and bringing in trays as they empty. Sounds simple, but it will be constant motion. Just more outside time than in the cave down here."

The smile that wanted to emerge would have been brighter than the sun that illuminated Coronado. She held it in, hoping that its heat didn't redden her cheeks and give away how very excited she was at this news. She gave, instead, a controlled grin and held two fingers to her forehead. "Aye, aye, Captain!"

"And one other thing."

"Anything." She hoped that didn't sound too eager.

"I had to let an employee go today, and I want you to take his place."

His? Kate wondered what job that could be. In general, the men had the best of the jobs.

Sean continued. "I need you to take special care of one of the actresses. The guy I'd assigned to her has been with me for more than a year, but he let this get to his head and made comments about her to other employees that I thought were unprofessional and ungentlemanly. So I decided to put a woman on the job. You."

"Thank you," said Kate. Her heart beat faster at the thought of getting this much closer to the moviemaking. To take care of one of the actresses! Granddad would be so proud!

"Yes." He sighed and looked both ways again, leaning in closer.

"You're the hardest worker I've seen in a long time, Kate Morgan. And this woman needs a lot of assistance. I've heard stories—she's really something else. You've got to bring her breakfast and motivate her to get out of her room and down to the set but without seeming like you're trying to direct her. Billy's already in a fit about hiring her in the first place, but they've shot too much film in Hollywood to start over."

The suspense was killing her, tempered only by the warm feeling that rose from her belly at Sean's compliment.

"The good news is that she's a late riser, so you don't have to be here until eight."

"Who is it?" Kate asked at last.

He whispered, "Marilyn Monroe."

Kate's knees weakened, and she had to grip the counter to keep from fainting.

She couldn't wait for the chance to tell Granddad.

At last, Kate got to see dawn peek over the eastern horizon. If she'd thought Coronado was beautiful when she arrived, she was left speechless by what it looked like now. Used to rising early now, she'd arrived at the hotel an hour before Sean needed her just to take in this majesty. Shades of purple, pink, orange, and gold such as none she'd ever seen displayed themselves in endless strokes like an aerial carpet being laid out before the sun.

The sun . . . The ultimate star. Lording over the ones who had taken up residence at the hotel.

Was it strange to feel so drawn to a place you'd only just seen? Like love at first sight?

Just after dawn, the crew began to emerge. It fascinated Kate to watch the tracks laid for the cameras and the lights hung. White canvas rooms sprang up, much like pictures she'd seen of the old tent city that had surrounded the hotel decades ago.

She watched the workers scurry about like full-size ants, orderly chaos that erected structures the like of which she'd never seen. Lost in amazement, she glanced at her watch, surprised at how quickly the time passed. She stood up, brushed sand off her clothes, and made her way to the employee entrance.

Sean was one of the first people she saw.

"Hey, bad news," he said as a greeting.

Oh no. She knew this had been too good to be true. "What?"

"I'm sorry," he retracted. He slowed his pace down the hall, still passing her but looking back. "Not *really* bad news. Just that having you work with Marilyn is delayed by a couple of days. She's unwell and not leaving her room. So just the runner duties. There's a list in the kitchen. I'll catch you later!"

His voice quieted as he made his way down the hall.

It was going to be another busy one.

Kate soon learned that she needed to be ready for anything that was needed. Until her reclusive charge was ready to show her white-blonde halo again, Kate ran back and forth between the kitchen and the beach bringing water, iced tea, and sandwiches to the cast and crew.

It was good to be so occupied. It distracted from her worries. Granddad's health. Her family's financial troubles.

And how she felt about Sean.

Every time she walked past him, a shiver went through her that felt contradictorily warm. But she diverted every such thought toward her current task, no matter how menial, in order to make an excellent impression on those she worked with. This would last only as long as the movie filmed here, unless she fashioned herself into someone they didn't want to let go of. And though the job was only a glorified version of what she did at Uncle Mike's, it was still here, in Southern California, a place she already craved as someone suffocating craved air.

In the late afternoon on the second day of working as a runner, Kate carried an overloaded tray full of lemonades out of the kitchen and down the hall. She turned around to push the door open with her hips, since she had no free hands. But as she stepped back, someone was coming inside. Kate tripped, spilling the tray and its contents all over the sidewalk. Glass shattered across the walkway, and she could see rainbows cast over the pavers as the shards caught the sunlight. It would have been beautiful in another circumstance.

"I'm sorry," she said, mortified, though there was no fault on either party.

"Let me help with that." The deep voice belonged to a most unusual-looking woman. She stood a whole head taller than Kate and was wearing an ill-fitting sequined gown. Her blonde curls sat close to her face, and her makeup was almost garish in its thickness.

The movie! She had to be a cast member. Kate had heard of cosmetics that went on like pancake mix, but up close it looked downright clownish. She supposed it must mellow into something resembling normal once the cameras picked it up. Kate felt a tingle of excitement. Hollywood had come to her.

The woman bent over and turned the tray upright, picking up cubes and placing them on it. She wobbled on her thick high heels.

"Thank you," said Kate. "But you don't have to do that. I'll grab a broom and clean up the glass. Just watch where you step. I wouldn't want you to get hurt."

"No trouble at all," came the strange voice once again. The woman stood up and handed the tray to Kate. "Serves me right for going off on my own to find a restroom away from the crowds. The bellhop directed me over here, but there are so many doors in this place, I'm not sure I'm in the right spot."

"There is one right down the hall there," Kate said as she pointed to her right. "It's just for employees, but I suppose it's OK for you to use it. I don't actually know the rules. I'm new here."

"Me too, honey. I just arrived yesterday."

Kate tried not to stare. She recognized those eyes. But from where?

The woman continued. "Tony made quite a contraption for this very kind of situation. He fixed a funnel to the end of the steel jockstrap and wound a hose around his thighs and down his silk stockings. Good idea in theory, but he claimed it was more trouble than it was worth. Too bad. I was going to ask him to make one for me."

A flush of excitement washed over Kate as the truth occurred to her. The woman was talking about Tony Curtis! And this was not actually a woman. This was Jack Lemmon. *Jack Lemmon!* She'd heard that *Some Like It Hot* featured a couple of men in drag, but until he—she—was right in front of her, she couldn't have imagined what it all looked like up close and in person.

First Marilyn Monroe. Then Jack Lemmon.

This was better than the Christmas that Mom and Dad had taken her to see Santa Claus at Union Square, and for a three-year-old that had been the very best thing imaginable.

Kate felt dizzy as blood drained from her head to her feet. This—*this!*—was what she had come here for. What Granddad wanted for her. To be more than a spectator. To be a *participant*, flesh and blood and celluloid, giving the world the gift of joy, even in this small way.

One glass of shattered lemonade at a time.

That sobered her, as did the image of the machinations of using a restroom for the actors in their getup. Must be daunting. But in some cosmic way, it seemed like the world would be set right on its axis if all men had a chance to step, quite literally, into the shoes of a woman and see how difficult it could be to belong to the so-called weaker sex.

Thank you, Billy Wilder, she thought. *For the gift of this movie.*

She took a deep breath and composed herself. She would never be taken seriously if she seemed to be no more than another giddy fan.

"Mr. Lemmon," she started, wondering if it was too forward to use his name. She felt like she should say something akin to *Your Majesty.* After all, he was Hollywood royalty. "I haven't seen anyone using that restroom down the hall, so I'm sure you can use it anytime you like."

"You're a dear," he said, patting her on the shoulder. "The crowds out there are supposed to be staying behind the ropes, but they've already spilled past it many times. This place might just have to be our little secret."

He smiled through red-colored lips, and Kate's heart pounded. She was helping out the great Jack Lemmon and had given him a place to find a brief respite among the hubbub that was brewing outside.

She was a tiny cog in the giant wheel of the moviemaking. But it was a start.

"Of course," he continued, "they're not here for me. It's Tony they're after. Billy Wilder says he's the handsomest face in Hollywood, and the ladies appear to agree. Doesn't seem to matter that he has a wife and child and another pip-squeak coming soon. And Marilyn, of course. They'll be after Marilyn like bees to honey as soon as she decides to come down."

Oh! Miss Monroe! She'd almost forgotten, wrapped up in the orbit of this man she'd always admired. Could it really be possible that Kate Morgan of Fisherman's Wharf could even *be* in a situation where she was juggling the needs of not one but *two* movie stars? "Do you know, Mr. Lemmon, when she might be making an appearance? I've actually been assigned the job of making sure that she has all she needs from the kitchen, but it's been two days and I've seen no sign of her."

Mr. Lemmon laughed. "There's one thing you'll learn quickly about Miss Monroe: she arrives on set when she feels like it, and if she doesn't feel like it, she doesn't arrive on set. Billy knew that when he took her on, but he insisted she was the only one he wanted for the role of Sugar Kane Kowalczyk. I think he's been licking his wounds since we started, though. We've been at it for weeks in Hollywood, and she's already delayed production more times than we can count."

Kate was speechless at being privy to this kind of insight from someone like him. If only her family could see her now. Even if they didn't share the love of movies that she and Granddad delighted in, they didn't live under a rock. They'd know who Jack Lemmon was and would no doubt be impressed.

She would love nothing more than to stay here all day, talking to him in the hallway as if there were no world outside it. But that would make her no different from the pushy girls pressing against the ropes outside. She wasn't here to fawn over the talent. She was here to distinguish herself as one who could work around them. She pressed her lips together to stifle a giggle and then spoke in a professional tone.

"If you'll excuse me, I need to go find a mop, and I don't want to hold you up. But is there anything I can bring to you when you're back out?"

He smiled. "That lemonade sure looked good. If you have another batch, I'll take a glass."

"Sure thing, Mr. Lemmon." She smiled at the coincidence of his name.

"And a straw if you can wrangle one. My makeup girl will have my head if I smear my lipstick one more time."

Kate held her hand up to her mouth and laughed.

He sauntered on down the halls, teetering on those shoes. One heel twisted, and he had to catch himself against the wall.

"I don't know how you gals do it!" he called out without looking back.

Kate rested the tray against her hip and shook her head in disbelief. There were not many people in the world who could say they'd had a moment quite like it.

It made everything it took to get here worth it.

~

The sun set late in Coronado. It was nearly eight o'clock, and the light that had just disappeared into the water still glowed. Kate tossed a towel over her shoulder and found a corner near the iconic red tower of the hotel. It was away from the sight line of the lawn in front of the beach, which was packed, even at this hour, with people who were eking out the last minutes before night descended. In San Francisco, she might be worried about walking a mile and a half in the dark, but Coronado felt like a safe oasis, and she had no fear walking back and forth to the carriage house room if it was too late for the bus to run.

After her encounter with Jack Lemmon, she was certain that she would be equally dazzled with every new person she met connected to the film. But in the frenzy of serving the buffet dinner, refilling waters, and taking orders for drinks she'd never heard of, it nearly escaped her attention when she saw Billy Wilder himself across the room and heard some cross words pass between Tony Curtis and his wife, Janet Leigh.

It was only here, looking at the actual stars that were starting to appear in the darkening sky, that she thought about all the ones she'd seen throughout the day. Indeed, they shone brightly when you sat in the comfortable cocoon of a movie theater. But here, even in this paradise, they were regular people who ate, drank, talked like everyone else.

Servers who had worked at the hotel for years commented on how busy it was. It was August, and families squeezed out a few final weekends before their children returned to school. Cast and crew filled many of the rooms, and movie fans who had sniffed out the location of the shoot took up whatever remained. Some even set up camp to the west of the hotel on the empty stretch of beach.

The Hotel del Coronado was at capacity. And Kate was exhausted from the constant activity.

But grateful to be here. It was all more than she could have imagined.

Breaks were scarce, but Kate had worked up the nerve to ask a guy she'd heard was a seasoned employee about the beautiful stranger. "A beautiful stranger?" he'd asked. "That doll on the beach in the pink bikini? That's a stranger I'd like to get to know."

She stopped asking for the time being.

"I see you've discovered my spot."

The words startled Kate, but when she looked up, she saw Sean standing on the step above her, a circle of light cast around him from one of the torches that framed the exterior of the hotel at night.

"Mr. O'Donnell." She started to stand and brushed her hands across her skirt to smooth it.

He stepped down and swept his hand in a gesture that told her to stay where she was. "Please don't get up for me. You've had a long day."

Kate returned to her place, and he joined her. He groaned as he sat, making him sound much older than his age.

"I've had a long day, too," he said. "I don't think my legs want to take me back inside just yet."

"Of course." She gathered her knees to her chest and hugged her arms around them. He'd said *my spot*, but it pleased her to think that, for this moment at least, it was *theirs*.

"I saw you working like a bee," began Kate. "You were darting about all day between the lawn and the ballroom and the kitchen and your office. Did you stop even once?"

He looked at his watch. "No. And I'm just realizing that I haven't eaten anything since breakfast."

Kate sprang to her feet. "Let me go get something for you."

"No, no," he said. "I'll be OK."

She almost listened. But she'd lived too many days after shifts at the restaurant where she felt depleted, poured onto her bed like day-old coffee, and she would have given anything for someone to bring her a small plate of food. As hard as she'd worked today, it wasn't anything in comparison to what she'd watched in him. He'd done so much for her in mere days—gotten her this job, clothes, the means to call her family once a week. This was something small she could do in return.

"I insist," she said. And she hurried off before he could stop her.

The kitchen was abuzz with the last of the servers loosening their cummerbunds and bow ties. Food that was left over was being discarded because it would have no use the next day. Kate winced at whole trays of deviled eggs being dumped into bins and thought about how many poor people in San Francisco they could have fed. But maybe homeless didn't have a presence here. Coronado carried an air of affluence about it, so who here would want to consume the remains of a picked-over buffet? She wondered whether San Diego was similar. Just across the bay, the city seemed a world away here on this tiny peninsula.

Before any more could be discarded, Kate grabbed a plate from the newly washed stack, still steaming from the heat of the water. She looked at the small dish and reached for a larger one instead. She was hungry, too.

She found the trays of food that were just waiting for disposal and heaped their goods onto the plate. Strips of sirloin, kebabs of chicken and tomatoes, an array of cubed cheeses, chocolate chip cookies. With her other hand, she grabbed the tallest drinking glass she could find and filled it with cold water from the sink.

Sean was still there when she got back to the beach, his head resting on folded arms across his knees. He sat up at the sound of her feet on the pavement.

"Here we are," she said. She set the plate on another step and handed the water to him.

"You are an angel, Kate Morgan."

She shrugged. "You looked as if I might have to carry you up the stairs if you didn't get something in your stomach, Mr. O'Donnell."

"And what about you? You need to get yourself back to the carriage house, right? Not an easy feat after a long day. Can you make it?"

Twenty minutes ago she'd wondered that very thing—the bus didn't run this late. But her energy felt renewed just by sitting here, looking at the ocean and talking to Sean.

She nodded, not admitting that by staying here with him, she would be violating the curfew of the strict Mrs. Rorbach. She hoped the woman went to bed early and wouldn't see Kate climbing the exterior steps to the room above the garage.

But she just wanted to sit and relax on this beautiful beach for a few more moments. And she liked his company.

"This is more than I could eat if I was stranded in a desert for a year," he said.

"I—Well, I haven't had anything since lunch. I grabbed some extra for me."

"Good!" He smiled, picking up one of the cookies first. "A real picnic, then."

Kate felt her cheeks warm. A moonlit picnic overlooking the ocean. It might have been romantic in another circumstance. But Sean was just her boss.

They ate hungrily, and the contents of the plate were half-finished before he spoke again.

"You know, if we're going to be friends, you can cut out the 'Mr. O'Donnell' stuff. Just call me Sean. At least when we're like this. Maybe inside we can return to the formalities. But I hear 'Mr. O'Donnell' all day long, and unless I call my mother, a whole day can go by where I never hear my own first name."

Kate wondered what his fiancée must call him, then. Or did he not talk to her every day? How odd. If Kate were in love, she wouldn't want to let a day pass without talking.

"Sean," she said, enjoying the familiarity of it.

"Thanks. I mean, otherwise, it makes me sound so much older. And there can't be *that* many years between us."

This seemed the right opportunity to ask him something that had intrigued her. "If I may ask a personal question, how did you get such an important job so young? Manager of—well, all that you are manager of. Not that you don't do it well. You do it really well. I was watching today. But I wouldn't have thought they would hire someone your age for that role."

"You're such a surprise, Kate Morgan." She liked how he said her name. "You come down all the way from San Francisco, leaving everything behind, persevere after being robbed, work all day long, maintain that beautiful smile, and still have the boldness to ask your boss a question like that."

Kate's heart sank. She'd not thought it too impertinent a thing to ask, but maybe it was. People could be funny about their ages. Maybe it wasn't limited to women.

"I'm sorry. I didn't mean—"

He patted her hand and then pulled away. "You misunderstand me. I *like* that about you. You're a girl who knows how to go after what she wants. I think that's a fine quality. We need more women like that in the world."

"Oh." She picked up a kebab and decided to eat it rather than respond. She didn't want to let on how much it pleased her to be thought of that way.

"Well, since you asked, here is the quick and uninteresting history of Sean O'Donnell. Besides what I already told you about my family when we were on the ferry, I was born and raised right here in Coronado. We only moved to the other side of the bay recently, because my dad's a building contractor and there are housing developments going up in Point Loma and the surrounding area that keep him pretty busy. He was tired of doing the ferry commute every day."

"So now *you* do the commute?" she asked.

"Yeah. But I don't mind. I usually bring a book. I enjoy that quiet time before heading into this chaos. Except for days, of course, when

I encounter young ladies looking lost in the boarding area and I get to come to their rescue." He grinned.

Her cheeks grew warm again. She hadn't felt like much of a lady when they'd met, having bathed in a filthy train bathroom just hours before. But now that she'd had a few good nights of sleep in a real bed, she was beginning to feel like herself once again. She no longer sensed the phantom rocking of the train when she lay down.

"Well." She grinned back. "Let's hope you don't make *that* mistake again."

"Right," he answered. "A man can only handle so many distractions."

"Back to my question," she said.

"Oh yes." He stretched out his hands, and she heard his knuckles crack. "How did I land such a job at this tender age, fresh out of kindergarten?" He laughed. "Well, I've been roaming the grounds of the Hotel del Coronado since I could toddle. My mother was a house cleaner here through each of her pregnancies, supporting the family while my dad started his building business. And—OK, don't blush, and this might be a totally inappropriate thing to say—but I happen to know that I was even conceived in one of the rooms. An unexpected present after a night of champagne when Dad was celebrating the first housing development he got a contract for."

Kate put her hands to her cheeks. What a thing to know!

His cheeks reddened. "I'm not trying to embarrass you, Kate Morgan. Just showing you that I have, well, a very long history at the hotel. I started running errands for the general manager when I was twelve, became a busboy by fourteen, chopped vegetables by sixteen, and six years after that I'm substituting for the events manager, who is on an extended trip in Europe learning about new cuisines we can incorporate into our banquet menus."

"Oh, I see."

"Disappointed?"

Kate smiled. "No. Not disappointed at all. I think that speaks very highly of you that they put you in charge of so much, especially in the summer season and now with the movie here and all that."

"Well, there's always Mr. Clark to help." Sean pinched his face and hunched his shoulders, making her laugh at the impression. "Actually, he doesn't like me because he thinks that once Mr. Bosel returns, I'm going to go after his own job. Little does he know, there's no such plan. My future is mapped out. And it doesn't involve being the events manager. In fact, it doesn't even involve working at the Del at all." Sean's face turned shadowy as he said this.

"Why not?" she asked.

He looked away from Kate and out at the water, and it seemed that he'd suddenly disappeared into a cave of his own. "Because as soon as the university is finished being built in San Diego, I'm set to go there to study business and finance. I have a guaranteed position at my future father-in-law's investment firm."

"Oh." Kate turned her eyes to the ocean as well.

"He and my father have been friends since before I was born. He financed Dad's earliest projects when no one else would give a young Irish boy a break. They've made a lot of money together. I don't think you've ever seen two fathers as happy as the day Cynthia and I announced our engagement. They toasted the merger, as they called it, and the wineglasses actually broke when they clinked them together. Cynthia's mother wasn't too happy. They stained her white lamb's-wool rug."

This had shades of Dimitri and Adara. Though in that case it was cultural. They barely knew one another—their betrothal had been planned years ago when they were in diapers. Adara still lived in Athens with her parents and planned to move to the United States when it was time for the wedding. Kate didn't know the circumstance between Sean and Cynthia, but she would have thought that a groom only weeks away from getting married would look a little more . . . excited.

But she had to admit her own inexperience with such things. Perhaps it was the approaching wedding-day jitters that she'd heard of. Or maybe it was the fact that the Crown Room was no longer available and he'd have to tell his investment-broker future father-in-law that news. If, in fact, he decided to give in to Mr. Clark.

Kate looked down at their plate. In this brief time, they'd cleared it off. All that remained were the wooden skewers of the kebabs and crumbs from the chocolate chip cookies. The moon sent its beams rippling across the waves. She could see the lights of the naval base in the distance at North Island, set in two straight rows along the ground, lining the runway. Coronado was an odd, magical place. The Victorian presence of the hotel. The piercing modern noises that came from the jets. The calming sounds of the eternal ocean.

"Want to know why they call it North Island?"

She was glad that Sean had changed the subject. "Why?"

He pointed toward the runway lights. "Back when J. D. Spreckels first invested in the hotel, that piece of land and this one were separated by a shallow bay. It was actually an island. They used it for hunting and horseback riding for hotel guests. They filled up the land in 1945 to better serve the base, but the name stuck."

"They're doing that in Northern California, too. There's a whole town called Foster City that is built on land they've created over water."

"My dad talks about that all the time," said Sean. "How the footprint of the state will change over time as coastal property becomes more expensive. They'll end up building where the fish live now, just for those views and that access."

"Our ancestors could never have conceived of such a thing."

"No, the equipment wasn't there for it. But Cynthia's dad speculates in coastal real estate and is already buying up water rights in places that he thinks will expand development. It's one of the projects he wants me to work on. In fact, he doesn't even care about me going to the university. He and Cynthia and my dad are laying on pretty thick the fact that they want me to come on board now. But I've been holding off, using school as an excuse. Saying that I want to have the education before I have the job."

Sean looked quite tormented, and this must have been front and center in his mind for him to have brought it up again.

"But that's not it, is it?" she prompted.

He looked at her and then turned to face the water again.

It crossed Kate's mind that water connected all the people who had stared at it centuries and millennia before, looking for answers, feeling the smallness of our problems in comparison to its vastness.

Sean broke through her contemplation. "Is it ridiculous to say that I feel like a piece of my soul is here at the Del? That I would be happiest if I worked here for the rest of my life? Even if I never advanced beyond what I'm doing. It's not what my position is. It's this place. This place—there's something about it that feels like it's a part of my very being." He shrugged and started to stand up. "I know that probably sounds stupid."

"Not at all," Kate said, staring at him in surprise. Sean had said exactly what had been on her mind ever since stepping foot on these grounds. That it stirred her soul. Like she belonged to it. Like it belonged to her. But she couldn't understand it herself, let alone put it into words. Sean at least had history here. It made sense for him to feel that way.

He took the plate from her just as she was picking it up, and their fingers brushed against each other. So lightly that it might have been a feather, but Kate still felt a shiver scurry up her arm like she'd touched an open circuit. She pulled away.

"I feel like I belong to this beautiful little piece of land," he said. "No wonder I don't want to leave it and don a suit and tie every day."

How does Cynthia feel about this? she wanted to ask. But it was not her place.

He sighed. "Well, then, Kate Morgan. I hope you don't mind my calling you that. It just still strikes me as funny that you share the name of our ghost."

"I don't mind." It only served to make her feel even more connected to Coronado.

Maybe that was all there was to it. She shared the name of some phantom woman who had died years ago and never left. It was a different Kate Morgan who belonged here, and this Kate shouldn't get the two confused. Her life was back in San Francisco, even if Coronado beckoned like a siren.

Sean lifted the plate and glass. "I'll take these back to the kitchen. Things should have wound down by now."

She stood up and followed him down the torch-lit path. But he didn't take her through the door where she'd met Jack Lemmon. Goodness—had that been only hours ago? It felt like years.

Sean walked in a different direction to a door she never would have seen if he hadn't shown her. "That other entrance is locked by this time. Here's another way in."

He opened the door for her, and she walked ahead. This hallway was not familiar. It seemed to lead to more administrative offices. Brass plaques bore the names of the various men who held positions at the hotel. The manager. The assistant managers. The accounting department. The sales department. The walls were lined with black-and-white photos that created a veritable museum of the history of the hotel and the area. Things she didn't even recognize today.

"Tent City—1901"
"Orange Grove, A Avenue—1897"

And on and on. Even a picture where, just like Sean had said, North Island was indeed separate and it was nothing but forestland.

Another wall held portraits of past general managers, and it was amusing to watch how the fashions had changed over the years—big handlebar mustaches in the beginning all the way to dark-framed eyeglasses today. Other pictures showed employees in times past being honored in one way other another for their service.

"HARRY WEST, BELLHOP—1892"
"IMELDA SKAGGS, HOUSEKEEPING—1902"
"EDDIE VAN DYKE, GROUNDS—1905"

Maybe this was the right time to ask about the beautiful stranger. Maybe the woman was some past employee—someone who could have worked here during Granddad's time.

But suddenly one photograph stopped Kate in her tracks, and she gasped. A close-up of a handsome young man and a stunning woman on his arm. She was smiling, and her hand covered her mouth as if she had just had a roaring laugh over something.

On that hand was a ring. A ring that Kate knew all too well. A silver globe on top of a thin band. Square diamonds on top, sapphires on either side.

That was Grandma's ring.

And that was Granddad George smiling at her.

But that wasn't Grandma.

The caption read, "George Morgan, Front Desk, and Mary Carter, Hotel Guest, on the occasion of their engagement on the lawn of the Hotel del Coronado—1908."

∾

1895

I am passing my third Christmas here at the Hotel del Coronado. To say it that way makes it sound like I mark the passage of time, but that would not be quite accurate. In the state in which I exist, where I am here but not here, there is no sense of that. I do not watch the clock. I do not acknowledge my birthday. I do not get bored. Instead, I watch the visitors come and go on their vacations, a perpetual fountain of joy for me that feels new and fresh each time the door opens and I observe their wonder. Especially at this festive time of year, I think one would have to be lacking a soul to not be moved by the beauty. And though my soul is in a limbo beyond my understanding, at least it is proof that I possess one.

The days and their twenty-four-hour cycles are far less consequential to me than the milestones of the holidays. Funny how we are so consumed by the seconds of the clock when we are living and our feet can touch the ground. How unnecessary it is later when the hands marking the time of your life have stopped.

I do hope that I am not in possession of anyone's pity, if I am remembered at all. It is rather the other way around. I am privy not only to the exuberance of the guests at the hotel but their heartbreaks as well. The mother who spent the family vacation in the bedroom because her young son caught the croup. The businessman who received a telegram that his wife had died of consumption while he was here working. The woman whose fiancé broke off their engagement and left her in tears on the very steps where my body was found.

No, I should not be pitied. I am liberated from those things that shackle the living. I do not know hunger. I do not know cold. I do not know sorrow. In truth, I don't even remember what those things feel like.

On this remarkable holiday, the hotel has put up an immense tree in the main hall and decorated it with candles. Tinsel and cranberry strands and garlands and ribbons hang around the railings that line the second story of the lobby. Carts of apple cider and hot chocolate send little tendrils of steam into the air. A pianist plays carols, and sometimes children join in when they know the words.

It is a charming sight. Storybook perfect in every way. Coronado already holds that kind of magic. Christmas only enhances it.

But last night—by the accounting of a calendar—something happened that felt as if an earthquake were rattling through me. I thought for a moment that I was being pulled from this place, going to whatever was next for one in my circumstance. Then I realized that the sensation was not one of being pulled outward but inward. It seemed as if a rope had been tied around my waist and I was being wrenched back into the world I used to abide in.

It was the presence of a young boy who entered the lobby. I watched, mesmerized, as he touched the ivory keys of the grand piano that stood in the middle. The boy was about six years old and he was darling, but no more so than any other child his age, so I did not understand at first why I was so drawn to him.

Bound to him.

He pulled his hand back when he heard the low bass G of the key he'd struck. He looked left and right, wondering, most likely, whether he would be in trouble for touching it. When no one came running, he played another note and another, finding more delight in the higher keys, whose notes were more joyful than the dirgelike ones of the lower register. As he felt more comfortable with the sounds of the notes, he began to experiment with them, seeming to have an instinct for what sounded right to his little ear. When he hit upon a tune he liked, he played it over and over, testing out the timing until he had a ditty that went like this: E-D-C, pause, C-E-A-G. And again, E-D-C, pause, C-E-A-G.

Memories flooded me. Sitting with my mother on the bench of the piano in my grandfather's house. First notes, then chords, then music.

So engrossed was the child in this tune that he was at first unaware that a girl about his age raced down the stairs to join him. She was dressed in a pink woolen coat with a fur muff around her neck and a matching hat across her head. But golden curls were splayed underneath it. She, too, was charming, but she did not hold the magnetism for me that he did.

The girl removed her mittens and banged both hands on the upper register of the piano in a discordant screech. The boy pulled away. "No!" he shouted. "Don't hurt the piano."

This sent the girl into tears, at which time the mothers swarmed from opposite sides of the lobby.

"Mary! Come get away from there. We're going on a sleigh ride."

The girl followed, though she looked back at the boy.

Next to Mary's finery and that of her mother, I noticed then how plainly clothed the boy was. Not that he was poor, but he was not quite as splendid as the others who were here for the holiday.

Another woman approached from the registration desk. "Come, now," she said in gentler tones to her son. "It's probably not meant to be played when there are a lot of people in the lobby. Maybe we can come back later this evening when the guests are at dinner."

"But—"

"No, dearest. Papa is waiting for us. I'm making your favorite soup tonight."

I drew closer to them, as I'd only been observing the exchange from the balcony. In a second I was next to the woman. I saw her rub her arms. I know I have that effect when I get close to people—they make mention of goose bumps or shivers that they can't explain.

If I had a beating heart, it would have stopped right then. I knew those blue eyes of hers. The dark-red hair that she wore in a bun. The sharp nose that was the only strong feature on an otherwise soft face.

Grace Morgan of A Avenue. How many years had it been, Grace? Six. Anything involving that family is the one part of timekeeping that I have not seemed to shed. In fact, it is only more pronounced where they are concerned. It has been six years, two months, and thirteen days since we have seen each other.

I look at the boy again. It has been just that long since I've seen him, too. Although with the way babies change, I would not have recognized him even a month after his birth. He looked a bit like the woman with him. The only mother he knew. Hooray for that. I'm sure it saved them from a myriad of questions. His eyes were a similar blue. But his hair was more fair, his nose less pronounced.

The pull I felt toward him intensified to the point that it was a supreme act of will on my part to not smother him entirely.

Oddly, he did not shiver even as I stood so close. In fact, he looked intently right in my direction. He held up a hand. To an observer it would have seemed as if his hand dangled in the air for no reason. But not to me—I took my hand and I placed it against his. Like mirror images. I don't know if he saw me, but he sensed me. Of that I'm certain.

"George, really," said Grace. "We must run along before Papa worries."

She took that hand of his, breezing right through my imperceptible one, and pulled him toward the door.

He looked back, his other arm trailing behind him. Reaching for the piano. No, not the piano. It was me he wanted, standing next to the piano, stretching my arm toward him as well.

Warmth filled my hollow being, so astounded was I at this most welcome and enchanting encounter.

They disappeared behind the large wooden doors that led to the roundabout.

The tie that seemed to bind me when the boy was here loosened, and I was again free to roam the hotel in the way I was accustomed.

But I wasn't really free. He had stood here in this place. Played these keys. Seen me with the inner eye of a child who still believes in that which is otherwise undetectable to an adult mind.

My George. My son.

Chapter Ten

Kate had trouble sleeping. She'd tossed in fits, punched the pillow into shapes that brought no comfort, cast the down blanket onto the floor only to pick it up again minutes later.

Despite the exhaustion of the day, the astonishment of seeing Granddad's photograph—and with a woman she'd never heard of, a Mary Carter—kept her up until just an hour before her alarm clock startled her.

Who was that woman? Why had Granddad never mentioned her?

Could *she* be the beautiful stranger? She wished she had thought of it in the moment—Sean might have been able to answer then and there, one question solved. But she was so shocked by the image and the plaque accompanying it that she'd thought of nothing else except this new mystery of Granddad's past.

The thought was sobering. She could be the answer, or she could be just another goose chase. Alive or dead. And would anyone at the hotel even remember a woman from so many decades ago?

But there was little time to ponder that as she hastened to fill a tray to bring upstairs. She couldn't stick around for answers if she couldn't perform the job she'd been hired to do.

Today was the day she'd meet Marilyn Monroe again.

A twinge of guilt niggled at her. How could she be excited about that as Granddad lay in the hospital and she *still* hadn't found the beautiful stranger? She was afraid that as the days ticked by, her reason for being here was getting muddled, tipping the scale toward her own interests and away from her family's.

And yet here she was, Kate Morgan from Fisherman's Wharf in San Francisco, about to serve the queen of all movie stars. Marilyn Monroe. Who *wouldn't* jump at that opportunity?

Kate poured a cup of steaming coffee, bourbon on the rocks, and a Bloody Mary, per the request sent down last night from the movie star. The only food was a vanilla pudding soufflé. No request for eggs or toast or bacon or anything she would consider a proper breakfast had been called down.

Kate looked at the room numbers, having committed Miss Monroe's to memory. At no point was it to be written down where it could be found by any of the hundreds of people in the crowd who gathered on the lawn hoping for a glimpse. Those who might trample each other for a hint of the whereabouts of the movie star. There were fewer doors on this penthouse level, but Kate was still jittery at the thought that she might knock on the wrong one.

The set call—she was picking up the production lingo—had been scheduled for nine thirty to account for the kind of natural light the cinematographer, Charles Lang, wanted to incorporate. He'd constructed a black net stretched across a frame so that it would filter the sun and illuminate Marilyn's white-blonde hair. Kate learned that if they lost the ideal light, they had to replicate it with lamps put on stands and metallic screens held by low-level assistants at angles that sent reflections and shadows just where they wanted them.

But doing so took time, and time was money—the mantra on the set. "Avoid the golden hours!" was a common phrase, meaning that the unions required production to pay additional money for overtime for cast and crew. Considering the number of people employed—and certainly Kate hadn't encountered all of them—and adding the cost of food and hotel stays for all, she could understand why the director jetted about the set in a constant state of frenetic movement. She wouldn't have been able to sit still, either, if so much were riding on her shoulders.

So much was, however, riding on the shoulders of Marilyn Monroe, who was late for the third day in a row. And according to Mr. Lemmon, that was just the Coronado part of the shoot. She'd set that precedent for herself in Hollywood, too.

Kate rapped on the door hard enough to alert someone inside of her presence without making a nuisance of herself. She held her breath to calm the jitters that radiated throughout her body like twinkling strings of Christmas lights.

The door opened, but to her disappointment it was not the legendary beauty who stood behind it. Instead, it was a short woman with gray wisps streaking through faded black hair. Her square chin seemed permanently set in a state of rigidity. Her big brown eyes might have been lovely with a touch of mascara thickening her lashes, but without it they looked shapeless and a little sad.

"Leave it over there and take the empty trays with you." Her voice was low, almost imperceptible, like a flesh-and-blood silent movie.

"Yes, ma'am."

Kate tried to maintain a professional demeanor, but it was impossible not to be awed by the scope of the suite of rooms. It was larger than the apartment she shared with her family in San Francisco. A spacious den opened to a wide balcony, though it was difficult to distinguish at first, since the wall-high shutters were closed. They let in light with horizontal streaks that looked like stripes across the floor. The rest of the room was darkened, though it was the time of day when the restaurant was already serving lunch.

What a wildly extravagant place. She had never seen anything like it. Not two weeks gone from the hot, greasy kitchen in San Francisco, and here she was in the most elegant place that may ever have been created. And somewhere in this suite of rooms lived, for now, the only woman who would ever be equal to it.

Kate oriented herself and figured that the view would have been an unobstructed panorama of ocean. Quite possibly the most beautiful thing she could imagine, and such a tragedy to hide it. Or from it.

The room to her left was almost unrecognizable as to its purpose. A long table for twelve people bore no room for company due to the piles and piles of clothes and cosmetics strewn across the chairs and tops. A scarf hung from a curve in the chandelier, and Kate had no idea as to how it could have gotten there. Lipstick containers sat open, and a bottle of nail polish had spilled onto the lacquered tabletop. Beyond the den was a door where she could see the rumpled linens of a bed and an indistinguishable figure moving within it.

Kate's mouth went dry. Could *that* be Marilyn?

"Leave the tray over there," the woman with the plain eyes told her. She pointed to a coffee table in front of a sofa and cleared away two tasseled caftans that lay across it. Her words forced Kate to avert her eyes from the bedroom door.

"Yes, ma'am," she responded. "Would you like for me to clear those?"

The mirrored bar was littered with half-drunk cocktail glasses and wineglasses and plates with food that had merely been nibbled.

"Please."

A tentative voice spoke from the bedroom. "Paula?"

That voice! Not the one from the movie screens or from the beach just last week. But that of a child—tired and timid. And yet just enough of a hint of the silk and velvet textures that made men swoon and women like Kate wish to emulate.

It occurred to Kate that Sean was duly justified in letting go of a male employee who had not treated this like the hallowed position it was.

She looked up to see Marilyn Monroe, and her breath stopped. But the woman no longer had the look of a movie star. Her face was plain, innocent. Trusting.

She wore nothing but a sheet from the bed pulled up to where she clutched it at her collarbone. The light in the bathroom was on, and it silhouetted her famous figure enough that the sheet seemed hardly purposeful.

The woman who'd answered the door turned to Marilyn, and Kate remembered reading about who she was. Paula Strasberg. An actress in her own right, though primarily onstage. She and her husband, Lee, were Marilyn's acting coaches. The trade magazines Kate devoured reported that Marilyn Monroe didn't make one move or film one scene without the approval of her mentors. In fact, Billy Wilder was supposed to have said that he might as well hand over the directorship of *Some Like It Hot* to Paula Strasberg, so thoroughly had she been involving herself.

Kate watched the interaction of the women as she might a mother and child. One would have never guessed that Marilyn Monroe had oodles of movies to her name. She looked as if she might be afraid to cross the street without holding someone's hand.

Kate's heart lurched at the star's unexpected vulnerability, and she felt the kind of parental instinct toward her that Mrs. Strasberg demonstrated. Maybe the old woman was not so much a sourpuss as a necessary counterweight.

"Paula," Marilyn said again. "When is Arthur arriving? I need Arthur." She did not seem to even notice Kate as she whimpered the question.

Paula put her hands on her hips. "Your husband isn't due for another few days. Don't you want to come out today, my dear? You'll be able to show him how well you're adjusting to Coronado. He'll be so proud of you."

From what Kate had heard, Miss Monroe hadn't started shooting at all.

"Must I go down there?" the movie star asked. "I have a rotten headache."

"Yes. You really have to. This has gone on too long. Billy is getting agitated. You're more expendable than you realize."

The women continued to take no notice whatsoever of Kate's presence. She was unsure of what she should do. Clear the glasses as she'd been told and then leave? Or wait around to see if anything else was needed? They seemed to exist in their own little dimension, and she had barely a peripheral role in it.

Kate assumed that she should be properly dismissed before leaving, though. She'd have to ask Sean what was expected of her in the future. In the meantime, she quietly emptied the bar of its debris, stacked the tray, and wiped down the surface until she could see her reflection clearly in it.

In the few minutes that took, Paula had wrangled Miss Monroe into a black sheath—right there in the open! Either modesty was a long-since-discarded habit or Kate was truly invisible to them, a forgotten spectator. The star's much-celebrated hourglass shape was even more pronounced in the dress, though she seemed to be carrying more weight than she had in other pictures. Tabloids were forever announcing that she was pregnant, but more reliable papers claimed that she'd suffered several miscarriages.

Poor Marilyn. On-screen she was invincible. But here in the flesh she seemed as fragile to Kate as a wispy dandelion. The kind she and Janie had called "wishing flowers" as children. One hint of wind and—poof—she might disappear.

Kate jumped at a squawk coming from the corner of the room and saw among the clutter the shape of a birdcage. A small parakeet flapped its tail feathers and hopped back and forth on a swing.

"I miss Hugo." Marilyn sighed and walked over to the pet, sticking a manicured finger through the rungs to try to touch it. She smiled at the bird, showing brilliant white teeth that hinted of her stardom. "You're no dog, but you'll do for now, my little man."

She turned and looked at Kate so abruptly that Kate didn't have time to look away. The brilliance of those eyes shot through her, and Kate felt heat rise in her throat as she drew the attention of the legend. She wished right now that she could blend into the wallpapered background. Being on the sideline felt far more comfortable.

"Oh, hello," said Marilyn in a singsong voice. "I didn't see you there."

"I'm heading out, miss," said Kate, hoisting the tray onto her shoulder. "I just wanted to see if there is anything else I can get for you."

She locked her legs so they wouldn't fidget. Despite everything she'd been witnessing, talking to Marilyn Monroe was the most *incredible* thing that had ever happened in her life. And she didn't want to blow it.

"Is that the Bloody Mary you have there?"

Miss Monroe walked toward her, and Kate felt the protective eyes of Paula Strasberg staring.

"Yes, ma'am. Just as you asked. And some water and a bourbon, too. And the pudding. May I get you an omelet, Miss Monroe? Or some toast?" Kate couldn't imagine starting a day with an array like this. Her mom always insisted on something hearty before heading out in the morning.

Mrs. Strasberg intervened. "We'll have exactly what she asked for and nothing else. You may go."

The actress sighed. "What I wouldn't give for a big, juicy fig right now."

Kate looked back and forth between them. Mrs. Strasberg had a wild, severe look to her that dared Kate to do anything except what she was told. On the other hand, Miss Monroe looked like she was desperate for a moment of connection. Was that the purpose of the bird? To give her a plaything so as to distract her from the loneliness that overwhelmed this room?

Because if there was any word that came to mind more abundantly to Kate in regard to Marilyn Monroe, it was that: *lonely*.

But it was not her place to think it, let alone say it out loud.

"Yes, ma'am," Kate said instead. She closed the door behind her, managing not to spill the tray full of spent alcohol glasses that she balanced on her shoulders.

~

An hour later, Kate was back on the lawn laying out trays of fruit and cheese. In the wake of meeting Marilyn Monroe, the movie set seemed tame and routine in comparison. Ropes cordoned off the sections where production was taking place, but throngs of people strained against them hoping for glimpses of stardom. Most were well behaved. Some, obnoxious. A good number of them were girls her own age who shouted, "Tony!" every time Tony Curtis was sighted. If he was in costume, he'd smile and wave. If he wasn't, sometimes he walked over and signed autographs for at least a few of them.

Kate realized the privilege of being here, though. Knew that each of those girls would give their right arms to trade places with her. Just a week ago, she would have been one of them if she'd lived anywhere in the area, yearning to be on this side. Yet here she was. The line in the sand, as it were. This had been the very definition of being in the right place at the right time.

She whispered a thank-you to Granddad, too many miles away to hear. The ache of missing him was like a knife. But the best way to love him was to be here.

"Waitress! Water over here."

That word brought Kate back to where she was and reminded her of her place. She was a part of the movie, yet not part of it. Her name would not appear in the credits as *Girl who served water on the hot August day*. But she would know as she watched it on the big screen in a few months that Joan Shawlee liked her club soda with lemon. Joe Brown preferred a Coca-Cola with extra ice and could make funny faces with that unusual smile of his when he said *thank you*. And that Jack Lemmon always gave her the courtesy of a hello.

The first time she saw him after that original incident, he'd said, "There's the lemonade girl. Surely you have a name."

Her face tingled with excitement that Jack Lemmon remembered her.

"Kate Morgan," she'd answered.

"Like the ghost here?"

"Like the ghost."

He was now the eighth person to make that connection. She really had to get used to just saying *Kate*.

Thankfully, he was too much of a gentleman to give her some sort of ghastly nickname like *Ghost Girl* and had the generous spirit to not only remember her name but call her by it every time he'd seen her since. The familiarity of it never ceased to leave her in a state of amazement.

There *were* kind, real people in Hollywood. Though they were far less than Kate might have originally imagined.

Tony Curtis looked like he was having the time of his life, but Kate often caught him chewing a pencil as he sat in a chair and looked at the script. He never turned the pages, though. Was he thinking about the scene? About his pregnant wife and his daughter? Things hadn't looked very cozy between them when Janet Leigh came to the set on that first day.

He was sitting pensively just now, in fact, across the lawn under a white tent. Today he was dressed as Shell Oil Junior. From what Kate had learned, his character was a saxophone player, dressed as a woman to remain incognito for some reason or another, but then he fell in love with singer Sugar Kane Kowalczyk, so he impersonated a millionaire oil heir in order to win her love.

If anyone could pull off a plot as crazy as that, it was Billy Wilder.

Tony's getup as the millionaire was a navy-blue jacket, a captain's hat, and a white cravat at the neck. He chewed a pipe like it was a candy stick and affected an odd accent, inspired by Cary Grant. And his ridiculous glasses served the disguise but made him look like his eyes were buggy.

Still, a Tony Curtis with buggy eyes was dreamier than almost any other man to walk the planet. Of all of them, he was, in person, the most like his presence on-screen, and Kate's cheeks warmed every time she walked past him. Definitely the dreamiest man in the movies.

A cheer erupted in the crowd, and all heads turned toward the sidewalk leading from the hotel.

Marilyn Monroe—the movie star, not the timid child Kate had seen just a bit ago—sashayed down the steps and toward the lawn. In her whole life, Kate had never used or contemplated the word *sashayed*, but it must have been buried there in the recesses in her brain for a moment such as this. Surely Miss Monroe knew that all eyes—male and female—were transfixed on her like glue. The girl had become a goddess again, and Kate was awestruck, as if this were the first time she was seeing her.

Miss Monroe put one delicate foot in front of the other in tiny steps. At one point she turned around like a model on a catwalk and let the caftan slip from her shoulders to reveal the black sheath that Paula had helped her with upstairs. She put her hands to her mouth and giggled, though Kate was sure that everyone knew it wasn't an accident to let the dressing gown sag the way it did.

She continued down the sidewalk, her deliberate steps sending a ripple effect up her body. It was as if she had a doctorate in how the female body should move and exactly how to attract attention.

Kate looked away, feeling somewhat garish staring at the facade that the cameras loved. She'd been more drawn to the girl-woman upstairs. That ache in Kate's heart for the lonely star returned. She saw Tony Curtis emerge from a nearby cabana. He rested his hand and chin against the pole of the tent, and the script sat forgotten on the chair.

He slid his glasses down his nose just in time for Kate to see a look pass across his eyes that mirrored her own.

He was not gawking at the star like everyone else. He looked concerned for her. It confirmed Kate's instincts.

This was a girl who needed protection.

But from what? Kate knew little of life yet, let alone adulthood and Hollywood and marriage, of which Marilyn Monroe had already weathered several.

Billy Wilder, whom Kate had not seen sit down in three whole days, nearly skipped over to the sidewalk.

"Marilyn, welcome!" His voice thundered even among the competing noise of the crowd.

The star flashed that smile she'd given to the parakeet. It was like a mask; Kate could see that now, having witnessed the woman's other, untouched face. The actress mask.

"Billy!"

He took her by the hand—her nail polish was bright red now—and led her toward the tent near Tony.

Tony shifted his weight and put the glasses in his pocket. Kate consolidated the trays so that room could be made for new ones—chocolate croissants were on their way out, she'd heard—but watched the interactions with keen interest.

From this spot at the table, she could no longer hear the nature of their conversations. But she could see everything. Marilyn played the role of star to the hilt—laughing, brushing her hands through her radiant hair. At first glance, one would think that she had not a care in the world. That she'd been kissed by fairies upon her birth and graced with their magic ever since.

Then Paula Strasberg emerged on the sidewalk, followed by a man with a bulbous nose and a thick white mustache. That must be her husband, Lee. They were Marilyn's shadows, pets tied by an invisible leash to their prodigy. Kate wondered, though, who was dependent on whom?

"Penny for your thoughts."

Kate heard Sean behind her. The smell of baked goods and yeast surrounded him, and she remembered that he'd been helping make the rolls for the dinner table tonight. He liked being a manager but missed his kitchen days and popped in to help when he had the opportunity. She preferred this scent of his over any store-bought cologne that a man could buy in a bottle and splash on himself.

"Hi, there," she replied. She hurried her pace with the trays so that he wouldn't think she was lingering without a reason. "I'm making room for the next round."

He put a hand on her arm as quickly as he took it away, and she felt the same electric charge that she had the first time he'd done it. She took a step back.

"Leave all that," he said. "You've been working for six hours. The state might fine me if I don't give you a break at regular intervals anyway."

Kate knew of no such rules. If so, Uncle Mike broke them right and left. She and Janie and her parents never took breaks. Not that Uncle Mike was unkind. Not at all. But after the other failed business in the family, they just didn't stop. Ever.

Which was why what Kate had done—hearing and following her own muse—must be so bewildering to them.

Kate wiped her hands on her white apron and let Sean lead her away from the movie set back to the place where they'd had their little picnic. She sat on the steps, hidden from view, and was surprised when he joined her.

He let out a groan as he stretched his legs in front of him. "Why do I feel eighty when I'm only twenty-two?"

"I know what you mean. Long hours on your feet will age you quickly."

"See, that's exactly the opposite of what everyone says. How exercise is so good for you. But by the end of the day, I feel like I've been wrung dry."

Yes, Kate definitely understood that feeling. She watched businessmen in their pressed suits walk to work and she'd think how easy they had it, sitting all day. Sean had that waiting for him. A ready-made job at an investment firm and a fiancée who wanted him to take it.

"So why do you do it? This kind of work is grueling," she said.

"How can I not?"

"You told me yourself you have another future ahead of you."

He smiled. "Do you see the sparkle in the sand?"

She looked where he was pointing. From this elevated vantage point, and with the angle of the sun, she could indeed see that the sand looked like there was gold hiding in it. Granddad had told her about it. But it was more beautiful than he'd described.

"I do."

"It's because of the mineral mica. I'm not a scientist, so I don't know the history of how that particular composition got here. But I do know that not all beaches have it, and it's one of the things that makes ours special."

Goldlike flecks in the sand. Who could not feel drawn to this place? Even Granddad was tied to it in ways that he never explained but were always apparent to her.

Sean plucked a blade of grass that was growing errantly in the cracks of the mortar. He stripped it down into thin ribbons as he spoke.

"Kate, the thing about mica is that if *all* that sand was made of it, there would be so much sparkle that you wouldn't even notice how special it was anymore. You need the plain, basic sand that makes up the rest of it to elevate the mica to shine the way it does."

"What are you getting at?"

He set the strips of the grass down and looked at her.

"I mean that I don't want to be the mica. I want to be the regular sand. The sand that bolsters the more important stuff. I'm happy organizing events or making food or arranging schedules so that my employees can work the way they need to. I'm happy walking the halls of a place that's many decades older than me and will be here many decades after me. Why isn't that enough? The world needs the regular sand just as much as it needs the mica. But we're pushed, pushed, pushed to be the mica. To outshine the next guy. To make the big bucks."

Kate didn't lose his gaze. She knew what he meant. Those businessmen might be important because they managed money and negotiated contracts and all sorts of things that didn't really matter to her. But when their toilet backed up, when their car broke down, when their bellies rumbled with hunger, who took care of them?

The Seans and the Kates and the blue-collar workers of the world. Maybe that was why she'd never wanted to *be* a movie star. She just wanted to be *around* it all. You couldn't have only the mica. The world wasn't built for unending sparkle. Someone had to admire it. Support it. Sean understood that.

"Have you told Cynthia how you feel? That you don't want to work in her father's investment firm?"

"I did. In fact, I called her last night."

"What did she say?" Kate's heartbeat thumped. Talking to Sean was different from talking to Dimitri. It had ease that felt natural. That she could just enjoy without the kind of hopes or expectations that had begun to overshadow the friendship of their adolescence.

The corners of his lips curled. Almost a smile but not quite. "Well, first she asked me what I was doing calling in the middle of the night. Apparently I'd woken her dormitory monitor, and she was afraid that someone in the family had gotten hurt. I'd forgotten the three-hour time difference. It was only ten o'clock here."

Ten o'clock was early by food industry standards. Kate knew that well enough. If she worked a dinner shift, she didn't get home until well after midnight. It was not just the serving but the counting of the drawer and the cleaning up. Only to do the same thing hours later.

"Oh, I'm sorry." Kate couldn't think of anything else to add.

"I apologized, of course, but I finally had her on the phone, so I wanted to talk while we could. She's been so busy out there with her classes that we haven't talked in a while. I told her that I'm doing well here while Mr. Bosel is in Europe. The hotel manager told me so and said that if I'm patient, he might be able to create a permanent position for me as Mr. Bosel's assistant so that I'm less of a floater. And when he retires someday, I might be able to take his place."

Kate hadn't known Sean for long, but she understood how happy that would make him.

"She must have been really excited for you."

He shook his head. "Not exactly. She talked sense into me. Any chance of a future in that line of work could still take years and years to make it to the top. And I have a ready-made position at her father's firm. I'll make a lot more money, I won't be so tired from working all these hours, and I'll have the regular holidays off that will allow me to be the husband and father I'll need to be."

"You make that all sound so very—clinical."

"I guess it is, isn't it?"

"Maybe you should take her here when she's back in town and show her the mica."

Like you're showing me, she wanted to add. But it didn't feel right to say it. Because this was the kind of romantic spot where lovers should sit, planning their future. Not an employer and employee.

Sean shook his head. "It just made so much sense the way she put it. That is not a future that everyone gets a chance to have, and who am I to refuse it?"

"But . . . ?"

"Why would you think there's a *but* there?"

Kate could sense his vulnerability as she answered his question, and she considered her answer carefully. "I don't know you well, Sean, but it's easy to see that you love it here and that you love your job—and that they love you right back."

"That's a lot of love." He grinned, and it made her skin tingle from her head to her toes.

"Exactly. I've been wondering if all we're meant for is to punch the clock at whatever place pays the most. What kind of epitaph is that?"

He pulled his knees up to his chest and rested his arms on them. "Probably one well before our time." His gaze seemed to be boring into her, but it might have been an illusion from the shadows cast from the turret above. "You're right, Kate Morgan. You are some kind of phantom after all. Or mind reader, at least. There is a *but*."

"What is it?"

Sean took a deep breath. "But I don't want to be an investment broker. But I want to work in the kitchen and manage the schedules and put my feet in this sparkling sand for the rest of my life. But I *like* the feeling of being exhausted at the end of the day. It makes me feel like I'm fully alive."

Yes! Kate clapped her hands. "Bravo!" She understood what he meant, because she felt that way, too.

He gave a slight chuckle. "Wow. That's the first time I've ever said any of that out loud."

She shivered with pride as a helicopter whirled above them, and Kate realized that it had become a habit even in this short time to pause conversations when aircraft flew overhead.

When it passed, its course set for North Island, they continued as if there had been no interruption at all.

"Tell it to Cynthia," she said gently. "She loves you—she'll want you to be happy in your work." She quieted the part of her that didn't want that to be true and made herself say the words that were the only right ones to say.

Sean pulled another blade of grass from the cement and twisted it around his finger. "Do you want to know what I also love about being here?"

"Of course."

He swept his hand around. "Just look in front of us. If you drew a straight line, it would be almost six thousand miles before you'd get to the next piece of land. Six thousand miles before you'd see anything but the blue waters of the Pacific. It's as if all the hassles of the rest of the country are behind us. Literally. I can come here and pretend that there is no nuclear arms race, no competition with the Soviet Union to get into space, no election fighting. But all that ends at the San Diego Bay, just before you get to this little island."

"You mean peninsula." Kate smiled.

"Funny girl. Yes, *peninsula*. If you count the tiny strip of land that leads to Imperial Beach. I guess it's a metaphor for life, if you want to get philosophical about it. Coronado—the magical place that feels like an island. But one little tendril of land to the south reminds you that you are still tethered to real life."

"Tethered. That's a good word for it. In just my short time here, the magic has almost made me forget all that I have to worry about."

"Your grandfather?"

"Mm-hmm." She drew in a sharp breath at the thought of him lying in a hospital bed hundreds of miles away. But she knew how much he'd want her to stay.

"You're welcome to use my phone to call him."

Kate warmed at how considerate he was, but she knew he could get in trouble if she overused the long-distance charges.

"No, thank you," she said. "I'll stick to our agreement. They'll know how to reach me if anything happens."

There were more worries than Granddad's condition, but she didn't want to distract from his concerns with talk of their financial woes.

A sound like an explosion ripped through the sky right above them. But already Kate had learned to tell the time based on when the jets flew over. Military precision.

"One o'clock," said Sean. "We should probably get back."

"May I ask you one thing before we go?"

She felt his eyes on her, and she turned to meet them with her own.

He said into the silence, "Anything, Kate."

She took a deep breath. She wanted to ask her question when no one else was around to tease her for such an unusual inquiry. And she knew somehow that Sean would take her seriously.

"This sounds crazy, but have you ever heard of anyone here called *the beautiful stranger?*"

She winced as she said it. It did sound as ridiculous out loud as it had in her head. Just as she had thought when her grandfather first said it.

But Sean surprised her.

"Of course."

Her heart leaped. Granddad had been right!

Sean continued. "The beautiful stranger is our ghost. The beautiful stranger is Kate Morgan."

~

1899

Little George and his mother came back the next Christmas and the next and sometimes in between. As far as I could tell, they still lived nearby, and as was the case with many locals, the Hotel Del was a beloved center point of life in Coronado.

Every time his feet took a step on the grounds, I knew it. I felt it. That cloudlike sense of airiness that made up my existence every day took on a kind of gravity whenever he was near.

The incomparable force of motherhood lived far beyond death, apparently.

Young Mary Carter and her parents visited every Christmas and usually the following summers. I learned that they lived in Houston, Texas. Her father speculated in oil and, from a conversation I overheard, he'd struck "black gold," as it was called. Now the family was quite well off, which is a proper way of saying filthy rich. Even my own grandfather's admirable wealth seemed to pale in comparison.

Whenever their visit coincided with George and his parents visiting the hotel, Mary and my son played together in the sand. I smiled as they attempted to build castles, which got better and more elaborate as time went on. Always, after hours of playing, George would beg his mother—his adoptive mother—to stop in the main hall so he could see the piano.

Of course, he was never content to merely see it. He had to touch it. It seemed he was drawn to it the same way I was to him. That gravity force that almost compelled him to reach out to those ivory keys.

And each time he continued with his little ditty: E-D-C, pause, C-E-A-G. And again E-D-C, pause, C-E-A-G. Two years in, he'd added some notes, rounding out the tune. E-D-C, pause, C-E-A-G. Repeated. Then, E-F-G-E-C, pause, C-A-D-C.

I'd begun to think that this was not a tune he'd heard somewhere but something he was composing, even at his tender age.

I wondered if he had a piano at home. Probably not, or I think he might have progressed even further with his fledgling song. And I had not known the Morgans, at least nine years ago, to have one in their modest home.

I have been remembering lately how the adoption of my son came about. It was not through normal circumstances—but when has anything about my life been ordinary?

When I first learned that I was pregnant with the child, I fled to California under the pretext of the good coastal air being a benefit to my lungs. And I had not told my husband about my confinement. Every time

I wavered in this decision, God's hand seemed to confirm it, for I would receive a letter from Tom—a scathing one asking for money, or accusing me of adultery, or any number of scandalous things. I'm certain he wrote them in drunken states. That's when he was always his cruelest.

I've witnessed funny drunks and mean drunks. My husband was the latter.

I sent money with each reply—almost the entirety of the allowance from my grandfather—and that seemed to hold him off and keep him from following me out west. It was well spent if it meant that he did not seek me out.

By the time I was only weeks away from giving birth, I was in the employ of a benevolent woman in San Diego, who suggested various places that would take children without asking questions. She believed me to be unwed—a misconception I promoted so as to hinder Tom from finding me again. But while her Christian generosity extended to giving me a position on her household staff, it did not go so far as to tarnish her reputation by raising the child of a wanton woman in her home. Or the distraction of having one underfoot.

She never said the word bastard, *but others would have.*

So I considered the option of an orphanage. This would have provided many benefits, including the rigorous—I assumed—interviews to ensure that the child would be placed in a proper and loving home. But on a Sunday after church, I delayed my return to the house and took a walk by the nearest one where children stayed until such time as the adoption could occur.

I saw no sign of the intentional abuse or neglect that sometimes make up the horror stories that one can hear about. But it was the sheer number of children in the play yard that astonished me, and the few adults who were present to supervise them. I witnessed one small boy fall from a swing, and none of the attendants ran over to him as I might have hoped—to pull him onto their laps and rock him and kiss him where he bled. He sat there crying silently. Something I could tell from his heaves, but which he must have learned from an even younger age, was that crying was not useful in attracting the needed attention, so overloaded were the workers. My heart ached for the small boy, and if I could have adopted him then and there, I would have. But that would have been entirely impossible and contrary to my purpose.

I could not go through with it. I could not send my child to a place where his scrapes might go unnoticed, nor could I risk that he might be passed over by a loving family because there were so many children to choose from.

Instead I had an idea that might sound ridiculous to some, but anyone who is a mother will know that a mother's instinct will compel her to places that she never would have imagined.

I had the notion that I wanted not only attentive parents for my child but a name that would forever connect him to me, even if he would never know of my existence. I scoured courthouse records looking—Farmer, Farmer, Farmer. The name I had before I was married. My father's name. But would you believe that even in a city as large as San Diego I could find only two people in the records with that surname? And when I hired a carriage at considerable expense and went the following Sunday to ride by those residences, I found that the two Farmer households were entirely unsuitable for a child. One was owned by an old woman who had what seemed to be a thousand cats crawling in and out of the windows of her small house. The other was a young man, perhaps newly graduated from college. I was able to walk close enough to him that I saw no wedding ring.

Maybe I was being particular, but I did want my child to have a mother and a father and as idyllic a childhood as I could provide for him.

I looked also for Chandlers, my grandfather's name. But there were none that I could find.

With only two weeks until I was due to deliver but not wanting to waver from my much-hoped outcome, I abandoned the names of Farmer and Chandler and looked instead for a Morgan. I told myself that in some providential way, it legitimized the boy to have the name of his father instead of sounding—though no one would have known—like a child born out of wedlock. There were four Morgans I could find in the area. So once again, I hired a carriage, aching with every bump the wheels drove over and fearful that I would give birth in its wretched cab. At the house of the first Morgan, the arguing between the husband and wife could be heard from outside, and their language was so vile that I did not even get out to speak to them. The two other Morgans were quite far—one in La Jolla and one very near it in Bird Rock. Perhaps if my condition were not so imminent I would have made the trek, so I decided that I might just write to them instead and see if a suitable response came back.

But the fourth set of names—Alan and Grace Morgan of 753 A Avenue, Coronado, did not seem so impossible to reach. Coronado was merely a ferry ride across the water, and the idea of the ocean air blowing against my face felt most welcome.

My employer granted me another day off the following week—without pay, of course—but my timeline was causing a sense of desperation that hindered my ability to work.

So you can imagine my enthusiasm when yet another hired carriage pulled up to a charming house. It was small—really a cottage, not a house. But it was perfect. A lush vegetable garden looked well kept. The fence boasted a fresh coat of paint, and smoke curled from the chimney, making me think of the cozy fireplace that must be inside. Perhaps there was a wooden mantel where they kept photographs of loved ones. And maybe an image of my child could sit there in the future.

The baby must have sensed the rightness of the place just as I did, for as I stepped from the carriage and entreated the driver to return in an hour, the child lurched in me, propelling me forward. I stumbled, catching myself on the pointed end of a fencepost and splintering my hand.

At once a woman ran from the door, wiping her hands on a towel. An apron was wrapped around her waist and was dotted with purple spots that I imagined to be the spoils of homemade plum jam.

"My dear, are you all right?" she asked.

I wanted to respond, but just then the child turned again and my knees buckled from the pain. A warm pool dripped from my legs. I feared that it was blood, or perhaps the breaking of the waters that I'd been warned was a sign of impending labor.

I will spare you the details. If you are a mother, you have already experienced the agony that it takes to bring a child into the world. And if you will be a mother someday, I will save you from the description that might frighten you away from this ancient necessity.

And if, by chance, you are of the male sex, then I promise that you will be thankful to me for keeping the mystery of this woman's burden from you. There is something of the feminine allure that should remain guarded.

So I shall abbreviate that part of my story and tell you this: that Mr. and Mrs. Alan Morgan of Coronado were heaven-sent. A middle-aged couple whose own previous experience with childbirth had ended in misfortune and rendered Grace unable to bear more. That my arrival was as opportune for them as it was for me. And that they helped me bring my son into this world and take him in as their own. And that as far as I can see from the vivacity of my now nine-year-old boy, the arrangement has continued to be as happy as a mother could possibly hope.

Chapter Eleven

Kate Morgan the ghost was the beautiful stranger.

Did that mean that Granddad wasn't crazy? Or did it confirm the confusion?

Because why on earth would he have been so frantic to insist that his granddaughter come down and learn this information? What was she supposed to do with it?

And why did she and the ghost share a name?

Kate couldn't wait to call home any longer.

It wasn't merely the ghost that unsettled Kate. It was Sean himself. Sean giving in to someone else's dream for him when it was easy to see how he fit so thoroughly at the Hotel del Coronado. Sean looking at her with those eyes that bore the tired look of resignation, when only days ago on the ferry she'd seen the brightness and optimism they were capable of.

Sean belonging to someone else.

Kate told herself that she was only here for a few more weeks. He would be married. She would be taking the train up to San Francisco to buy back Grandma's wedding ring. And what would come next was a mystery. As much as she wanted to stay here and to make this place a part of herself, she didn't know if she could take leaving Granddad again if his health declined. Maybe life would return to slathering fish fillets in peppered batter for hungry tourists and this would all be some blissful memory. Or something to try again later when . . . when taking care of Granddad wasn't a concern anymore.

But the thought of returning home for good kept her up at night. Because now that she had smelled the salty air of this place, seen its gold-flecked sand, met people who descended from screen to set, it seemed impossible to imagine a life that didn't happen here.

Kate had asked Sean last night for the morning off to buy some clothes so that she could return the pieces that belonged to his sisters, having counted her earnings and realizing there was just enough in her budget to purchase something simple. Shops here opened at ten, and Miss Monroe preferred her breakfast to be delivered to her room around eleven.

But before that, there was a more urgent task.

She made her bed and laid out the clothes that she'd need to wash before giving them back to Sean. Then she headed to the hotel to use the bay of telephone enclosures to make her call.

The booths were lined up against a wall one floor down from the registration desk. They were narrow—Kate couldn't imagine how someone with a frame any larger than her own slim one could fit. But their perforated doors closed tightly and offered privacy.

She deposited several nickels and gave the operator the extension. She could hear it ring on the other end. It was too early for customers, but she might catch someone else at Uncle Mike's.

"Mike's Fish and Chips," came the familiar voice.

"Mom!" Her mother's voice sounded like chicken soup on a cold day, all warmth and comfort.

"Kate!" Her mother's voice was frantic with joy, but it was only a matter of time before it would settle into the more usual tone of worry. "Katherine Margaret Morgan, I don't know whether to blow you a kiss over the phone or grab this spatula and tan your hide when you get home."

Kate smiled at the greeting, though her mother's voice only made Kate feel guilty over leaving without saying goodbye. But she knew they would have tried to talk her out of it. And would have succeeded.

She rested her head against the wall of the booth and twirled the cord around her finger. "I miss you, Mom." She bit her lip to keep from crying.

"When *are* you coming back to us?"

"I've got a good job here."

"You've got a good job *here*. With your family."

"I know."

How could she explain that this place made her happy? That she wanted more than the life she had in San Francisco? It would break her mom's heart. She would think that *they* weren't enough. That Kate wanted something more than *them*. Only Granddad had ever understood. Maybe because he'd been here. He knew the world that lay beyond the northeast corner of the City by the Bay.

Kate heard the stirrings of the restaurant in the background. The opening of the massive refrigerator, the pouring of the ice into the tubs that would receive the fresh fish shortly. For one second, she pined for its familiarity. But then she looked at the lush carpet beneath her feet and remembered how much she already craved this alluring world down south.

"How is Granddad doing?"

Her mother sighed, and it sounded so close to Kate's ear that it felt as if she were right there. She closed her eyes and pretended she was.

"He's stable right now. They're keeping him at the hospital awhile longer, and I think the medicine they're giving him has been good."

Kate could only imagine the bills that would pour in after this. All the more reason she needed to earn a higher paycheck than what she made at Uncle Mike's. And even working at the hotel wouldn't be enough. Maybe they'd have to give the ring up and keep the money to pay for it.

"Give him my love? Please?"

"Of course. Or you could come back and see him for yourself. He's more lucid than normal. He's been asking about you."

"He has?" Kate's stomach knotted at the idea that she wasn't right there next to him.

"Yes. Maybe you'll know what this means. He keeps asking the same question. 'Has Katie-boots found the beautiful stranger yet?'"

He remembered! And he knew that she was here. Maybe if she could talk to him, she could find out more information. Even though Sean had told her that the ghost who shared her name was the beautiful stranger, it shed no light on why she would be important to Granddad.

"He said that? Has he said anything else? Please, Mom. I'll take any detail you can remember."

"Are you eating well down there?"

Her mother believed every problem could be solved as long as you were eating enough.

"Mom. First. Please. Did Granddad say anything else?"

"Well, only one other thing. The letter *A* over and over. A-A-A-A-A. I can't make anything of it."

Kate felt her body deflate and hadn't realized how tightly she'd wound herself. "I need to talk to him. Do you think there's a way I can talk to him while he's in the hospital?"

She heard a clamor over the phone.

"Oh, honey, the potatoes are here. I'm going to need to start peeling them. But to answer your question—no, the only telephone I know of is in the nurses' offices, and I don't think they're going to let him use it."

"Mom, please. There has to be a way."

The shouts of men became deafening as they hauled in what she knew to be enormous plastic tubs full of the spuds. If she were there like normal, she'd be receiving them with her mom. They'd fill the sink with soapy water and soak them for half an hour while they prepared the other parts of the kitchen for the day. Then they'd drain the water and rinse the potatoes and peel them one by one until their hands were chapped. And they'd talk about the same things they always did. If the weather would be good enough to put the tables outside. If the daily special would sell out before one o'clock.

Every day. Day after day after day after day.

Hearing the noises of the restaurant made Kate miss her family. If her life were a movie, the sounds would be the film score in the background. But more than that, it reminded her of all the mornings she'd stood there at that sink and peeled those potatoes with a force that was greater than the task required. With every stroke, she'd wished herself away from there.

"Kate? Are you there? Is the line cut off?"

"I'm here, Mom."

"Oh, it was silent. I thought we'd been disconnected. You know I'm not used to these telephones. Mike insisted on it, and I'm just not sure how it works."

Her mom's brother had always been one step ahead of everything. He'd been the one to see opportunity in San Francisco and move there fresh out of high school, escaping the doldrums of Bakersfield. Mom followed and met Dad in May of 1937 on the day that the Golden Gate Bridge opened to pedestrians. Car traffic would follow a few weeks later, but her parents often regaled them with the tale of that first day when thousands gathered for its inaugural beginning. Two hundred and fifty carrier pigeons were released, intending to fly to all corners of California to announce the news, but the birds were frightened by all the people and swooped into the nooks and crannies of the bridge.

One dropped what Mom always called a "present" right in the curls she'd set so precisely just for this very occasion. A good-looking young man saw what had happened and pulled a handkerchief from his pocket. According to her story, he touched her hair with such delicacy, seeming to appreciate all the work she'd put into it. And to use a cliché, as was often Mom's fallback, the rest was history.

Some people said that pigeons were nothing more than flying rats, but the Morgan family had always thought otherwise.

Kate ran her free hand through her hair and tried to shake off the nostalgia. This would all be so much easier if she were not as close to her family as she was. How was she supposed to follow her heart when it was torn in two opposite directions?

"Kate?" her mother asked again.

"I have to go, Mom, and I know you do, too."

"Yes, honey. Please call us again soon. We miss you so much."

"I will. On Monday. My boss will let me call from his office."

"How nice of him."

Kate rubbed her eyes. She wanted to curl up in her parents' bed and tell Mom all about Sean. About how he made her feel the kinds of things she'd only seen in movies. And how he was engaged to someone else. Mom would listen and brush her hands through Kate's hair, give her some good counsel, and then suggest they go get ice cream.

"He's a nice man, Mom. The best."

She heard the water of the sink start and the recorded voice of the operator demand another dime.

"I love you."

Kate hung up before her mother could respond. She was afraid that if she heard the words come back to her, it might tear at her just enough to make her consider coming home earlier.

She pulled a few more nickels out of her pocket. She had just enough to have a short conversation with Granddad if she could get through to him. And that still gave her plenty of time to head into town and pick up the clothes she needed.

She inserted the coins into the slot, and after a maze of connections with various operators and ten minutes spent on the ordeal, she reached the nurses' station on Granddad's floor at the San Francisco Memorial Hospital.

"Sixth floor."

"I need to speak with George Morgan. This is his granddaughter calling from San Diego."

"I believe they're about to serve him his breakfast."

"Can it wait? I don't know when I'll be able to call again."

"There's no telephone in his room. I'd have to ring for a wheelchair so that we could bring him over here."

Kate's alarm pulsed through her veins. "A wheelchair? Is he so ill that he can't walk?"

"No, it's just hospital policy."

"Damn hospital policy," she said. And then she covered her mouth in disbelief that she'd let those words slip from her lips. She never talked like that.

"I'll not have that attitude, young lady."

Kate lowered her voice. "I'm sorry. I'm so sorry. It's just that I'm worried, and it's *urgent* that I talk to him. It was hard enough to get through to you, and I'm running out of coins for this pay phone."

The woman sighed, and for a long spell, Kate was worried that she'd ruined her chances. But the nurse spoke at last.

"I'll see what I can do."

She was gone before Kate could say thank you, and during the wait, Kate searched through every pocket she had until she found a dime. She'd used up nearly all her coins just getting to this point.

"Hello?" A shaky voice came over the phone at last.

"Granddad! It's Kate!"

"Who?" She heard him tap on the phone like he didn't even know what it was.

No! She didn't have time for pleasantries or to wait for his lucidity to return. She had to try to jar his memory and find out something that would be useful. "It's Katie-boots. I'm in Coronado. I found the beautiful stranger. But I don't know what you want me to do about it."

"Who is this?"

Kate pulled the telephone away from her ear and rested her forehead on the receiver, her eyes burning with tears. *Please, please, please,* she whispered to whomever might be able to listen and help.

"Katie-boots, Granddad. Remember? You call me Katie-boots because of the pink rain boots you bought for me when I was six. In Union Square. They had ladybugs on them and I wanted them so badly, and even though you couldn't afford them, you bought them on lay-by and surprised me at Christmas. I wore them everywhere, even when it was hot outside," she rambled, hoping something would connect. Two years in, and it still ripped her heart out to have to explain over and over things that once meant so much to them. That still meant so much to her. But she was careful not to let that frustration reach her voice. Only patience upon patience for his sake.

Silence.

Then, "Katie-boots? Is that you? Are you here?"

At last! She took a deep breath, making up for the shallowness she'd felt in her chest since they first started talking. "No, Granddad." She repeated herself. "I'm in Coronado, just like you told me. I found the beautiful stranger. We have the same name. Kate Morgan. Why do I have the same name as the ghost of the hotel?"

"Are you doing all right? How's the weather there?"

"Perfect. The weather is perfect. Janie and Mom told me something about the letter *A*. You kept saying it. A-A-A-A-A. Does that mean anything?"

"Yes, the weather is always perfect there. Sunshine every day. I haven't been there in so long, of course. Mary always loved it. The sunshine. Do they still have that big piano?"

Mary! Kate's heart beat faster. She'd lived her whole life without that name ever escaping his lips, and now he'd said it so casually. It was like his past was moving away from the shadows, revealing itself bit by bit. Letting her get to know a whole new side of him.

And the piano! Kate passed one every time she walked near the reception desk, but she didn't know what it might have to do with Granddad. The fact that he remembered was remarkable. Maybe she'd learn something that got her closer to her answers. She felt excited that they were finally getting somewhere.

"Who is Mary?"

Of course she remembered. The girl in the picture. But she hoped the question would prompt the kind of answer she needed. Granddad had been engaged to someone before marrying Grandma. Why had they never known any of this?

But he ignored this question, too. Or maybe he hadn't heard. She didn't know what else to ask.

Kate checked her wristwatch. The seconds were ticking, and the operator would come on any time now to tell her that her time was up. She was out of change and didn't know if the nurses would be very agreeable if she called later. This was her chance—maybe her only chance—to find out more.

And yet all she really wanted to do was ask him how he was, if he was comfortable, if they were feeding him the red Jell-O he liked, if he'd be home soon. Maybe she could send a copy of the San Diego *Evening Tribune* to add to his fire-hazard collection. At least it would give him something to do. And maybe reading about the area would even spark a memory he could share that would make her task seem less impossible.

"Katie-boots, are they feeding you well? Want to come over for a grilled cheese?"

Oh, no. She was losing him.

"Granddad. Think. Kate Morgan. Coronado. Mary. The beautiful stranger. San Diego. A. A. A. What does *A* mean?"

"A? Did I ever tell you that I grew up on A Avenue? My mother and father were good people. Of course, they weren't really my mother and father."

The line went dead.

~

1899

    I don't know by what miracle or phenomenon this is possible, but George came into the hotel for an ice cream with his parents, and while Alan and Grace were talking to each other, my son looked right at me, just as he had before. The first time, I'd thought I was imagining it, though it had seemed so very real. But for it to happen a second time—that meant he could see me! I blew a kiss at him, and he smiled.

    Could this pull I feel toward him, this attachment whenever my son is in this place, be apparent to him as well?

    The moment was all too fleeting. He scratched his head and looked confused, as if he doubted what he just saw. And then Grace spoke to him, and his attention was pulled away.

    But it left me wondering. If I am more intentional, might I be able to communicate in some way with my dearest George?

Chapter Twelve

Kate was flooded with emotions as she hung the receiver back in its cradle.

It was all so much to take in. Granddad had a fiancée before he married Grandma Kitty. His parents weren't his parents. That part alone was almost too much to take in. Then there were small things like knowing about the piano. Giving her a street name.

And that was not to mention the beautiful stranger—the hotel ghost—for which she could not make the connection.

No answers. Only more questions. And what was the endgame? *Find the beautiful stranger,* he'd said. Why?

Why? It was giving her a headache.

Even more, it pained her to envision Granddad being wheeled down the hallway in a hospital and to be eating what was probably unappetizing slop when she could be home sitting by his side and sneaking in something he'd been told he shouldn't have.

But on the other hand, he'd given her some information she hadn't known before the call. The A-A-A he'd said to her mom wasn't just a letter. It was a street! And though he hadn't said specifically that it was in Coronado, she knew that such a street existed here. It was one of the less astonishing things she'd learned from him but was one of the few concrete things she might be able to follow up on.

She closed the wooden telephone door behind her and raced up the main stairs to the reception area. She had not yet met anyone in that department, so as far as they were concerned, she might as well be a tourist asking a question.

A tall man came out when she rang the small bell. He looked down at her over a large mustache.

"Miss?"

"Do you have a map of the island I could see?" She had adopted the local sense of thinking of Coronado that way.

"Certainly."

He bent over and reached beneath the counter to bring out a large scroll. He laid it flat on the desk, and she could see the gridlike streets of this place she was continuing to get attached to. Sean had told her how much of the island was taken up by the naval base, but now that she could see it laid out like this, she realized how little of it was residential.

So it didn't take long to find A Avenue. But much to her disappointment, it was not a dead-end street or a cul-de-sac or anything that would have narrowed down what it would take to locate one single home for which she didn't even have a house number. A Avenue stretched north to south, from the top end of the island to the bottom. Ten long blocks. It wasn't the idea of the distance so much as it was the sheer number of houses that must sit along the street. Was she to go door-to-door asking if the residents happened to know if a George Morgan once lived there?

And how exactly did Granddad end up with the Morgans if they weren't, like he said, his *real* parents?

Once again, new information only led to more questions. Who were they, then? And what happened to the ones he'd been born to?

Or—would their name have even been Morgan? Maybe that was his birth name and she'd be on even more of a wild-goose chase by not knowing what their last name was.

What the news confirmed was that pre–San Francisco, Granddad was a vault of secrets, and Kate didn't know why. She felt saddened by this. She was as close to Granddad as anyone in the world, and yet she'd learned more about his life in the past twenty-four hours than she'd ever known before.

~

Shopping for clothes in Coronado was not the easy task Kate had hoped. The island being a resort area, the boutiques were quite expensive. Kate pictured Maisy wearing her crocheted pink sweater or selling it to someone who would never appreciate all the time it took her mother to make it. Was that what thieves did? Did they steal for their own use, or did they hock items somewhere else? Either way, the sweater was gone for good.

This would all be so much easier if she hadn't been so trusting and hadn't gotten herself into this predicament in the first place.

In the end, Kate had enough time merely to scour some of the sale racks and find a couple of still-overpriced tops and a pair of slacks. But it was enough for now, especially since most of her hours were spent in the hotel-issued white blouse and black skirt.

She *could* ask Sean if she could borrow more of his sisters' clothes or keep the ones she had longer, but there was an intimacy to the notion that made her feel that it was more than an employee should ask of her boss. And she had to continue to think of him that way.

She returned to the hotel kitchen just in time for the day's orders. Miss Monroe had just called down for a gin and tonic, and Kate was scheduled to work the lunch buffet on the set.

It surprised Kate that she wasn't light-headed at the thought of going into Marilyn Monroe's room as she had been at first. And even working around the set—though exciting—had become comfortable. Already the actors were people just like everyone else. They left their sandwiches half-eaten, their drinks fully drunk, their cigarette stumps ground into the sand.

Jack Lemmon was undoubtedly the kindest person here. And that wasn't to say that others weren't, but they were often too preoccupied to mingle. Kate had never seen Billy Wilder sit down in his tan leather director's chair. Not once. He hopped about like a nervous kangaroo, always working, always fixing. And Tony Curtis retreated to his trailer every time a scene was finished. Someone had said that he liked to review the script over and over before shooting the next scene.

Kate noticed that Mr. Curtis did come out whenever Marilyn Monroe was outside. Even from across the lawn, Kate could see him watch her with an expression that seemed something like concern.

And it would have been justified. Kate, too, was worried about the star. She pined for her husband, never ordered food, and always arrived late.

But Mrs. Strasberg, in her array of black dresses and sun hats, hovered over her pupil as a mother bear might guard her cubs. Kate learned not to ask questions when alcohol was ordered for breakfast or when the tray she brought back downstairs bore more empty highballs than anything she'd brought up.

~

The next day, she clocked in at eight as usual. Sean walked into the kitchen just as she was arriving. Her heart did the little flutter that happened every time she saw him, despite her best efforts to tamp it down.

"Good morning," he said. "What's new in your life?"

Kate smiled. She knew he was kidding. They were at the hotel morning to night. There was no life outside the movie set. And given much more time, maybe that would seem like drudgery. But it was everything she wanted for now. It *was* her life.

She traced her finger down the day's instructions. "My notes say that Miss Monroe wants her tray at eleven again."

Sean reached for the same piece of paper, and for a second their hands brushed against each other. Was it her imagination that his eyes lingered on hers for a second longer than necessary? Did he feel the shock that went through Kate at their touch?

"No, I have different orders. She is to get a breakfast tray every morning at eight thirty from now on. Eggs, toast, bacon. And she can still have her vanilla pudding soufflé. But no booze."

"But that's not what this says." She held it up to the light in case she'd missed something.

"No matter what request might be on there, those are our instructions. Straight from the top. Billy Wilder himself."

"Billy Wilder is ordering her breakfast now?"

Sean folded his arms. "Yes. He says that every hour she delays filming costs the producers seven thousand dollars. He's enlisting our help to facilitate that in any way we can."

"Facilitate that?" Kate had visions of trying to rouse Marilyn Monroe from her luxurious bed and imploring her to come downstairs. It seemed that not even Mrs. Strasberg could succeed in that area. "Not very likely if we don't get her cooperation."

He shrugged. "He knows that he's asking the impossible, but the man is trying everything to get this film done on time. It's not just the costly delays. When she's late, they also lose the optimal morning light and have to scramble for artificial substitutes. He's already got enough to deal with, since the navy jets fly overhead every twenty minutes. All that combined gives him a very narrow amount of time in which to shoot a scene."

Kate smiled. "Don't you sound like quite the film expert?"

Sean grinned and unfolded his arms. "I've picked up a thing or two. Kind of hard not to with all that's going on."

"I know what you mean." Kate wadded the paper into a ball, tossed it into a trash bin, and felt her cheeks redden when he applauded the shot. "It's like movie sets have their own lingo. *Apple box. Key grip. Golden hour.* If I ever applied for the foreign service, I might be able to list it as a known language. Who knows what other terms I'll have learned by the time I leave?"

Saying the words out loud made her feel like the sands of the hourglass were pouring much too quickly.

There was no question that Sean's eyes lingered longer than usual this time. Was it what she'd said about leaving before long? Did that mean anything more to him than the need to find a replacement when she left?

"Kate—" he started.

"Yes?" Her heart pounded as she wondered what he might say next.

"I, um." He looked down at his feet and then up again. "The film crew is going back to Hollywood next week, just for a week. Everyone has come together so well to make this a success, so the hotel manager is going to throw a barbecue on the beach for employees. Probably next Tuesday night. I just thought you'd want to know."

She let out a slow sigh. "Thank you. I'd love to come."

Janie would have told her that it was silly to read meanings into things, especially where men were concerned. *Women have a habit,* she'd once told Kate, *of trying to interpret every little word and gesture a man says, when in reality, men are exactly what they appear to be with no subtext at all.*

How Janie would have acquired this knowledge, Kate had no idea, though she never missed a chance to sound like the wise older sister. She might have read it somewhere. But she was probably right, as she was, frustratingly, with most things.

Kate decided to heed the advice. Sean meant nothing more by it than what he said.

"Good," he said. "I'll let you know when the time gets worked out."

Straightforward words. But she still kept feeling there was some-thing more he wanted to say.

She looked at the clock above the main stove. It was easier than continuing to look at him. "It's almost eight fifteen. I'd better get her new tray prepared."

She turned around and walked over to the sous chef to tell him about the food order and kept her back turned to Sean until she heard him leave the room. If he'd seen her face, he might see the quiver of her bottom lip. She cared about him. That was the best way she could describe how he made her feel. She cared about his kindness to her; she cared about his dreams.

The sous chef handed her a plate of scrambled eggs and bacon and the soufflé. She walked over to a toaster and slid in some bread slices. When they popped up, she placed rose-shaped pats of butter on their golden tops, and the intoxicating smell of it all reminded her that she hadn't eaten yet.

She took a service elevator up to Miss Monroe's floor, and for a moment she thought she'd gotten off in the wrong place. A man was coming out of her penthouse room. He was wearing a long raincoat with its collar pulled up so that it half covered his face. His black hair looked like a tangled mop, and, as if he'd read Kate's mind, he ran his fingers through it. He glanced to his left, and Kate stepped back just as he looked to his right.

He started toward her, and she put her hands to her mouth to stifle a gasp.

What was Tony Curtis doing in Marilyn Monroe's room so early in the morning? Kate may not have been experienced in the ways of the world yet, but she was fairly certain they weren't running lines together.

This was the kind of thing that would make the cover of the gossip rags. At home, Kate took every opportunity to go to the grocer not just because it was a break from the restaurant but because she'd stay ten extra minutes to flip through the magazine articles.

An affair between Tony Curtis and Marilyn Monroe would be a sellout. The Kate of two weeks ago might have been scandalized by it, but now that she'd met the actress and seen her loneliness, now that she'd seen how concerned Tony Curtis seemed to be about her, Kate realized that it wasn't simply salacious fodder for reporters. These were two people, flesh and blood, with much more at stake than mere physical attraction. It was not an excuse for adultery, but it certainly put context to that which would have been relegated to a cheap headline.

She watched him open the door to the stairway, and she waited a few minutes to make sure he wasn't returning. The breakfast was going to get cold even under its stainless steel dome, but she didn't want to get caught up in something she shouldn't be a part of.

When the hallway remained silent, Kate gripped the tray and walked toward Miss Monroe's suite. She steadied it on her hip and knocked on the door.

There was no answer, but she heard a faint rustling sound from inside. She waited a moment, still uncertain whether she should turn back, but she had instructions to deliver this. Who was really in charge? Sean? Miss Monroe? Billy Wilder?

She opted to knock again. This time she heard the rustle come closer. Someone fumbled with the lock inside. Maybe Paula Strasberg was in there, and Kate stiffened in readiness for facing the tiny but formidable woman. Then again, Miss Monroe would likely be alone, given that Tony Curtis had just left and taken such precaution to conceal his face.

The door opened an inch. "Tony?" came the childlike voice. But Miss Monroe's radiant smile dimmed as she realized it was only Kate.

Kate cleared her throat. "Your breakfast, Miss Monroe."

"Oh." She sounded like a little girl who had just been told the truth about Santa Claus. "I don't want any breakfast, but thank you."

The door shut.

What was Kate to do? Again she wondered—should Miss Monroe be able to choose her own plans for breakfast, or should Kate press on?

She knocked again but spoke through the wood, not knowing whether she could be heard. "Miss Monroe, I'm sorry, but I was given direct instructions to deliver your breakfast. If I don't do that, I might get fired, and as much as I would like to respect your privacy, if you could only let me in enough to set this tray on the table, I would be so grateful."

Kate doubted that Sean would fire her, but he was not the highest one on the chain. And Billy Wilder seemed determined to rein in his star no matter what.

The rustle again. The door opened, this time wider.

Marilyn's cheeks were rosy but not from the rouge that would be applied so thickly later in the day. Her lips were full, her eyes red. From lack of sleep? Crying? Or did people look like that after a night of lovemaking?

Kate blushed at the thought.

The woman was dressed only in a bedsheet, just as the first time Kate had seen her. With the amount of clothes strewn about, she could have grabbed something to put on. Or did she always wander around her room wearing nothing?

Miss Monroe's shoulders were flawless. Like bone china. Not that Kate had ever seen bone china, but she imagined that it was the very definition of perfection. There was not a wrinkle, not a freckle, not a blemish that stained her perfect, creamy skin. It was as if she'd arrived from somewhere else—maybe a lost goddess wandering this earth among mortals like Kate.

"Just set it over there," Miss Monroe whispered.

Kate walked over to where she'd been pointing. The table in front of the enormous sofa. It had endless scarves on it. Kate balanced the tray on one hand and scooped up the scarves in the other. She hoped that was OK, but it was better than spilling on them. Just one probably cost more than Kate would ever hope to see in a year.

"Thank you," said Miss Monroe. Keeping the sheet around her, she delicately sat down on the sofa. But then she didn't move, as if she didn't know what to do next if someone didn't tell her.

Kate knew she should leave. But there was something about Miss Monroe, something about how helpless she seemed, that made her hesitate.

She lifted the lid and arranged each item on the table. Orange juice, silverware, napkin, plate.

Stalling.

"Can I get anything else for you?"

Miss Monroe looked up at her. Her eyes were small but beautiful, void of the mascara that would illuminate them on-screen.

"Figs."

She'd mentioned those the first time. Kate thought about the kitchen, taking a mental inventory. "I don't think we have any figs downstairs, but I can probably track some down for you."

The star sighed and waved her hand. "No, don't go to the trouble. I guess I'm just missing Ida and Wayne right now. They raised me, since my mama was sick in the head. And they grew the most wonderful figs."

Kate wondered whether this was a symptom of nostalgia or some odd craving that would confirm that Miss Monroe was indeed with child, as rumors were saying.

"Can I do anything else for you?" Kate said again.

Miss Monroe looked at her with pleading eyes. "Stay?"

Kate's heart stopped, stunned at the request. That was not what she'd expected to hear. Was that OK? Would Mrs. Strasberg enter and report her? But the invitation was too tempting to say no to. To not risk everything for.

Miss Monroe spoke again, the lilt of confidence growing in her voice. "Yes. Stay. And please sit down."

Kate did as she was told and sat on the other side of the table, still in disbelief.

"I'd like you to eat this for me. Otherwise I'll flush it down the toilet, and it would be such a shame to waste it."

"You want me to eat it *for* you?"

"Yes, and quickly, please. The smell of eggs nauseates me."

Point two for the pregnancy rumor.

"I—I don't think I'm supposed to do that."

Miss Monroe leaned forward, still clutching the sheet around herself. Kate didn't think she could ever be daring enough to have company over wearing nothing but bed linens. "What is your name?"

"Kate. Kate Morgan." She held her breath, waiting for the inevitable response. *Like the ghost?* But it didn't come. Maybe Miss Monroe didn't know about her.

"That's a pretty name. Is it your real one?"

"My real one? Yes. Well, it's Katherine Morgan, if I'm going to be specific, but I've only ever been called Kate by my family." She'd always been told that Granddad was the one who'd suggested her name, and she'd assumed that he simply liked it. But now that she knew there was some kind of connection to the beautiful stranger, she wondered if there was more to it.

"Have you ever wondered if there's anything in a name? Like what Shakespeare said about a rose?"

A thought came to Kate: Marilyn Monroe herself was a *beautiful stranger*. How little anyone really knew about her. Of course, Kate had read all the movie magazines like any girl her age, and even the trade ones, but up close, without makeup, the woman was entirely different.

Kate answered the question. "I don't know."

Miss Monroe continued. "Funny how something that will stick with us our whole lives is beyond our control. Something as important as a name. Well, except for my case. I never liked my given name. Norma

Jeane. Can you just see that on a marquee? *Norma Jeane Mortenson.* That would be quite a mouthful."

"Why did you change it to Marilyn Monroe?"

She didn't answer the question. She just turned it back to Kate. "What would you call yourself if you could pick your own name?"

The surreal feeling of who Kate was talking to returned, dividing her thoughts in two—one that was actively engaged with talking to the woman in front of her. And one that wanted to scream with glee that this was *Marilyn Monroe.* The two personages were difficult to reconcile into one.

Kate returned to the question asked. She'd never thought about it. Hers suited her just fine. It was simple and short and plain, much like herself. She remembered reading *Anne of Green Gables,* where Anne renamed herself Cordelia, but Kate didn't have such fancy notions.

"I don't know," she answered. "I can't imagine being anything other than plain old Kate."

Miss Monroe leaned even farther in.

"Oh, but are you content with that? Is your life everything you want for yourself?"

"Is yours?"

As soon as Kate said the words, her hand flew over her mouth; she wished she could take them back. She was under no illusions that this was a conversation as meaningful to Miss Monroe as it was to her, and to have asked such a thing might be taken as rude. Was her life, though, everything she wanted for herself? Wasn't that the very question Kate had grappled with when deciding to come to Coronado?

Miss Monroe stood up. She walked over to the dining room table, where one of the many kimonos was laid out. She put her arms through it, pulled it around herself, and in one motion dropped the sheet and tied the belt around her waist.

Had Kate offended her?

Miss Monroe walked to the bar and set out a highball. She opened a freezer that was hidden behind some cabinetry and pulled a chilled bottle of vodka from it.

"You want some?" she asked, pulling out a second highball.

Air shot out of Kate's lungs with her relief—that she hadn't alienated Miss Monroe. That she was still wanted here. But she had never had vodka and didn't think that nearly nine in the morning was quite the appropriate time to start.

"No, thank you."

Miss Monroe proceeded to fill her glass with ice and pour the liquor. She came back to the couch and gestured for Kate to start eating. So Kate picked up the toast and tried to take bites without getting crumbs all over the white upholstery.

"You asked if my life is everything I want for myself, and I will tell you that it's not."

Kate felt the sharp edge of the toast scrape against her dry throat. Why on earth was Marilyn Monroe confessing to her like this? Was she so friendless that an anonymous girl from the kitchen was an acceptable substitute for a proper confidante?

"It isn't?" She didn't dare to pry more than that. Kate glanced into the open door of the bedroom where the bedcovers—minus the sheet, of course, that lay pooled on the floor by the bar—were tousled far more than they would have been if Miss Monroe had simply been sleeping in the bed. The covers were clinging to the corner of the bed closest to the door—more like they'd been tossed aside. In the way.

Miss Monroe and Tony Curtis had spent the night here together, and she was saying that her life wasn't everything she wanted from it?

Well, of course. Both of them were married. You didn't have an *affair* with someone else if you were happy in your own marriage.

If Miss Monroe intended to tell her anything else, Kate would never know, because the door to the suite jostled and Paula Strasberg, wearing black once again, entered the room. Kate bristled, fearing that she would be reprimanded for being here when she'd been told to leave the food and go.

Mrs. Strasberg's eyes widened, then thinned as she saw them sitting together. The star bolted up and hid her quickly emptied glass behind a cushion.

"Good morning, Paula."

"Marilyn. You're not dressed yet."

"I'm just finishing my breakfast."

She sat back down on the couch across the table from Kate and picked up the tiniest bit of scrambled eggs with her fingers. Kate could see her wince as she put them in her mouth and put her hand over her stomach. But, the consummate actress, she pushed through it and smiled.

"What is she doing here?"

She was Kate, of course. Did Paula know that Tony Curtis had left just minutes before? What would she say to that? Or would she ignore it?

"She brought me my breakfast."

Paula pointed at Kate. "*You* may return to the kitchen. Miss Monroe has to prepare for today's shoot."

"Of course." Kate stood up, leaving the tray in its place, feeling duly chastised. The food had barely been touched, and she suspected that Miss Monroe would indeed flush it down the toilet at first chance.

"And take care," Mrs. Strasberg said as Kate passed, "not to presume to sit here with her in the future."

Kate looked at Miss Monroe, hoping for some kind of defense, but she cowered in the presence of her mentor, and nothing that cleared Kate of the accusation was forthcoming.

"Yes, ma'am."

"See that you don't. Or your boss will hear about it."

Kate didn't look back as she hurried out of the room. She knew what she would have seen. Miss Monroe curling up in a fetal ball while

Mrs. Strasberg selected her clothes for the day. And the star would come down to the lawn later looking resplendent, wearing the made-up face that the world knew and loved. But she had just shown Kate something else. That there was a girl inside named Norma Jeane who worried that life wasn't always what she'd thought it would be. A girl who was a shadow to the millions of admirers who thought they knew her. Indeed, a beautiful stranger.

One whom Kate would very much like to help.

~

1903

The celebration of the turn of the century was only slightly more elaborate than it'd been on any other New Year. In truth, though I observed that people were quite taken with the notion of the "00" at the end, there was also much talk that we were a mere hundred years away from a brand-new millennium. This was said wistfully, of course, as none would be alive to see it. At best, their grandchildren might be around to ring in that particular milestone.

Will I still be here at the hotel wandering its halls at such a time? Honestly, I can't imagine what a hundred more years could bring upon us, and I'm not sure I even want to know. Perhaps we will have sprouted wings and humankind can fly here and there. Or maybe they will have discovered how to cheat death.

I digress. I meant only to say that the years passed one after another no matter what the numbers preceding AD said.

There is one item of note. It is small, perhaps, but quite extraordinary in my life, such as it is. In seeing little George grow, I longed to do more than just observe the boy. I held no real hope that I'd ever be able to break through this divide and embrace him, but it occurred to me that if there was ever some way, no matter how tiny, to make my presence known, I would certainly want to do it. As it was, I had all the time in the world at my disposal, nor did I require sleep, so it was merely a matter of pondering what exactly I wanted to accomplish. And how.

I'd heard of poltergeists in my childhood. Particularly on All Hallows' Eve. Tales of ghostly specters who scared mortals and disrupted their worlds. I didn't believe it at the time, nor do I consider myself akin to such nightmares. But it occurred to me that there might be an element of truth to the stories that I could use.

For example, was it truly possible for one in my state to touch the material world?

I tried with a paperweight on the hotel manager's desk. Trembling at the possibilities if I were successful, I reached a finger out to touch it. But I felt nothing as I stroked its glass surface, and it didn't budge so much as a hair.

I experimented on other items. A vase, the fringe of a rug, an egg in the kitchen. But I had the same result every time.

Nothing happened.

Discouraged, I was about to give up on my futile effort. But then, without even trying, I found success.

I was curious one day about the room that I'd occupied. I'd heard that the hotel had changed out some of the furniture and draperies. I wandered over to 302. The door was open, and a housemaid was placing clean sheets on the bed. It must not have been among those receiving a refurbishment yet—it was exactly the same. The brick fireplace where I'd burned the documents from Tom. The velvet chair where I'd doubled over in pain from the sharpness in my abdomen.

Then two things startled me. First, I caught my own reflection in the windowpane. It was fleeting. And it was hazy. But I saw enough to recognize myself as I was eleven years ago. Except that the dress I'd worn when Tom murdered me was black. And since then—why had it only occurred to me now?—that same dress was white.

I don't know how I would not have noticed in all this time that my dress was white. It is another indication that behind this veil that hangs between life and death, nothing is exactly as it was. Time is arbitrary here, and so are details, though it takes simple things like this to remind myself of it.

But the eternal bond I have to my son feels exactly the same, no matter what side of the veil. A mother is always a mother.

The second thing. It was insignificant. Almost laughable. But as the housemaid finished the room, I noticed a slight wrinkle on the coverlet she'd lain over the finely made bed. I reached out to it without thinking and pulled it straight.

And it moved.

It moved! I cannot tell you that I felt it. No, its silky texture eluded me, and I recalled it only from the days when I had flesh-and-bone hands. But nevertheless, it moved.

I might have thought I imagined the whole thing, but the housemaid screamed.

Another one ran from the hall. "What is it, Rose?"

"There," said the girl. She pointed to the bed with a trembling finger. "Someone pulled the coverlet straight."

The other one looked around. "But there's no one about."

"I know!"

"Did you take the drink last night, Rose? You know what the manager would think of that."

The housemaid put her hands to her hips. "I am a teetotaler, as you well know. It was not the drink. I am not making it up. I saw the coverlet move all on its own."

"Then the room either has a rat or it has a ghost."

The housemaid pressed her hands against her apron and then crossed the room to pick up the broom. "I don't believe in such things."

But as they left, the housemaid looked behind her from the doorway. She made the sign of the cross over her shoulders and shut the door with a loud thud.

I didn't know what it all meant. But I had a feeling that something was about to happen.

Chapter Thirteen

Kate arrived at Marilyn Monroe's suite at the same time she had yesterday. Eight thirty on the nose, tray in hand, same breakfast. She paused at the door in case Tony Curtis was in there again. And, indeed, she did hear the voice of a man.

But it didn't sound like anything particularly intimate was happening, and knowing Billy Wilder's strict orders about Miss Monroe's meals, she knocked.

To her surprise, a different man answered the door. With a start, she recognized him as Miss Monroe's husband, the playwright Arthur Miller.

He was tall with dark hair and a large, round nose and wore thick-framed black glasses on his face. He'd already dressed for the day in a suit without a jacket and a skinny black tie that fell at his waist. He did not smile when he saw Kate but acted like she was an interruption.

"Breakfast for Miss Monroe?" Kate offered.

He sighed and turned around, where Miss Monroe was sitting on the white couch in another of her kimonos. This one was blue with embroidered cardinals.

"That's exactly what I'm talking about, Marilyn," he said. He scooted past Kate without another word and trotted away down the hall like a horse.

Kate watched until he disappeared and wondered what they'd been arguing about.

"You may come in," said Miss Monroe.

Kate closed the door and set the tray on the table once again. She turned to leave.

"Stay with me a bit?"

The sound of Miss Monroe's voice had changed since yesterday's childlike tone. Instead she lounged on the couch, arms stretched out on either side of her. She'd done a little of her makeup. Her eyes looked bigger, and her hair was brushed out. She had a grin that spanned from ear to ear, and she looked like she was ready to go out for an evening.

"I shouldn't, Miss Monroe. I'll be due downstairs soon."

"Nonsense. Have a seat." No trace of concern over what Kate had just witnessed.

She patted the couch next to her. There was a gravity to the star that pulled one into her orbit on- and offscreen, and Kate dismissed the worry that Mrs. Strasberg might report her if she walked in to see them conversing again, and she obeyed.

"That was my husband." Miss Monroe waved an arm in the direction of the door. "Arthur Miller." She sighed. "That man is more attractive than any I've ever known."

And yet Tony Curtis, considered the best-looking man in Hollywood, had been in her suite only yesterday morning. Kate's money would have been on him. Miss Monroe was full of energy this morning, though, and Kate had no desire to contradict her.

"He's here to check up on me, you know. He never wanted me to take on this film in the first place. But Billy practically begged. 'You'll not play the dumb blonde again,' my husband said. He didn't stand in my way, though. Could you hear us bickering through the door?"

Kate shook her head. "Just talking."

"Well, I didn't know how long you might have been standing there. Arthur left his previous wife for me, you know. At the time, I wanted to give all of this up and be a housewife. I even converted to Judaism for him. Of course, they banned my movies in Egypt after that, but what is Egypt compared to the *whole wide world*?"

She waved her arms around the room, and her porcelain-white skin showed as the kimono sleeves fell toward her shoulders. Bracelets dangled at her elbows.

"Why are you telling me all this?" Kate shifted in her seat. It was beginning to feel like talking to a friend. Maybe they both needed one.

"Because we have to talk about *something* while you eat the breakfast." Miss Monroe pulled the silver dome from the plate. "Eat, eat. Or, as I learned when I was in Italy, *Mangia, mangia.*"

Kate hesitated. "Miss Monroe, I'm not supposed to be eating your breakfast. *You're* supposed to be eating it. Billy Wilder's orders. We could both get into trouble." Kate's ears were attuned to the possibility of hearing Mrs. Strasberg's key. No one could touch Marilyn Monroe. But Kate could get fired if a big enough stink were made.

But, boy, it did smell good, and Kate's own breakfasts were bits here and there between working. Miss Monroe looked at her with absolute faith that her whims would be acted upon, and Kate found it impossible not to do exactly what she wanted. Marilyn Monroe could speak with her eyes—implore, cajole, beg—all with a look. Maybe that's why she was such a sensation.

So Kate started eating. Small bites at first, and then larger ones.

"*I'm* not going to get into any more trouble with Billy than I already am," the actress continued. "And as for you, do me this favor, and I'll do one for you in return."

Kate looked up, startled. "What do you mean?"

"Name it! I owe lots of people favors, but they rarely collect. They don't take me seriously. But I mean it. When you're ready for my help with anything, just ask."

Kate flushed at the offer, one that was probably just said out of kindness. But still, it was extraordinary to have someone like Miss Monroe say something like that.

She nodded, not acknowledging it for fear that it was a throwaway statement. "Would you like me to bring up something a little different tomorrow? Is it that you don't like scrambled eggs and toast?"

The only thing the actress had seemed interested in all these days was the vanilla soufflé.

Miss Monroe shook her head, and her waves of platinum curls swirled like the kind of twirling dresses Mom had sewn when Kate was little.

"I can't keep anything in my stomach right now. I told you I'd flush it down the toilet yesterday, and I did. Only it backed up, and Paula had to call a plumber. I got quite the lecture. So I promised her I wouldn't do that today." She giggled. "I omitted that I still have no intention of eating it. That's why you're such a good helper to me."

Kate nodded, her mouth full of toast. The sous chef had put marmalade on it today, and it was divine.

"Tell me about yourself, Kate Morgan. And before you do—isn't that the name of the hotel ghost? I don't believe in ghosts myself, of course, but one does hear such things."

Kate sighed. She'd hoped there might be one person who wouldn't make the reference. But maybe it wasn't a bad thing. All it would take was one person knowing something about Kate Morgan the Ghost and why Granddad would have been so insistent that she be found.

"Yes. As luck would have it, I share a name with her." A week ago, she'd brushed it off as a coincidence. Not anymore.

Miss Monroe laughed. It sounded like tiny bells. "There are no coincidences in this world. Arthur's faith taught me that, at least. I'm starting to believe that there is some bigger hand at work over everything. Otherwise, it's all just some cosmic accident."

Talking like this—like real people—Kate began to feel truly comfortable in Miss Monroe's presence. She curled her own legs up onto the couch and thought that this was like chatting with an older sister, though different from talking with her own, Janie. Marilyn Monroe was, well, *Marilyn Monroe.*

"You want me to tell you something?" asked Kate.

"Dash it, don't keep me waiting! Anything's better than running lines. Paula will be over too soon to do that, but it's a bore."

Kate's heart skipped at those words. She wanted to be well cleared out of this room, tray and all, before Mrs. Strasberg appeared. Something told Kate that the woman would retaliate at any encroachment upon her hold over the star.

"Well . . . all right." Kate didn't know where to begin, what to tell Marilyn Monroe about herself that the star would actually want to hear. But words started spilling out, and before she knew it, she had told her everything that had happened in the last week. Everything that had to do with Granddad, at least. The part about Sean—well, there was nothing to say there.

"A Avenue," repeated Miss Monroe when Kate had finished. "And you say that's here in Coronado?"

"Yes," Kate answered. "But it's such a long street, and I don't know where to begin. And I don't even know what I'm *looking* for. People move about these days. Am I to knock on every door asking if someone had heard of George Morgan decades ago?"

"Of course!" said Miss Monroe. "That seems like exactly the thing to do."

"But I don't have enough days off before I go to San Francisco. That's a big undertaking."

"Finish that last bite."

Kate looked at the plate and realized that she'd continued eating and that only a piece of egg remained. She prodded it with the fork and ate it.

"There," said Miss Monroe. "You've finished my breakfast. And now I owe you a favor. This will be the favor."

She stood up and walked over to a drawer and pulled out an enormous stack of photographs of herself. They were all signed: *Love, Marilyn.*

"Now," she said. "Take these to your room and enlist some of your friends here to help out if you want this to go faster. Write fifty notes, or a hundred notes, or however many you think is necessary to blanket A Avenue. Say something like, 'Marilyn Monroe most humbly requests that you present her with any information you might have about a George Morgan who lived on A Avenue many years ago. If your information is deemed important to what she is trying to learn, she will invite you to the set of *Some Like It Hot* as her personal guest. Please be prompt—shooting will be finished soon, and the information needed is of a timely nature.'"

Kate had to consciously keep her jaw from dropping open. What a magnificent thing to offer! Kate from San Francisco was a nobody. But Marilyn Monroe could snap her fingers, and people would hop.

"Wow! I don't know what to say."

"Well, it's as much as I can think to do, other than going door-to-door myself, but that would hardly suit dear Billy, would it?" Miss Monroe grinned. "Although it *would* be a good deal more fun, to tell you the truth."

Kate smiled with her. "No, I don't think he's ready for you to leave the set and peddle for information."

"Oh—you'll need these." Miss Monroe walked over to a desk and pulled out a bundle wrapped in brown paper. "Here is some stationery. It's awfully expensive stuff, and you don't want to write important letters like that on just anything. Not if you want an answer. So have it all." She opened her wallet and pulled something out. "Here's twenty dollars for postage." She pulled out another and crossed the room to hand them to Kate. "And another twenty for you to go do something nice for yourself."

Kate's throat tightened. Sean had said there might be tips, and Jack Lemmon had slipped her a dollar here and there when she refreshed his lemonade. No one else had been as considerate. But this was unbelievable. Miss Monroe did it as casually as if she were handing Kate a licorice.

"Why are you doing this?" Kate asked.

It was the first time today that Miss Monroe grew serious. She rejoined Kate on the couch, straightened her posture, and seemed to age from child to adult in a moment.

"The role of an actress is to get under the skin and understand a character from the inside out. They have to be a good observer of people. People may underestimate me, but I do know how to read people. And I can read you, Kate Morgan. It's like looking in a mirror. You want something more from life. And you're not going to get it without some help. And also because I'm straddling my own choices right now. If I had someone to tell me which way to go, I'd be ever so grateful. Actress or wife. Movie star or stepmother. This isn't the lark that I thought when I first came to Hollywood, and I'm starting to crave the roots that Arthur can give me. But it's all so much to think about. Your little project will be a welcome distraction, and just the kind of good deed that might come back to me and help me find my own answers."

Kate was stunned at this admission, something that seemed the intimate confidence of friends, not two young women who'd met under these most unusual conditions.

"I—I don't know how to begin to thank you."

"Just succeed, Kate. Whatever you find will be a much-needed diversion. For both of us."

Kate heard the jingle of the keys.

"That will be Paula," said Miss Monroe. "You'd better take the tray and go."

~

1904

I tried to make sense of how I was able to move the coverlet and how I might try to do so again. And I wish that I could tell you that there was some pattern to my successes and failures. Some method that worked when others didn't.

But in the past year—by the timeline of the material world—I have tried again and again with coverlets, flowers, papers. After having startled the housemaid, though, I do try to wait until a room is empty before I attempt to interact with an item. No need to frighten anyone unnecessarily.

I have had some successes—minor ones but not predictable ones. Still, there is an elation that pierces my otherwise isolated existence and gives me hope. Hope that somehow, someday, I can reach out to my son and he will know I am there. And who I am.

I'm not to be pitied. I know I am asking for a mountain. But what mother with endless time at her disposal will not try absolutely everything to be with her child?

Enough of that, though. I do want to tell you about an extraordinary encounter that happened today. And really, it should have eclipsed every other anecdote.

This is the time of year that families arrive for their summer vacations. And the luckiest of them remain for several months. Usually the fathers are present at the very beginning and the very end, leaving their wives and children in the capable hands of nannies and friends.

My son is now fourteen years old. I have heard him mention to Grace that he would like to start working at the hotel soon, and she showed great enthusiasm. I have not yet seen him in any capacity but a sporting one— playing on the beach—though he is probably too old for me to call it playing any longer.

There was a particular family who arrived today. One I had not seen before, but the patrons and employees of the hotel were quite abuzz about their arrival. It was a fine-looking man and his wife along with their four sons. The boys were not little—in fact the last two looked to be around George's age. I overheard several housemaids swooning over the presence of such up-and-coming gentlemen.

Do young people still say swooning?

What was remarkable about this family was that the father was the much-celebrated L. Frank Baum, the author of The Wizard of Oz. That book was not published until well after my death, but in the past few years, I hardly observed a nanny or a child who had not packed a copy of the bright-green book, and I'd heard it said that it already had several sequels and a Broadway musical in the works!

The hotel is accustomed to celebrities, certainly, and I felt immune to that particular excitement. But Mr. Baum—or Lyman, as I heard his wife call him—was one of the most remarkable men I had ever encountered. Children gathered around him like some kind of Pied Piper. And while I would have expected that he would shoo them away and tell them that he was on holiday with his family, he did quite the opposite. Every night he sat near the piano, and the children staying at the hotel would gather at his feet while he'd tell all sorts of stories.

They were often related to the books of Oz, but I was under the impression, based on conversations I witnessed, that these were tangents to what he'd already published. He spoke of green glasses that made everything look like emeralds. A home printing press that his father bought for him when he was too sickly to go to school. Trading stamps. And acting. The man had done everything, it seemed, that a person could do, and he could spin a tale about it that would fascinate the most hardened of men.

I was enraptured, but on the third evening of his storytelling, I felt that familiar and welcome pull when the door to the hotel opened. George had arrived.

I did not see Grace or Alan, but then again, George was now old enough to be at the hotel independently. I saw the eyes of my boy dart around *the room until they rested on the lovely vision of Mary Carter, who had arrived only that morning. I thought the two might sit near Mr. Baum and hear his tales, but instead they nodded to each other and made their way to an exit that led to the beach. I wanted to follow, but although I would have been unnoticed, I am not one to pry. So I stayed in the room with the piano.*

But as they reached the back door, I saw George take Mary's hand.

Chapter Fourteen

Just as Sean had said they would, the cast packed up and left for some filming that had to take place in Hollywood. Kate had heard Billy Wilder say that it was terribly inefficient to do so. But Marilyn Monroe's delays had set the Coronado filming behind. If they didn't head back north, they would lose various monies they'd put down on some Hollywood locations, and he couldn't afford that. So as far as Kate knew, he'd worked out an arrangement with the hotel to keep much of the equipment there and retain all the extra staff who would be needed again upon their return.

The barbecue for all the employees was almost here.

With Miss Monroe gone for the time being and the cast and crew as well, Kate's schedule had been reduced to the part-time hours she'd originally been hired for. She gathered the photographs and stationery and continued to work on the project of sending letters to all the owners along A Avenue. It was tedious work, but she had to admit that she didn't have any better ideas. Aching for scenery outside the boarding-house room, she brought it all to the hotel and headed outside to the spot where she and Sean had eaten their impromptu picnic more than a week ago.

It was her favorite spot not only for its secluded area from which to look at the ocean but because it was where she and Sean liked to talk. She'd begun to think of it as *their* spot.

"What are you up to?"

Her heart beat faster at the sound of his voice, as if her thoughts had summoned him. Kate set her pen down and shaded her eyes in the sun. She saw his silhouette.

"I'm writing letters."

"May I join you?"

"Of course."

Kate scooted over to make room for him on the brick steps. Sean sat down and picked up one of the *Love, Marilyn* photographs.

"Kate, your responsibilities to Marilyn Monroe do not extend to having to do her correspondence. She must have people who can do that for her."

She smiled. "It's not what it looks like. She's actually helping me."

Kate explained the nature of the project, and Sean whistled.

"That's quite an endeavor, judging by how big that stack is. Want some help?"

She would have loved his help. But she didn't want him to feel like he had to, just because he'd found her here again.

"You have a lot of responsibilities. You don't need to be doing this."

"I'm off the clock early today. Cynthia was supposed to come in from Philadelphia, and I'd requested the time off to go pick her up from the airport. But she had a change of plans. Her mother is whisking her off to Los Angeles instead for some shopping before the wedding."

Kate's first thought was that if she hadn't seen her fiancé in a long time, she'd be aching to spend time with him, but she shouldn't presume that everyone felt the same way. It wasn't as if she had personal experience with that kind of relationship.

And the romanticism of movies seemed further away the closer she got to the making of them.

"Here you go." Kate handed a pile of notes and envelopes to Sean. "I've already written everything out, and they just need to be stuffed, sealed, and stamped."

Sean picked up an envelope. "They all say the same thing: *Resident of A Avenue*. How are they going to get delivered that way?"

"That was my dilemma exactly. But I went to the post office the other day, and the postmaster was so helpful. He was able to tell me that there are a hundred sixty-four houses along A Avenue and that if I just addressed them generically like that, he would see to it himself that one was put in each mailbox."

Sean's eyebrows lifted. "You've written out a hundred sixty-four of these?"

"Mm-hmm."

"And Marilyn gave you that many pictures?"

"Yes. She had stacks and stacks of them. This barely made a dent."

He saluted her with two fingers against his forehead. "You must have writer's cramp. And a helluva dedication to this."

Kate shrugged. "How could I not? As amazing as it is to be in this paradise, to be doing a job I love, to have made friends like . . . you"— she took a breath and continued—"there is another reason I'm here, and I can't lose sight of that. I have to solve whatever it is my grandfather's trying to convey to me. And not only for my own curiosity, or for the good of my family, but for him. I don't know why, but he said it was important."

"How so?"

"Well, I've been thinking about it. What if the loss of his memory is like some puzzle piece that's missing, and if I can find it, it will help fill in the things that are missing? Maybe I can bring the old Granddad back."

She saw Sean bite his lip before releasing it.

"I know what you're thinking," she said, lowering her voice. "That it doesn't work that way. That you can't cure dementia by just quilting together all the forgotten facts."

"I didn't say anything."

"You don't have to. And at least you had the courtesy to pretend I'm not out of my mind. My sister would have had plenty to say."

Sean crossed his arms over his knees. "No one should contradict your dreams, Kate. And if they're not a little far-fetched, how much of a dream can they really be?"

"I should embroider that on a piece of silk and frame it on my wall."

"I'm serious," he said, acting wounded.

"So am I." Kate leaned back on her arms. "And what about your dreams?"

He shifted on the step and glanced at the water. "We've already covered this." Then he dropped his hands to his lap. "It's kind of hard to discuss this with Cynthia when she's so preoccupied."

Kate's heart leaped, but just as quickly she felt bad about it.

"I've never planned a wedding myself, Sean, but I imagine that it's quite an ordeal. Especially when it's happening so soon. She probably figures she's going to have all the time in the world with you after the wedding and is overseeing a lot of details right now." She had to force out the words, no matter how sincerely she meant them.

His cheeks grew red. "This isn't some trifle over what color the flowers are going to be or who's going to sit at what table. This is my *life*. This is *her* life. We'd better make sure we can reconcile this before we walk down the aisle."

He was hurting; that was easy enough to see. This was no doubt just the male version of the prewedding jitters. But his words brought an ache to her heart for what could never be. The easy way out would be to excuse herself and walk away, but if she were a true friend, she would help him through it.

"I think I know what you need," she said.

He turned his head and looked at her. The hint of a smile formed on his lips. "What's that?"

"Come with me. I have an errand to run."

~

Kate left the pile of letters in her locker in the employee lounge and then rejoined Sean outside. She led him around the east side of the hotel, past the large white house called Millen Manor. Sean resumed his original role as tour guide while they walked down Glorietta Boulevard.

"That was the home of John Spreckels," he said. "One of the original investors in the Hotel Del. I think it's a bed-and-breakfast now."

Kate took in the charm of the mansion and pictured what it would be like to sit on one of its columned porches as the bay breeze wafted through. There were seven of them. Three on the front, spanning the whole width of the house, divided by billowing white curtains that could close them off or open them into one long one. Another protruded from the second floor, and two flanked the sides. The rooftop appeared to be one enormous porch.

It's Tuesday, so I'll read on the west-facing patio, she thought.

"What are you smiling about?" Sean asked.

She hadn't realized that she was. "I had just noticed that the house has seven porches. You could sit in a different place every day."

"Shall I bring you tea on the central terrace today, Miss Morgan?" he said, holding his hands up in the air to signify a tray and serving set. He spoke with exaggerated British formality, and she answered in kind.

"No, no, my good man. Don't you recall? I had tea there yesterday with the earl of Shireham. Tonight we'll dine at sunset on the roof."

Sean laughed, and she hoped it meant that he was forgetting his earlier woes. "Who is the earl of Shireham? I hope he has honorable intentions."

"The earl of Shireham is my betrothed, and I do hope that not *all* his intentions toward me are honorable." She smiled.

"A wanton! Is there something wayward about our Miss Morgan that I don't yet know?"

Kate's heart skipped a beat as the conversation slipped toward a flirtatious tone, and she faltered in the charade. A navy jet blasting through the sky saved her, interrupting their banter. Nothing like an afterburner to change the mood.

They quieted, shielding their eyes from the sun as they watched the vapor trail dissipate into nothing. Kate's heart pounded, maybe from the wake of the deafening sound, maybe from how *right* it felt to be taking a walk with Sean as if neither had any cares outside this moment. She wondered if he thought the same thing, because he put his hand down and looked at her, his eyes widening as they might over a realization about something. But she remembered Janie's words of caution about how women could read too much into gestures.

Maybe inviting him along was a bad idea.

His voice softened. "We should keep going."

They didn't speak as they walked. Glorietta Boulevard traced the perimeter of the new municipal golf course. She could have cut over to Pomona, but this route was more scenic, even if it added a half mile or so to their destination. From this street she could see not only the great expanse of the green course, the golfers considering their swings, the balls whizzing through the air, but she could also see Glorietta Bay on the horizon, with its tall palm trees lining the water and boats floating in and out.

She'd noticed this about Coronado in her two weeks here—that the water view changed depending on where you were. From the hotel, it was the vast ocean—six thousand miles from Japan, as Sean had told her. But to the north was the San Diego Bay, which the ferry crossed, sailing to the other side with its businesses and its buildings and its bustle. On this eastern side, marinas, warehouses, vessels, and fishermen and vacationers launched from its docks.

For a small place, there was much to see.

They made their way up farther, commenting only on scenery and nothing of substance. Safe things.

When they got to Fifth, Kate took a left and walked one more block before stopping.

"Where are you taking me, the moon?" asked Sean, the joviality of earlier returning to his voice. "We've walked far enough that I should almost consider myself your hostage."

"I assure you that if this is what it was promised to be, you'll be glad you came." She liked being a little mysterious. It was a new feeling for her.

Her methods for finding this place were not all that crafty. She'd merely asked the local grocer for some advice. He told her about Miss Margaret, and his description of the woman and her home intrigued Kate enough that it was all she could think about until she could get there.

Kate pulled a piece of paper from her skirt pocket and checked the address against the house in front of them. It was large, made of white stucco with a Spanish-tile red roof, much like others in Coronado. A stucco wall lined the perimeter, and an iron gate stood in its center.

"This is the one."

Sean opened the gate and waved Kate through first.

The courtyard was so lush that the day seemed to darken as overhanging branches blocked the sun. After stepping inside, Kate had the sensation that they were far away from anything else. Trees were laden with abundant fruit—mostly oranges and lemons—and their limbs sagged from the weight. The brick sidewalk was set in a herringbone pattern, and beds of small white flowers flanked it.

Kate and Sean made their way to the front door, on which hung a hand-painted sign on a piece of driftwood.

MARGARET'S GARDEN OF EDEN

"You're full of surprises, Kate. I thought I knew every inch of this island. But I've never been here."

Kate knocked on the door. "I asked around."

"For what? What are we doing here?"

"You'll see." She smiled with what she hoped was Mona Lisa intrigue.

They heard the creaking of a floor inside just before the door opened. An old woman answered. Her wispy white hair was held up in a loose bun, and the curvature of her spine made her hunch forward as she leaned on a cane.

"You here to sell me something? I've already got an encyclopedia set, and I can hardly see that one as it is." Her voice was not unkind, but maybe she'd encountered more than her share of door-to-door solicitations over the years.

Kate spoke. "I talked to you yesterday on the telephone, Mrs. Linden."

A look of recognition washed over the woman's face, but not in the same way as it might for Granddad. With him, there were wide swaths of forgetfulness. For Mrs. Linden, it seemed like she just had been caught up in doing other things. And to her credit, they had not set an exact time.

"Ah, yes. Aren't you prompt, dear? I didn't think you'd come until later, but you young people probably don't sleep late into the morning. Things to do. Busy, busy. I have some baskets ready, and Lord knows the trees need picking. Meet me around back."

She closed the door, and Kate and Sean followed the brick path around the side of the house. Kate heard Sean take a breath, matching her own awe. If the front courtyard had been stunning, the back was, indeed, a Garden of Eden. A half circle of grass extended from the back of the house, and nine paths emerged from it. If one could fly above it like a bird, it would probably look like a sun and its rays.

Each path contained a row of trees. More lemons and oranges like what they'd seen up front. Some fruits were not recognizable, as they were just green bulbs in the infant stages of growing. Two rows were filled with what she'd come for—figs. Their deep-purple color made them look like large, plump olives. But on closer inspection, Kate could see the faint green and beige stripes that lined the fruit.

"This might be the most beautiful place on the island," Sean said in a worshipful tone. "And that's saying something."

Kate closed her eyes and inhaled the robust scent of the garden. "Isn't it magnificent?"

"I can think of at least a hundred words for it, but that one would top the list," said Sean.

"Then I'm glad it was a good surprise. I heard this is the best place for fifty miles to pick figs. And I know that Miss Monroe has been craving them."

Sean's eyes grew wide, and she sensed his approval. "Thinking like a hotel concierge. Maybe you're in the wrong line of work."

She smiled. Little did he know that if Dimitri had his way, she'd marry him and work in the hotel he was going to build. She did want to work around people but not in the hotel business. Not even at the Del. But she didn't know how to combine this love she had for Coronado with her love for the movies. Still, she was closer than she'd been before. Closer than if she hadn't promised Granddad to come here.

A screen door slammed. Kate turned to see Mrs. Linden hobbling toward them with the promised baskets. "Ah, you found the right trees," she said. "Are you sure it's just the figs you want? Everything needs picking, and you'd be doing me a favor to take as much as you want."

"Thank you. But we walked from the hotel, so for today, I'm just going to take what I can carry."

The old woman set the baskets on the ground. "Well, have at it, then."

Kate jingled the coins in her pocket. "Oh, I forgot to ask. Do you charge by the pound or by the number of pieces?" She would have been happy to take bushels and bushels home if it were not for the walk. Or the cost. And she didn't want to be overly eager in her picking only to come up short of money.

"What the good Lord has blessed me with, I can't take money for. I just enjoy visiting with anyone who comes to pick the fruit."

Sean and Kate looked at each other and then at Mrs. Linden.

"You can't mean that," said Kate. "That's too generous. Let me pay you something for them."

The old woman waved her hand. "Look at these trees. You would be doing me a favor to take everything you can. See how the branches sag in some places? I'm not young like you, and I can't make it out here to pick them as fast as they all grow."

"Surely there's something we can do to repay you."

Mrs. Linden pressed her lips together and nodded. "Just promise me to come by now and then for a little company. Maybe have some tea with me and visit awhile. And you can have all the fruit you want."

Kate's mouth watered at the prospect.

The woman set the baskets down and looked back at the house. "I'm expecting a telephone call from my daughter in just a few minutes, so if you will excuse me, I need to get inside. If I'm not finished by the time you fill those, just let yourself out the front gate and come again soon."

She paused and took a step toward Kate. She raised her hand, thin, dotted skin stretched across bones, and stroked the younger girl's cheek. "You're a beautiful one." Mrs. Linden turned to Sean. "This one's a keeper. I can tell."

Kate felt her face grow warm. She didn't dare look at Sean after a statement like that. Instead, she picked up one of the baskets and started down the path to the fig trees. She'd worn her hair in a ponytail today and hoped that her ears and neck didn't look as red as they felt. But she sensed that Sean's eyes followed her from behind.

She set her basket down in front of a particular tree and ran her hand along one of its star-shaped leaves. The veins of the leaf extended, yellow against green, like five skinny fingers. The leaf was a palm spread out, and there were hundreds of them beckoning them in to pick their fruit. The Garden of Eden, indeed.

Kate squeezed the fruits for ripeness, and although she'd never selected figs at the market, they seemed to be like any other fruit. The deepest-purple ones gave way at once, secreting juice onto her hand. She plucked a few and set them aside on a rock. She'd bring those back for herself and set them on top so as not to be squashed by other ones. She felt the skins of green ones, but some were still hard to the touch, and she figured they might have weeks to go before they were ready to eat. But the in-between ones were just right for her purposes. Their color was a shade darker than lavender. They softened at her touch without fully yielding. These were what she was after—figs that would keep until the movie people came back to Coronado. Her little surprise for Miss Monroe in gratitude for the tremendous favor she'd done by giving her the pictures and stationery and lending her name.

Kate felt Sean moving behind her and peeked to see that he was facing a tree in the opposite direction. Being taller than she was, he was able to reach figs that were much higher, and there seemed to be the bounty of the most ideal ones.

She watched him as he stretched up for those, the calves in his legs tightening. It felt like a stolen moment, seeing him without being noticed. His hair had grown a little longer since they'd met two weeks ago, the edge of it brushing against his shirt collar. He'd been too busy for a haircut, but she kind of liked it this way. She could let herself imagine in this tiny paradise that she could run her fingers through that hair, that he would pull the fruit from the top of the tree and encircle her with those arms. Kiss her forehead and laugh about a joke they'd shared earlier and make plans for dinner later that night.

Sean stepped back, and she shook off her daydream, not wanting to be caught with eyes that would have told him how much she was beginning to care. Not wanting to come between him and his fiancée.

"How's the harvest over on that side?" he asked.

"I've picked as many as I think I can take back for now."

"Me too. I think I'll take some to my mom. She makes the best fig preserves in the world, and she'll go nuts for these."

He bent over the basket and dropped an armful into it. But he kept two, colored the deepest of purples. He walked toward Kate until there were mere inches between them and she could see the flecks in his green eyes. Her heart beat faster as her mouth went dry.

Sean held a fig out to her. "I saved the best ones for us."

His words were innocent enough, but Kate's chest tightened when the tone in his voice slowed. Like maybe he felt, too, that this garden was miles away from anywhere else and it was just the two of them and time existed outside it. She looked at the fig and had to brush off the feeling that she was Eve accepting an apple. Or was it the other way around? Regardless, there was something forbidden underneath these branches. The way they swayed in the breeze allowed flickers of light among the shadows.

She took the fig from him, taking care not to touch his skin with hers, taking care not to ignite what she was beginning to believe might be a mutual spark between them. His eyes had not left hers, and they carried an intensity that far outweighed the occasion.

She took a bite, and it was the most outstanding thing she'd ever tasted. The tiny seeds rested on her tongue, and she managed this time to keep the juices from dripping. Instead, they formed a pool of the sweetest nectar in her mouth, and she thought that if there was such a thing as the food of the gods, this was it, without question. No wonder the fruits were such a fond part of Marilyn Monroe's childhood.

Sean bit into his as well, but it fell apart, sending pulp down his chin and onto his shirt. Kate took a breath before laughing, not knowing him well enough to tell whether he would see the hilarity in it. But she was grateful for the respite from the impossibilities that had been going on in her head.

He wiped the debris from his face, and Kate saw his eyes sparkle a half second before his shoulders began to quake. And then, the laugh.

Sean's laugh seemed to originate in his stomach. It was not the shallow kind but took him over completely, cutting through the silence. Then Kate gave way to her own, wrapping her hands around her waist and bending slightly. He held up his hands as if he didn't know what to do with this fruit that had just *erupted*. She pulled a tissue out of her purse and wiped his chin, but it was too flimsy to do any good. It wasn't until she put her hand down that she realized she'd stepped even closer to him in her attempt to help. The tip of her shoe brushed against his, and she pulled it back. But the rest of her stood there just as close.

The laughter stopped, and the solemnity of the previous moment returned before she could even brace for it. Sean placed his hands around her elbows and pulled her toward him. He closed his eyes just before she closed hers, and she could feel the heat of his breath as she raised her face to his lowered one.

The screen door slammed and startled Kate as fiercely as an electrical jolt might have. She jumped back and looked in that direction, flushed with embarrassment over what had almost happened.

Mrs. Linden stepped out of the house, waving two towels in the air.

"Dear me," she said loudly as she approached them. "I forgot to tell you what little mischief makers those figs can be when they're this ripe. I thought you both—" She stopped midsentence and looked at Sean. A smile spread across her wrinkled face.

"Well, either I'm too late or just in time, depending on how you look at it. Seems you're already well acquainted with how temperamental the purple ones can be."

The old woman didn't seem to be aware that she'd just broken up a moment that could have steered an entirely new course for Sean and Kate, but she'd saved them from that danger and bought time for level heads to return once they were outside the garden. For that, and for everything about this place, Kate was grateful.

She dared not look at Sean, though, the second time in minutes that she'd avoided his reaction. If she saw in his eyes the depth of feeling in the afterglow of an almost kiss, she might lose all hope of keeping between them the line that needed to be there.

But he mustered up a voice that sounded steady, unruffled, and responded to Mrs. Linden as if an invisible earthquake had not shaken each of them mere seconds before.

"Just in time," he answered. "I'm long overdue for a trip to the Laundromat, and these were the last clean pants I have. Good thing it didn't get past my shirt."

Mrs. Linden looked as charmed as Kate felt. This particular smile brought out tiny dimples that she hadn't seen on Sean before. She thrust her hands into her pockets and balled them into fists, digging her nails into her skin to try to keep from blushing again.

"Come over to the hose," said Mrs. Linden. "Let's get you cleaned up before you head back."

Sean gestured for Kate to go ahead of them, and they followed her to the side of the house. She turned the spigot, and a trace of water sputtered before fully flowing. She handed the hose to Sean, and he wet his hands just enough to clean his shirt.

He looked at Kate, his eyes lighting up as if they were carrying the laugh he dared not emit. There were no words Kate could conjure that described the range of things they'd experienced in so short a time, but Sean seemed to understand.

The old woman turned the hose off and wiped her hands on her apron. "Those baskets aren't going to seem very heavy now, but they will be if you walk them all the way back to the hotel. My daughter said she needs to call back in half an hour, so that's just enough time for me to drive you over there."

Kate was about to object but thought better of it. Not because of the burden of all the fruit they'd picked, but because a half hour alone with Sean might be very awkward. Would he apologize for almost kissing her? Would she? Would they just be silent in mutual remorse, or—she felt chills run down her arms—might they become swept up enough in each other's company to continue what had been interrupted?

Sean spoke first. "Normally I would say no, but I'm needed in the banquet room later, and I'm going to have to grab a shower and a change of clothes before then."

He'd told Kate earlier that he had no plans for the afternoon. She wondered whether he was making excuses to avoid the same situation that she'd imagined.

"Bless your heart, I like a man who doesn't have to be proud all the time. I was married to a no-good rascal for too long. Scoot on in. The car's unlocked."

Kate and Sean walked over to the driveway, where veinlike cracks scattered across broken concrete. The only blight on an otherwise perfect oasis was a reminder that there was no real perfection in life. Not in lush, fruit-filled gardens. Not in Coronado. And not in love.

The paint on Mrs. Linden's enormous mint-green Chevy Bel Air was so glossy it reflected the trees that towered over it, and save for a minor dent near the fender, it was in excellent condition. It was the kind of car Kate's dad had always wanted, but they didn't need a car in San Francisco. And they couldn't afford one anyway. Jeez, he'd love this ride, and Kate wished he were here to see it. Three more weeks and she'd be home to see him again.

But did it really feel like home anymore?

Sean put the baskets in the trunk and then opened the passenger door for Kate. Maybe he was just being a gentleman. Or else it was a subtle message that it wasn't a good idea for them to sit together in the back seat.

The door closed with a solid *thud*, and he ran around to open the driver's door for Mrs. Linden. But instead she was pulling back the white cover of the car.

"Let's enjoy it the way God intended. As a convertible," she said.

Kate smiled as sunshine began to peek into the open space. She closed her eyes and could picture cruising along Ocean Boulevard. She doubted the wind would blow through her hair like it did in the movies if they were only poking down Orange Avenue. She put her sunglasses on like Audrey Hepburn.

Mrs. Linden returned to the driver's seat and backed out of the driveway at a snail's pace. Kate rummaged through her purse and found the new lipstick she'd bought a few days ago. She leaned to her right, just enough to catch her reflection in the side-view mirror. But the coral color she'd wanted was more of an orange than had been advertised on the display, and it would have looked much better with Janie's brown curls. It made Kate look like some kind of clown. She put the lid back on, catching a glimpse of Sean in the mirror. They both froze for a second that felt like an eternity before looking away.

What did take an eternity was driving the mile back to the Hotel Del. Mrs. Linden clutched the steering wheel and peered over it as if she were combing a beach for shells.

Kate looked at the odometer. Seven hundred sixteen miles. This car was at least five years old, based on the models she'd seen her dad pore over in the past. Mrs. Linden was a kind soul who deserved this car and much more, but Kate winced in disappointment that it wasn't getting as much use as it could.

As they pulled up to the hotel, Mrs. Linden put the brake on, and Sean hopped out to get the baskets out of the trunk.

"It's been such a joy to have you both over to my house. I hope you'll come back soon. I have quite the bounty, as you've seen!"

"We will. Thank you for a delightful afternoon," said Sean.

Mrs. Linden put her speckled arm on Kate's. "Isn't this silly. In all the time we were talking, I didn't catch your names. Yours and your boyfriend's."

Kate flushed at the notion but didn't look at Sean to see his reaction to the word.

"I'm Sean. Sean O'Donnell."

"And I'm Kate Morgan."

Mrs. Linden's eyes widened, and her skin turned pale. "That's the name of the ghost."

Kate pursed her mouth and nodded. That made at least ten times now. "Yes. I've heard that."

The old woman continued. "But not just the ghost. My beloved friends Grace and Alan. And their son, George. They were Morgans, too."

Kate's chest tightened, and she felt a chill run from her head to her toes.

"You—you knew them? You knew George?"

A smile grew on Mrs. Linden's thin lips, one that was tinged with something like sadness. "Yes. Yes, quite well. You see, George was engaged to my daughter Mary."

∽

Over the years, the Hotel del Coronado has played host to many notable people. I find it amusing to watch the staff become all atwitter when a famous guest is due to arrive or if the filming of a movie is to take place here.

Names that inspire giddiness for residents of Coronado meant little or nothing to me, as cinema was something that became popular long after my husband ended my life. But you might recognize them—Clark Gable, Bette Davis, Greta Garbo, Rita Hayworth, Bing Crosby, Jimmy Stewart, and Mary Pickford, for starters. There were sports figures as well—Babe Ruth and Jack Dempsey—and others who drew throngs of people who were dazzled by whatever athletic feats they had accomplished.

That's really just a snippet in comparison to all who come through creating sensation. In fact, renowned people are more the standard than the exception. Especially during the bewildering period called Prohibition. That brought an especially raucous crowd who used Coronado as a launching point to head to Mexico and indulge in the vices that our country had made illegal.

There have been some standout visitors who've caught my attention. Most memorable were a comedy team, Desi and Lucille Arnaz, who also happened to be married. I overheard them having a discussion that for the purposes of television, she would be called by her maiden name—Ball. They were quite a mismatched couple, just by the looks of them. She had wild red hair that seemed impossible to tame. He was the more serious-minded one when it came to their work. Cuban, I believe, and heavily accented. I often missed some of his words. But I had great enjoyment watching as they sat on the large porch and crafted a routine that they hoped to pitch for television. A vaudevillian actor they called Pepito guided their scripts, and eventually they decided on a storyline where Desi would play a grumpy bandleader and Lucille would play his crazy wife.

It warmed my heart to see them. A team coming together to produce something good. Tom had wanted me to be a partner to his antics as well, but they were for dastardly ends, and I would not participate.

I saw Desi and Lucille a few years later. Apparently their television show had become popular, and they returned to the Hotel Del to film an episode with their two sidekicks, Fred and Ethel. It was one of the few moments I longed to be flesh and bone again to watch the ordeal that production was, the endless days, to film something and then to view it on a television set. Especially a program so funny as theirs.

The hotel did eventually put televisions in the bedrooms, but I never ventured into places that were private. I am not a voyeur.

Presidents caught my attention, as I was far more aware of their accomplishments than of anything in the entertainment realm. People were endlessly chattering about politics, and newspaper headlines shouted opinions in dark, bold letters. So their names and faces were familiar to me. As was His Royal Highness, the Prince of Wales, who visited in 1920.

I admit that the presence of a prince did create a stir in me, to the extent that sort of thing was possible. My mother used to read fairy tales by *candlelight, and my grandfather frequently bought beautifully bound books full of fantasy stories and tales of adventure. So I was not immune to the illusions that a young girl has about being rescued by someone who could lift her from her troubles. I thought for a time that Tom was my prince.*

But he was actually the trouble.

Prince Edward was more handsome than in pictures I'd seen in newspapers. He smiled like a little boy, and his eyelashes fanned out from soft eyes. He walked with his hands held behind his back, and he leaned in as he talked with people, appearing, at least, to give them all his attention. Some years later, he became king, only to abdicate the throne for a woman with the mannish name of Wallis.

Isn't that a romantic notion, though? Relinquishing a kingdom in pursuit of love? I suppose I did the same thing, albeit on a smaller scale, and while it didn't work out for me, I hope it did for them.

I still believe that love is worth sacrificing for. Tom could not rob me of that.

Certainly the most memorable—and meaningful—visit as long as I've been attached to the hotel was that of Thomas Edison in 1904. He was decidedly less charming than the prince I witnessed years later. Edison's mouth was grim, a permanent frown placed either through biology or through attitude. He was not unkind. Overly serious, perhaps. But the man had brought light to the world in the most literal sense possible, so I suppose there was every reason to make excuses for his demeanor.

Edison, I learned, had been to the Hotel del Coronado before. During its construction, in fact. Five years before my stay, he had personally overseen the installation of the lighting system, the one that my husband, Tom, had been so keen to see. He—Edison, not Tom, mercifully—returned seventeen years later in 1904 to throw the switch on the first Christmas tree to be placed in the hotel.

I was quite excited that day because Christmastime always brought Alan, Grace, and George to the hotel to see the decorations. And undoubtedly Mary Carter's family would arrive for the season as they always did.

I could never pinpoint the exact day, but this year, for the momentous occasions of Edison's arrival, I was certain they would all make a point of being here.

And I was right.

The Carters arrived first. I was in the lobby, one of my favorite places in the hotel. I loved to witness the joyous arrivals and the tearful departures. The lobby was the heart of the hotel. Its floor was covered in thick red Oriental rugs, its ceiling framed in dark wood, its elevator made of gold lace.

The Christmas tree was already set up. Atop it sat a glittering star that missed the ceiling by mere inches. Shiny ornaments and burgundy velvet ribbons adorned it in such abundance that its green branches were barely visible. The lights were already strung. I'd watched Edison oversee the process himself. The strands had been pulled from wooden crates decorated with painted pictures of Santa Claus. Across the box were large red-and-white letters—GLASS. HANDLE WITH CARE.

They'd started from the top, men holding rickety ladders while others took turns climbing them. There were three at a time, creating a pyramid around the tree. A man would attach the lights on his side and hand them around to the next and the next, ever widening as they made their way to the middle and the bottom. It seemed precarious to me, as did the idea of outfitting a tree with electricity. Wouldn't a spark set it on fire? But given that the previous tradition had been to light the tree with candles set in clips, perhaps it was a needless concern.

I saw Mr. Carter before I saw his family. I'd noticed this about him before—he walked ahead of his wife and daughter instead of behind them as you would expect a gentleman to do. I made a comparison to Tom. Perhaps that was unfair—I knew almost nothing of Mr. Carter other than the understanding that their money had come from oil. But the way he paraded through a door and left Margaret and little Mary to manage the luggage with the bellman made it appear that he thought himself to be more important than they were.

He walked to the registration desk and spoke in brusque tones to the poor man on duty—Harold Cotes, who'd been there for three years and who had never lost his patience with patrons whom I might have given up on far more quickly.

"Mr. Carter," said Mr. Cotes. "We are delighted to have you and your family stay with us once again. Your rooms are nearly finished, and we would be happy to serve you a drink over in the bar while you wait."

"They should be ready now. We had a reservation for yesterday."

"Yes, sir. But when we received word that your train was delayed, we opened those two rooms to other guests. The hotel is booked, as you can imagine. Everyone wants to see Mr. Edison."

"But those rooms were paid for."

"Yes, sir," said Mr. Cotes again. Not a trace of frustration in his voice. "And of course the hotel will reimburse you for last night."

"This is unacceptable. I am tired. My wife is tired. My daughter is tired. And I have business to attend to."

"Of course, Mr. Carter. It shouldn't be more than ten minutes. I see the bellman coming in now with your bags."

Margaret and Mary Carter entered the lobby, both looking immediately at the tree. My first thought was that little Mary was not "little Mary" any longer. It had been only a few short months since their summer visit, but she seemed absolutely transformed. A couple of inches taller, but that was only what was obvious. What I detected was a maturity that had developed. Her cheeks were pink, likely by cosmetic aid. Her jawline was somehow more pronounced, as if she had an expectation of what this trip would bring. And her eyes—her eyes were filled with anticipation that was not satiated by the sight of the tree.

Could it—could I dare hope that the new look to her had anything to do with dear George? The last time they'd been together here, they'd held hands. I wondered if they'd written letters to each other during the months between. They were fifteen now. Not yet adults but not so terribly far off from it.

Only minutes later, as promised, Mr. Cotes announced the news that their rooms were ready, and they made the trek up the gold elevator to the fourth floor.

I watched them go, Margaret and Mary walking to the back corner, Mr. Carter standing at attention as he leaned against his walking cane. His posture suggested importance, his demeanor that of a man with little time to waste.

Suddenly my attention was pulled toward a side door, and I recognized the feeling that only one person could evoke in me—George. I never ceased to wonder at the invisible bond of a mother to a son across this chasm. George walked in and looked around with the same eager eyes I'd just witnessed in Mary, and I knew in my heart that it was no coincidence.

My son walked over to the piano and played the notes that he'd worked on for all these years. But each time, the composition possessed more layers. He'd added chords on the bass line, changed the timing of several notes. The tune repeated itself, but the sound transformed as each repetition started. I listened carefully. It was the pacing. That was the difference. I knew little about music composition—had he inherited it from Tom's side?—but I'd heard enough of this song over the years that I could tell where the changes were.

The first time through, the notes sounded even. I didn't know if that was a musical term, but it's the only way I can describe it. Each note seemed to last as long as the next. It reminded me of dawn. The slow, steady rise of the sun.

The second time, though, same notes, different pacing. Some were short; some were drawn out, evoking an entirely different feeling. Like the quickening of a heartbeat, followed by a slow, lingering pace. Love? Was this a song that reflected the stages of love? And did he think of Mary when he played it?

As I've said, I'm a romantic.

The elevator bell rang, and its heavy doors opened. Mary Carter stood there. She must have dropped her luggage and hurried down. Could she have heard the piano from the fourth floor? Surely not, but maybe the heart knows when the object of its affection is near. Yes, I realize that it is poetic silliness to think such a thing, but then again, I exist in a space that I previously would not have believed possible, so maybe there is an unspoken connection that exists between us all if we only home in on it.

Mary walked toward George, who was so engrossed in his piece that he did not seem to hear her. She placed a gloved hand on his shoulder. He continued to play but sat up taller and cocked his head to the right so that his ear rested on her fingers. He slowed the last few notes and played a final, featherlight one on the high end of the scale. Only then did he stand up and turn around. He looked at her with an affection that seemed far older than his mere fifteen years. Her took her hand in his, removed the gray leather glove, and kissed her pale skin.

George and Mary seemed to be unaware that they'd collected a small audience. I saw eyes glance up from newspapers and down from felt-rimmed hats, the men judging, the women smiling, and the scene became poisoned by my worry for George and Mary. Surely Mr. Carter would not allow this fledgling relationship to continue. He might be new money, but in my experience, new money emulated old money. Unless the culture in Houston was vastly different from my own background of wealth, the daughter of an oil tycoon had no business dallying with the adopted son of an older couple who tended a picket-fenced garden on the tiny island of Coronado.

Mary withdrew her hand and gestured for him to follow her down the hallway to a corridor I knew to be seldom frequented. I did not follow the young couple, wishing for them the privacy they'd missed just now. But I'd read enough fairy tales to know what happened next, and I hoped their first kiss was the happily ever after that mine was not.

Chapter Fifteen

It was a good thing she wasn't driving. If Kate had been behind the steering wheel hearing Mrs. Linden's revelation that she was Mary Carter's mother, she might have slammed on the brakes and caused an accident or even careened into the sidewalk in total shock.

Questions poured into her head. Why was her name Linden instead of Carter? Was she widowed? What had happened between Granddad George and Mary? The idea that someone might have known Granddad all those years ago was exciting and overwhelming all at the same time. It seemed a tragedy to Kate that he was losing his mind and his memories just as she was becoming old enough to realize how precious those things were.

Mrs. Linden had to be years older than him, and yet she seemed as sharp as anyone Kate had ever met. Granddad was sixty-eight. Ancient to someone Kate's age, but faced with Mrs. Linden, she realized that he really wasn't very old. Which made his dementia all the more unfortunate. He could have many more years of good physical health even as he lost everything that made him uniquely himself.

"Are you unwell, my dear? Did I say something wrong?"

Kate looked out the window and realized they were already at the Hotel Del.

"Yes. I—I just don't think I expected you to say what you said."

"About George and Mary? How is it that you know George, anyway?"

The sun was setting behind them, and it reflected in the rearview mirror. The light was almost blinding, so she couldn't see Sean's reaction to the conversation.

"George Morgan is my grandfather."

She held up her hand to shade her eyes and see Mrs. Linden better. Were those tears on her cheeks?

"Bless me, yes. Yes! I knew George had a granddaughter, though I didn't think her name was Kate. Something starting with a *J*."

"Janie. She's my sister. Wait—are you in touch with my grandfather?"

Mrs. Linden pulled a handkerchief from her pocket and dabbed her eyes. "Miss Morgan, I think you and I are going to have a lot to talk about. And if I didn't have this phone call in ten minutes with my daughter, I would stay a little longer."

"Mary's calling you?" Mary was alive? Why had she and Granddad broken up?

She dabbed her eyes again. "No. Not Mary. We'll talk about her sometime. My younger daughter, Elizabeth. She lives in a small town called Pismo Beach. I'm supposed to go visit her tomorrow, and I have to catch her call so I can get directions."

With the low mileage on this car, Kate guessed this was the first time Mrs. Linden was driving there.

"When will you be back?"

"Not for a week. It's her fortieth wedding anniversary, and she and her husband are going to Lake Tahoe to celebrate. I will be staying with their dogs while they're away."

A whole week! Kate felt parched for information. Mrs. Linden held the glistening pitcher of refreshing information that would answer everything she longed to know. A week was a lifetime.

"Would we be able to talk by telephone? I have so much I want to ask you." The sun shifted just enough that Kate was now able to see Sean in the mirror. He looked as anxious as she felt.

Mrs. Linden sighed and rubbed her hands along the steering wheel. "I apologize for disappointing you, but I think this is a conversation I'd like to have in person."

Sean spoke up. "Did—did something happen to Mary?"

Mrs. Linden turned and looked at him. She opened her mouth as if to speak and then closed it back up. She hung her head and then shook it.

She lifted her wrist and peered at the watch. "It's going to have to wait until I get back. Elizabeth is on a party line, and it might not be available later. I need to get home and take her call."

Kate's hand trembled as she reached for the door handle. She opened it and turned her body to step out of the car, her head full of something like the fog that always descended on San Francisco. She followed Sean to the trunk of the car and pulled out the baskets, but her limbs seemed to move independently, because she could think of nothing more than how very long this next week was going to feel.

Mrs. Linden stepped out and pulled Kate into her arms. She smelled of citrus and strong tea and tobacco, which blended into something that made Kate squeeze her eyes to keep tears from falling. She reminded Kate of all she missed about her own grandmother.

"When you've lived as long as I have, you learn that time moves like lightning. And if you try to lasso it, you'll only get burned." She kissed Kate on the cheek and squeezed her as if they'd known each other for a very long time. And indirectly, they had. Or at least their histories were entwined in ways that Kate couldn't even imagine right now.

But as impatient as she was, Mrs. Linden's embrace worked its magic. It was then that Kate remembered how much there was to look forward to in the next few days—the employee barbecue and her next phone call with her family.

Sean stood next to Kate as they watched Mrs. Linden roll away in her beautiful car. Neither moved, and in their silence, the ocean behind them sounded like unrelenting thunder. In San Francisco, she and Janie would sometimes take the bus to Half Moon Bay, where the water lapped their ankles like an eager puppy. But here the waves roared with no break, no pause, and the sea's fervor said everything Kate couldn't.

$\sim$

The next afternoon brought sunshine, which was the standing order for Coronado. Indeed, God must have smiled particularly on this tiny piece of land, named as it was for martyrs. Kate didn't know which ones—the booklet she'd found at the registration desk didn't give details. But the Crowned Ones, as martyrs were called, lent their name to this paradise, perhaps to reflect the one they were promised by giving their lives for their God.

Kate decided that she could spare a few dollars to buy a swimsuit, thanks to Miss Monroe's generous tip. Maisy had taken off with the only one Kate owned, and in any other circumstance she would have said *good riddance*, as it was a hand-me-down from Janie and threadbare at best. But the barbecue was coming up, and having one would be necessary for the beach.

She headed to a shop on Orange Avenue on her way to the hotel. The summer offerings were a burst of color—towels of the brightest pink, white sunglasses with thick frames and dark lenses, yellow umbrellas to block an even more yellow sun.

The shopkeeper walked over to Kate. "May I help you?"

Kate stroked the terry cloth of a robe sitting on a hanger and glanced at its price tag. Eight dollars. Such a fortune! Not even with the tip would she spend anywhere close to that. The majority of it was going to get saved along with everything else she'd earned.

"I'm looking for a swimsuit," she answered. Though all she wanted to do was escape through the door. She felt out of place even breathing the air in here.

But the woman tugged at the measuring tape hanging from her neck like a piece of jewelry and wrapped it around Kate's bust—smaller than Kate would have liked. Then her hips. The woman stepped back and looked her over.

"I have just the thing."

She headed toward a rack in the middle of the store and returned with a small suit clipped to a hanger that she twirled around her finger. Kate's eyes widened. It was a two-piece, in leopard print. She'd never worn a two-piece. Or leopard print. And she didn't know if she had the courage to.

"You have just the figure for this. You can try it on behind that curtain."

"Thank you." Kate took it and walked as if in a trance toward the dressing room. This kind of life was surreal. She didn't aspire to be wealthy, but to shop in a place like this, even occasionally, would be such a treat.

Kate closed the curtain and turned her back to the mirror. Stepping out of her clothes and laying them over a leather ottoman in the corner, she slipped on the high-waisted bottom half and then the top, tying it behind her neck.

She squeezed her eyes shut and turned around, not quite ready for whatever image would face her. Opening them slowly, she caught her breath. It looked amazing! Could she really pull off a suit like this? Something about the way it was cut gave her the bust she barely had, and the bottoms showed off the curvy hips that she did. She slid her hands down her hips and turned around.

It was amazing how something like a silly, stretchy fabric could manufacture confidence.

What would Sean think of me in this? she wondered. But she pushed the thought away.

Then her hand found the tag. Six dollars and seventy cents. She swallowed hard. Buying something like this would greatly cut into the interest she owed the pawnshop, and no piece of clothing was worth that.

But if one were, it would be this.

She rolled it off, wishing she had a camera with her to at least remember what she looked like in that beauty. She clipped it back to the hanger and put on her clothes, which suddenly felt simple in comparison.

"How did that work out for you?" asked the hopeful saleswoman.

Kate took a breath and decided to be honest.

"It's perfect. You were right. But"—she lowered her voice, though the store was empty—"I'm afraid it's a bit too expensive for me."

The woman frowned, but seemingly out of pity not disappointment. "It *is* special, isn't it?"

Kate nodded. The woman stepped closer and whispered, "I used to be your age. Just starting out. And I know it's difficult. If you take a right on Eighth, and then a left on that diagonal street called Olive, you'll see a little shop there called Daisy's. She sells some thrift items, and since it's nearly the end of the season, she should have some of the swimsuits that have been brought in by people who finished their vacations already. Would that help?"

Thrift store. It would be just like receiving a hand-me-down from her sister. But at least it would be from a stranger, and she wouldn't have memories of Janie wearing it first.

Thanking her, Kate headed to Daisy's and found that it was exactly as described. There was a whole rack just for swimsuits that looked like they'd seen some sun, but the elastic was still firm. Probably just worn this season by women who could get new ones every year. There wasn't anything like the leopard-print one, but maybe that was better. No matter how she'd looked in it, she wasn't sure if she had the courage to wear something in public that showed her belly. It would have been like wearing a bra and underwear in front of strangers. But that seemed to be the fashion.

She tried on the first. Blue-and-white gingham with a skirt that lay across the hips and a wide band that formed a V at the neck. It wasn't the man-catcher that the two-piece was, but Kate often wondered why it was the goal of nearly every woman to get married and why they spent so much effort on its pursuit. Certainly, she wanted that, too—love, marriage, babies, the whole thing. But she also wanted to learn about herself first. Her dream had always been getting to Southern California. And now she was here, with very little time left to figure out what it all meant to her. Letting a swimsuit encourage her in being a coquette was not part of her plan.

Though she would not mind if Sean thought she looked attractive in one.

Then she tried the other. It was the lesser worn of the two. White with bold red poppies, appearing to be a one-piece from the front but cutting across the back like separates.

A perfect compromise. It was daring enough to be a departure from Kate's more conservative style but safe enough to keep her from feeling embarrassed.

She checked the tag—only two dollars and forty-five cents, just over an hour's worth of work. That she could manage, plus fifty cents for a white sundress that had a small tear in the hem. After paying for them, she finished her walk to the Del and headed straight for the back.

The beach was particularly stunning today, the sun brighter, the seagulls louder, the breeze milder. Kate walked far out of her way to enter the lawn because she loved seeing the hotel from this angle. It was especially festive this afternoon, with colored banners and strung lights that had been set out for the occasion of the barbecue. Today marked the exact middle point of her time here in Coronado. Each hour, another bit of sand descended in the hourglass of her five weeks. She wished she could fill time with all the sand on this beach and stay here forever.

As she walked, she counted twenty-six sand dollars, their wriggly pink bodies looking nothing like the hard white skeletons that were sold as trinkets in gift shops. If only they were actual dollars, she could comb the beach every morning and become wealthy enough to save Mom, Dad, Janie, and Granddad George. Maybe then she could make this her home.

The beach was littered with white shells, and she stooped to pick up a few, flinching once when a particularly cylindrical one turned out to be a discarded cigarette butt. She had no idea why someone would mar the beauty of this place with such a revolting remnant.

She ascended the wooden steps that connected the beach to the hotel grounds. The party was in full swing, and as she approached, she noticed with glee that it was not merely a barbecue but a luau. She'd heard of those—the kalua pig being roasted underground. This one had just been lifted from its pit. The head of the swine was placed on a plate with an apple in its mouth. One last supper before it became supper for the rest of them?

With any luck, they would have plates of the pulled meat at a side table—there was a grotesque nature to looking your dinner in the eye. Even a lifetime working at Uncle Mike's hadn't cured her of the squeamish feeling of looking at fish heads.

But she tried to put all that aside and get swept up in the atmosphere the hotel had created. Hawai'i was another dream long into the future, and in the meantime Sean and his kitchen team had re-created it in a most spectacular way.

Many of the faces were familiar, but few names were known to her. The entire staff had been invited—the bellboys, the laundry girls, the maids. Some could only come briefly so as to not be torn away from their duties. After all, the hotel was still full at its summer capacity. Kate was grateful in this moment to have been hired merely as extra help for a movie that was currently on hiatus. It gave her the time to enjoy the slower pace of these few days.

"Kate!"

She turned her head in the direction of Sean's voice. He was wearing a Hawai'ian shirt—green with white pineapples—and the color complemented his freckled skin in a way that made it seem that he was born to live outdoors.

"You came." He trotted down the steps, a drink in hand. He extended it to her. "I saw you from up there and got a lemonade for you. I hope that's what you like."

She took it from him. "Thank you. I love lemonade."

"What were you doing all the way out there?"

"I wanted to see the hotel from the beach."

He smiled. "That's my favorite view, too."

She could feel herself blush.

"Sean?"

A new voice spoke from the top of the stairs. A beautiful woman stood there. Her blonde hair was bobbed, and she wore a smart skirt-and-jacket suit in pale pink. Pearls surrounded her neck and graced her earlobes. But as elegant as she looked, she was completely out of place in this setting.

"Cynthia—darling," said Sean, his voice flattening. Or maybe that was just Kate's imagination.

"Are you coming up?" said his fiancée. "Don't leave me here alone. I don't know anyone."

"Come down. I want you to meet someone," he responded.

Kate noticed Cynthia's tall heels. The woman teetered on the steps as she met them halfway. Her own lemonade sloshed on the sides of the glass, reflecting her unease.

"Cynthia, this is Kate. She's one of our temporary employees, and she's from San Francisco."

"Good to meet you," Cynthia said without even looking at Kate. "Sean, what time did you say this would be over? We're expected at my parents' for dinner at five."

Sean's cheeks turned red, an easy feat for his fair skin. He spoke under his breath. "I didn't agree to it, though. I told you I'm in charge of this event, and I'll stay through the end. Cleanup and all."

"But they're serving filet mignon with blue cheese sauce. Your favorite."

"I didn't ask for that, Cynthia. I need to be here tonight."

She continued as if Kate were not anywhere to be seen, telegraphing what Kate assumed to be a perception that all this was a mere trifle.

That *she* was a trifle.

"They'll manage without you, Sean. And this will all be over in a few weeks anyway. You have an overdeveloped sense of loyalty."

"Isn't that what you want in a husband?"

Kate didn't think she belonged in this conversation. "Excuse me," she said and made her way up to the lawn, grateful to be wearing sandals instead of heels.

She picked up a plate, saying hello and all the expected pleasantries with coworkers who she wouldn't see again just weeks from now. She felt anchorless—she belonged here and she didn't belong here.

She looked back and saw Sean and Cynthia still talking. They stood there for at least twenty minutes. Kate glanced over once in a while, and only once did she see any deviation in their actions. Sean reached his hand out to Cynthia and rubbed her arm, still folded across the other one. But Cynthia shook her head and looked out to the water. Then she shrugged him off and hurried up the stairs, walking right past Kate without saying anything. She walked around the hotel, presumably to the parking lot.

Sean didn't run after her. Instead, he walked down to the beach, heading toward North Island. He became smaller and smaller until he disappeared completely into the horizon.

Kate looked at her plate, which was now only filled with the crumbs and traces of barbecue sauce from a meal she'd barely tasted. She set it down.

"Kate, right?"

One of the girls she recognized as a coat-check attendant spoke to her.

"Yes."

"A few of us are heading into the ocean. Want to come?"

"Sure." She stood up and started to follow the girl back to the steps. Anything to distract her from what she'd just witnessed.

"I'm Ellie. This is Sasha, and that's Mabel. You looked so sad over there. Everything OK?"

Kate nodded, embarrassed to have worn her feelings on her face. "Yes."

"Do you say anything more than one word at a time?"

"Yes." Then she laughed, the tension of the last half hour escaping. "Yes. Usually my family is telling me that I talk too much!"

"I'll have to see that to believe it."

"Thanks for asking me."

"You're one of the temporary girls, right?" asked Sasha. Her black eyeliner was expertly drawn into the catlike curve that was starting to grace the magazines. She wore a red two-piece, one that showed far more than the one Kate had tried on in the store, and she fit into it better than anyone Kate had ever seen.

"I am." Two words. See, she could do it.

"No sense holding back from the fun just because the gig is only for a few weeks. You have a beau back home?"

"I don't." Two words again. Why did she let these stylish girls intimidate her when they were only being nice?

"Just as well. There are plenty of catches here. More than the fish out there!" She laughed at her pun, and Kate finally smiled. She'd always wanted to be someone bold like Sasha but lacked the nerve. "Should we find someone for you?"

Kate shook her head. Falling for Sean had made the idea of leaving hard enough.

"How about we just swim, and I'll think about a beau later?"

"Even better." Sasha looked back to Ellie and Mabel. "Race you there?"

All four girls skipped down the beach, leaving footprints in the sand. Kate felt the sharp edge of a seashell brush her right foot, but she didn't stop to check on it. It felt too freeing, too joyous to run into the breeze, and she didn't want problems—big or small—to interrupt the reverie.

In San Francisco, she barely had time to make friends and only kept the company of her own sister and of Dimitri, who'd lately made his hopes for them more and more apparent. And her pals from high school were either married, working their own jobs, or—the lucky few—attending college. All too busy, just like Kate.

It was nice to have some girlfriends again.

When they got to the beach, Kate shed her sundress and reveled in the feel of the sun on so much exposed skin. She felt positively modest in comparison to Sasha, but soon enough they'd made their way into the water and all that could be seen was their heads bobbing above the surf.

Kate couldn't help but scan the far reaches of the beach, but she didn't see him.

The water felt amazing. So much warmer than Pacifica or Half Moon Bay. It was hard to even catch sun up north, and she and Janie spent their occasional day trips to the coast moving their beach towels out of the shade that crept over them every half hour or so. Not so in Coronado. The sun was consistent, as if tied here by an invisible thread, and she was grateful. Her swimming skills were rusty, so she stayed closer to shore, admiring the girls who felt so bold as to venture far enough that they were almost out of sight.

Kate felt more shells underneath her feet and even the occasional brush of tiny minnows that swam by her legs. She followed one school, intrigued by the way they swam in groups through the glasslike water. When she looked up, she realized she'd ended up quite a ways from the hotel. It was just as beautiful from afar as it was up close, though at this distance she could more easily see the way its red-roofed turret pierced the blue sky. The sun cast a huge swath of light across this particular part of the beach. She stepped out and found a piece of sand that was not inundated with shells.

This part of Coronado looked so different from the cluster of buildings that had sprung up around the Del. Here, lots were of the estate size with large, expensive houses that must be owned by millionaires seemingly trying to outdo, outbuild, outshine each other. The homes were beautiful, and she wondered what it would be like to peer through some of those diamond-shaped leaded windows. But nice as they were to look at, she'd be overjoyed just to live in a simple cottage off Orange Avenue.

This moment was too perfect to do anything but relish it. She stepped onto the sand, unconcerned with the way it plastered her wet skin. She could get into a shower soon enough, but she would not always have this opportunity. The coast at home was better explored with a heavy sweater and hearty shoes.

She sat down, realizing she'd forgotten a towel, but she could retrieve it later. She'd gone enough of a distance to be noticeably alone but was still close enough to observe the details of the lives of other beachgoers. It was a cycle, really. A pair of lovers walked hand in hand, the woman kicking an arc of water with her toe, the man wrapping his arms around her slim waist and twirling her around, both laughing. Honeymooners, maybe, or an even newer love.

Then a family, the by-product of young love. Father reading a newspaper, mother fanning herself with a book that she tried to read, but her attention was on the little ones building sandcastles. A teenage daughter lifting her oversize sunglasses to look at the lifeguard while he scanned the horizon. The lifeguard turning his head toward the girl once she'd looked away.

Then an older couple. Also holding hands but not gripping them like the lovers. Perhaps making just enough of a connection to keep from tripping in the unevenness of the sand.

Kate lay back, her eyes closed, blocking the light, though she could still feel its heat through her eyelids. She thought about all the other people here. She'd not seen anyone else enjoying it in solitude as she was, and though she'd been a part of a group for a few minutes, she found that it was a welcome change from the bustle that her life in San Francisco demanded. Slowly, slowly, she drifted into the drowsy state that sunshine could impose.

And then nothing.

~

1908

Blessed, joyous, welcome news! My George has proposed to Mary Carter and, fittingly, he did so right in the lobby of the Hotel del Coronado. Had it been anywhere else, I would not have been there to witness it, and I whispered a word of thanksgiving to whoever lords over this in-between state of mine.

I began to sense that something was going to happen when I saw both Alan and Grace Morgan enter through the front door, dressed in the finest clothes I'd ever seen them wear. When I first met her, I'd noticed that Grace was handy with a needle, and she'd put her talent to good use for today. On closer look, I'd seen her dress before—Christmas, probably. But she'd appliquéd a bird design onto the shoulder, sewn a wide sash across the waist, and attached felt flowers to what would have otherwise been a plain hat.

The finest women, in my opinion, are those who can innovate and improvise.

Not long after, Margaret Carter appeared at the elevator door. She, too, was dressed in finery—the kind that was no doubt tailored to meet her exact measurements. She looked around the lobby, and when she saw the Morgans, she hurried over to them, arms outstretched.

"Alan, Grace, so good to see you again."

"Mrs. Carter, welcome back to Coronado," said Grace. "I hope you had a pleasant journey from Houston."

"Please call me Margaret. We're going to be family now. And yes, the journey was pleasant enough, but I'd prefer to simply move here and not have to travel at all! But Richard won't hear of it."

"How I wish you could!"

As did I. Mrs. Carter was such a pleasant person and would make an excellent friend for dear Grace.

Margaret continued. "I've planted a garden on the small patch of land Richard would give up to me. Avocados, figs, oranges. Sometimes I sit in the middle of it and pretend I'm back here in lush Coronado."

"And how is Mary?"

"Well, she's excited to be here, but she doesn't know of George's plan. I don't think it will be a surprise, though. Those two have been inseparable since they were children."

The two women still held hands. Alan, ever the quiet one, put his arms behind his back and rocked on his heels, looking around the hotel as if for the first time. He'd always seemed overwhelmed in the company of women. A quiet, charming shadow.

The family certainly had more of a connection to the Del than they had ever known before—George had recently been hired at the front desk. Five days a week, my son would come to work in the only suit he owned, greeting guests, smoothing out problems, making everyone welcome. He had a gift for it. Friendly boy. I saw so little of Tom in him that if I hadn't known better, I would have questioned whether he even shared blood with that rat. Instead, George reminded me of my grandfather. My kindly grandfather. How I wished my son could have known him.

Grace continued. "So Richard accepted George's request to marry your daughter? I hope you don't mind my saying, Margaret, but that does surprise me a little."

A dark look came over Mrs. Carter. "I intercepted the letter, and I wrote to George that we were so pleased and gave our consent. But no, Richard never saw it."

Grace dropped her hands. "Do you mean to tell me that the children do not have Richard's blessing? Margaret, he will make a scene!"

Margaret stepped in closer to Grace and linked their arms. "The only thing Richard would dislike more than Mary wedding herself to someone he didn't choose is a moment of public disgrace. I encouraged George in my note to propose to Mary here in the lobby. I know Richard. He might be steamed, but even if he never forgives me, he will act the part of the happy father so as to save face."

"But what about afterward?" Grace wrung her hands, her beaming look melting into one of worry.

"I'll handle him afterward. This is all my doing, Grace. I'll take the wrath for it."

"Why are you doing this?"

Margaret turned to Alan. "Alan, dear, would you mind if we excuse ourselves? I'd like to take a stroll with Grace for a few minutes."

"My pleasure, ladies. I'll just sit here and read the newspaper."

The women continued to link arms, and I walked behind them, never more in want of the ability to be part of a group than I was now with this dear one. Margaret leaned in close to Grace.

If I could not be a friend, I could be a hovering specter. A guardian angel of sorts.

Their heads were almost touching. "I sense that you're a forgiving soul, Grace. That you believe in love. And so I hope that you'll be able to look past what I'm going to say and allow the children to have their happiness."

"I can think of nothing you could tell me that would prompt me to want anything but that for them."

Margaret took a deep breath. I trembled on her behalf, though I did not have a hint of what she was about to impart. "I was in love before I wed Richard. To a soldier. He'd come through Houston with the army on his way to fight in Coahuila. They were delayed and stayed for several weeks to do additional training. We met at a dance hall. A perfectly respectable one, not one of those that people whisper about. My father didn't approve of dancing, though. I was raised as a strict Baptist. But I saw nothing wrong with it and spent my evenings there with some of my friends. That's where I first saw Matthew. And the long and the short of it, Grace, is that we fell in love during those weeks. But then the orders came through that it was time to go to Mexico. It was supposed to be a short campaign, and he would be back soon to marry me."

"I see no scandal in that, Margaret."

Margaret lowered her voice even more. "I discovered that I was pregnant on the same day that his unit posted his name on the casualty list."

"Oh, my dear!" Grace stopped and turned to the other woman, tears forming in her eyes. It was exactly that kind of compassion that had made it easy—as much as possible given the circumstances—to leave my infant son in her arms. She took those arms and wrapped them around Margaret, the secrets of women forming yet another bond in the tapestry of shared sisterhood. They stood like that for longer than a man ever would have, and it was one of those few times when I wished I had the ability to touch another human being instead of floating in this half existence. Tom had forbidden me the company of other women—or the company of anyone, for that matter—and I'd long ached for such companionship. I would have dearly loved to call Margaret and Grace my friends.

"Richard worked for my father," Margaret explained. "We were not wealthy, or I should say, we had a great deal of land but little cash. Richard was in charge of the migrant workers from Mexico who came through to work the fields. He always behaved as if he were far better than them, and I loathed him for it. He'd made many advances toward me ever since he'd worked there, and though I'd rebuffed him at every turn, I was now desperate for my child to be raised with a father and mother who were married. So I visited Richard in his office one night and let him . . . Well, you can imagine. And when I 'discovered' that I was with child, he married me. It's

what he'd always wanted, anyway. A way to possess our land. To possess me. And I handed it right to him just because I'd lost my head over a soldier."

"Oh, my poor Margaret." Grace's eyes had grown red with tears and radiated love for her companion.

Marriage has been such a beguiling institution throughout history. We imagine that it is about love and romance when it is often about power and secrecy. My own example of marrying for love had been disastrous, but I had only to look at my grandparents, my parents, Alan and Grace, George and Mary, to know that there was hope that it could be all that we dreamed it to be.

"You are too generous, dear Grace, to offer me your kindness when I'm so undeserving of it. And I hope you won't let my tale of misdoing change your mind about George and Mary."

"Of course not. Anyone who has seen them over the years knows that they belong together. But, Margaret, what does this have to do with your husband? I still fear that he will make a scene, since he was not informed ahead of time. I'd always been under the impression that he had bigger plans for Mary."

"Is there a bigger plan than love?"

Grace smiled. "Of course not. But you know what I mean. Wealth plans. You enjoy an enviable status out in Houston."

"Richard has had airs ever since I've known him. Money from the oil found on our land only heightened it. But regarding all this, leave him to me. I know for certain that he will not say anything publicly when George proposes to Mary. And if he tries to break it up in private, I will tell him the truth after all these years. That Mary is not his daughter and that he has no right to interfere."

"You've never told him in all this time?"

"Despite his flaws, I don't hate the man. I hope I didn't leave that impression. He took my father's fledgling business and turned it into an industry that has taken excellent care of us, as well as many others. And it was his idea to drill when that concept was merely in its infancy. He has

moments of tenderness that are near enough to each other than I can eas-
ily forget the things that anger me. And I wouldn't wish heartache on any
creature. Still, I've often wondered if he has figured it out."

Her soft face grew serious. "But Mary is my daughter, and I will ensure
her happiness with everything I have."

"You're treading dangerous waters."

"It wouldn't be my first time."

The women embraced, holding on to each other with more than mere
regard. It was as if they clung to the hope that love would win and they
would be its helpers.

But as they walked back toward the lobby for the appointed hour, I saw
something troubling pass over Margaret Carter's face.

Fear.

Chapter Sixteen

Kate's eyes were still closed, but she slowly became aware of her surroundings. The sounds were different—the seagulls less active, the waves more so. She must have fallen asleep, and given her state of grogginess, it had likely been for some time. Her back ached from the grit of the sand, and the glow of the sun through her eyelids seemed dimmer than it was earlier. A shadow blocked the light, and she awoke fully.

"Oh!" she said, startled. Then she realized who it was and brushed the dried sand from her arms, embarrassed. "Sean, you scared me."

He grinned. "Sorry about that. I didn't mean to. Wow—you were really out. You were even snoring."

Kate felt her cheeks flush, and it could not have been from the heat, because the sun was beginning to set behind North Island.

"Janie never told me I snore. And she wouldn't have hesitated."

"I know what you mean. My sisters are quick to point out all my faults. But I dish it right back to them. I'm kidding, though. Merely trying to get a rise out of you. But let's just say you *were* breathing in a deeply sonorous way."

"Deeply sonorous way? Oh my goodness, do you spend all your spare time reading the dictionary?"

She picked up a handful of sand and threw it at his feet. He was bending over her, his shirt, only halfway buttoned, fluttering in the light breeze. The hair on his chest was a shade lighter than that on his head.

Her stomach stirred from the Adam and Eve kind of feeling that arose from sitting alone in this evening paradise.

Sean sat down next to her. He picked up a seashell and turned it over in his hand. "No. I spend all my spare time thinking about the beautiful girl who came to work here a few weeks ago."

Kate inhaled a quick breath and held it. In that silence, she could almost hear the rapid beat of her heart.

From any other man, Kate might have thought it was a misguided line, but from Sean it held all the sincerity she would expect from him. But sincerity did not excuse its impropriety.

"You can't *say* things like that, Sean. You're getting married in a few weeks."

"Not anymore."

Blood rushed from her face while those two words repeated in her head as if in an echo. So it was true!

She straightened her back and held her hand up to her eyes to shield them from the descending sun that was at just the right height to seem blinding.

With his free hand, he reached out to her and placed a strand of loose hair behind her ear, sending a shudder through her body. Such a small gesture but laden with the intimacy of two people who'd grown close amid all that separated them. She shivered, despite the warm weather, and leaned in. Sean smelled of coffee and salt air, and it was intoxicating. He whispered, "I broke things off with Cynthia a little while ago."

He was so close, she could feel the warmth of his breath, and his words left her dizzy. It was too much to take in, and she didn't know how to respond.

Sean pulled back and wrapped a towel around her shoulders, perhaps misinterpreting her reaction as one of cold.

She attempted to rub some of the sand off, but as the water had evaporated, it left a fine layer of sea salt stuck to her skin. The rough texture reminded her of exactly where they were. And all they needed to talk about before she could revel in this turn of events.

"I saw you having, well, a heated discussion, but I didn't stay and watch. I figured that was private."

He pulled his knees to his chest and crossed his arms over them. He sighed. "A conversation like that should have been private, but she kept pushing and pushing for me to go to her parents' house for dinner. Even though I'd told her I couldn't make it tonight. She doesn't understand how seriously I take my job here, especially since everyone seems to think I'm leaving after the wedding to work for her father."

"And aren't you?"

"No. Some girl from San Francisco reminded me that Coronado is where I belong."

Her cheeks warmed at these words that she'd wanted to hear ever since she'd met him. But her concern battled the elation she desperately wanted to give in to.

"I don't want that on my conscience, Sean, if that's a better choice for you. You would be just across the bay if you worked for your father-in-law. It's not like you'd be up in Alaska or something."

"The bay might as well be five thousand miles away if I'm sitting at an office window every day looking out at that red turret and wishing I were here."

Kate wanted him to say *here with you*, but she knew he meant the hotel and the job that made him happy. And he knew that she was leaving soon. The things they might have said were unspoken, because no other path was possible. Her family needed her there. He needed to be here.

She looked down at a seagull feather that had drifted over. She picked it up and used its shaft to draw circles in the sand. "I know what you mean. I'll be all the way in San Francisco dreaming about gold-flecked beaches and palm trees and—"

She almost said *you*. And if he'd said it first, she might have. "And being at the Del."

"Yes. The Del." Sean lowered his voice again. They each seemed incapable of speaking in normal tones when the underlying sentiments remained mute.

"Kate," he said. He placed her hand in his and stared into her eyes. Her heart beat more rapidly, outpacing even the rapidity of the waves, and she had to steady her breathing before it overcame her.

"Sean . . . we can't."

"Kate. You've convinced me that this is where I'm supposed to be. I was *made* at the hotel, remember?" He laughed, and Kate smiled at the thought that was both charming and embarrassing. "How can I convince you that maybe you belong here, too?"

Kate felt her blood pulsing, racing, the kind of thing she'd only felt before in the darkness of a movie theater as an observer—hoping, imagining that it would happen to her one day. But now that it was so close, she was afraid and hoped he couldn't feel the quickening through her skin. "Here in Coronado?" *Or here with you?*

He didn't let go of her hand. And she didn't try to take it away.

"Here in Coronado, for starters," he said in a slow cadence. "I *see* you, Kate. I see the difference from the nervous girl I met on the ferry a few weeks ago. The salt air has gotten in and made itself a part of you. Do you know that we're mostly made of water? Sixty percent, I've read. That's why you feel so fully yourself here. I know because I feel the same way about it."

He spoke words that defined what she felt. That there was something almost *elemental* about being here. Vital, even. Here by this water. And by him.

She smiled. "We have water in San Francisco, too."

"But is it like this?" He released her hand and swept his arm across the horizon, where the sun was now a half circle behind the naval base.

"The Bay Area has its own kind of beauty," she said, defending her hometown. "The Golden Gate Bridge, the Palace of Fine Arts, Lombard Street." But as she listened to herself, she realized that she was merely rattling off the kinds of places one would find in a tourist brochure. She didn't mention the things that spoke to her heart, which, if she had to list them, were topped with family. Not with places.

San Francisco was one of the most enviable places in the world. But she'd never felt like she belonged there even though, until now, she'd never been anywhere else.

"But," she added, sensing that she'd let the conversation run away from her, "you're right. There is something about Coronado that I have never felt in San Francisco."

They both danced around the word that hovered between them like a thick, humid cloud: *you.* Kate could almost taste that word in the air, on her tongue. But she didn't say it. She didn't say that she wanted to stay here . . . with him. Wasn't two weeks too soon to speak such things? To feel them?

But then, it had happened instantaneously with her parents on the Golden Gate Bridge. They were never apart after that day. Was it so foolish to believe that a soul could recognize its match in so short a time?

Sean turned to her once again. The sun had disappeared completely, its green flash appearing as quickly as it left, leaving only its rays as a remembrance of its light. It cast even more beauty into the sky and across the water with its pinks and purples and oranges. Though he was sitting right in front of her, the details of Sean's face were silhouetted by the scene behind him. But the feeling of electricity that went through her as his body sat so close to hers told her more than his expressions would have.

"Kate," he said. He pulled her up to her feet and put his arms around her waist, drawing her close. His hands touched her back, which was bare in the swimsuit, and she shuddered at the unexpected intimacy of it. Rubbing against the salt, his fingers sent another shiver up to her shoulders.

"Are you cold?" he asked.

She nodded, not wanting to admit that he was the source of all these new sensations.

"Sean," she answered, stepping into his embrace.

He leaned down to her, and now he was close enough for her to see the determination in his jaw, the longing in his eyes.

This was so much better than anything that had ever played out on a screen.

In the distance, the soft whir of helicopter blades cut through the air, but she didn't hear it the way she might have otherwise. All her senses were concentrated in the anticipation of something she couldn't put words to.

Sean's hands moved up her back, and his lips brushed hers, slowly. An invitation. Her head went light, and her knees weakened. She lay back down on the sand, unable to stay upright. He followed, hands and lips never letting go. Still tender, but she felt his muscles tighten, and she knew he was holding back. Feeling the same fire that was rousing in her a thousand feelings she'd never known. She stopped breathing—stopped thinking.

She wanted to give herself entirely to the waves rushing through her, matching the rhythm of the ocean pounding behind her with increasing intensity.

The noise of the helicopter grew louder, and she might have pulled away to look, but then Sean's hands skimmed the sides of her hips, and nothing else existed except delirium.

Her lips parted as if they were completely independent of her head.

His breath quickened, and from head to toe, a rush of warmth engulfed her. It was something like drowning. Drowning, drowning, wanting to catch a breath. Wanting to die in this most glorious way.

At last she put her arms around his waist, just outside his loose-fitting shirt. A flimsy sheet that was her only defense against losing herself entirely. Because she was afraid that if she touched his skin, she would be finished, and there would be no question of returning home to her family.

This was home. *He* was home.

Sean pulled her up closer to him, and she felt them sinking into the ground, or maybe that was just what it seemed like. She sensed his fervor and became aware of the language between bodies, because she had no doubt that if they were anywhere more private than this, there would be a fluency between them that would be exquisite.

Her trance was interrupted when the smell of smoke—of fire— came from nowhere and encircled them. Sean pulled away first, and Kate looked up in horror as the helicopter raced toward them. Too low to make it to North Island. Panic flooded her body so quickly that she forgot everything else.

"Run!" he said, grabbing her hand and pulling her away from the encroaching surf.

The pilot was heading toward the water, and the aircraft banked right and left as he attempted an emergency landing. Kate felt herself pulled toward it like a vacuum. She screamed, and Sean gripped her arm with ferocity. She stumbled after him as they headed to the seawall that separated the ocean from the expensive houses.

"Stay here," he shouted. But she could only read his lips beneath the thunder of the helicopter.

The smoke was thick, and she breathed in knives as it shrouded the beach.

"Sean, stop!" she yelled into deafening noise as he raced toward the water. Her chest tightened, and she coughed until her lungs felt like they would explode. Her knees buckled as she crawled toward the water, but a wave overtook her, disorienting her from what was up or down. Her heart felt like it was going to shatter as she held her breath in the surge, and fear for Sean and for the pilot and for herself mingled as one terrible thought. When at last she pushed herself up and gasped for air, she turned around to look back at where Sean had run to.

The ocean water had put the fire out upon impact, but a new wall of impenetrable smoke took its place.

And Kate couldn't see either man emerge from its grip.

∼

1908

George's proposal to Mary could not have been more idyllic, though in looking back at all that happened afterward, the glossy memory is singed with the burn of anguish.

But sometimes I try to remember it just as it was, pristine as that Coronado day.

Mary came down to breakfast in the gold lace elevator. She stepped out looking even more resplendent than ever. It was not her fine dress, though, but the youthful blush in her cheeks as she saw her beloved. My son, sitting at the grand piano.

Margaret and Richard Carter followed, arm in arm, and her smile bore the dual looks of joy and sorrow. I watched Richard's jaw tense as they followed their daughter through the lobby. A small crowd began to gather on that vast Oriental rug, drawn in, perhaps, by the invisible gravity of love that speaks to hearts even when words are absent. Only four people knew what was about to happen—George, Margaret, Grace, and myself.

Then George began the first notes of the song he'd composed as a boy. Those once simplistic notes of E-D-C, pause, C-E-A-G had bloomed over the years into a melody that was rich in its complexity and magical in its soulfulness. It was the anthem of George and Mary, and he had been writing it since childhood, since before he realized that she was the other piece of him.

Mary had heard the song over the years, of course, for George had always played some version of it. But never as thoroughly as this one. It was complete. She glided over to him, and without stopping or missing a note, he slid to the far end of the bench to make room for her. She swept the fullness of her skirt to her side and sat next to him. Her perfectly set curls bounced as she joined him. Then she removed her gloves, starting at the fingertips, as any properly trained young lady might do. With her right hand, she played slow notes in the highest octaves that complemented the song in an even more glorious way. The ivory keys sounded like petite bells, laughing high above the richer ones below them. Not unlike George and Mary themselves. A marriage of seriousness and delight.

When the last notes were played, their fingers lingered, having the effect of the sounds fading into nothingness. They looked at each other, seemingly unaware that an even larger crowd had surrounded them. I could only see his face from where I was, and it was beaming. He leaned in beside her and whispered something into her ear. When he pulled back, her shoulders straightened, perhaps in surprise, and then she threw her arms around his neck.

I couldn't help but look over at Richard. His arms fell at his sides, and his fingers flexed back and forth, making fists and releasing them. Margaret's smile widened, but her eyes twitched, likely in the worry she'd expressed to Grace earlier.

As for Grace and Alan, they clasped one another, surely hoping for their son—my son—and his bride to share the lifelong happiness that they had discovered either by some divine blessing or fortunate happenstance.

Richard stepped toward them with an angry stride, but the hotel guests and staff who had gathered around the happy couple began applauding. It echoed throughout the cathedral-like hall, sounding like a roar.

He pulled back.

The manager of the hotel came from around the desk carrying a small black case in his hands.

"Step aside, step aside," he said. And the crowd moved as a whole, giving him just enough space to approach. "What a momentous occasion to

witness the young love of our own George Morgan and one of our favorite guests, Mary Carter."

You are right, if you are wondering when the announcement was even made, for George had spoken his words for only Mary to hear. But the meaning was clear, and no explanation was needed beyond the looks on their two faces.

Or Richard's. If you were watching closely, as I was.

As I've told you, I've practiced through the years the art of touching objects in the material world. The bedsheets were just the beginning, an accident, but my attempts were slowly, slowly becoming intentional enough that I believed if I'd had to intervene, I would have been quite capable of picking up one of the beautiful vases that sat atop the tables in the lobby and smashing it on that man's head.

The manager opened his case to reveal an accordionlike camera. Black with burgundy trim and a brass metal frame. The lens was shiny, either brand new or well cared for. But as I had not seen many of these, even among this moneyed set, I assumed the former.

This was confirmed when he had trouble getting the contraption to operate, but with the help of a nearby stranger, he managed to get it working.

"George, Mary, sit just like that. Look at me. Slide over just a bit to avoid the sunlight. That's perfect."

He took three photographs—a generous thing, since I understood film and the development of it to be costly.

The photograph was hung in a downstairs hallway some months later. I would pass it daily. Brushing my hand across its glass, aching to be able to feel its smooth surface. Triumphing when I was, at last, able to.

For it was the only record of their joy together, and the last time we ever saw Mary.

Chapter Seventeen

Kate spit sand from her mouth and wiped it away with her hand, only to leave a trail of more in its wake. She coughed out water and breathed out smoke, but these were nothing compared to her panic over Sean and the pilot.

The smoke began to dissipate, its plume ascending over the white-caps into the otherwise spotless sky. And at its base, she saw them at last. Tears flooded her eyes, washing away the grit of the sand, and giddiness pushed an inopportune laugh from her throat.

Sean was bent over as he struggled through the surf. The pilot's arms hung limp around his neck. Kate stood on now-steady legs and raced over to help him, and together they pulled the waterlogged man to safety.

Sean collapsed onto the beach, his arms stretched wide and limp, all energy spent on the task. Kate barely noticed the chill setting in as the sky continued to darken. His coughs sounded like choking, and Kate's brief respite from fear returned in full force, a strain of terror rushing back through her veins.

"Sean," she shouted. "Sean, you can do this!" She crawled behind him and laced her arms under his, pushing him upright. Pressing her body against his to keep him in that position, she slapped her palms against his back until, at last, he spit out gobs of water and flecks of seaweed.

But she couldn't let herself pause. The danger wasn't over.

Sirens wailed from both North Island and the area around the hotel, but they might not get there in time. Both men needed her. Sean, at least, was breathing, so Kate turned to the pilot. She wiped her arm across her forehead and began, though she had no idea what she was doing.

She rubbed his sides, then pumped his arms up and down, hoping that the movement might expel water or encourage breathing. But he didn't stir. She opened his mouth, hoping to force air to revive him. She blew into it, his cigarette-saturated breath overwhelming her. But she continued on. Never in her life had her lips touched a man's, and now in the course of minutes, she'd tasted the exhilaration of her first kiss and the desperation of a life draining beneath her.

Kate heard Sean begin to rouse from his stupor, but she could only see him in the periphery. He curled onto his left side, sand falling from his skin, and dragged himself over on drenched arms. Her relief was marred by the urgency of the pilot's needs, but down to her toes she was thrilled that Sean was alive and moving. He began to turn the pilot over and pounded on his back. And just as the first ambulance pulled up to the street, their patient lunged forward and spewed water and seaweed bits onto the ground.

Exhaustion washed over Kate, and Sean collapsed back into the sand.

"Hey, there. Are you all OK?"

More voices joined that one, and what seemed to be an army of men hurried toward the beach.

"I'm fine. It's them." This was as much as Kate could manage to say. She stood up on wobbly knees and looked around for the towel Sean had brought for her. She wrapped it around her arms. It was soaked from the last rush of water that came to shore, but she felt uncomfortable in the swimsuit, especially with so many men coming down from the street. Her teeth began to chatter, faster and faster until it seemed almost inhuman in its speed.

It quickly became difficult to determine who was official and who was a spectator. It seemed as if all of Coronado had descended on this deserted stretch as soon as they saw the helicopter having trouble. She and Sean hadn't even noticed. It had only been the two of them, distracted in the extravagance of their kiss even as the pilot was struggling to maneuver the aircraft to the unpopulated ocean. Kate swallowed guilt at the thought of it.

Maybe it was a sign that they'd been too carried away doing something that couldn't end well. There was little hope she could stay here, and how could they be together otherwise?

Soon she couldn't see Sean or the pilot at all. Not until they were both carried out on stretchers. She got as close as she could, her worry eclipsing how very cold she was.

"Sean!" she called out. But he probably couldn't hear her over all the voices. She hoped he didn't think she'd abandoned him.

Sean and the pilot were both awake, though, and for that she breathed a sigh of relief. The pilot had surely suffered some injuries after the impact in the water, and in regard to Sean, she heard the words *smoke inhalation*. Someone could survive that, couldn't they?

The men were taken away in separate cars. The one with the pilot sounded a red siren and turned left toward North Island. The car with Sean did not speed away, but it did turn right. Were they taking him to San Diego? If so, it only made sense. That's where Sean's family lived. And if he'd directed them that way, she hoped it meant two things.

That he was conscious enough to speak. And that the choice to take the ferry meant they weren't in a terrible hurry.

∼

Kate's morning schedule was light, since the cast and crew of *Some Like It Hot* were not due back until tomorrow. The hot shower last night had served to warm her after that chill, but it left a headache in its place that made it impossible to sleep.

But if she were being honest, the headache wasn't a side effect of last night's accident. It was worry over Sean.

Today was her day to call her family. It was tough to find the right time. They were at Uncle Mike's all day and almost too exhausted to speak in the evening. So she would try them this morning instead. Just when they'd be getting to the restaurant.

Kate turned her body toward the window and sat up slowly so that she didn't feel too dizzy. She got like that when she didn't sleep, unlike Janie, who shot up like a rooster at the first hint of dawn. The sun hadn't yet risen, though. In fact, last time she saw the sun, she was locked in the heady embrace of Sean's arms. The night that had descended since felt like it would never end.

She threw on clothes and gave a cursory brush to her hair and teeth before catching the bus to the hotel.

It was early enough to still be quiet. Her footsteps fell without sound as she walked on the plush carpet. She wondered about all the people sleeping behind those doors. People with the money to stay here, the time to vacation. She had no illusions that they lived perfect lives, but maybe on this day, maybe this morning, they would wake up to the euphoria that came with being a guest of this glorious place and with their cares as far away as wherever their homes were.

But for Kate, she'd bitten her nails down to stubs with concern about her family, her grandfather, and now Sean. Not to mention the pilot.

She took the staff elevator down to the level where the kitchen was just beginning to stir. This had always been her favorite time at Uncle Mike's. Before the customers came. When the only sounds that could be heard were the fishermen coming in from their runs and the splash of water as she rinsed the potatoes.

This kitchen was not as rustic as that. Nor did the smells leave her feeling like she lived inside a can of tuna.

Though she had not yet worked down here this early or had anything to do with the preparation of the food, she hoped they wouldn't turn down extra help. She simply could not stay back in the carriage house room in the dark with her thoughts.

As if they were waiting for her experienced hands, a barrel full of potatoes waited near the sink. The lights were on. Someone else was up and about, but for the moment, the kitchen was empty.

Kate put on a nearby apron and washed up to her elbows, not surprised that even the soap in the hotel kitchen was more luxurious than the ammonia-scented one that left her skin raw at Uncle Mike's. This one smelled like oranges and must have had some kind of lotion in it.

She scrubbed the potato skins, harder than necessary, and then peeled them. Her mother had often told her that she daydreamed too much while doing this task, and in fact her thoughts were often lost in whichever movie she'd last seen. She'd take the peeler and trace the asymmetrical curves of the tuber instead of attacking it with the vigor that Janie would, eager as she was to move on to the next job.

But today Kate was Janie, and the poor potatoes became unwitting victims of her frustration.

"What did they ever do to you?"

A voice echoed from the other side of the kitchen. Kate completed the stroke of the peeler and set it down on the cutting board. She turned. It was the manager, Andy Fletcher.

He was smiling, and it made her realize her own ridiculousness.

She let out a deep breath. "You're right. I shouldn't take things out on them."

He approached and washed his hands at the sink across from her.

"Having a bad day already? It's only a few hours old."

"I never slept, so it's still yesterday as far as I'm concerned."

"Sean?"

Kate met his eyes and then looked down at her apron pockets. She nodded. "How did you know?"

Andy picked up a towel and dried himself. "I've seen the way he looks at you. Ever since the first day you got here."

She watched his eyes for any concern that two employees of the hotel had even a hint of romance between them, but she saw only compassion.

Kate wished she could hide behind her veil of hair, but she'd put it up in a ponytail. Had her attraction to Sean been equally obvious? If other people were sensing something between them, maybe there was truth in it. But she would hate for her first foray into a romance to be so publicly known or to get either of them in trouble.

She managed to look up at him with eyes she hoped seemed nonchalant, but she couldn't keep the quaver out of her voice.

"How—how is he?"

Andy folded his arms and leaned against the counter. "He'll be fine, Kate. His mother called about an hour ago from the hospital in San Diego. He suffered from a lot of smoke inhalation, so they're going to keep him for a few days. But he expects to be back by next week."

That was good news. Great news! But by the time he returned, she would have only one week left.

Still, she smiled. "He can't stay away from the hotel for very long, can he?"

"From the hotel? Or certain people *at* the hotel?"

Andy was playing with her now, though it made her uncomfortable to be the subject of the ribbing. She looked away so he couldn't see the hope in her eyes.

"Although," he added, "I don't think Cynthia is going down without a fight."

Kate looked up sharply. "What do you mean?"

Andy pursed his lips as though he were making a decision. "I mean that when I spoke to Sean's mother, Cynthia was there as well."

"In the hospital room?" Kate brushed her hand across the counter and knocked a knife onto the floor. She picked it up and hoped Andy didn't see her hand shaking.

"Yes. Apparently she came right over when she got the call."

Kate felt like the potato peeler had just pulled back the thick skin she'd grown around herself and exposed the very tender feelings she was trying to protect.

Andy unfolded his arms, and an uncomfortable silence descended in the already quiet kitchen. He didn't come over and give her a hug and tell her that everything would be all right. Because everything wouldn't be. Sean would be moved by Cynthia's devotion and realize that she would be a perfect wife, despite their recent disagreements. And the few days that would remain upon his return would remind both him and Kate that this had been a fleeting flirtation, a pause on the lives they lived and the people who had claims on them.

What had she been thinking?

Again, the guilt of being lost in that kiss—even as the helicopter pilot was in such peril—nauseated her.

Kate missed her family. She wanted to run back to the routine of familiarity that promised no surprises. Or heartbreak. It was not the most exciting life, but helicopters didn't crash in Fisherman's Wharf. The worst calamity was the pickpockets who loitered.

She looked up at the clock above the main sink. It was still early enough to call her parents before the morning ran away from them.

Andy walked to the end of the kitchen to start taking inventory of the pantry, so Kate took the chance to leave and slip into Sean's office.

The door closed without a sound, and Kate marveled that even the employee wing was so well cared for. She looked behind her as if she might be caught, although it was written into her contract that she could make this call in this office once a week. On the previous times, Sean had stepped out to give her privacy, though she didn't feel the need to keep anything from him. So to sit in here alone was not unfamiliar.

Except for the fact that Sean was not waiting on the other side of the door. He was not there to ask her how her grandfather was doing or how her family was holding up in her absence. Inquiring about people he'd never met but suggesting that because they were important to her, they were important to him. Instead, he was lying in a cold hospital room—or so she imagined it to be—with his doting fiancée at his side.

Kate couldn't imagine that this incident would do anything but make Sean reevaluate things—between them, as well as staying on at Coronado. Maybe he'd even see it as a sign from fate.

The phone rang on the other end.

"Hello?"

"Janie?"

"Kate! Why are you calling so early?"

Because I can't sleep. Because the man I love is in the hospital. Because calling home is about the only thing that will keep me sane right now.

Kate shrugged even though her sister couldn't see the gesture. "I didn't want to interrupt once customers came in."

"Hold on. Do you want to talk to Mom or Dad?"

"In a minute. I'd like to talk to you, too. Mom always gives me the *we miss you* line, and Dad blows a quick kiss into the phone. But I figured you'd give me the straight scoop on things."

"I don't think you want the straight scoop." Janie's voice was terse.

Kate's heart stopped.

"What do you mean? Has something else happened?"

"Something else? You mean something *besides* you running away, scaring everybody, and taking our grandmother's heirloom ring with you?"

It was becoming such a tired conversation. Kate rubbed her eyes, emotions threatening to unsteady her voice. She hadn't yet told any of them that Mary Carter wore the ring first. She wanted to know the complete story first rather than to relay mere snippets.

"I don't want this bitterness between us, Janie. Please. We may not agree—I'll have to be OK with that. But I hope you can trust that I'm here for good reasons. Haven't you ever been curious about the pieces of his past he's kept hidden?"

She didn't try to explain that Granddad had also encouraged her to come pursue her dream of working in movies. Only a few weeks ago, such a thought was an unimaginable luxury. But now—now that she was so close, Kate realized the *necessity* of discovering what she was meant to do in the world. It was as vital as air, as elemental as her draw to the water. And without it, suffocation. She hoped her sister and her parents might come to see her way of thinking—for their sakes as well as her own.

"Have you found the beautiful stranger yet?" It was an accusation from Janie. Not a question.

Kate sighed. How to explain that every time she got closer to an answer, more mysteries appeared? The beautiful stranger was the ghost. Kate Morgan. But this was not a problem on a school quiz. Fill in the blank with the correct word. She needed to know what lay beneath it—the whos, the whys, the whats. And there were things that had happened that were beyond her control—Mrs. Linden's absence. The helicopter crash.

Janie must have covered the mouthpiece with her hand, because it sounded like she was talking in a cave.

"You left to help *you*."

It felt like a slap. Janie could get down to the core of something, and there was truth in it.

Kate sighed. She'd always heard that siblings who fought in childhood would become the best of friends later on. This had not yet proven true between her sister and her. Though she hoped someday that might change.

She decided against defending herself. Janie might never understand her reasons, and she could see why her sister was upset. It was an impasse they couldn't cross for now. "Tell me about what's been going on with you, Janie. We've never gone three days without seeing each other, let alone three weeks."

The silence on the end led Kate to believe her sister had hung up. But just as she was going to do the same, Janie spoke.

"Don't be mad, Kate."

Mad? About what?

"Dimitri and I have been out a few times together." Janie's voice softened at this confession.

Kate let out a breath.

Dimitri and Janie. It was about time.

Janie was a much better partner for him. Smart and hardworking and so very content with her life as it was. Not tinged by the restlessness that had gripped Kate for as long as she could remember. And if Dimitri's parents could ever accept that Janie wasn't Greek, they would not be able to find a more ideal girl for their son to date.

An unexpected feeling of warmth washed over Kate. How good this would be for her sister! She hoped it was something more than a flirtation—that there could actually be a future for them. But the simplicity of their being together shone light on her own complications with love at the moment.

"Tell me more," Kate whispered.

"He came in looking for you a few weeks ago at closing time, so I told him to sit down and got him some fries and explained what you'd done."

"And what did he say?"

Janie was quiet at first. "His exact words were 'Good for her.'"

Yes! That was the Dimitri she knew.

"He was always so understanding."

"He understands a lot of things, actually. He came in the next night and the next, and we kept talking, and, well, I think it could lead somewhere." Janie's tone had changed to one that sounded like chatter among girlfriends. Was there hope that the sisters' recent challenges could return to something more congenial? Maybe the lightness of new love would set a new course for them.

"I'm happy for you, Janie. Really happy."

"You are?"

"Yes. You two could be perfect together."

Janie's smile on the other end didn't need to be seen to be understood. The whole tone of her voice softened. "I think we could, too. Hey, I'm sorry for being hard on you. Maybe it's because I'm a little jealous."

Kate leaned forward, her ponytail falling into her eyes. She pushed it back. "You're jealous of me? You've always scoffed at the idea of coming down south."

"No, I'm not jealous of you for being in San Diego. You're right—I don't really have any interest in going there. But if I'm honest . . ." She took a breath before continuing. "I admire the leap you took to follow your dreams. Dimitri helped me see that, though sometimes I'm still mad. You're doing what you set out to do. And I'm not sure I even *know* what I want to do. Until you left, I assumed we'd always just work at Uncle Mike's, and I was fine with that. But you and Dimitri have both made me realize I can consider other things."

"You know Dimitri is going to be building a small hotel. Can you see yourself helping him to run it?"

"I said that we're spending time together, Kate. Not that we're getting married." She hesitated and then added. "But it has crossed my mind, yes."

Kate grinned at the answer. She didn't speak, though, as she counted the seconds on her stopwatch, racing toward the end of her fifteen minutes. It was too fast. She wanted to be able to talk to her sister like this forever. To listen to Janie gush about these new feelings. To tell her about Sean. Even to ask for her advice.

But her time was almost up.

"Janie, I have to go. But please know that I think this is really good news, you and Dimitri. I'm really happy for you. And I—I would like to tell you about what has been going on down here, too. Can I call you this evening from the pay phone?"

"I won't be here later. Dimitri is taking me to a movie. *Vertigo*. Maybe tomorrow?"

Funny, ever since being here, Kate hadn't thought about going to a movie at all. She was *living* in one. On the set. And off.

"OK. Have fun. Give my love to Mom and Dad. But, Janie—"

"Yes?"

"How is Granddad?"

She heard the clatter of pots in the background and for half a second feared there was something Janie wasn't telling her. But her tone said otherwise.

"He's home. We're taking turns spending the night with him. He's doing well physically. But his rantings are getting more frequent. More urgent. It's not just the beautiful stranger stuff. Or the A-A-A. He's repeating something else, Kate. Over and over and over. *'Save her. Save her.'*"

Save her.

∽

1908

The messages of congratulations from strangers who had gathered lasted for nearly an hour. No doubt the vacationers were delighted to have experienced this romantic gesture. In their circles, proposals of marriage were more often done privately in parlors. First the father was approached. Then the girl. The mother, of course, had little to say in the matter.

So to have seen George's love for Mary played out through the piano music and then to witness his question bucked all tradition. And I applauded my son for being so modern.

With the exception of one, the faces reflected the jubilance of my son and his bride-to-be.

The one, of course, was Richard Carter. Even when the much-celebrated L. Frank Baum and his wife offered their happiest wishes to the couple, he was unmoved. Had God himself descended from the heavens, I believe Richard would have stood there in statuelike anger and ignored even that blessing.

For the first time since I saw my husband, Tom, walking toward me on the steps of the hotel all those years ago, a sense of dread consumed me, and it was as close to hell as anything I'd experienced. A feeling of abject helplessness.

Poor Margaret was right about only one thing: Richard was not going to make a scene in public. But it was not going to be the end of it.

As the crowd dissipated, Mary and George sat on the piano bench together. Her pale-yellow dress contrasted with the red embroidery on the seat. She held out her left hand, and it was only then that I could get close enough to see the ring.

The ring . . . Dared I hope that it was . . . ?

It was!

It was the ring I'd entrusted to Alan and Grace all those years ago in the blue velvet bag. One of the few mementos I'd kept when I left the Midwest to escape Tom. It had been my grandmother's wedding ring, the one she'd worn ever since my grandparents married in their home country of England.

I don't know if it was worth a great deal of money. My grandfather was not born a wealthy man. He was in service—a stableman to an earl in Cornwall—and my grandmother a kitchen maid. But he saved enough for that ring and for two passages to America to better their station in life. It was in Iowa that his ancestral roots of farming bloomed in him—evidenced by our surname—and he became a corn farmer of some repute.

The jewels in it were mere chips—possibly cast-offs of much larger pieces for much wealthier people. A diamond on top of a lacy silver sphere with square sapphires on either side. It was unique, to be sure, and meant so much more to me than its modest worth in cash. But it was valuable enough, I'd hoped, for Alan and Grace to buy some meals for George in his youth. So the surprise that they had preserved it for this kind of day rendered me delirious with gratitude.

To see the ring placed on the delicate hand of a girl as lovely as Mary redeemed all the years of struggle and sacrifice it had seen in its years in my family.

After some time had been spent between George and Mary whispering and laughing with one another, Richard approached them. His hands rested in his suit pockets, and I could imagine that they were balled into fists that would have been unseemly in this elegant company.

"Mary," he intoned. "I have made reservations for lunch at Le Soleil. We must be going."

Mary sprang to her feet. "Oh, Papa. You know I've always wanted to go there." She turned to George, who'd stood up after closing the lid over the piano keys. "It's supposed to be a delightful place that overlooks Point Loma."

"Not him," insisted Richard. "Just you. You and me."

The girl looked at her fiancé and then around the lobby, probably for her mother. "But it's in San Diego across the ferry. We'll surely be gone the rest of the day and, well, considering the occasion, shouldn't we go as a family?"

Richard's voice softened, but I observed a steely intent in his eyes.

"Shouldn't a father be able to take his daughter out for a nice luncheon upon hearing the news that she is to be taken from him?"

Mary laughed, no doubt covering up her embarrassment. "Of course. I didn't mean to be inconsiderate of your feelings. May I run upstairs and get my shawl? The breeze is swaying even the tallest of the palm trees today, and it will be cold on the ferry."

"We're leaving now."

Richard turned his back and started striding toward the main door. Mary and George exchanged confused glances. My son removed the suit jacket he was wearing and put it over her shoulders, grazing her cheek with his lips. He whispered something to her that I could not hear. She nodded and then followed her father.

Mary never returned to the Hotel del Coronado, and since then its shimmering elegance has borne a tarnish that still saddens my ill-fated heart.

Chapter Eighteen

Granddad's words—*Save her. Save her*—haunted Kate's thoughts night after night with an urgency that wouldn't dim with the knowledge that whomever she was had needed saving decades ago. Mary Carter and Kate Morgan were the only possibilities she could think of. Unless she was wrong altogether and this rant was just a product of Granddad's failing mind. She wished Janie was adept at reading his eyes the way Kate was—she could always tell when his declarations had merit and when they were delusions. But she guessed the former.

Still, what could she do with that information? The most she'd been able to find out about the ghost was that she was an unfortunate woman who'd committed suicide on the steps of the hotel in the last century and that she was sometimes seen in white wandering the halls. But what did she have to do with Granddad? And Mary Carter was a dead end until Mrs. Linden returned and could tell her more.

Until then, Kate had to sit on her hands and practice the art of patience. There was little time left here. The family from Mexico would be arriving soon to reclaim their carriage house rental—nanny and all. The movie was about to finish filming and return to Hollywood. With the exception of kindly Jack Lemmon, no one from the set had even noticed her, let alone offered her a job that could let her follow them back.

And even if they had, Kate was no longer sure what exactly it was she wanted to do. It had been fun, and she would never sit in a movie theater again and wonder what it was like to be there. But Kate realized it was Coronado she loved. Sean she loved. Maybe the rest was just some providential way to have led her to the place that made her feel so completely herself.

And though Coronado would remain—those beautiful beaches, that cloudless sky—Sean's love was in question, and even that required forbearance until he was back from the hospital.

In the meantime, she'd use these waning days to enjoy the outdoors when she wasn't working. Because next week, she'd be off to San Francisco. Maybe for good. With nowhere to live and no job once the set closed down, she could not stay in this enchanted place.

When she'd arrived four weeks ago, Kate had nearly suffocated under the weight of inferiority as she compared herself—her clothes, her schooling, her worldliness (or lack thereof)—to the stunning women who paraded around the palm tree–lined streets of Coronado. Wide-brimmed hats, oversize sunglasses, and pointy bras that made their breasts look like horizontal mountain peaks. And there she was, a runaway of sorts, a thief in the eyes of her sister. Payback coming in the form of the loss of her suitcase at the hands of Maisy in the Los Angeles train station. Borrowed clothes from Sean's sisters and nothing to call her own except her undergarments and some items bought on sale.

It wasn't that San Francisco was some kind of cow town in comparison. Nor was Coronado akin to the runways of Paris. But the role of the waitress from Fisherman's Wharf recast as assistant on a real-life movie set had seemed all too impossible to believe. And yet, here it was.

Now, though, with just one week to go, she felt she belonged here as much as if she'd been conceived in the rooms of the hotel, as Sean had. Excellent clothes and money to vacation in style were only half the battle—and maybe not the battle at all.

It was like Sean had told her—human bodies were made up of a majority of water. And the endless ocean on all sides, the rolling waves that mimicked the rocking people knew so well as infants, gave a sense of oneness with this place that had changed her forever.

And love—yes, she was willing to call it that—even a love that had been borrowed, awakened something in Kate that made her crave it again. Not to settle for the safe arrangement with a friend like Dimitri. But the kind that roused the blood in her veins and electrified her every thought.

Sean, recuperating in the arms of his fiancée, would soon be settled across the bay, and if that were what he wanted, then Kate had to accept it and would not interfere. But the way he'd made her feel created a picture of what love and passion looked like, felt like, and it had changed her. Made her unwilling to settle for less. But how to find that again?

These musings, which had begun to nip at her with each waking moment, were now gnawing their way through the remnants of her dreams and convincing her to do the proper thing and return to her family and the job she'd be in until she was an old lady.

But at least she would return—she hoped—with this gift for Granddad and her family. Answers. History. Mrs. Linden had returned from her daughter's house, and they were due to meet this afternoon. Kate looked outside her window, which had a slivered view of the beach if she opened it and looked far to the right.

On any given day, the summertime vacationers spread across the wide expanse of the beach from the Hotel del Coronado to North Island. Sandcastles dotted the landscape, some at the hands of gifted artists whose work could rival Michelangelo. Others were pedestrian— drippy castles, as Kate liked to call them—the result of soaking sand in a bucket and sprinkling it into drooping little towers.

Sean had told Kate a couple of weeks ago about the annual sand art festival that would take place shortly after she left. He described the masterpieces that could be seen. Castles so intricate in their detail that you half expected miniature people to walk out any moment. Mermaids with scales on their tails and fine strands of hair on their heads. Dragons that seemed to breathe real fire, especially when the mica glistened in the sun.

How she wished she could stay to see those marvels, to go to the famed costume ball. But like them, her stay here was temporary. Sometimes such beauty wasn't meant to last for long.

When she thought of Sean, she could not help but think of Cynthia by his bedside. Consoling him, caring for him, convincing him that he belonged in a situation that was more predictable than a life spent on this shore. Hadn't the crash of a helicopter proven the necessity of playing it safe?

Despite the timeline that Andy had proffered, Sean had not yet come back to work, and no news had been passed along. Kate couldn't help but feel responsible—if she hadn't strayed from the party, if she hadn't fallen asleep, if Sean hadn't felt he had to come find her, he would be here. He'd be in the kitchen preparing for today's return of the cast and crew.

But then she thought back to the pilot. If things had not transpired just as they had, he might be dead now, because Sean wouldn't have been there to rescue him.

No one would want that.

Kate slipped on some white capris and a blue shirt, the last of her clean clothes. She should have done laundry during these few days before it got busy again, but instead she'd spent the time after work walking around Coronado. Memorizing every palm branch and eucalyptus tree and flower before time ran out and she returned to city life.

But today would be different. The cast and crew were returning to the set, and she'd have one last chance to enjoy that particular experience.

When she arrived downstairs, Kate heard Miss Monroe's laughter before she saw her.

The throngs of people who normally fanned across the beach had all gathered on the lawn in clusters of excitable chaos. Surely the actress was somewhere in the middle, and not for the first time Kate reflected that stardom might not be the glamorous existence she and millions of girls around the country imagined it to be.

But Miss Monroe was a professional. Kate could see the top of her shiny coiffed hair bobbing over all the other heads. At one point, she stuck out her arms, autographing a photograph up in the air. Kate wondered how the pen could work against gravity.

The singsong voice spoke. "That's all. Thank you, everyone. You're so very darling. But I must be going."

Kate glanced at her watch. It was only nine in the morning. In her brief experience, she'd never seen Miss Monroe come downstairs before eleven, despite the director's best efforts. Why hadn't she been asked to bring up breakfast like all the other days?

Billy Wilder walked over and held his arm up as if he were Moses with a staff. And just like the old story, the crowd parted, and Miss Monroe walked—*sashayed*—through them like a queen. She wore another thin caftan, and underneath it Kate could see her hourglass shape hugged by a pink polka-dot bikini.

Miss Monroe breezed by Kate and flashed her a huge heart-shaped smile, but Kate had the distinct sense that it was meant as it would be for any other fan. She saw no sense of recognition for the girl who brought her tray every morning or cleared out the evidence of long nights of drinking.

Did she even remember giving Kate all those photographs and envelopes, conspiring together to entice residents of A Avenue to come forward with information about George Morgan?

A sense of emptiness consumed Kate. Had their conversations, so intimate at the time, held little meaning to Miss Monroe? It reminded Kate that everything here was an illusion—the lights that replicated the sun, the cosmetics that concealed the flaws, the maneuvering that replaced true relationships.

Marilyn Monroe had made a lasting impression on Kate. And Kate's impression, if any, had been fleeting—just one of many.

The star turned and waved a manicured hand to the crowd as an adoring cheer rose. She took the brick path back to the employee entrance of the hotel—the one where Kate had first met Jack Lemmon.

Kate had never seen her go that way before, but maybe she was already weary of the public. Kate waited a minute to give her a head start and then followed, turning to the left, where the kitchen was.

Andy was stirring a wooden spoon in a large pot. He added some salt and then walked over to the sink.

"Going to be a busy week, Kate Morgan," he said.

"They're back. I wonder what scenes they shot while they were up there?"

"I heard it was gangster stuff."

"Gangster stuff?" There had been no sign of that storyline here at the hotel.

"Yeah." He looked left and right as if he held state secrets. "I heard a little bit about it from one of the cameramen. I found him a Russian vodka he had a weakness for, and after that, he told all. The characters played by Jack Lemmon and Tony Curtis are borrowing a friend's car from a public garage in Chicago. They accidentally witness the Saint Valentine's Day Massacre, and in an attempt to escape and hide from the perpetrators, they dress as dames in an all-girls' band and hightail it to Florida."

"Florida? Not California?"

"Nah. The Hotel Del is subbing for the Seminole Ritz."

"How disappointing! I almost feel a little betrayed on behalf of Coronado."

Was anything true in the movies? It was even being filmed in black and white to evoke the era of the 1920s, not the color that represented a truer picture.

Andy shrugged. "Maybe there's a reason it has to be Florida. I don't know. But it's awfully easier to come down here from Hollywood than to pack up and shoot on the other side of the country."

"I guess you're right."

"Anyway," Andy continued. His eyes lit up, and his hands moved faster as he washed the dishes. "I heard there's a real slammer of a scene. They have a meeting of gangsters, and they roll in a huge birthday cake. A mobster pops out with a tommy gun and shoots up everyone in the room."

Leave it to a guy to get worked up about a scene like that.

It sounded completely opposite to the serenity of the beach scenes here and the antics of Tony Curtis and Jack Lemmon dressing up in women's clothes. Could that really be the same movie? Maybe in the month here, she'd learned less about moviemaking than she'd thought.

"Well," she answered, "I guess we'll just have to wait until it's released to see how that all comes together."

"Yeah. You going to be around? I think it's coming to theaters in the spring."

Kate folded her arms and shook her head. "No. I'm going home next week."

"Next week? Does Sean know?"

She tightened her arms around herself at the mention of his name and knew that Andy understood more than he let on.

"Of course. He's my boss. I was only ever here temporarily. I have to get back to my family. And besides, the filming will be done, and he won't need the extra help anymore."

Andy set a plate down on the kitchen counter. "That's not what I meant."

She played dumb. "What are you talking about?"

"Kate. I think you and Sean are due for a long talk. Did you know he called this morning?"

Her heart sped up. "He did?" *Is he coming home soon?* She wanted to ask but kept up the useless pretense.

"Yes. With two instructions. One: to tell me he'll be back at work tomorrow. And two: to release the Crown Room to Billy Wilder for the cast party. There will be no wedding there next week."

~

Kate had been anticipating Mrs. Linden's return for days, but now that Andy had dropped this bomb on her, she couldn't think of anything else.

He'd said there would be no wedding at the hotel next week. Did that mean it was canceled altogether? Or just that they'd made another plan? Or merely given way to the cast party that Billy Wilder wanted? Janie would probably say, "You're such a ninny, Kate. Of course it means the wedding is canceled."

And she'd probably be right. But Kate didn't dare hope for more. Not until she could talk to Sean and be convinced.

She walked up to Margaret's Garden of Eden. It still felt like a paradise within the paradise of this island, and even since last time, the jasmine around the doorframe had bloomed. It had a Hansel-and-Gretel feel to it, except with flowers instead of candy and a dear old woman inside instead of a greedy witch.

Kate took a deep breath. She hoped this visit would be the end of the road as far as the Granddad George part of this adventure went. Where the answers didn't produce more discoveries to explore and just told the end of the story. Whatever that was.

She knocked. And waited. She could hear someone inside and worried for a moment that Mrs. Linden was hurt. But just as she put her hand on the knob, the door opened. Mrs. Linden was there, smiling and rosy cheeked.

"Kate, my dear," she said. "You're right on time. Come in. I've invited someone to join us. Someone you need to meet."

~

1911

George has a new girl. He brought her in to the hotel today, and their ease with each other suggested they had already been friends for some time. She doesn't have Mary Carter's natural beauty, but then, I am biased, as I knew sweet Mary ever since she was a young child, and I grew an affinity toward her that nearly matched what I felt for my son. Perhaps because I had a mother's instinct that she would be the one he chose. And he did. But then she was gone.

This girl's name is Kitty. But she doesn't resemble a cat. Not even a little. Her eyes are round and full of trust and innocence. Her hair is dark red— almost brown, until the light shines and its crimson shades reveal themselves. She is pretty in the most conventional sense—that is to say that her features are simple, symmetrical, universal. But I see something in my son's eyes that is new. I cannot think of a word for it, but it gives me a feeling of peace.

And it is a relief to see that his long-dormant spark is returning. And that he is returning at all. He has been away from the hotel for far too long. Three years by his calendar.

If George is happy, I am happy. He is all that matters to me in this limbo.

I look at my son and study him. I once had the joy of seeing him nearly every day when he worked here at the hotel. But today he doesn't touch the piano. He doesn't even look at it. He's changed from the optimistic young man he was back then to a fully grown adult.

Loss can do that to a person.

Kitty is probably a nickname held over from childhood. Back in Iowa, I'd known a fellow named Dab. He had a younger brother who hadn't been able to say his name properly when he was first learning to talk. So Thaddeus Richter became Dab, and the name stuck. Or maybe Kitty is George's nickname for her. I almost hope that it is—it would indicate an affection that I dearly wanted to return into his life.

Time will tell. Time. I have nothing, but I have that in abundance.

Chapter Nineteen

Kate entered Mrs. Linden's house, not knowing what to expect or who was there to see her.

If the outside of the Garden of Eden was lush and even overgrown, the inside was its twin. The entryway had wooden floors that creaked under her footstep, and it was adorned with a lone waist-high bookshelf on the only wall that had space for it. From there, three hallways extended to the rest of the house. To the immediate right, a parlor. Beyond that, she saw a dining room, and beyond that, the kitchen. She assumed the one to the left led to the bedrooms.

Every wall was covered in paper, each room with a distinct floral print. The dining room had a long mahogany table that looked like it could seat twelve. Around and even above it on the ceiling was red paper with huge white magnolias. The kitchen appeared to be yellow with painted green vines. From somewhere she could hear the scratchy sound of opera on a Victrola.

Mrs. Linden, with her long, dated dress, looked exactly right in this place that seemed frozen in a period from decades ago. It was part of her charm. A benevolent Miss Havisham.

"Let's sit in here, dearest. Ruth is making some tea and will join us in the parlor."

Mrs. Linden put her arm through Kate's with no explanation as to who Ruth was. She smelled like violets and mothballs, and it made Kate miss her own grandmother. Grandma Kitty had stored her wools in a cedar closet with mothballs, and Kate had always associated the smell with it. As a child, she would wrinkle her nose at the smell, but now it only brought a melancholy wave of nostalgia.

The parlor was covered in paper, walls and ceiling. This one was dusty pink with white and yellow daisies. An organ was placed in the corner, covered in a green velvet overlay, completely free of dust. On the opposite end of the room, a leaded-glass window in the shape of a diamond cast rectangular rainbows across the floor. The rainbows fluttered as she and Mrs. Linden crossed the room.

Kate had never entered into any other homes of the residents of Coronado, but she imagined that this unusual place was unique among them. If Kate lived here, she would paint everything white and let the natural colors of the outside bring their beauty in.

At Mrs. Linden's invitation, Kate sank into a large cushioned sofa, covered in burgundy chintz.

"That was my mother's Duncan Phyfe," the old woman offered. "My sister was nearly born on that sofa, but my father returned home just in time to carry her to the bedroom."

Kate brushed her hands along it. Old furniture, old houses, old people had histories that were so difficult to imagine. That was the tragedy of Granddad George's decline. She hadn't appreciated the stories he might have been able to tell back when he could still tell them. And now that she wanted—*needed*—to know more, he had little to say. Just confusing fragments. She hoped that today, and in this final week, she could piece those bits together and discover his story. Before he was lost to them forever.

"Ah, here comes Ruth now."

Kate stood. "May I take that tray from you?" Always the waitress.

"No, dear. I'll just set it on the table."

Ruth looked to be about the same age as Mrs. Linden, but then, once time had turned hair white and wrinkled the skin, how could one tell the exact number of its passage? The two older women could be a day apart. Or a decade.

What Kate marveled at, though, was that both were older than her grandparents. They'd outlived Grandma Kitty's body and Granddad George's mind. Was it the salt air that Sean was so wild about? The casual life of days spent in the bliss of Coronado? Kate's grandparents had worked hard—backbreakingly hard—their whole lives. What a difference it might have made if they were able to pass their days in a place like this. They might both still be here, whole and happy.

The one difference in Ruth was that she did not seem to favor Mrs. Linden's penchant for dressing and living in the past. Her attire was much more up-to-date, and if anything a bit *too* youthful for her age. She had a thin waist that Vivien Leigh might have envied. A round-collared blouse in white, a belt in orange leather, and then a billowing, pleated green skirt with blue stripes. Chic.

But Kate knew these observations were mere distractions as she waited for these women to tell her what she most wanted to know. She folded her hands together and pressed them into her knees so she wouldn't fidget.

Both sat in chairs opposite the sofa, and after serving up peppermint tea and white sugar cubes, Mrs. Linden started.

"I'm sorry, Kate, that I had to leave just as you were most eager to hear this story, but I believe it is better this way. I had the idea that you might want to speak with Ruth as well, and this gave me time to write to her and invite her to join us."

Ruth smiled. "Let's take her out of her misery, Margaret." She turned toward Kate. "My name is Ruth Goldberg, and I lived next door to Grace and Alan."

Kate's face must have shown her confusion. She did not recognize these names.

Ruth and Margaret looked at each other, and then Ruth continued. "Grace and Alan Morgan. George's parents."

Kate sat up straight, as much as it was possible to in this sinkhole of cushions. Her great-grandparents? Granddad had never mentioned them. Or maybe he had and she'd been too full of the self-absorption of childhood to remember. But she didn't think so.

"Kate," said Mrs. Linden softly, as if she were approaching a scared puppy. "Is it unreasonable of us to assume that you don't know what we're talking about?"

Kate smiled and sank back into the sofa. "I'm sorry. I know so little—maybe even less than I assumed. Now that I hear them, I feel silly to not know these names."

Ruth chimed in. "Please don't be embarrassed. Every family is different. Some are so known to each other that it's smothering. And others prefer to leave the past in the past."

That sentence could almost describe the difference in the appearances of Margaret and Ruth.

She continued. "Let me start from the beginning, then. Grace and Alan Morgan lived in a cottage on A Avenue ever since it was first built. A sweet place. Light-green stucco. A white picket fence. Alan sold pens and advertising doodads to businesses, and Grace kept house. She used to tat the most beautiful lace until her hands became too arthritic. Then she made do with crochet, though I know it pained her almost as much."

Mrs. Linden interjected. "Let's stick to the point, though, Ruth. We don't know how much time Kate has to give us today. And you know that we old ladies could prattle on for hours."

"Oh, please," insisted Kate. "I only had a morning shift. I have all day for this." She ached for these tiny details. Pearls in the vast ocean of all that she didn't know about her family's history.

Ruth smiled. "She's right, though. Let me tell you the important things, and then you may ask me anything else. And I'll just hope I can remember the answers!"

Mrs. Linden topped off their teacups with more of the steaming liquid while her friend spoke.

"I moved in next to Grace and Alan right after I was widowed. Their son, George, was only two years old. And he was the most beguiling child I'd ever seen. Like Grace, I had miscarried several children, so George was the apple of our eyes. And when I learned how he had come into their lives, I found myself wishing that a guardian angel would have walked up to my door just like that!"

Kate sipped at her tea, her lips burning. "I don't understand. What do you mean, how he had come into their lives?"

"Why, Kate Morgan, of course. A young woman of great misfortune. She found Grace and Alan in a county register. She wanted her son to share her surname, but she could not take care of him."

"Why not?" Kate's heart was racing, but she hoped she'd kept her voice steady. Ruth had to be speaking about the hotel's ghost. There could not be that much commonality of names. How did the woman who haunted the hotel figure into this story?

"Mrs. Morgan's husband was quite abusive. At least, that's what she shared with Grace and Alan. It was imperative to her that they know her son wasn't a bastard. That he was conceived in a marriage, although it was not a happy one. She was afraid that her husband would take the child, and she believed she had to prevent that at all costs."

Kate jumped in. "This might be an odd thing to ask, but is she the same Kate Morgan who is supposed to haunt the Hotel del Coronado?"

It was not quite as coincidental as she'd thought four weeks ago. If she were to believe Ruth—and why would she not?—then this Kate Morgan was her own blood-related great-grandmother. The pieces were all coming together but had not yet formed a picture that she could understand.

"Indeed," said Ruth. She set down her teacup. "It's tragic, what happened to her. Several years after giving them George—right about the time I'd moved to the island—the unfortunate girl committed suicide on the steps of the hotel. She had not even told poor Grace and Alan that she was back in town. When news spread that a troubled young woman had taken her life on the steps near the ocean, it broke their hearts to learn it was George's mother."

Sean had told her about the suicide, and it had become part of the lore she'd learned about the hotel. But to know women who'd been much closer to the situation shed light on it as if it were a new story.

Kate's fingers tingled with the hope of learning more.

"But why would she do such a thing?"

Mrs. Linden answered. "Why would anyone do such a thing? It is a desperate act, and I cannot begin to imagine the anguish that leads to that kind of decision. But I will say, if it puts your mind at ease, that there has always been doubt surrounding it."

"What do you mean?"

"I've read the documents from the inquest. I think anyone who was curious did the same thing. Though they ruled it a death by her own hand, the testimony was gaping with holes. For some time, they weren't even sure they had the right name for her. They thought it was some passer-through named Lottie Bernard."

"How else could she have died, then?"

Mrs. Linden and Ruth looked at each other, mirroring frowns.

Then they turned to Kate.

"Murder," said Ruth.

"Murder," Kate whispered in echo, horrified at the notion.

So her great-grandmother had either taken her own life . . . or had been murdered.

"Yes." Mrs. Linden nodded. "My family started coming to Coronado from Houston just a few years after it happened, and even then it was a much-debated topic. Even to this day, those steps are often photographed by curious tourists and ghost hunters."

"H-have you ever seen her?" whispered Kate. Was it such a frivolous thing to ask, seeing as she was not the first person to be fascinated by the ghost?

Mrs. Linden's jaw tightened, and she took a breath before answering. "I have not seen her. But I believe I've been in her presence."

Kate leaned in, and Ruth had a sparkle in her eyes. She'd clearly heard this story before.

"At the height of the spiritualist movement several decades ago, the one promoted by Sir Arthur Conan Doyle, some adventurous souls decided to try to call her out and conducted a séance in the lobby of the hotel. I was there dining with Mr. Linden, my late husband, and excused myself to use the ladies' room. I came upon their little session."

She removed a handkerchief from her pocket and put it to her nose. "It was all very amateur. Not that I've been to one before, but it seemed quite unorganized, and there were even arguments among the group as to how to go about it. I had the distinct feeling they were disappointed with the outcome, and they left almost as soon as they'd arrived."

"What happened?" asked Kate. That did not sound like much of a story.

"During dinner, a colleague of Mr. Linden's stopped by our table and invited him to the patio for a cigar, so I said I'd wait in the lobby, as I'd brought a book with me. The men stayed out quite a while, and soon the lobby was lit only by the dim glow of the main chandelier and the sconces on the wall. Most diners had returned home or to their rooms, and for some time, I was quite alone. But then—"

"Oh, Margaret. You always tell this so well," interrupted Ruth.

"Then the grand piano started playing."

Kate felt a shiver creep up both her arms, and every peachy hair stood up. "Did you see something?"

Mrs. Linden shook her head. "No. But the keys depressed. Rather slowly, as if they were weighted. At first, the notes were simple—E-D-C. It could have been the beginning of any song. Then, C-E-A-G. And just like your arms, dear Kate, mine filled with goose pimples that made it look like I'd gotten the pox."

Kate looked down at her arms, embarrassed that Mrs. Linden had noticed.

"It repeated," the woman continued.

Kate knew nothing about music except for the radio songs that came on that she and Janie were so fond of. Elvis Presley. Doris Day. She could not begin to decipher the notes.

Mrs. Linden closed her eyes and began to hum a little tune, and Kate assumed she was following the pattern she'd spoken. It was sweet. And familiar.

It was the song that Granddad always hummed under his breath!

Ruth spoke. "Tell her, Margaret, what it meant."

Mrs. Linden's eyes shot open as if she'd been woken from a dream. "It was the song that young George composed when he proposed to my daughter Mary."

Chapter Twenty

At the name of her grandfather and the recognition of the tune, another shiver made its way across Kate's skin, all the way to her neck, as if the ghost herself were present in this room.

Mrs. Linden returned the handkerchief to her nose and dropped her head down.

"Shall I continue, dear?" Ruth asked Mrs. Linden. "I know this part is hard for you."

She nodded and then excused herself. She walked down the hallway Kate had assumed led to the bedrooms.

What was so terrible that she couldn't talk about it?

Ruth waited until they'd heard a door close and then turned to Kate.

"Even after all these years, she finds it difficult to speak of. And as I've never been a mother myself, I can't begin to imagine."

"What happened?" asked Kate. Her voice had lowered, as if there were something sacred about their conversation.

Ruth sank back into the plush chair. "I was not there to witness these events. Though George was quite dear to me, and Grace wrote that she was expecting him to propose to Margaret's daughter, I was away from Coronado for several weeks tending to my sick mother in Santa Cruz. So everything I heard came later, both from Margaret and others who were there."

She poured herself a new cup of tea, this one less steamy, as the water had cooled.

"I don't know how much you know from your grandfather, but he and Margaret's daughter Mary were quite close ever since childhood. Every time the Carters—that was Margaret's first marriage—visited Coronado, George and Mary drew together like magnets until at last, he proposed during one of their summer vacations. He worked at the hotel, of course—his whole life seemed to be tied to that place—and so it was fitting that he do so in the very place they first met. He played this song for her that he had written, and the whole thing drew a crowd of admirers. From what I heard, the applause and cheers were quite grand. Fitting for such a place. But there was one person who did not approve. Margaret's husband Richard. Mary's father."

Kate felt like a sponge, soaking up all this history. No, Granddad George had never spoken of any of this. Had never even told them that he'd worked at the hotel. Only hinted at having even lived in the San Diego area. Kate felt like she was floating—as if she were somehow looking in toward the story as an observer rather than someone who had a true right to hear it.

Ruth continued. "To hear Margaret tell it, she'd been quite nervous about Richard's reaction, but when he said that he wanted to take Mary out to lunch to celebrate, she thought she'd misjudged him. Until he insisted that it be only the two of them. Her instinct was to argue, but you have to understand, dear, that marriage was quite different back then than it is now. A wife had little room to have an opinion—and particularly in their union—so when Richard spoke, Margaret obeyed. But she was terribly nervous the whole time they were gone, and with good reason."

Kate held her breath, and for one second it occurred to her that it was strange that the body could have the same reaction to love as it could to fear. She felt this same thing when she was near Sean—the breathlessness that made a room spin.

"Richard returned alone, though. He came through the hotel lobby looking quite bereft and, from all accounts, quite ashen. Margaret ran to him and asked where Mary was. 'She's gone,' he said. And Margaret asked, 'What do you mean, gone?' He collapsed onto one of the sofas and began to bawl. Margaret had never seen him so broken. He was finally able to tell her that he and Mary had a row over the meal. He'd refused to allow her to marry George. He had a business associate back in Houston who had already approached him about marrying her, and the boy at the hotel was simply not good enough for his daughter. To which Mary began to cry and protest and even refused to listen to him. The long and the short of it is that they argued so vehemently that the steak she was eating slipped down her throat. Too large, it seems. At first, Richard saw her eyes widen and her face turn red and he assumed that she was having some kind of fit over this discussion. Too late, he realized that she was choking. He told Margaret that he'd tried to save her, but by the time he'd overcome his own anger enough to understand it, she'd turned all shades of blue and then gone limp. She was gone."

Gone. Just like that. Just like Sean racing into the water to save the pilot or the helicopter crashing in the first place. These tiny, unexpected twists could have enduring impacts, and it was luck that dictated whether or not one survived. It stirred something in Kate. Life was too short to spend it doing what you didn't want to do.

Ruth leaned in. "Poor Margaret was inconsolable. She just cried out over and over, 'I have to save her! I have to save her!' She went running for the door, but George caught up with her and pulled her into his arms as she collapsed right at the entrance."

Silence descended in the living room, and the heaviness of the wallpaper and the velvet and the church organ suddenly made the room feel like a tomb. Only then did Kate look at the table to her right and see a photograph of a stunning young woman with light-colored ringlets in her hair and a smile that was angelic. This was the same girl Kate had seen in the engagement photo back at the hotel. Mary Carter.

Her heart clenched in sorrow over George and Mary and the tragic end to their love story. But at the same time, she realized that she would not be here—would not even exist—if things had not played out the way they had. These were not mere tales; this was history—*her* history—and one miseaten bite at lunch had shifted the entire course of Granddad's life. There would have been no Grandma Kitty for them. No Dad, no Janie, no Kate. Mom might have married some other man—maybe even met someone else entirely on the Golden Gate Bridge that day. Who would Mom have been? What children would George and Mary have had?

The possibilities were daunting, and the questions of love and marriage led her to think again of Sean. Was he to end up in a tepid marriage with Cynthia? One that would please the business interests of her father but leave him a shell of the person he could have otherwise been? Though it was still so soon after their meeting, could Sean and Kate kindle the kind of love that George and Mary had known?

None of the great love stories began with *He and she were wed even as the ink on the business partnership was drying, their fathers shaking hands in satisfaction.*

No! The great love stories made your heart pound, your dreams soar, your sense of daring heighten as you risked all for the person who put fire into your life.

Fear and love were, indeed, woven together.

Kate resolved that the next time she saw Sean, she would run into his arms and tell him how she felt and hope, hope, hope that his canceling of the Crown Room was indeed a canceling of his wedding. And that it meant he loved Kate instead. Everything else could be figured out. Family. Distance. Details.

"Kate? Are you all right, dear?" Ruth spoke, and Kate looked up to see that Mrs. Linden had reentered the room.

"Yes. I'm sorry. I—This is all so much to think about."

Mrs. Linden's eyes were red, her cheeks puffy, but she returned to her seat and spoke. "It is. And I can only imagine that this will have you up late at night, as it did for me for so many years." She cocked her head and looked at Kate sideways. "You might have been my own great-granddaughter."

"But that's not possible," said Kate.

Mrs. Linden smiled. "I know that, my girl. *Biologically*, as people might say. But you're George's granddaughter, and I can imagine that he and Mary might have had children and that a sweet thing like you would have come along. An old woman can still dream."

Kate smiled at the thought. "Mrs. Linden, if you're up for it, I have two questions."

"Only two?" Ruth laughed. "Dear, I would expect you'd have dozens after what we've just told you."

Kate nodded. "I do. But two especially."

"I'm rather tired," said Mrs. Linden. "So I think that sounds just right for today. What would you like to know?"

"Well, first, if this is not overstepping anything, how did you come to stay here? And become Mrs. Linden?"

The old woman smiled, but not the joyful kind. The nostalgic kind that was dusted with wistfulness and sorrow.

"Something about Mary's death emboldened me to tell my husband things I'd wanted to say for many years. Secrets I'd kept from him for the good of everyone. It ended with telling him that I wanted a divorce, and the short end of the story, Kate, is that I simply refused to leave Coronado. We buried Mary at Mount Hope Cemetery in San Diego, not far, coincidentally, from where Kate Morgan was laid to rest. I like to think that they look after each other."

"So you never went back to Houston?"

She shook her head. "Never. Quite a lot of our money was mine, as Richard had married into my father's company, not the other way around. I agreed to let him keep the majority of it if he didn't contest the divorce, if he packed up all my clothing and some of my furniture and even our macaw, Mr. Hobbs."

Kate gripped the handle of her teacup. "Mr. Hobbs was *your* macaw?"

"Yes. Or rather, he belonged to Mary. The bird was a birthday gift to her from our British housemaid, Mrs. Hobbs. He had one word— *blimey*. Don't tell me the rascal is still around!"

Kate nodded. "Yes. He's Granddad's bird. He's had him since I was born."

"Longer," answered Mrs. Linden. "I gave Mr. Hobbs to your grandfather in memory of Mary. I always suspected he'd outlive us all."

This was one more piece of Granddad's history that fell into place. But Kate had more to ask, and she didn't know how long the women might be up for the visit.

"So Mr. Carter didn't protest your staying here?"

"Of course he did, along with my insistence of a recurring allowance to buy myself this little house, start the garden, and take care of my simple needs. But I held my ground, and before long, Mr. Carter wanted to marry again, so he released me on my conditions. Soon I met dear Mr. Linden. He was quite a bit older than me, but we had a daughter and were quite happy up until his death. As you know, my Elizabeth lives north of here, so I am left with my plants to nurture and my friends to annoy."

She laughed at the last bit, and Ruth rolled her eyes.

"I hope you annoy me for many more years to come, Margaret."

Mrs. Linden patted Ruth on the arm. "You're too good to me." Then she looked at Kate. "What else did you want to know?"

Kate cleared her throat. This was the most important question. To her, at least.

"How did my grandfather come to meet my grandmother Kitty?"

Mrs. Linden looked to her friend. "Ruth, I think you would be the right one to answer that."

"I agree," the other woman said. "Since Grace and Alan were my good friends and my neighbors, I witnessed this part of his story. After Mary died, George quit his job at the hotel and told his parents that he needed to get out of Coronado for a while. He didn't know where he was going, but he promised to keep in touch with them so they wouldn't worry. Over three years, he sent them postcards. Each time a new one came in, Grace would call to me through windows that faced each other, and I'd come over for tea. We'd mark a spot on a map she'd bought just for that purpose."

"Where did he go?"

"All over. He took a train across the country to New York at first. We figured he wanted to get as far away from here as possible. He worked at the Waldorf Astoria in their laundry department. Sometime later, he went up to Boston and worked at the Parker House. Then Chicago, but that one, I think, was at a restaurant not a hotel. Indianapolis for a short time, Denver for almost a year. Grace began to hope that he was working his way back to California. He sent a postcard from Salt Lake City, but by then he'd saved enough to take a little time off, so he just spent two weeks hiking there. Then he went to San Francisco, and Grace was beside herself with joy that he was so close. She wanted to go see him, but by that time, the cancer had spread throughout her body, and she was unable to travel."

"Cancer?" Kate felt like a parrot, repeating her word, but she also didn't want to stop Ruth's story.

"Yes. Grace had cancer in her bones, and soon I took up all her gardening because the poor thing couldn't walk far down her own brick path for fear of falling and breaking something. Alan was a prince—he always was anyway—and treated her like a princess. But she was fading quickly."

"Why didn't George—Granddad George—hurry back then?"

"She didn't tell him. Grace wanted him to come home when he was ready to, and the very fact that he was as close as San Francisco told her that he had almost healed his broken heart. But he stayed and stayed. He sent postcards and letters all the time. And after what seemed an eternity, he returned to Coronado. With Kitty."

∾

1911

It had been so long since I'd seen George, though three years was as three days or three minutes to me. I had an awareness only because of the comings and goings of the people in the hotel.

I did feel a connection to him, though, by that grand piano. At night I would sit at its ivory keys while the hotel spoke only silence. And my fingers would hover over it, remembering the tune George had played.

Only once did I cross that unseen barrier. I'd grown more and more skilled at connecting with the material world. There was little use to this ability, and it was far from perfected, but at the piano on one particular evening, I was able to press the keys and play the simple notes of George's composition. Only when I had finished did I notice that Margaret Carter, now Margaret Linden, was sitting in the nearby chair. She looked my way, and I was startled by the possibility that she might be able to see me. Not with her eyes—eyes are only one way to see. I know that she sensed me. Or sensed something—heard something—and I believe it was our shared motherhood, our shared losses, that strengthened my ability to play the tune and play it accurately.

Grace did not fare so well in George's absence. There is something to be said for no longer being captive to the forces of emotion, as I am in this state. Watching Grace reminded me of how painful they can be. She came in to the hotel only occasionally. Eating in its dining rooms was more than I knew she and Alan could afford. But sometimes she came in, just as Margaret would, and sat in the lobby. Presumably to be near George in the only way she was able.

Once, Grace and Margaret were there at the same time, and it occurred to me that it was on the anniversary of the proposal and Mary's death. They did not speak but nodded at each other before walking their separate ways with their united memories.

Each time I saw Grace, she seemed to be in decline. She grew thinner. She walked with a frailty that had never inhabited her before. If I hadn't thought it would frighten her, I might have concentrated all my limited ability to touch the world and try to stroke her arm in consolation as a friend might have.

But the day that George returned with Kitty, Grace's color filled her cheeks again, and her smile spread across her face. Alan joined them, looking a good bit older himself.

The four sat in the garden restaurant together. George explained that after all his years of wandering—I'd assumed as much by his long absence—he'd made his way to San Francisco. He'd planned to come right down to San Diego, but on the day he was due to leave, he sat down at a lunch counter near the train station and was beguiled by this sweet girl who served him battered flounder and the best potatoes he'd ever remembered eating.

So he'd stayed on in San Francisco, feeling the first happiness he'd known in three years. Kitty's family owned the small restaurant and hired George when he mentioned the need for a job. Through the weeks, Kitty took him around the city, slowly resurrecting since more than eighty percent of it had been destroyed in the earthquake five years prior.

She'd lost a sister and a cousin, two of the three thousand who'd died. And she'd promised herself to take happiness where it could be found, as life was fleeting and the chances for joy few.

In George, she'd found that happiness, and he'd found his in her.

At this point in their story, George took her left hand and placed it on the table.

"We've married," he announced.

If I'd had a voice to gasp, I would have, for on her hand was the very ring he'd given Mary. The ring that had been mine and that I'd thought to have been buried with Mary Carter. I presumed that the always-considerate Margaret had taken it from her daughter's hand and returned it to George. A remarkable thing, especially in light of the certain devastation she must have felt.

It was all George had of me, though I didn't know if Grace and Alan had ever divulged his true history to him. Still, I delighted—as much as was possible for me—to see it on Kitty's hand.

She must be very special to him to wear the ring he'd given to Mary.

Grace excused herself at one point, and I followed her to the ladies' lounge. She fell into one of the chairs and buried her head in her hands. At first I thought she was upset at this turn of events, though it seemed to be something that would warm her motherly heart. Only as I stayed with her did I realize that she'd been feigning health throughout the dinner. In fact, she was quite ill. In this light, I could see that her skin was the lightest shade of pale I'd ever seen on someone who lived in the perpetual sun of Coronado. She took breaths that attempted to be deep but were shallow and labored. When she'd stayed away as long as she dared, she pulled from her bag a small box of rouge and applied the rose-colored powder on her cheeks.

I had not taken Grace for such vanities, but then it occurred to me that she was playing a role. Pretending to be full of glowing health so as to celebrate with her son and not distract him.

I did not know that evening that it was the last time I would see all of them. Grace, Alan, George, Kitty.

Well, not George. I did see him once more.

Chapter Twenty-One

Kate tucked a loose strand of hair behind her ear and brushed a hand over her cheek. She held the tray in her left hand, all her years as a waitress refining this particular trick. That you had to balance it in three places on your hand, whether you used your fingers or your palm. It was like *life, liberty, and the pursuit of happiness*. Without one, the rest toppled.

With her other hand, she knocked.

She was fifteen minutes late to Miss Monroe's penthouse room. She didn't mind facing the actress. Marilyn Monroe was never known to be on time. But Mrs. Strasberg was another matter. She still struck fear in Kate like a creature from a bad science fiction flick.

But to Kate's surprise—and relief—it was Miss Monroe who answered. She wore nothing but a black silk robe, and her white skin stood even in more contrast than usual.

Before Kate could speak, Miss Monroe held a manicured finger to her puffy lips. "Shhhh . . . ," she said.

Kate tiptoed in while Miss Monroe held the door open, wondering if someone was sleeping in the bedroom. The husband, Arthur? Tony Curtis? The actress's nest of white-blonde hair fell around her face in a shroud, not revealing anything.

She set the tray on the table, which was surprisingly only half-filled with empty liquor bottles. Miss Monroe put her fingers to her lips once again and then beckoned Kate to one of the windows.

"Look," whispered Marilyn. "A little spider."

Indeed, there was a small brown spider making its way up the windowsill to a tiny mass that looked like cotton. But as Kate watched, her face so close to Miss Monroe's, she saw that it was the beginnings of a web.

Miss Monroe's voice sounded like a small child's, even when she spoke softly. "Have you ever wished you could be a bug? To go about your life with almost no one noticing, just making your home and eating and being left in peace?"

Kate did not interject what she was thinking—that in her view, the life of a bug was one of fear that it might get squashed, trampled, or run over, and that its diet was not exactly enviable. But there was something in her companion's tone that was full of innocence, and she didn't want to shatter that magic.

Marilyn Monroe was the most complex and the simplest person Kate had ever met.

"That would be lovely," she said instead.

Miss Monroe stood up, and Kate followed her to the couch. To her surprise, the actress began to eat the meal in front of her, and Kate's stomach groaned in hunger—she'd come to expect that Miss Monroe would want her to eat on her behalf. At least there would be plenty in the kitchen later.

"Have a seat," she said, gesturing to Kate. "I've quite forgotten your name. If it was three hours later, I might remember it, but every husband I've had has told me that I'm worthless in the morning."

"Kate Morgan."

Marilyn clapped her hands. "Yes! Like the ghost. Now I remember. Some letters came for you. Looks like you mailed out all those photographs. Good girl. I'll get those for you later."

Kate's heart lifted at Miss Monroe's words. Maybe their interactions had meant a little more to the star than Kate had feared.

She didn't think she had any more capacity in her head, filled as it was with the conversation from yesterday with Mrs. Linden and Ruth. But now her thoughts extended into wondering what the letters might say. Were they all attempts to meet Marilyn Monroe, or were they real offers of more information about her grandfather?

Coming to Coronado had indeed revealed more than she'd ever expected, but she was eager to learn more.

Miss Monroe did not elaborate. Instead, she spoke with the distraction of someone who was intoxicated, but she appeared to be perfectly— or at least *mostly*—sober.

"Andre used to call me his *little mushroom.*"

Andre? Kate didn't ask.

"He'd take me on drives and I'd make a picnic basket and we'd pull over when something struck us as beautiful. He liked that I'd fawn over things like spiders and ladybugs and wild mushrooms. We had a little song we loved. It was called 'When You Were Sweet Sixteen.'"

And she began to sing the lyrics, unfamiliar to Kate, but simple in their phrasing. Off the movie screen, her voice was sweet like a bird's, no pretense of the sultry bombshell who was captured on celluloid.

"Who is Andre?" Kate ventured after all.

Miss Monroe blushed and crossed her legs. Her silk robe had fallen open, nearly revealing all that men across the world would pay vast amounts of money to see, but at the mention of his name, she became like a schoolgirl.

"My first real love. He loved Norma Jeane, and she loved Andre, and we looked at the *M*s on our palms and forecast what they meant for our future."

Miss Monroe continued as if she were her own audience. Kate glanced at the clock and wondered when Sean was coming back, when she might be expected downstairs. But she'd been hired to help Miss Monroe when needed, and the lost soul seemed like she needed to talk to someone.

"Andre said a fortune-teller told him that the *MM* lines on his palms would be significant to him someday. He thought it stood for *memento mori—remember that you have to die*. But once when we were stranded in a snowy cabin, he said it meant *marry me*, so right then, I decided to divorce my husband and become engaged to the photographer."

Kate remembered reading that before she came to Hollywood, Marilyn—or Norma Jeane, at the time—had married at age sixteen. A neighbor named Jim Dougherty, to spare her from returning to the orphanage when her guardians had to move out of California for work.

"But after our two weeks driving through the state, he took me to Hollywood and we went to Schwab's and I tasted the life of the actress, and *Marilyn Monroe* was born." She tossed her curls as she said it.

Nowhere in Kate's movie-star magazines had there ever been a mention of an Andre.

"I wonder," mused Miss Monroe, "what it would have been like if we'd never gone to Schwab's and had instead driven straight to Las Vegas to get married. I would be Norma Jeane de Dienes, housewife. Probably living in a little cottage with five children and cooking dinner for my husband."

Some women might think it sounded appalling compared to the penthouse life overlooking the Pacific Ocean, but it did not seem so on Miss Monroe's face. Quite the opposite. She looked like she would switch places with that dream in a flash.

"Take love where you can get it," she said. But it was as much to herself as it was to Kate.

Miss Monroe proceeded to act as if she were alone in the room, singing another line of the ditty about love, swaying her robe as if it were a gown. Maybe she was more intoxicated than Kate realized, and Kate didn't know what she was supposed to do. The early morning breakfast was meant to encourage Miss Monroe to get down to the set on time, and Billy Wilder had specifically tasked Sean's team to be in charge of this.

But watching her was like watching an entirely different person. The other beautiful stranger, just like she'd thought that first time in the suite. In seeing Norma Jeane prance around nearly naked and give raw glimpses into things never in print, Kate was privy to the details of a life that the public craved. That *she* had craved and would have spent fifteen cents for at a magazine stand mere weeks ago. But the movie star was no more than an orphan who'd chased love and attention from places that built her and then broke her. Had she indeed found real love before she found Hollywood, and had she forsaken it in order to fill her emptiness with something larger and cheaper?

Take love where you can get it, she'd said. And Kate became even more anxious for Sean's return.

She looked at the clock again. It was nine thirty already, and Miss Monroe was no closer to leaving her trancelike state and preparing herself for the shoot that started in thirty minutes. Billy Wilder would be livid if he lost his light in these final days of filming. Kate knew that today's scene was important—the one where Marilyn would join Tony Curtis and Jack Lemmon and Joe Brown on a boat as they escaped the gangsters Andy had told her about. Billy had coordinated with all sorts of agencies to keep boat and ship traffic away from the hotel for two hours while he got this shot, and he would not stand for it to be ruined by having traffic in the background all because of a difficult star.

She had to intervene, not only for herself but for everyone waiting four stories below for the star's grand entrance.

"You said you had letters for me, Miss Monroe?"

This jolted her out of her reverie.

"Yes." Miss Monroe pranced over to the desk. She pulled out a shallow drawer that held a small stack of envelopes, as well as a few photographs that were already autographed. "I haven't read them, but I hope they'll help you find what you're looking for."

Kate took them from her and put them in her pocket and tucked the pictures under her arm, taking care not to wrinkle them. Realizing that she was dismissed by the fact that Miss Monroe took to the bathroom, she picked up the tray. The bacon had been left untouched, so she ate one piece to tide her over until she could take a break.

When she returned to the kitchen, it seemed as if all the employees were gathered, buzzing about with dishes, trays, breakfasts being thrown out, lunches being prepared. No one noticed as she walked in, so she slipped out and found a corner in the hallway. She slid down the wall and sat cross-legged, removing the envelopes from her pocket.

Most were useless, taking the opportunity to feign knowledge of the Morgan family from A Avenue. They weren't even craftily worded—indeed, they were eager attempts just to meet Miss Monroe. Little did they know that when she'd made that offer to Kate, there was no real chance of making good on it. She couldn't even recall Kate's name this morning, and Billy Wilder went on and on about how she didn't remember her lines.

But her intentions had been good, and though the stack of envelopes appeared to be useless, Kate appreciated what the actress had at least tried to do for her.

One envelope, however, contained a letter that was different from the others. It did not address Marilyn Monroe in any kind of starstruck manner but in the language of someone who worked in business.

Arthur Freeman
501 Seventh Street
Coronado, CA

September 1, 1958

Marilyn Monroe
Hotel del Coronado
1500 Orange Avenue
Coronado, CA

Dear Miss Monroe,
I was most appreciative of your letter, as I have been hoping for some time to speak to someone in connection with Alan and Grace Morgan. My father was their lawyer, and he left me with information that would be of vital importance to any of their descendants. I urge you or any party related to the situation to set an appointment with me as soon as possible so that we may discuss the matter.
Yours,
Arthur Freeman

Kate reread the letter three times, heart pounding at the thought of being so close—*so close!*—to answers about Granddad's history. This did not seem to be the fiction of a fan of Miss Monroe's who was eager for an audience but of someone who had long waited to pass along . . . to pass along what?

What did he know about Alan and Grace that was important for her to know?

She had three days left. Three days before the filming ended here. Three days before she had to return home and reclaim her grandmother's ring with everything she'd saved. And three days to find Sean and tell him how she felt.

She put the letter in her pocket, stacking it on top of the useless ones, and stood up. She turned the corner and heard the voice she'd been longing for all week.

"Kate."

"Sean."

~

1912

George returned to the hotel the following year, and the moment he entered the lobby, I felt the familiar pull that drew me in every time my son was near. He was alone, and I wondered about Kitty. His demeanor was dour, bereft. Until he saw some old pals at the reception area. Then he brightened up.

"George, old man, it's been ages. What are you up to?"

This from the bellboy. I'd seen numerous bellboys come and go in my day. This one was named Chester. I liked the gap in his two front teeth, and he showed it off with every jovial grin.

The men shook hands.

"I'm up in San Francisco now, working with my wife's family in a restaurant near the train depot."

"Ya got a caboodle yet?"

George laughed. "Kitty is expecting our first child within weeks."

A child! My grandchild. I was to be a grandmother. Where George was concerned, my state of existence was always rattled, overcome by the maternal bonds that seemed to transcend every other tie. And already I experienced the bond between myself and this child who lived so far—too far—away.

Chester punched George in the arm. "Way to go, old man. You're on your way to a dynasty now."

"If you call early morning restaurant hours and aching feet when I'm still in my twenties a dynasty, then maybe so."

"Ya don't like your work?"

George folded his arms. "I like my work, and I love my wife. But there is something about this place." He looked around the magnificent room.

He didn't finish what he was going to say. But he didn't need to. There was something about this place. Something that kept my spirit tethered, that kept the Carters and the Baums of the world returning every year. That kept George longing for it.

He turned back to Chester. "But I'm here on sad business. My mother, Grace, died just after Kitty and I married. And now my father is in his last days."

Chester's smile closed. "Geesh, pal. That's rough. Your old lady's up in San Francisco about to have a baby, and you're down here with your dad. Did she mind?"

"No," said George. "Kitty is a peach. She insisted I come."

They caught up on things that interest menfolk, and George promised to get away to smoke a cigar on the patio with him if time permitted. But I didn't see George again. I presumed that Alan died and that George settled what little estate there was. But he didn't return to the Hotel del Coronado, and for the first time since I'd made my permanent home here, my heart fell into shadows.

Chapter Twenty-Two

Sean's return filled Kate with relief and joy after learning so much about Granddad's grief-filled history. It was all she could do to keep from breaking down and throwing herself into his arms. But despite Andy's message that the wedding had been called off, she needed to hear it from Sean himself.

She said his name again.

I love you. We'll make this work. Don't marry Cynthia. These and all the things she wanted to tell him remained unspoken, because as soon as she spoke his name, laden, she knew, with the emotions that it carried, he pulled her back into the corner of the hallway and kissed her.

It was a magnificent kiss. Her back pressed against the wall, and Sean bent over to put his mouth on hers. Familiar because it had been only a week since he'd done so, new because it seemed like forever. Even in this embrace, he was a gentleman, but Kate could tell that he wanted more as much as she did.

This was not the kiss of a man engaged.

"Kate," he said. And she didn't want him to pause. Not to say her name, not to breathe. No matter what anyone might think if they were seen.

Sean pulled away, and she looked into his eyes. Kate put her hand on his cheek. "I've been worried about you."

"I've been worried about *you*," he answered.

"Why? You were the one in the hospital."

"But I knew I was going to be all right. I didn't know how you were doing. I wanted to call, but Cynthia was *always* there."

"Andy said you canceled the reservation in the Crown Room."

She said so with just enough caution to protect her heart just in case, but she no longer thought there was much cause for worry.

"Darling," he said, kissing her forehead. "I've called off the whole wedding."

At last. The words she'd known were true, but she'd needed to hear them from his lips.

"But what about Cynthia?"

"I told you on the beach, silly, that we'd broken it off. Or that *I* had. Then I was stuck in the hospital, and I think she figured that if she never left my side, I might, I don't know, change my mind."

"But you didn't?"

All the things she'd imagined. Cynthia nursing him back to health, helping him sip broth. Winning him back.

He touched a finger to Kate's nose. "She's going to be better off in the long run. And I was bewitched by a pixie from San Francisco weeks ago, and I've thought of no one else since."

She smiled, relief making her head feel light. "It's good to have you back."

He leaned down, his lips so close. He whispered, "It's good to be back."

His mouth grazed hers, but they jumped apart when the rattle of a serving tray started coming down the hall.

"Meet me on the beach tonight?" he whispered.

Kate nodded.

"Ten o'clock. The dinner for the crew will be cleared and dishes put away, and we can sit in peace and talk."

Kate nodded. There was much to talk about.

~

She'd hoped to get a break and walk over to the office of Arthur Freeman at some point, but with the shoot finishing soon, Billy Wilder was going frantic. The day was overcast, and he wasn't happy about the light even though Marilyn Monroe came downstairs *almost* on time, in no small part due to Kate's encouragement. The navy planes must have been requiring extra practice, and generally nothing was going right in Movieland.

Eager to respond to his letter, she wrote a note of her own.

> *Mr. Freeman. Miss Monroe passed your letter on to me.*
> *I am the great-granddaughter of Grace and Alan Morgan.*
> *Their adopted son, George, is my grandfather. He lives in*
> *San Francisco now and has for many years. I have come*
> *down to Coronado looking for the history of my family, as*
> *he is no longer able to recall such details. I will call on you*
> *as soon as I am able to get away, but in the meantime,*
> *I was quite anxious to let you know that I am looking*
> *forward to being in touch. I hope to be by tomorrow.*

Kate no longer had the bait of a meeting with Marilyn Monroe, as she was quite sure the actress had forgotten that part of the deal. But she would apologize when she met Mr. Freeman and hope that he would be understanding.

She found a boy just slightly younger than herself standing by the rope, looking longingly at Marilyn Monroe. The star was dressed in an evening gown, part of the scene they were attempting to shoot. It was sheer black, and its thin, sparkling material stretched to its limits across her curves. The illusion from this distance was that she was not wearing anything on top, and the gathered crowd, men and women all, could not look away.

Kate approached the boy. He turned to her with effort. His chin had broken out in the acne that plagued boys newly discovering the men they were.

"How would you like an autographed photo of Marilyn Monroe?"

Now he looked interested—little did he know that Kate had about twenty of them in her locker at the hotel.

"Gee, yes. You can get me one?"

"Yes," she said. "That and a dollar if you'll run an errand for me."

"Anything! That's swell!"

"Here. Please bring this note to 501 Seventh Street. You know where that is?"

He nodded, looking back at Marilyn before returning his attention to Kate. "Yeah. I live pretty close to that."

"Good. The photo and the dollar will be waiting for you when you return. Just come find me."

It wasn't until he ran off that it occurred to her that she had no way of knowing whether he would actually make the errand or if he would just come back and say he had. She didn't know enough about teenage boys to tell if they were trustworthy. But she had nothing else to do except hope for the best.

He returned almost an hour later, and she made good on her promise, hoping that he had, too.

And she knew he'd done his job when late in the afternoon, after the last shots had been taken, the movie stars were resting, and Billy was fidgeting over some panoramic takes, a tall man approached her. He wore a linen suit, a material she'd never seen a businessman wear, but other than it wrinkling at this late hour, it seemed exactly the right fabric for the hot Coronado sun.

She saw the man approach Sean first as he carried a tray back toward the hotel. Sean lifted it above his shoulder and, with his free hand, pointed Kate out to him. Sean and Kate made eye contact, and she shrugged, telling him from across the lawn that she didn't know who he was.

But when he approached her, he said, "Miss Morgan? I'm Arthur Freeman. Forgive my intrusion, but I thought it important to talk to you now."

~

1958

I am marveling at the fashions that are now acceptable at the beach. In my day, a lady's bathing suit was quite bulbous, with yards of fabric that couldn't decide just how to conceal the curves of her body, and we even wore stockings so that almost no part of the skin showed. Some claimed that it was to preserve delicate skin, but we young women all knew that it was to protect us from the lusty glares of men.

But just now, I've seen a group of young women exit the elevator with towels wrapped around their frames. And when one girl drops hers, I am astonished to see that she is wearing nothing but a top and a bottom, exposing nearly everything to onlookers. But she appears to have no shame and picks the towel up as casually as one might do for a parasol that has dropped, and she continues on with it slung over her arm.

I am at once surprised and delighted, secretly cheering on the women who have made themselves equal with the men, at least where the beach is concerned.

But my attention is pulled away by that magnet that I have not been drawn in to for quite some time. Forty-six years, by your calendar, though it amounts to a moment for me.

George? If my George has returned, he must be an old man now, and excitement builds in my chest. But as I look around, nothing is different. Life in the hotel is continuing as normal, as if something momentous has not just happened. I hurry around, feeling the pull stronger and stronger when I near the back of the hotel. But it is only Sean, one of the junior managers, and a pretty young girl following him into the area reserved for employees as he gives her a tour of the grounds. She's carrying nothing but a small bag and a look of exhaustion. But I see how she is looking at him—like one who has quickly fallen in love. Though if I go by hotel gossip, I think he is engaged.

I believe in love, even after how it has treated my son and me. I'm going to root for them. They would make a charming couple.

I am confused by the pull I feel toward her, though. Only George has had that effect on me before.

Why would this girl do the same?

Chapter Twenty-Three

"It's nice to meet you, Mr. Freeman," said Kate as she shook the hand he'd extended. "I'm so sorry that Miss Monroe cannot join us, but shooting is behind schedule, and she's needed on set."

She did not let on how very excited she was to see him, but she was certain that if he'd come down to the hotel instead of waiting for her tomorrow, there must be something worth hearing.

"Is there somewhere we can talk?" He'd made no mention of Marilyn Monroe, and Kate had the distinct impression that he wasn't here for the prize of meeting the movie star or visiting the set.

"Yes," she answered, looking around. It wouldn't do to have him sit on a chair on the lawn. It might crumple his suit even more. And while she was on the clock, she wasn't supposed to be dining in the garden café. But she only had two days left here, and this man might have vital information. She'd mark down the time and ask Sean to remove it from her pay.

He followed her to the café, where they each ordered iced tea and finger sandwiches.

As they were being served, Kate took the opportunity to observe Mr. Freeman. He was about the same age as her parents, though with a bit more gray in his hair than Dad. He wore a vested suit and a bow tie. She smiled to herself. She could never picture her father in such a getup.

"Forgive my intrusion," he said again. "When the boy brought the note, I asked him to wait while I read it in case the sender needed a reply. And when I read it, I asked him who'd sent him. So he described this girl at the hotel. I finished up with my last client and came over straightaway."

Kate just nodded. She didn't know what else to say.

"I was so glad to hear that you'd received my letter," he said, making no gushing remarks about Marilyn Monroe at all. "Before my father passed away some years ago, I moved here from Los Angeles to help with his business. He gave me files he had for several of his clients. And on the top of one was written the name Morgan."

Mr. Freeman added two sugar cubes to his drink. "He briefed me on all the cases, but it was the Morgan case that stood out."

He went on to tell her about the other Kate Morgan. The terrible marriage she was running away from. The suicide that might have been a murder. How she'd left her son in the care of Grace and Alan. These things and more she'd learned at the Garden of Eden with Margaret and Ruth, but she didn't interrupt, hoping there would be a snippet of a detail that they hadn't told her.

And then it came.

"Kate Morgan was her married name, of course. Her maiden name was Farmer. After the inquest, her parents arrived from Iowa. They'd wanted to take her body back to their home, but she'd already been buried in San Diego, and they decided not to exhume her. She'd always written them letters about how much she loved California, and maybe this would give her the peace that had eluded her ever since marrying Tom."

He paused to take a bite, and Kate noticed that her own plate was nearly full. She'd barely touched anything.

"As it's been told to me, they met with various people on the case and learned something from the coroner that had not been revealed in public records, as it had no bearing on the case."

"What was that?"

"During the autopsy, the coroner had made notes about the marks stretching across her abdomen, consistent with a woman who had carried a baby before. He mentioned this as a matter of fact to the family, assuming, I supposed, that they'd known about a child, for the marks were several years old."

"But they didn't know."

Kate's hands grew clammy at all this new information.

"Apparently not. According to my father, whom they met as they were looking for a lawyer to handle some wishes of theirs in regard to Kate, the news was entirely a surprise to them. They hired him to find the child, but with so little information to go on, it was an impossible task. It took him to several places throughout California—different employers she might have worked with. But as she'd changed her name so many times and tried to hide herself from her husband, there were too many dead ends. He was never able to find out about the child. But—"

He paused to take another sip, and Kate dug her nails into her hand to keep from begging him to just continue.

"But they never lost hope. In fact, they put aside some money in the name of this unknown child in the event that he or she would ever be found. They weren't what you'd call dripping rich but quite comfortable, as my father described it. And they hoped to leave of substance something for their grandchild."

That would be Granddad! Kate's heart beat quickly; she was so excited to learn even more about this part of the family's history.

"And you never found him?"

Of course Kate knew the answer to that. If they'd found Granddad George and there was a trust in his name, then the family wouldn't have worked themselves to the bone all these years.

"We did find him."

Kate dropped her glass, spilling droplets on the white tablecloth.

"What do you mean, you found him?"

"My father found his adoptive parents, Alan and Grace Morgan. Just some sleuthing and asking of questions. It turns out that after writing letters to all sorts of leads in California, the answer was right here in Coronado. It's a small town. People talk, and when he was telling someone at a barbershop about his search, a neighbor of the Morgans overheard and said that he believed they had some connection to the woman who'd died."

Kate was listening but still thinking about how Granddad George could have known all this and never told his family.

"He met with Grace and Alan, and even met young George, who was about thirteen years old at the time, and out the door to school as he arrived. He told Mr. and Mrs. Morgan about the money and, with them, helped them to establish it as a trust on behalf of the Farmers. He drew up all the legal paperwork they needed to be able to access it for the purpose of raising him, and my father was appointed as the trustee. So much time had passed, and Kate Morgan's family did not want to disrupt the boy's life by taking him from the only family he'd known. From what I understand, Grace faithfully sent letters and photographs to them, but as far as I know, George never knew about all this."

Kate thought about this. If Granddad *didn't* know, then why would he have sent her down here to look for the beautiful stranger? He must have known something. Or found something that he couldn't understand through the haze of his dementia. Anything was possible in that maze of things he'd saved.

"When Alan Morgan passed away," Mr. Freeman continued, "my parents were vacationing in Europe. When they returned, they learned that George had been there with Alan during his last days, and that he'd hurried to empty out the house and put it up for sale because his wife was due to give birth any day and he had to get back."

"Get back to San Francisco," Kate said. "That must have been my father being born."

Small puzzle pieces were putting themselves together.

"But surely it would have been easy to find George," she offered. "San Francisco is not Mars."

"You would think," said Mr. Freeman. "But back then, a trip to Europe was an endeavor of many months. The train ride to New York, the ship passage across the Atlantic. The tour itself, and then all the way back. By the time my parents returned, the house had been sold, and there were no traces of notes or books that might have led them to George. And neighbors didn't know of his whereabouts, either. But it turns out that not only had Alan and Grace never touched the trust money, they'd mortgaged their house significantly to raise George. The market at the time was slow, and the money after the sale and real estate commissions was nothing. So George signed that paperwork and returned home without leaving a forwarding address. Once again, my father could not find him."

Kate's tea had grown watery as the ice melted, and she filled it up again. She tried to think through the series of events. If Granddad had emptied out the contents of Alan and Grace's house, surely he would have found some record of the bank statement that held the trust money.

Then again, he'd had to rush home for the baby's delivery. And knowing Granddad, he'd taken any paperwork he'd found and set it aside in some ever-growing pile of newspapers to be read later. Which never happened.

To think that all these answers might have been sitting in Granddad's apartment all this time!

Anyone who'd ever seen Granddad's fortress of periodicals would find it easy to believe. But she couldn't be upset. Granddad had never had time to get to those things because he'd always been so busy working to take care of the family.

"Is that all, Mr. Freeman?" she asked.

"There is nothing else. Until I received your letter, the Morgan file had been collecting dust, even as the money in the trust has grown. Not significantly—my father put it in some very safe investments, but still, there is a useful amount of money there."

Kate's mouth went dry at the possibility that there might be some salvation there for her family. That finding the beautiful stranger would be an answer to a prayer they'd grown weary of praying. But she dared not hope until he could give her some kind of confirmation.

"You mean, no one has ever touched it?"

"No one. And the good news is that you've come along before it expired. Part of the stipulation of the trust was that if it was not claimed within sixty years, it would be donated to various local charities, at the discretion of the trustee, and in the name of Kate Farmer."

Kate tried to do the math, but without knowing the year that it was set up, she could only guess.

Mr. Freeman answered her unspoken question. "It was established in 1903."

She nodded. It wasn't as narrow a margin as it could have been. But still, if a few more years had passed, this conversation would have taken a most disappointing turn.

"Why sixty years?" she asked. The number seemed arbitrary.

"It brought George's age into one where a young man might get married and have a child of his own. And added the life expectancy of the time, which was fifty years. Beyond that, I imagine there would have been concerns about having a new generation and an unknown number of descendants to consider."

She folded her arms. "Sounds pretty legalistic."

"Many families set up trusts with similar provisions so that money doesn't go unclaimed in perpetuity."

Kate wondered if somehow Granddad had come upon the bank paperwork and recognized it as important but not known why. And set it down again, to be swallowed in the mountain, and forgotten it. But the remnant of it had stirred the urgency that there was *some reason* Kate needed to get down to Coronado.

It was the only thing that explained why finding the beautiful stranger seemed so important to him.

Perhaps she could ask him in a moment of lucidity. Or perhaps it would remain one of those mysteries that would be forever lost. Like too many things about Granddad's life.

Maybe the death of Grandma Kitty had freed him to sort through those piles of memories and think about those days again.

"What am I supposed to do next?" she asked.

Mr. Freeman cleared his throat and set his napkin on his lap. "We will, of course, need to verify everything you tell me about your family so that we are certain we're handing the trust over to the right people, but if that is all clear, then we will turn the twelve thousand dollars over to your grandfather."

Twelve thousand dollars! Kate hadn't even thought of an actual number, and she wouldn't have dreamed of picking one from the sky. Mr. Freeman was right—it wasn't the kind of instant fortune that would make them rich. But Kate had never aspired to that, nor had anyone else in her family that she knew of. It was *plenty*, however, to improve their lives. To help her parents buy their inn and move Granddad in with them. Maybe even a car like Mrs. Linden's for Dad. The Morgans would always work hard. But at least they could pay their bills, and that was a wealth better than diamonds.

She had one other question. "What about the Farmers in Iowa? Are they still around?" The idea that they had more family than their own little unit was intriguing.

Mr. Freeman pursed his lips and thought. "I would have to look into that further, but I do believe my father said that Kate had been their only child. There might be some distant cousins."

Yes—after several generations, the bloodlines could be quite thinned. With more time on her hands, perhaps Kate would someday take on the project of writing letters in the hopes of finding them. But for now, she was two days away from seeing her own family and hours away from planning her future with Sean.

She chatted politely with Mr. Freeman for a few more minutes, but they'd each said what they came to say. He gave her his telephone number so they could work through the details of transferring the trust money.

Then she ran to Sean's office, happy that her fifteen-minute call was due today. She couldn't wait to share the news.

~

1958

The mystery of the girl was solved over the course of the next five weeks. Her name is Kate Morgan, like myself, a tidbit I learned on the first day. But at first she seemed equally as bewildered by whatever connection there is to me. Still, I know that there is something about her drawing me in.

She calls her family every week, and it was in the first call that I discovered her grandfather's name is George. And slowly, the pieces of what she said answered my questions. I began to understand that this sweet creature is his granddaughter. She talks frantically about her grandmother's ring, and I can only assume that it is the same one that was mine and my grandmother's before me. I am delighted that it is still in the hands of the family, or will be when she "buys it back," whatever that means. But she seems determined that it will happen.

I learned, too, that she came here with the dazzle in her eyes that most do for the glamour of Southern California and the movies and the like. I have had enough of entertainers—I've seen plenty in my time at the hotel. They remind me of Tom, to be honest. He would have preferred the term actor *to* swindler, *and while they don't endeavor to rob trusting souls, this movie business is still just a flimflam that shows people what they want to see and takes their ticket money in return. I harbor no ill feelings against it all—did I not also enjoy the occasional theatrical production in my home-town? But I am glad to see that this Kate has seen the smoke and mirrors that put it all together, and she has set her sights on greater substance.*

Love.

I married for love, and it was my undoing. But not because of love itself. It was that I chose a bad apple, and I guess not everyone can win every time or the earth might spin off its axis. I still believe in love, and I have enjoyed watched this budding romance grow.

Tonight they met on the beach, hours after Kate's lunch with the lawyer Freeman, where I believe she learned as much as I did. I was so moved at how my family tried to find my son, though I don't know that I could have done anything to facilitate the success of the search.

The boundaries of my confinement do not allow me to walk farther than the lawn, and as Sean and Kate step beyond that into the sand, I can-not hear their words, and that is best, because whatever they have to say is meant to stay between them. I think of myself as a distant angel, wishing the powers of the heavens to grant them the happiness I didn't have. They are out there for quite some time, standing close, conversing deeply. And just before they alight the steps that will lead them back to the hotel, he kisses her, and I turn away, satisfied that they have resolved whatever was necessary to stay together.

Chapter Twenty-Four

April 1959

"I thought you'd never get here," said Kate as Sean walked up to her apartment.

"Sorry. My sister asked me to watch my nephew, and she didn't get home in time, so I missed the earlier ferry. But here I am."

He took her left hand, the one on which she wore the old silver ring. He'd wanted to buy her one of her own when he asked her to marry him, but she begged him to let it be the ring that had been in her family for so long. She'd offered it to her sister first, but Dimitri had bought her a one-carat sparkler. And besides, Janie admitted that if it had not been for Kate's ambitious adventure to Coronado, none of this would have come about. Even as she and Dimitri planned to have a little apartment on the grounds of the hotel they were building, Mom and Dad had found a bungalow near Union Square. And though they hadn't yet decided to take the leap to open an inn, it was a step forward. It even had a second bedroom for Granddad George. They'd thought it would take a miracle to get him to part with the myriad of newspapers he'd collected, but it had taken less cajoling than they'd expected—when Kate told him the story of her time in Coronado, some piece of his memory must have relaxed, because he no longer held on to things as he always had. This alone had made her whole trip worth it.

"It's going to be weird, isn't it?" asked Sean. And as it was with people in love, Kate didn't have to ask what he meant.

"Uh-huh. To have seen all the behind-the-scenes work and then to watch the film on-screen as if none of that existed. I don't know what to expect."

"Well, we only saw a piece of it. Most of it was filmed back in Hollywood, so maybe there will be more surprises than you realize."

They turned a corner onto Orange Avenue.

Kate had found her calling. When an aging general store came on the market, she had the idea to use her portion of the Morgan money to put a down payment on it and converted it into a one-screen theater. She had plans to expand and renovate as she could afford it, but for now, residents and visitors to Coronado no longer had to take the ferry to San Diego to catch a flick.

It was perfect, and she couldn't imagine life being any better than living in Coronado and marrying Sean and running the little enterprise that gave her the only connection to the Hollywood world she really wanted to have. The only thing better would be to have her family living here, but they already had plans for a visit. And San Francisco wasn't really so far away. Especially if they drove in Dad's new car.

"But it's not just the storyline," she continued. "It's knowing that Joe Brown liked his Cokes, that Tony Curtis tried to fashion a contraption to help him use the bathroom while he was dressed as a woman. All those details."

She didn't mention Marilyn, but they both thought of her. The Marilyn she'd loved and grown protective of didn't exist on the screen. Movie star Marilyn Monroe would glitter and smile as she always did. And Norma Jeane, recovering from a miscarriage and suffering from public difficulties in her marriage to Arthur Miller, was somewhere hundreds of miles north trying to reconcile her private pain with her public persona.

It didn't take long to get to the cinema. After all, Coronado was a small place, and that's exactly how Sean and Kate wanted it. They were under contract to buy an apartment on A Avenue, a few blocks over from where Grace and Alan and George had lived. They were planning the wedding to coincide with the closing.

And the reception would be not in the Crown Room but on the beach under a white tent, with sand dollars for witnesses and friends and family for celebration.

But all that was in the future, and though plans for it often took over her day, she set them aside for this evening. As the lights in the theater dimmed, Sean took her hand and squeezed it. Kate looked at him and smiled. The credits flickered, the hexagonal United Artists card appeared, and the big-band music blared, trumpeting the beginning of the movie that felt like the beginning of her life.

～

August 5, 1962

The day is ending, and so begins the nighttime at the hotel. It is quiet and peaceful. Tonight, Kate and Sean and their little son, George, came to the hotel for ice cream. He is a precious child. He just turned two years old and loves the piano just like his great-grandfather did. Earlier, they'd spent time on the beach together, Kate looking charming in a two-piece leopard-print swimsuit that I would have enjoyed wearing at her age.

I watch George slip from Kate's grip, and when she sees that he is only feet away at the bench of the instrument, she smiles and turns back to her husband. I sit next to my great-grandson, and he looks as if he sees me.

Perhaps he does.

Children, I've learned, are far wiser than adults.

He places a tiny finger on a key. E. Maybe that's a coincidence, and maybe not. By now, I have gotten even better at connecting with the material world when I want to, though I avoid it most of the time, cautious about frightening people.

But children have not yet learned to fear the unknown. While conversations abound around us, I play the next notes.

E-D-C, pause, C-E-A-G. And again, E-D-C, pause, C-E-A-G.

Little George repeats them with prodigious accuracy, save for the final two, where he hesitates. But that's OK. He has many years to learn, and I have forever to teach him.

The silence is disrupted by something I cannot explain, but I sense that there is someone else with me. Someone not of the material world. Instead, a soul that has suddenly attached itself to the paradise of the Hotel del Coronado.

I almost don't recognize her at first. She looks to be about nineteen, with chestnut-brown hair and innocent eyes. Her teeth are perfect and white, but it is the voice I recognize, and I meet her with both welcome and sorrow.

She is all too young to be here. Whatever turned her into the white-blonde beauty and whatever—or whoever—took her life and sent her to this place is unknown to me, but I will make sure that she finds peace here. I will make sure that she is not the restless soul that she was on this earth.

"I'm Kate Morgan," I say.

She answers.

"And I'm Norma Jeane."

Author's Note

Writing historical fiction is just that: history and fiction combined. Sometimes, to make the story compelling, an author has to weigh the two. Or to fill in where there are gaps. I have done so in several places with *The Beautiful Strangers*. Kate Morgan was a real woman whose body was found on the steps of the Hotel del Coronado in 1892. The prologue in which she discusses her husband, her various aliases, and the circumstances of her presence at the hotel are almost completely found in inquest records and surrounding interviews. Her death was ruled a suicide, but there was much about it that was questioned. It is even debated whether it was an entirely different woman who died! So it left a wide berth for a fiction writer to make decisions about one possible version of the truth. The latter parts of Kate's story are fictional. Though she *is* the famous ghost at the hotel, and there have been numerous reports of sightings, telling a story from the point of view of a ghost is, of course, made-up. I did not actually set out to write it that way. Her perspective was originally going to be limited to just the prologue. But something about her character kept crying out to me—to tell her story, real or not. Who she was as a mother, a woman, even when circumstances were beyond her control.

It dawned on me—doesn't every woman feel constrained in some way, from boundaries surrounding her that she must live within? Maybe it wasn't so strange to attach this particular characteristic to someone. Her boundary was that she was dead.

Interestingly, some people believe that the ghost of Marilyn Monroe haunts the hotel as well, and I had fun writing the last lines where the two meet. Marilyn's death, too, has always been in question—suicide or murder?

It is reported as well that Miss Monroe haunts the Roosevelt in Hollywood, her old house, her Cadillac, and the White House. She appears to be having a very busy afterlife!

There was also much room as a fiction writer to expand upon the goings-on of the filming of *Some Like It Hot*. I hope readers will excuse the liberties of scenes taken between fictional Kate as a waitress with the celebrities who were all, in fact, real. Books reported Jack Lemmon, for example, as being kind and funny. And Tony Curtis's autobiography details his on-set affair with Marilyn. I strove to write the *essence* of their characters when facts were few. Did Joe Brown enjoy drinking Coca-Cola? I have no idea. And though I had a sketch of the timetable of filming while they were in Coronado, I allowed it to be fluid in my plotting. I cannot say that one scene was filmed on one particular day or that the dates of filming exactly match the calendar in how they happened. But I think that is inconsequential in comparison to relaying the story.

So thank you, dear reader, for giving me room to use my imagination here as I took true elements of real people and events and played with them until they fit into a story that I hope you enjoyed. If you are fascinated, as I am, by ghost stories and Hollywood tales, there are lots of nonfiction and biographical works out there that can tell you more about Kate Morgan, Marilyn Monroe, Tony Curtis, Jack Lemmon, and so on. I encourage you to read them and picture for yourself that bygone world that intrigues us all so.

Acknowledgments

As a child, I had only ever dreamed of writing one book, but I am so grateful to my agent, Jill Marsal, for believing in this as a career for me and shepherding me through ideas and all aspects of the book world.

To my developmental editor, Tiffany Yates Martin, you are a-m-a-z-i-n-g at what you do. You have been the very best writing teacher but, more than that, a treasured friend.

To Chris Werner, editor extraordinaire at Lake Union. You are a fantastic advocate, and I am beyond grateful to be working with you. Thank you for the guidance, encouragement, and unwavering support!

To Danielle Marshall and Gabe Dumpit and Alex Levenberg for all that you do for me and for Lake Union, and to all extra supporters of the book—copy editors, proofreaders, cover designers, etc.

To my husband and kids, thank you for holding down the fort when Mom heads into a writing zone. Your patience, love, and support mean a great deal to me!

I am really grateful for the social media groups that have been so supportive, many of the people becoming dear friends in "real life." My Lake Union author friends are exceptional, and I get so much joy out of groups like Great Thoughts Great Readers (Andrea Katz), A Novel Bee (Kristy Barrett and Tonni Callan), Suzy Approved Books (Suzanne Weinstein Leopold), Baer Books (Barbara Khan), Sue's Booking Agency (Susan Peterson), In Literary Love (Jen Cannon), Linda's Book

Obsession (Linda Levack Zagon), The Romance of Reading (Sharlene Martin Moore), Confessions of a Bookaholic (Jennifer O'Regan), Good Book Fairy (Lauren Blank Margolin), and so many others. I also love being a founding member of My Book Tribe!

To Ann-Marie Nieves of Get Red PR, you are fantastic, and I'm so happy to have you in my corner. Authors—call her!

To some particular authors, thank you so much for your friendship: Rochelle Weinstein, Chanel Cleeton, Aimie Runyan, Joy Jordan-Lake, Steena Holmes, Heather Burch, Christine Nolfi, Heather Webb, Fiona Davis, Barbara Davis, Teri Wilson, Sally Koslow, Rebecca Rosenberg, Michelle Gable, Patricia Walters Fischer, Thelma Adams, and Jane Healey. I have greatly enjoyed visiting with all of you this year.

I'm also thankful for my super-supportive readers and grateful we have the opportunity to get to know each other through social media. I can't do what I do without you! As a reader first, I love being part of an awesome book club, The Happy Bookers.

And finally, I love my community over at Instagram. There are so many wonderful people to mention, but thanks especially to @outofthebex, @saltwaterreads, @marisagbooks, @_the_bookish_blonde_, @beauty_andthebook_, @susieormanschnall, @travel.with_a_book, @bookwineclubtoronto, @beauty_andthebook_, @texasreadergirl, @basicbsguide, @shereadswithcats, @reading.between.wines, @katerocklitchick, @jennsbookvibes, @mwladieswholit, @_thatswhatsheread, @jess_reads_books, @booksandchinooks, @rendezvous_with_reading, @lattesandpaperbacks, @lisaandliz, @the.wanderlust.bookshelf, @amylynnlifestyle, @hippiechickreads, @fictionmatters, @abookorafewandjavatoo, @thejoyharris, @my_book_journey, @judithdcollins, @motherofcooper, @goodgirlgonered, @silversreviews, @thepulpwoodqueen, and @cyruswebbpresents. Follow them for amazing book pics!

About the Author

Photo © 2018 Christina Orosco

Camille Di Maio always dreamed of being a writer. Those dreams came to fruition with her bestselling debut novel, *The Memory of Us*, followed by *Before the Rain Falls* and *The Way of Beauty*. In addition to writing women's fiction, she buys too many baked goods at farmers markets, unashamedly belts out Broadway tunes when the mood strikes, and regularly faces her fear of flying to indulge in her passion for travel.

She and her husband homeschool their four children and lead an award-winning real estate team. They recently moved to Virginia, where she can finally live near a beach. Connect with Camille at www.camilledimaio. com and on Instagram, BookBub, Facebook, and Twitter.